TWIN SISTERS LIVINGSTON

❖ AND ❖

THE MYSTERY AT MADAME MOLINEAUX'S

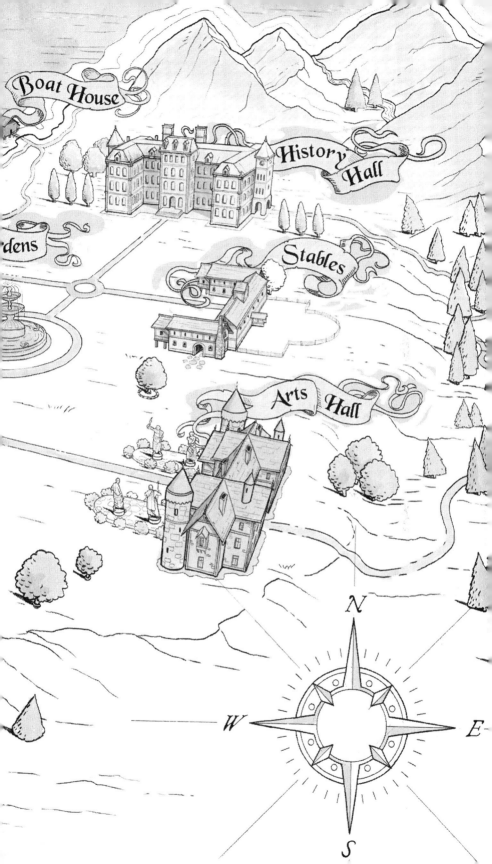

TWIN SISTERS LIVINGSTON

✧ AND ✧

THE MYSTERY AT MADAME MOLINEAUX'S

BY MARY KNIGHT

ILLUSTRATED BY DEREK CLARKSON

For the Pilot and his Songbird

With Special Thanks To:

Alan Samuel Cohen
Clara Chow
Harold Clarke
Beth and Larry Knight
Jessica Knight
Michelle Lamison
Chrissy Livaudais
Heather McCormack
Corbin Pon
Jody Revenson
Alisha Rutledge Alonso
Ava Seave
Laura Wallendal

CONTENTS

Two Exceptions to the Rule

Two figures sat across from each other at a desk, silhouetted by the last rays of sunlight passing through blue stained-glass windows. The woman, after shuffling through a stack of papers, read aloud quietly as she scanned the letter once more.

"I tell you, they are perfect," the man said in his thick French accent. "Smart, curious, talented . . . both of them speak a little French and Latin, and they even play music. I assure you," he insisted, tapping his index finger twice on the desk, "their parents are nothing short of brilliant. Professors them-selves, archaeologists. And," he added with an exaggerated nod, "they're offering quite a lot of money for their girls to attend."

The woman peered out over her silver-rimmed glasses. She met the man's hopeful stare and, after a few moments, let her gaze drift up to the relics that adorned the wall behind him. Her tired brown eyes darted from trophies and plaques to portraits of former professors and photographs of students. She sat up in her tufted leather chair and addressed the man sternly.

"Henri," she scolded, absentmindedly tugging on the worn hem of her jacket sleeve. "Since the beginning, we've only accepted students from Europe. Earlier this year, you convinced me to admit girls from outside the continent, and now this? Americans?" She let go of her sleeve and softly hammered her fists on the desk. "There were *rules*, Henri."

He smirked and shook his head.

"We've gone over this, Klara. Again, and again, and again. Certainly, a woman in your"—he hesitated and shifted his eyes away from hers—"*unique* position can see the advantage of bending those rules? Your situation has not changed. In fact," he said, standing up to count the portraits behind her silently with his outstretched finger, his gaze settling on an empty space, "it appears to be worsening. Besides, you haven't even asked me how much their parents are willing to pay." He pulled a note card from his coat pocket and slid it across the desk.

Klara picked it up, glanced at it, and laid it back down.

"American dollars?" she asked, searching Henri's face for evidence of a trick or some sort of joke.

"Yes, American dollars," Henri replied, pausing for effect. He leaned in closer to her. "Each."

Klara tried to stifle a cough and looked down to regain her composure. She took the letter off the desk and unclipped the black-and-white picture from the top-right corner of the page, tilting her head back and forth as she studied it. In the picture, two smiling girls dressed in short pants and jackets sat on a boulder jutting up from the shrub-covered ground.

"Are they . . . are they in the jungle in this picture?" Klara asked.

Henri nodded. "With their parents on one of their archaeological digs."

"You say they're twins?" she pushed further, taking off her glasses and examining the photograph more intently. "They don't even look like sisters." She thought for a moment about what the money could mean for her beloved school. "Well, I suppose rules are just rules, meant to be broken. Isn't that what they say?" She looked at the man and shrugged her shoulders. "Perhaps we could find a place for them here," she said in a lilting tone.

Henri, finally satisfied with her answer, took his hat from the desk and placed it on his head. "Bent, broken, it doesn't matter . . . just as long as you get the money. That's what I always say."

She pursed her lips and then offered a knowing smile. "I'm a lady, so I won't ask for the details of your involvement. But let's not pretend you aren't getting something out of this as well, hmm?"

He winked at her and flashed his most charming smile. "As always, Klara, I am inspired by your grace and goodwill." He bowed politely and made his way to the door.

"Are they coming directly from the jungle?" Klara asked cautiously before Henri's hand touched the doorknob.

"Oh, yes, they are. And I forgot to mention: They're bringing their pet snakes with them."

Klara looked alarmed, but managed to reform her expression into a smile. "Well, I suppose the snakes could live in the conservatory," she said slowly, trying to remain optimistic.

"Come now, Klara," Henri said, laughing out loud.

She sighed with relief and shook her head apologetically as he stepped through the door. "Oh—I"—she stammered—"I just wanted to be sure these American girls know how to behave at a school like Madame Molineaux's."

Henri poked his head back into the office. "Not to worry, old friend. Of *course* they're not coming from the jungle," he said, raising his eyebrows and tilting his hat up. "They're coming from the desert."

CHAPTER ONE

SUNSET ON THE EXCAVATION

The bottom of the blazing orange sun slipped beneath the horizon at the ancient Roman ruins. Hundreds of yards away, several gazelles gathered to graze under a lonely tree, its shade giving them refuge from the heat of the Moroccan afternoon. Other than the whisper of the hot summer wind, the only sounds in the desert were the clanking and shuffling noises coming from a small archaeological camp. Canvas backpacks and water canteens rested against an old military ambulance, and a makeshift table piled high with dusty tools and notebooks threatened to topple over at any second.

Martha Livingston took a moment to look up from the broken pot she was trying to wrap in burlap cloth. "Girls," she called, cupping her hands around her mouth. "I said *hats on*."

A petite blond girl turned around and squinted at her mother. "But Mom," she complained, "the sun is almost down! And we've made it all day without getting sunburned. Can't we take them off now?" *We're twelve, Mom, not five,* she thought. Madeline—or Maddie, as her family called her—stared down at the wide-brimmed safari hat she'd been wearing since that morning. "Besides," she continued, "I think a family of beetles has made mine their new home." Indeed, three small beetles clung to the chin strap, having enjoyed the free ride all afternoon.

Josephine, tall and brunette, approached her twin sister to inspect the hat's new inhabitants. "Yep, she's right, Mom. Maddie's hat is now the finest bug hotel this side of the ruins!" She tossed her own hat like a saucer toward the campsite.

"Jo, we talked about this," Martha said, taking canvas bags off the table and blowing the dust off the surface. "I need those hats on. It's about to get as cold as the winters back home."

"Don't worry, girls," sang their father, Tom, hoisting bundles of wood out of the old military ambulance. "As soon as I get the banquet fire going, off go the hats and on go the crowns."

Maddie and Jo smiled and put their hats back on without protest. It was, after all, their favorite day of every summer, as far back as they could remember: The End of the Excavation Banquet.

"Who's coming to our banquet again, Dad?" Maddie asked, searching the barren landscape around them for potential table decorations. "Harry? Henry?" she guessed as she tried to remember the name she'd heard a few days before.

"It's *ahn-Ree*," Tom said, emphasizing the syllables. "Henri is spelled a bit like Henry, but with an *i* instead of a *y* at the end. And you don't pronounce the *H*. He's an old friend of mine and your mother's." He looked down at his wristwatch. "And he'll be here in an hour." He walked faster with the bundle of wood toward the firepit.

"Just in time for the lantern lighting!" Jo chirped, excited to have a guest see the ceremonious beginning of the Livingston family's last meal on the excavation. "Why is he coming?"

"Oh, well . . ." Martha's voice trailed off as she wrapped more clay pots in cloth. "Henri is always full of the latest archaeological news. And besides, he's always set up our summer excavation trips." She glanced at her husband nervously, then quickly smiled back at her girls. "But mostly, we're just excited to see our friend. It's been almost seven years that we've been communicating by mail. You girls remember his letters from all over the world, don't you?"

"Colored envelopes with pretty stamps, right?" Maddie asked, vaguely recalling stacks of them in her parents' office, tied in bundles with twine. "He should have sent chocolates, not letters," she giggled. "I'd *definitely* remember those. But at least we finally get to meet him."

"Well," Martha drew out the word, almost singing it. "If I'm not mistaken, Henri has a few souvenirs from Paris for you this time."

"Paris!" the girls exclaimed in unison. Maddie held the back of her hand to her forehead and pretended to faint, and Jo clasped her hands under her chin in delight.

"I can't wait to go to Europe," Maddie gushed, sauntering down an imaginary promenade. "Maybe next summer?" She stopped and posed for an invisible photographer, giving her most sophisticated expression.

"Yeah, Dad, why haven't we been there yet? There must be heaps of ruins in Europe," Jo insisted, taking her trusty compass out of her pocket and tucking it into the front of her pack. As she traced the engraved edges with her fingers, she envisioned all the summers she and Maddie had spent abroad with their parents: Mexico, Australia, South America, and now Africa. *Europe is next on the list. It just has to be,* she thought.

Tom shrugged and managed to give his daughter a crooked smile. "Soon—err—I mean, *someday,*" he stammered, his voice shaky and unsure. He dropped his armload of wood onto the firepit, becoming very interested in the pile of sticks.

Martha picked up where he left off. "Only a matter of time, girls," she assured her daughters as she slapped her dusty hands together. "But for now, let's get the table set, and the lanterns made. Let's show Henri that Paris isn't the only place to have an incredible meal!"

The End of the Excavation Banquet was not something that the Livingston family took lightly. It marked the end of each summer's worth of digging, dusting, sweating in the heat, and dragging their finds back to camp. It had never been glamorous, but they did their best to find ways to make it feel special. And this year would be the first time they'd have a guest of honor.

"That makes five," Maddie called out, admiring the arrangement of dishes on the makeshift table. She picked up an old, parchment-colored pillow from the ground and beat it against a table leg until it refused to cough out any more dust. "Henri gets the chair with the cushion," she laughed, placing the pillow on the metal chair at the head of the table. "The most luxurious seat here at chez Livingston!"

Jo walked over to inspect her sister's design. At each rustic place setting, there was a chipped white porcelain plate, a mismatched fork and spoon, and a dented tin mug. She placed a fan-folded square of burlap in the center of each plate, weighing down the center of the cloth with a smooth stone.

"Perfect," Maddie whispered, crouching down to eye level at the table to see where the flat parts of the knotted wood were. "We can put the candles here"—she paused, laying down a tiny wreath woven from twigs—"and here." She set the second tiny wreath at the other end of the table, and Jo twisted thick candles into each one.

"Think you can find something to do with these?" their father asked, approaching the table with a thicket of Mediterranean saltwort stems lush with dark pink flowers. "Your mom is using leaves and the shoots for our dinner, but I couldn't let these go to waste."

"They're beautiful," Jo crooned. "Perfect for our last night in Morocco." She took a closer look at the woody stems and petite flowers, wishing she could take some of them home. "Do you think they'd make the trip back?"

"Don't be silly, Jo," Maddie scolded. "They'll be dried up by the time we land in Boston." She turned to her father. "Right, Dad?"

"R-r-right," he stuttered. "Those aren't going to make it back to Boston, Jo." He picked up a few of the woody stems and fashioned them into two loops. "But I think they'll make some beautiful crowns for the banquet." He placed the halos of flowers on his daughters' heads and stepped back. "There they are, my desert princesses. All grown-up, I'm afraid."

Martha joined him. "You look beautiful, girls," she sighed, taking a long look at the tall brunette and the petite blond standing back-to-back. "And quite grown up indeed. Henri will barely recognize you." She took Tom's wrist and turned his watch face toward her. "Five minutes, everyone," she said, scrambling back to the bubbling pots of food over the firepit. "Time to string the lanterns!"

Maddie and Jo picked up the lanterns they had made from glass jars, spooled wire, and the colorful silk scraps they'd picked up at the street market just days before. Each jar had been wrapped in silk, and was nestled into a wire harness.

Maddie threaded rope through the wire loops, making knots on each side to keep the glowing jars in place. "I'll do this part and you can hook them to the tents," she instructed her sister.

But even Jo couldn't reach the tops of the tents surrounding their camp. She dragged a steel shipping drum over to her parents' tent, stood on top, and reached up to the highest part of the hooked poles. "Got it!" she called. "Ready when you are, Sis!"

Maddie stood next to the shipping drum and carefully passed the rope and dangling lanterns up to Jo, who slid them over the hooks at the end of each tent pole.

"On to the next tent!" Jo sang, wondering how the pretty lanterns would look when they were finally lit. She gazed at the sunset in the distance as the pink and purple clouds became darker by the minute. *I wish the sunsets in Boston were as pretty as this,* she thought, and stared for a moment longer before turning around to jump back down to the ground. But just as she hunched over and bent her legs to squat down, she heard an engine sputter in the distance. Jo shot up straight again and looked out over the military ambulance.

"What? What is it, Jo?" Maddie asked, jumping up and down to try to see over the ambulance. "Is it a truck? Is it Henri?"

"It might be Henri," Jo said slowly, still staring out into the desert. "But it's definitely not a truck." She hopped down from the shipping drum and took her sister's hand. "You're going to want to see this," she said, and the girls ran to the front of the camp.

CHAPTER TWO

UNEXPECTED GUESTS

Martha and Tom were already standing out front, and they shielded their faces as the cloud of dust from the approaching car blew toward them. A shiny black Rolls Royce slowed to a stop in the desert sand. It was the kind of car Maddie and Jo had seen outside the fanciest hotels in Boston. The twins stood behind their parents, peeking around them to see who would emerge.

The car door swung open and a man stepped out, looking down as he brushed off the sleeves of his tailored cream suit. He stamped his fancy brown leather shoes in the sandy dirt, kicking up yet another cloud of dust.

"I am only making things worse," he muttered in a thick French accent before coughing twice. He stopped shuffling, straightened his jacket lapel, and lifted his head. His skin was tanned, his features were chiseled, and his blue eyes sparkled as they darted back and forth between the familiar faces in front of him. "Tom, Martha," his low, velvety voice boomed as he stretched both arms out toward the Livingston family. "It has been too many moons!"

Tom sprang toward his old friend, and the two men embraced, patting each other's backs for a few moments. Tom stepped back and looked Henri's car up and down.

"Only you could get a car like that in a place like this," he said, running his hands over the shiny silver hood ornament. "Where did you find it?"

"Oh, a local business colleague owed me a favor," Henri answered nonchalantly. "So, I borrowed his car." He walked around Tom to greet Martha.

"Mmhmm. Does the poor sap know you borrowed it?" Martha teased, turning her cheeks to accept Henri's airy kisses.

He hugged her and looked her straight in the eyes. "Of course he knows, my dear, but"—he paused and winced—"even if he *didn't* know, I'd have the car back before he returned from Casablanca. *Qu'est la différence?*" He let go of Martha and walked backward a few paces before placing his hand on his chest and taking a small bow. "Maddie and Jo Livingston, I presume?"

Maddie and Jo giggled, and inched toward him.

"We get that joke a lot in Boston," Jo said timidly.

"But this time, we're actually in Africa," Maddie thought out loud, smiling. She brushed her dusty hand against her shorts and extended it to the stranger in front of her. "I'm Maddie, and that's Jo," she explained, pointing to her sister.

Henri let out a belly laugh and crouched down. "Young ladies, I knew you when you were crawling around the Mayan ruins of Copán! No need to introduce yourselves to me. You are both as lovely as I remember, especially in your flower crowns." He raised his head to meet Martha's eyes and winked. "I told you, Martha, that Madeline would grow into that nose and Josephine into those spindly legs, didn't I?"

The girls opened their mouths to protest. Maddie pulled on her button nose to make sure it was the same size as before, and Jo looked down at her legs, wondering if they could still be considered spindly.

Henri stood up straight and shook his head once more, smiling with satisfaction. "Ladies, I'm only teasing. Pushing your legs, eh?"

"I think you mean *pulling* our legs, Mister Henri," Maddie corrected him.

He nodded and threw up his hands with a sigh. "All of your American sayings," he said, laughing. "I shall never learn every one of them." He pulled two small tin boxes of violet pastille candies from the pocket inside his coat and handed them to the girls. "Why don't you try and spoil your dinner with these while I talk with your parents?"

"Are *these* our souvenirs from Paris?" Jo asked sweetly. "Mom said you'd be bring—"

"I think you meant to say *thank you*, Jo," Martha scolded. "Henri has come a long way to be here tonight. Why don't you girls go and check on dinner?"

"Heavens, no!" Henri addressed Jo, walking toward the passenger side of the car. "The candy is just a cheap bribe for some moments alone with your parents. When Henri brings a souvenir from Paris, Henri brings the finest dr—"

He stopped talking and whipped around toward the sound of yet another engine in the desert. But unlike Henri's fancy car, this looked like an army truck, and it roared up the sandy roads at racetrack speeds.

14

Henri pulled his jacket cuff back from his wrist and looked at his watch. "*Zut alors*, why are they here already?" he spat before changing his expression, forcing a smile. "Ah. Maddie, Jo, check on dinner like your mother asked." He pushed the girls toward the firepit, grabbed Tom and Martha by the elbow, and hurried them away from the camp, speaking quickly as they went. After a few moments, Martha and Tom halted, smiled at each other briefly, then looked on with worried interest as they watched the vehicle approaching.

The open-roofed army truck skidded to a halt outside the camp, and a man and a woman, both wearing sunglasses, climbed up on the seats and leaned over the dusty windshield. The man was dressed in work boots, khaki pants, a collared, long-sleeved, linen beige shirt, and a leather work belt—the same kind Martha and Tom wore to hold their tools. The woman, looking as out-of-place as Henri on the dig site, was elegant in a tan pencil skirt and a white blouse. The curls of her blond hair had been tied back in an orange-and-cream printed scarf, which matched the bright swath of color on her lips.

Henri ran over to the truck, waving hello to the new guests. "Right on time," he shouted, looking back nervously to read Tom and Martha's faces.

"What on earth . . ." Tom whispered slowly to his wife, squinting his eyes to make sure the man in the truck was the man he knew from back home.

". . . is *he* doing here?" Martha whispered back.

"Tom, Martha," Henri called as he reached up to help the woman out of the truck. "You remember Michael Prescott, no? From your work together in Rome? Here, Mademoiselle," he insisted, motioning for the woman to take his hands. "Allow me."

The woman smiled, placed a pair of cream-colored high heels in Henri's hands, and hopped out of the truck by herself, wearing what appeared to be military boots.

"Thanks," she chirped, and took the heels back. "I knew these weren't going to work in the desert, but I figured I'd bring them along on account of this fancy dinner." She looked around at the camp for a moment. "I'm Elizabeth, Elizabeth Averil. Is there somewhere I can change my shoes?"

"*Enchanté,*" Henri said, bowing slightly before looking back up at her. "Truly," he murmured, and almost went to kiss her hand before stopping himself. "I am Henri Lemaître. Eh, Maddie, Jo," he called, trying to regain composure. "Can you show Elizabeth to the table so she can change her shoes?" He wiped the sweat from his brow. "Come, Michael," he said quietly as he guided the man toward Tom and Martha. "And remember, you heard the news *this morning.*"

CHAPTER THREE

New Friends and New Adventures

Maddie and Jo hadn't moved since Henri had shoved them off to check on dinner, but they both snapped out of their reverie when he asked them to help Elizabeth.

"Uh—sure," Jo said, forcing a polite smile. She walked toward the table to pull out the chair with the cushion on it for Elizabeth.

Maddie watched the graceful woman pass by. *Easy to look nice when you don't have to do any of the real work out here,* she thought, feeling more underdressed by the minute. But she joined Elizabeth and Jo at the table anyway.

"Must be exciting, getting to travel to all these exotic places with your parents," Elizabeth gushed as she took off her boots, pouring the sand out of each one the way a waiter might pour milk into a cup of hot tea.

"It is," Jo blurted. "I mean, well, it was. We're going back to Boston tomorrow. We have to start school, and Dad has to go back to Harvard, and Mom has to—"

Maddie kicked her sister's ankle under the table. "I'm sorry, Miss Averil," Maddie interrupted. "How did you find out about our banquet?" She realized after speaking that she sounded rude and tried to recover quickly. "That is, I would have set extra plates at the table had I known you were coming."

"Oh dear, don't fuss over us, we'll squeeze in somehow," Elizabeth insisted. "We didn't even know about it until today. Michael said something this morning about an archaeology something-or-other he's involved with, but you know how that goes. Travel here, pick up camp, travel there, and then do it all over again. It's wild getting to tag along, don't you think?" She slid her stockinged feet into her high-heeled shoes and laced the straps through the tiny gold buckles at her ankles. "There!" she sighed. "Now I feel dressed for a banquet. I wish I'd known tonight was crown-optional," she said, leaning in to take a closer look at the girls' floral adornments. "Those are beautiful."

Maddie adjusted her floral headpiece. "We could make one for you, if you like, but our Dad—"

"Is Michael an archaeologist, too?" Jo interrupted.

"And is he your husband?" Maddie jumped in.

"And are you from Boston?" Jo finished, hoping that she might be. Elizabeth radiated style and sophistication, and she imagined how fun it might be to shop around town with her.

"Inquisitive, you are." Elizabeth nodded at the twins. "I like that." She stood up at the table and stamped her feet a few times, her heels digging slightly into the rugs on top of the sandy ground. "Yes, Michael is an archaeologist. And no, he's not my husband." She held out her left hand to show off an ornate engagement ring. "But he *is* my fiancé."

Maddie and Jo bent over to inspect the big, beautiful diamond ring sitting on Elizabeth's finger. It sparkled from every angle, even at dusk.

Elizabeth drew her hand back playfully. "Don't worry, girls, I'm sure you'll get your own diamonds one day."

She pulled a silver tube from her handbag. Taking off the cap, she turned the bottom edge back toward her, using it as a mirror while she reapplied her orange lipstick. "And we're not far from Boston. We live in Providence, where Michael is a professor." She turned her head to the side and winked at the girls. "I don't suppose you'd like some?" she asked, waving the lipstick. "You're about that age now, aren't you?"

Maddie and Jo smiled at each other and stepped toward her, pleased that this new friend had realized how grown-up they were.

"Yes, we're about that age," Maddie said before pursing her lips.

Dinner was about to be served, and everyone had taken their seats. Since Michael and Elizabeth had come for dinner unexpectedly, the girls agreed to sit opposite Henri and share the only extra plate and the only extra piece of furniture at the camp. They fought each other for what little space there was on the lid of the rectangular basket that served as their shared chair at the end of the table.

"Stop pushing me, Jo," Maddie hissed under her breath.

"I've only got one leg on," Jo insisted. "*You're* the one taking up all the room!"

Martha interrupted them. "Girls, why don't you light the lanterns? The adults have some things to talk about." She looked around the table uneasily.

The girls stood up, and Jo drew an imaginary line down the center of the basket lid with her finger.

"*That's* the middle. Right there. When we get back, stay on your side."

Maddie scoffed and pulled her sister by the hand to the other side of camp.

"Something's wrong with Mom and Dad," Maddie whispered as they lit the lanterns around the first tent. "And they don't want us to know what they're talking about."

"I don't think Dad likes Michael very much," Jo added. "He's been frowning since they arrived." She squinted to see her parents' faces, dimly lit by candlelight. "Why do you think Henri brought them here?"

"Maybe they're doing another dig together," Maddie answered. "Henri asked Dad if he remembered Michael from Rome."

"And Michael's a professor, just an hour away from Boston in Providence. Maybe they know each other from there, too?" Jo proposed as she stepped back down.

"No idea." Maddie cupped her hand around her ear and tried without luck to pick out words from the conversation at the table. "We've got to get closer. Come on." She pulled at her sister's hand again. "After we light the lanterns, we'll go to the far side of the tent and listen. Whatever's wrong, they're not going to say it in front of us."

Jo stepped out from the darkness on the side of their sleeping tent. "Maybe if we get closer to the firepit, we can hear better," she said.

Maddie shook her head. "The fire's still too bright. They'll see us for sure." She tugged on Jo's shirt and pulled her back into the shadows.

Just as she did, their mother got up and headed toward the makeshift camp kitchen. Back and forth, back and forth she went until the rustic dinner was on the table. She turned her head to look for her girls before Henri stood up, clutching a bottle of champagne in his hand.

"I do love a happy ending," he said sentimentally, and popped the cork with ease. "I told you this would all work out, didn't I?" Everyone lifted their tin mugs, and he poured until the bottle was empty. "*Santé*, ladies and gentlemen! To new friends and new adventures."

Tin mugs clinked together, leaving Maddie bewildered.

"What, now they're all friends?" she whispered to her sister.

Martha put her cup down and stood. "I'm going to go and find the girls," she said, and walked swiftly in the direction of the first tent.

Maddie and Jo moved out from the side of the far tent and walked toward the table, intending to sit down before their mother realized they had been hiding. But just as they were halfway there, Elizabeth stood and raised her glass again.

"And here's to shopping in Paris for nine months' worth of winter clothes! Hats, gloves, coats, and the rest. I hear it's much colder in Siberia than New England," she laughed. "Are you sure you're ready for the weather, Tom?"

The girls froze.

"*Siberia?*" Maddie mouthed to Jo, her thoughts racing. She didn't know exactly where Siberia was, but it wasn't near Boston.

Jo didn't answer, already on the move and running up behind her father's chair.

"Dad?" she said cautiously. "Where are we going? Are we not going back to Boston?" She looked at the faces around the table. Elizabeth looked dreamy, as if she were still thinking about shopping in Paris. Michael flashed Jo a toothy smile and raised his eyebrows. Henri held his napkin to his mouth and looked down at his plate to avoid her eyes.

"Well, honey, I—we—" he stammered.

Elizabeth gasped daintily and leaned over to Michael. "They haven't told them?" she whispered.

Henri stood up and motioned toward the cars. "Let's give them some time."

Martha put her hands on both of her girls' shoulders and crouched down to be at eye level. "We didn't find out that we had been selected to go on this project until Henri arrived," she said in her most soothing tone of voice. "Your father and I, and Michael and Elizabeth, were chosen from many, many talented archaeologists to spend the next nine months in Siberia to study ancient cave dwellings. It's the opportunity of a lifetime for us."

Jo's voice quivered when she spoke. "But where is Siberia?"

"It's in the Soviet Union, in northern Asia," her father answered, squeezing Jo's arm the way he always did when he had less-than-good news to share.

"What about *home?*" Maddie cried. She couldn't steady her shaky voice. "What about our *friends*, and our *school?*"

Tom leaned forward and took the girls' hands. "Boston will still be there when we get back. It's only nine months," he reassured them. "We'll be back home by next May. Our town-house, your school, your friends, they will all be there when we get back."

Maddie and Jo looked at each other and sniffled for a few moments. Jo shuffled her feet and tried to put on a brave face.

"I guess maybe we could live in Siberia," she choked out as best as she could. "Do we have to go to school?"

Tom and Martha suddenly realized that they had told their daughters only half the story. Martha braced herself and collected her thoughts.

"Girls, my girls." The words came out in a sigh. Martha shook her head slowly with her eyes closed. "Yes, you *do* have to go to school. And that's why . . . well, that's . . . ."

Tom jumped in to finish the sentence his wife couldn't. "That's why you're not coming with us."

CHAPTER FOUR

A Change of Plans

The words echoed in Maddie's ears.

You're not coming with us.

Her emotions bounced between shocked and fearful to giddy and excited. *Mom and Dad are going to leave us somewhere.* The fact that *where* was still a mystery calmed her somehow. A hundred different possibilities flashed through her mind. *Perhaps Jo and I will be taken back to Paris by Henri to attend the finest ballet academy. Or maybe we'll stay in Morocco, and live in a beautiful hotel while we're taught by a fancy governess. Or maybe—*

"What?!" Jo wailed, bursting into tears and interrupting Maddie's daydreams. "What do you mean we're *not coming*, Dad? What are we supposed to do? Where are we going when you and Mom go to Siberia? Why can't we go there, too?"

Martha and Tom stayed calm. As much as they wanted to abandon their plans for Siberia, scoop up their daughters, and return to Boston the next day, they knew this would only sting for a little while more. The work they were about to begin, and the new adventures for Maddie and Jo, were worth the initial sadness.

"It's not that you *can't* come to Siberia, girls," Tom explained, pausing for a moment to consider another option. "If you like, you *can* come. But you won't be able to go outside and play, you won't have any friends, and you won't be able to go to school. Siberia is freezing cold, and no one lives in the region we're going to. Even your mom and I aren't looking forward to the icy weather, the snowsuits, and the isolation. But if you insist, well!" He tossed his hands up and smiled at his wife. "Honey, I think we should let them come—Ow!"

Martha elbowed him in the side. "Uh . . . thanks, Tom," she said as her husband rubbed his ribs. "*Or*," Martha said, a smile forming at the corners of her mouth, "you could go to Europe, just like you asked to do earlier."

The girls' expressions changed. Jo's chin lifted as she waited for her mother to tell her more, and the wheels in Maddie's head stopped spinning for a moment.

"Henri knows of a boarding school," Martha said quietly. "It's a marvelous place, just for girls. He assured us it would be perfect for you. They're expecting you soon."

By now, Martha was crouched down on the ground. Maddie and Jo, temporarily forgetting their sadness about being left behind, sat cross-legged in the sand so they could put their heads on their mother's shoulders.

"Boarding school?" Jo asked. "Does that mean we would live there?"

"Yes, Jo, with lots of other girls your age," Martha replied. "Doesn't that sound like fun? Like when your friends stay over, but it will happen every night."

Jo began to imagine nightly ghost story sessions, pillow fights, and cookie making—just like when she and Maddie had a birthday party in Boston.

"Mom, Dad," Maddie asked, "where is the school?"

Tom reentered the conversation now that Martha had pacified their daughters. "It's in Switzerland, in a tiny town called Saint-Marcel. Henri says that it's beautiful, on the banks of a sparkling blue lake, high in the mountains. It's called Madame Molineaux's School for Girls."

Jo sounded out the name. *"Madame Mo-Lee-Noe's?"* she asked, exaggerating the syllables. "Is that a French name?"

"It sounds like it," Maddie said, turning to her mother with a new reason to be concerned. "Do we have to speak French there? Do they speak English?"

Maddie and Jo had had French lessons back in Boston and had even gotten to practice with some of the Moroccan locals, but they could only carry on light conversation.

"Not to worry, girls," Martha said. "Most classes are taught in English. There will be others there who don't speak French, and you'll take French lessons with them. I bet by the end of the year, you two will sound like you were born in Paris!"

Jo thought about how long it had taken to get to Morocco in the first place. "But how would we get to Switzerland? And how long will it take? And where are our things? And—"

"Speaking of Paris," Henri interrupted from a few feet away. "I didn't have a chance to give you these earlier." He stood behind two tall white boxes, each tied with blue-green satin ribbons. "Maybe these will come in handy on your way to Switzerland."

Maddie and Jo inched away from their parents toward the large gifts, momentarily distracted from the grave discussion of their fate for the next school year.

"Which one is mine? Or are they the same?" Jo asked solemnly, wishing she felt more excited about receiving such a huge present from Paris.

"Of course they are not the same," Henri insisted. "Even though you are twins, you ladies are as different as can be. The one on my right," he gestured with his hand, "is for you, Maddie, and the one on my left is for you, Jo."

The girls crouched down and untied the satin ribbons, letting them fall to the sand. Jo squeezed the sides of the box lid and lifted it into the air. "Look, Maddie," she whispered as she ran her fingers over the raised golden lettering of the card that sat atop layers of yellow tissue paper.

"Wait for me, Jo!" Maddie complained, struggling to lift the lid off her box. "I'm not looking at yours until I get this open."

But she couldn't resist catching a glimpse of her sister's gift out of the corner of her eye as she tugged more insistently on the box's top.

"It's so fancy!" she chirped as she finally slid the lid upward and laid it next to her. "And mine is *blue*," she marveled, looking up at Henri. "How did you know our favorite colors?"

"Uncle Henri knows all things," he said playfully. "Well, *most* things." He exchanged smiles with Martha and Tom. "I have help from time to time."

Jo held the card at the corners, doing her best not to bend or scratch it. "House of Fournier," she read aloud.

"Fiona Fournier?" Martha exclaimed. "I've seen her dresses in fashion magazines. I didn't know she made children's clothing."

Henri smoothed his hair underneath his hat. "Children? I don't see any children here, Martha." He winked at Maddie and

Jo. "Besides, Fiona is a personal acquaintance of mine. She was delighted to have such youthful clientele."

Maddie and Jo pulled back the layers of tissue paper to reveal their dresses—ball gowns perfectly tailored to each twin's favorite style. Maddie stood and pulled her gown out by the sheer blue sleeves, gently shaking out the gathered silk skirt. "It's gorgeous," she breathed, holding it up to her shoulders to inspect the beaded details.

"They're *both* gorgeous," Jo chimed in, hugging the bodice of her yellow gown to her torso and kicking her legs in front of her to spread out the layers and layers of tulle on the long ballerina skirt.

"I don't suppose you bought one for me?" Elizabeth's voice called out from across the camp. She walked up to the girls and curtseyed. "I'd like to be a princess, too, Henri," she joked.

"Can you make it in fur and leather for the trip to Siberia?" Michael asked, joining the group and laughing with Elizabeth. "Maybe something out of *The Snow Queen*."

Maddie despised the thought of wearing animal fur, but she couldn't help but imagine Elizabeth draped in white rabbit pelts as the Snow Queen, ordering her parents and Michael around on an icy slope.

Henri smiled and cocked his head. "I'll inquire with Fiona the next time I'm in Paris. But for now," he said, pulling back his jacket cuff and looking at his watch, "we must be on our way."

"On our way *where*, exactly?" asked Jo. "And do I need to wear my new dress?"

"No, no, Josephine," Henri assured her. "Your desert clothes are fine. You'll wear your dress on the ship."

"The ship?" Jo repeated. Last time she checked, Switzerland didn't have any port cities. "The ship from where? To where?"

"I'll explain everything as we drive. We'll be on the road in just a few minutes."

"A few minutes?" Jo asked, her heart sinking as she folded the delicate dress back into its box. "We haven't even started our dinner!"

Martha beckoned her girls back to the table. "You can eat while Henri and your father load your things into the car. Hurry up, girls."

Maddie and Jo plopped down and ate begrudgingly, each bite taking longer than the one prior. Elizabeth walked over with warm bread and laid a piece at each girl's plate, trying to be helpful.

"Thanks," Jo mumbled, not sure if Elizabeth would be the friend she hoped for at first.

"But what about dessert?" Maddie asked, trying to stall for more time with her parents.

Henri walked by them, holding the two large dress boxes in his arms, and turned back toward the table. "Don't worry, ladies, I know of a great place for dessert in Fes. We'll stop on the way."

Maddie fidgeted with the buttons on her light jacket, intentionally taking longer than usual to put it on. She and Jo had never been away from their parents for more than a few days, and that had always been to stay with family.

"Mom?" she asked. "Why didn't you tell us earlier this summer? I want one more day with you and Dad before we go."

"We haven't known for long, Maddie. We first heard about the special dig a few weeks ago in a letter from Henri. It wasn't for sure, and we didn't want to worry you girls if we didn't get chosen, so we waited to say anything. But Henri did insist that, if the deal went through, we'd have to leave in a hurry. Of course, your father and I want more days with you," she said to her daughter, staring into her eyes. "But this is how it has to be—and why Henri made such careful arrangements for you and Jo."

Maddie stared at the ground and searched for ways to see them sooner than the following summer. "Will you and Dad be visiting us over Christmas?"

Martha shook her head.

"No, darling. We'll be too far away. It would take nearly three weeks to get to you from Siberia! Henri will make sure that you have a wonderful holiday. But we *will* be writing to you, every month. And remember," she said, holding Maddie's head in her hands, "your father and I love you and Jo so, so much."

She pulled both girls to her sides and hugged them tightly. Jo began to tear up, and Martha stepped back and addressed her daughters like young ladies. "Now, you listen to me, Jo. You, too, Maddie. We're all a little scared, and believe me, I've been just as frightened as you are now. Once, when I was a girl, your grandfather put me on a train in New York and sent me all the way to Chicago, all by myself."

Maddie and Jo had a harder time believing that their mother was ever a little girl than the story about the train ride.

"But we're adventurers, right? I made it to Chicago just fine, and you're going to have an exciting year in Switzerland. Wipe those tears now, Jo. We'll all be back together before you know it."

Maddie took her flower crown from her head. "I guess these stay here," she said softly, and tossed it onto the table. Jo followed suit.

Tom joined the group and wrapped his arms around the girls. "You'll always be my princesses."

The Livingston family held one another together for just a few more moments, then moved quickly across the sandy camp. The sun had finally set, and the festive lanterns, with flames glowing through the brightly colored silks that draped the glass, felt oddly out of place. Maddie and Jo looked up at the twinkling Moroccan sky as they made their way toward Henri's car, the passenger door open, the engine idling in a low rumble.

"We love you, Maddie and Jo," Tom told his daughters as he kissed their cheeks one last time. "Be safe, be brave, and above all, take care of each other."

Martha kissed their foreheads and fixed their hair, just as she would have in Boston, shooing them out the door for another school day. "Be good girls for me, okay?"

Henri placed both hands on top of the open car door. "In you go, ladies. It's time to leave."

Elizabeth approached the car, tugging at Michael's arm to come along. "Bye, girls," she called apologetically. "It was awfully nice to meet you. Hope we get to chat again someday." She shook Maddie's hand, then Jo's, lingering there for a second.

Jo felt something cool and metallic on her palm. She opened her hand slightly to reveal the lipstick from earlier, and flashed it to her sister before closing her fingers around it again. Both girls tried their best to smile at Elizabeth in thanks.

Elizabeth winked twice, then turned her head while the Livingstons exchanged their final quick hugs. "This is hard to watch," she whispered to Michael, whose expression didn't change.

The girls tucked themselves into the leather bench in the back of the car.

"I love you, Mom and Dad," Maddie said, struggling to be brave.

"I love you, too!" Jo called out. She wiped her nose on her sleeve.

Henri closed the back seat door, bid a hasty farewell to his friends, and climbed into the driver's seat. After the tires spun a few times in the sand, the car drove away from the camp. Martha and Tom grasped hands as they waved and blew kisses toward their daughters, stopping only when they could no longer see the red taillights. They turned around toward Michael and Elizabeth.

"You've done the right thing," Michael reassured them. "The girls will be happy in Switzerland, and we'll all be famous for what we discover in Siberia."

But Tom and Martha couldn't force a smile. It would be a long nine months without their girls.

It was quiet inside the automobile as Henri drove the girls through the desert, its headlights cutting through the darkness to reveal the tire tracks it left on its way in. Jo reached for her sister's hand, squeezing hard as Maddie inhaled a heavy breath of air and started to cry.

"Maddie, please don't cry or I'll start," Jo said, curling up next to her sister and finally letting her tears fall freely. The girls, finally realizing what had happened in the whirlwind of news that ended their banquet, were beginning to unravel. By now, they were miles away from their parents.

Henri glanced at them in the back seat, struggling not to get choked up as he watched the girls cry. Though he had hardly seen them during their childhood, he loved their parents dearly, and felt that Maddie and Jo were the closest thing to daughters he would ever have. Seeing them so distraught was unbearable.

"Ladies, ladies," he pleaded softly. "I know you are missing your parents now . . . but understand they did what they thought was best for you. You believe that, don't you?"

There was no answer from the back seat, just a sniffle here and a sigh there.

"I understand if you don't want to talk," he continued. "I'll tell you what I am going to do. Let's stop and get dessert in Fes, like I promised. And while you eat, I'll tell you the story of how I met your parents."

He held his wristwatch at an angle to catch the moonlight, and, after checking it twice, pushed his foot harder on the gas pedal.

Wham!

Maddie's shoulders jerked as the slam of the car door woke her from a fitful nap. It felt like hours since she'd nodded off on Jo's shoulder, and she wiped her tear-stained cheek with the back of her hand. She blinked to focus in the dark. Henri's shoes made a scratching sound on the gravel drive outside, and Maddie watched as his silhouette moved to the back of the car.

Maybe he's leaving us here with our trunk, she thought, suddenly aware that Henri could, at any moment, decide to change their plans again. He was, after all, a stranger to them—a faint memory from childhood, a name their parents dropped into conversations here and there, and, until now, someone who felt more like a ghost or a character in a storybook than a trusted guardian.

Henri rustled around in the car's trunk for a few minutes, cursed softly, and slammed the trunk, startling Maddie and waking Jo.

"We're here," he sang as he opened the door for them to step out. "Time to have some dessert." He looked around. "Dessert in the *desert*," he stated proudly. "Hey, that's funny, like a joke, right? Dessert and desert?" He helped Maddie out of the car.

Jo squinted in the back seat and stretched her legs until her feet were hanging out the door. "Kind of," she said thoughtfully. "But your accent makes the words sound exactly the same, so . . . not really." She shrugged before springing out of the car and onto the ground. "Where are we? It doesn't really look like the desert out here."

"You're right, Jo," Henri said, and winced playfully. "My jokes, they need more practice, I suppose. But," he encouraged the girls, "look around you. We're on one of the liveliest streets in all of Fes." He held his arms up and spun around slowly, nodding and waving to strangers in the crowded street. "The night market. Enchanting, yes?"

Maddie peered down the cobblestone road as far as she could see. Above the noisy merchant tents, the stars twinkled in the blue-black sky. Sellers peddling spices and leathers called out to passersby from their carts. Lanterns flickered near every doorstep, casting a soft orange light on walls and plants. She took a few quick breaths in through her nose and squinted.

"It's beautiful," Maddie agreed, "but the air is a bit . . ."

"Overwhelming?" Henri laughed. "You'll get used to it. They're tanning leather all around us, after all, and the fragrance is . . . rather pungent." He walked to a nearby doorstep and pulled two bouquets of mint sprigs from a stone pot. "Here, hold these under your noses until we get to fresher air."

"I thought you said the place we were eating dessert was a secret," Maddie reminded him, wondering why the street was so full of people at such a late hour. "It looks like everyone here already knows."

"Patience, Maddie. This is as far as we can go by automobile," Henri said, taking a quick look inside his jacket lapel before locking the car. "We'll have to make the rest of the trip on foot. Stay close," he warned. "It's easy to get lost in all these people."

The girls linked arms, held their mint bouquets to their noses, and stayed only inches behind Henri. With his large frame, he moved easily through the crowd. The shouting of buyers and sellers, the clanking of pots, and the hoisting of heavy sacks onto carts drowned out even the loudest of the street musicians. Maddie considered sacrificing her mint bouquet in order to cover one of her ears.

With a quick turn to the left, Henri cut through the market onto a quieter path, and the clatter began to fade. They slowed their pace and strolled uphill until they reached a narrow alleyway nestled between two arched doorways. Henri ushered the girls to the dark entrance.

"In we go!" he ordered. "Ladies first."

"In *there*?" Jo protested. "I don't think I'll fit."

"My dear Josephine, if *I* can fit, *you* can fit. Now come on, we have to keep going."

"Okay," she said, nodding. "We can all fit. Sure we can." She took a deep breath and jumped behind Maddie. "You first, Sis." She placed both hands on Maddie's shoulders and walked her to the edge of the entrance.

Of course, me first, Maddie thought, wondering why being the first-born twin had somehow automatically signed her up for doing *everything* first. She held on to the front of the alleyway entrance with both hands and leaned into the darkness. She thought she could see a faint glow off in the distance, but the more she squinted, the more it faded. *More like dessert in the dungeon,* she thought.

Henri nudged the girls forward and whipped his head around in both directions to make sure no one was watching before following. "Hold on to the walls, Maddie," he instructed, turning sideways to fit his muscular build into the tight space. "And walk toward the light."

Maddie pressed the palms of her hands into the walls, walking them forward as she took one step at a time. As the light from the street faded, her other senses were heightened. She could feel every bump in the stone walkway through the soles of her shoes, and she noticed every crack and crevice in the earthy walls as she swept her fingers over them. Her ears picked up the faint sounds of muffled voices and clinking glasses in the distance.

"Shouldn't we have a torch or something?" Jo whispered in complete darkness.

"It's not much farther," Henri coaxed. "I know where we're going, and we're almost there now. See how it's getting lighter? You're excellent excavators, just like your parents!"

Jo bounced back and forth between her sister and Henri, ramming her elbows into Maddie's back or accidentally kicking Henri's shins when she took unsure steps forward. It was almost easier with her eyes closed. Trying to navigate in the dark was making her dizzy.

At last, Maddie could make out the end of the path a few dozen steps in front of her. Within moments, the trio emerged from the alleyway and into an underground courtyard.

"Whoa," Jo breathed as she stepped out of the alley. They'd arrived in a large rectangular room, full of arched doorways and tiled fountains against the walls. The roof, a dome-shaped assembly of blue, green, and clear glass panes, let the twinkling stars shine through as it reflected the serene scene below.

A man taller and wider than Henri stood at the largest of the arched doorways, the faint noises from what seemed like a party escaping from the spaces behind him. His deep brown skin shined with sweat, and his bright eyes widened when he recognized Henri. He smiled, held his arms out in front of him, and shook his head.

"I just broke up a brawl and sent two Frenchmen flying out of here," he insisted. "Can I have a moment's peace before I have to do it again?" He laughed and hugged Henri before pulling back with a more serious expression. "It's good to see you, friend. You know he's here, right? He's been looking for you and—"

"I know," Henri interrupted. "Allow me to introduce my, ah, nieces: Madeline and Josephine." He pushed the girls forward. "Girls, this is your Uncle Henri's, ahhh, *business partner*, Olu." He locked Olu's gaze. "I just brought the girls for a late dessert at my favorite spot in Fes."

"You thought this would be a great place for *children* to come and have *dessert*?" Olu asked, looking at Henri sideways. "Okay, then. Well." He bent down to greet the girls and gave a warm grin. "It's very nice to meet you, ladies. I hope you enjoy your dessert."

"Well, I did tell them that this was the best café for pastries in all of Fes," Henri stated.

Maddie and Jo smiled as the towering man stood back up. "Thank you, Mister Olu," they said in unison. But already, they both felt as if something wasn't right.

Henri scooted the girls through the doorway, then hung back near his friend for a moment. He opened one side of his jacket and then the other, finally finding a small envelope. "I need a quick favor. Here are instructions and payment, I'm sure you'll find someone to take care of this while we're inside." Olu took the envelope and nodded. "As far as *him* being here," Henri said in a lower tone of voice, "I'm well aware, and I'll find him when I'm ready. Try to keep him and his men occupied while I have dessert with the girls."

Olu flipped through the envelope of bills and smiled. "Anything else?"

"Not that I can think of. But, just in case I have to make a sudden exit, I'll bid you farewell now."

Olu patted him on the shoulder. "When have you *not* had to make a sudden exit?"

"*Au revoir*, Olu. Until next time." He straightened his jacket and walked quickly to catch up with the girls.

Jo coughed for the third time at the table. Clouds of cigar smoke made her eyes water as she looked around. *Why did I drop that mint bouquet?* she scolded herself, wishing she had something more pleasant to sniff.

The café was noisy and dark, and small groups of people chatted loudly and erupted into laughter. Men crowded around a card game and cheered or shouted angrily after one of the players made their move. A three-piece band played traditional Moroccan music in the corner, and women dressed in long headscarves, midriff-baring tops, and floor-length ruffled skirts danced to the beat of the drums while their gold jewelry jingled in time.

Henri and the girls had been taken through the café to a quieter table with two benches covered in orange fabric. All eyes seemed to be on them as they passed, and Henri, looking uncomfortable, instructed the girls to duck down as they walked, citing cleaner air lower to the ground as his reason. But Maddie and Jo suspected otherwise.

"Are we *allowed* to be here, Henri?" Maddie questioned him from across the table once they sat down. "I don't see any other children here, and everyone stared at us as we came in."

"Don't worry, Maddie, it's perfectly fine that you're here, and we won't be long," he assured her. "In fact," he said, raising his hand and gesturing to a nearby waiter, "your dessert and my coffee will be arriving shortly."

"This place is . . . well . . ." Jo tried to find the word as she observed all the happenings around her.

"Charming?" Henri chimed in. "I know, it's been one of my favorite places for years."

"I think she might have meant *uncouth*," Maddie spoke for her sister after remembering a word she'd learned at her school in Boston. "It means 'a bit rough.'"

"Rough? This crowd? Certainly not." Henri looked over his left shoulder, glimpsed a group of men in suits a few tables away, and immediately ducked down closer to the table for a moment. "But it really is smoky in here, that's for certain. You might do as I do," he encouraged them.

"Are you . . . are we *hiding* from someone?" Jo asked, more curious than accusing. She sat up on her knees, rocking the upholstered bench she and Maddie shared as she looked around the room.

"Of course not!" Henri protested. "It is simply your Uncle Henri's habit to always be aware of my surroundings without anyone being aware of me," he said as he tugged on Jo's arm to bring her back down to the table. "I've had business meetings with almost everyone in this room. But there are people here who—"

"Here you are," the waiter interrupted cheerfully as he placed water and a small plate holding a honey-covered pastry and a fork in front of each girl. "And your regular, Henri," he said, setting down an espresso with a lemon twist and a tiny piece of chocolate.

"Ooh, baklava," Jo gushed.

"Actually, it's a special dessert prepared by the chef's mother, just for you," said the waiter. "It's called briwat."

Henri nodded in thanks and looked over his shoulder again. The men in suits were gone. He twisted the spiral of lemon peel above his strong coffee, sending shiny droplets of lemon oil onto the rim of the jewel-toned cup.

"I know you must be a bit confused . . . shocked, even, at the events of tonight. Missing your mother and father already. So let me tell you a story I think you might like," Henri offered. He sipped his espresso and waited for the girls to lift their heads, which they did, albeit slowly.

"It was twenty years ago, eight years before you were born. I was sixteen years old, beginning to go on my own adventures, just as you are now." Already, the girls looked more interested in his story. "I worked as a dishwasher in a street café in Paris. Can you believe it?" he scoffed. "Your Uncle Henri, washing dishes!"

Maddie smiled and Jo giggled through a closed mouthful of briwat. Henri softened his posture a bit and kept going.

"One day, an American couple, maybe ten years older than you are now, sat outside and drank coffee for hours, looking frantically at maps, books, and articles. My English was decent, but their French was horrible. I cleared the empty coffee pots from their table and overheard them arguing over the meaning of a particular headline in a newspaper. The man was trying to translate from French into English, and the woman just kept telling him that he was wrong."

"Mom and Dad?" Maddie asked, trying to picture her parents in their younger years.

"Yes," Henri answered. "Your mother stopped me before I left the table and asked me to tell her who was correct. In fact, both were wrong about the translation! For your records," he said, leaning closer, "*évidence* means neither 'evidence' nor 'proof,' but means, 'the obvious nature of something.'"

Maddie and Jo furrowed their brows.

"Sorry, ah, just a quick French lesson for you, so you don't make the same mistake as your parents did. But, back to the story!" Henri quipped. "I set the empty dishes on a table and sat down to help them for a moment."

Jo raised her arms and plunked her elbows on the table. "What was the article about?" she asked.

"Your parents were searching for a journal—the diary of a French treasure hunter. It was rumored that he sank his own ship full of treasure to hide it from his enemies, but . . ." Henri paused before raising his eyebrows and speaking slowly. "He died before returning to find it, or so the legend goes."

Now, it was Maddie's turn to lean forward. "Treasure!" she exclaimed. "Did they find it?"

"Ah, no, Maddie, they did not. If they had, well, all our lives might be very different now, as it is worth a fortune," he said, sighing. "But they were not looking for the treasure. They were looking for the journal. You see, this treasure hunter fancied ancient artifacts, too. Your parents considered him an archaeologist first, a thief second. He hid his historical finds all over Europe, and the journal contains riddles and puzzles that direct the reader to his hiding spots."

"Well," Jo persisted, "did they find the journal at least?"

"No, they didn't find that either. No one has found it yet, and believe me, there are others looking for it . . ." Henri once again looked over his shoulder, pausing for a moment. "But," he continued, "it was the search for the journal that brought your parents and me together. After that day in the café, they asked me to translate more and more documents. I worked in exchange for your mother's cooking and your father's endless history lessons in their tiny apartment. It was our first project together, and we have been friends ever since." He popped the small chocolate on his saucer into his mouth and tipped his espresso cup back, finishing it swiftly. "Now then. Why don't you girls finish your desserts while I say a quick hello to a friend?" He stood up from his bench, patted his jacket lapel, and walked away. "Stay there until I come back," he called before he was out of earshot.

Maddie pushed her plate away.

"You don't like it?" Jo inquired, hoping this meant there would be more for her to eat.

"I like it just fine," Maddie said, facing down. "But I don't want this."

Jo pulled her sister's plate toward her own triumphantly.

Maddie didn't flinch. "I want the sandy, hard muffins Mom made at the dig site. I want them with the spoiled milk that Dad tried to convince us was clotted cream. I just want to be back at the camp, packing up to go home."

Jo chewed for a moment and swallowed. "I know," she said, putting her hand on Maddie's shoulder. "But you've got to admit, this is kind of exciting. I mean, look around." She motioned to the dancers as they moved through the crowds with elegance and poise, waving scarves in the air and jingling the coins on their waist belts. She pointed to the card game where what seemed like fifty men hollered in disbelief at the same time. "We've never seen this back in Boston. And we're finally getting to go to Europe."

Maddie nodded, then moved her head rhythmically to the beat of the music. A smile grew on her face as she and Jo started to relax and enjoy their exclusive look into the hidden nightlife of Fes.

"See?" Jo asked, looking at the various vignettes taking place around them. Her gaze settled on a beautiful brunette woman in a silver dress, who took turns scolding and then showing her outstretched hand to her stylish male companion. "I bet she's saying, 'Look, darling, look at my plain, unjeweled hand. You should have bought me that ruby back at the night market!'"

Maddie laughed and joined in the game. "Look over there." She turned Jo's face with her hand, pointing out an irritated man wearing a silky Moroccan Djellaba robe shouting at the waiter. "I'd swear I just heard him say, 'I ordered your finest spiced lamb dish, not this peanut-butter-and-jelly sandwich!'"

Jo doubled over laughing and sat back up, determined to make a better joke than her sister. "Look at that man running through the crowd toward us," she giggled. "I bet he's saying—"

"*Allez vite!* Run!!" Henri belted out, zigzagging in and out of onlookers like a slalom skier. He threw his arms around furiously as he motioned for the girls to get up from the table. "We have to go," he panted at them, looking behind him to see how much time they had. *"Now!"* He pulled the girls off their bench and pointed to a door behind a group of waiters. "Through the kitchen door!"

Without time to think, Maddie and Jo scrambled in the direction he pointed.

"Excuse me!" Maddie cried out as she pushed through the waiters like velvet drapes. Jo bowled along after her, and they both crashed through the swinging door ahead of them, spilling onto the tiled floor.

"Up we go," Henri barked hastily as he yanked them both off the floor by the arms. "There's a side door there—" he instructed them, and pushed in front of the girls. "Out of the way!" he shouted, barreling through the sea of bewildered cooks with the girls running behind him.

The hot kitchen air made it even harder for Maddie to catch her breath, and each inhale made her lungs feel tighter and tighter. Luckily, they were almost to the side door. Henri threw it open, and suddenly, they were back outside on a quiet residential street.

Jo panicked. "Where's the car!" she demanded, whipping around frantically to catch sight of their escape vehicle.

"And who's chasing you? Who's chasing *us*?" Maddie hissed, her eyes permanently fixed on the side door out of which they had just exploded, waiting for someone to burst through it again.

Henri looked surprisingly calm. He twisted his neck to one side and then the other in an attempt to stretch, but was hindered by his necktie and collar. He walked to a nearby side yard and pulled a burlap cover off a covered military truck. Peeking into the back, he nodded and looked back at the girls. "It's all here," he assured them. "Now then. Let's go! You have a boat to catch in the morning."

Maddie didn't need a second invitation. She rushed over, climbed into the truck, and looked into the back. "How did our things get here?" she asked as her sister jumped onto the seat with her.

"Olu always comes through," Henri replied as he slid into the driver's seat and started the engine.

"That Olu?" Jo asked innocently, peering out the screened back window of the truck. "The one holding those men back?"

Henri sprang up and stood on the outside edge of his seat, hanging on to the door frame to look out over the top of the vehicle. "Yes, *that* Olu," he said as he dipped back inside the truck. They could all hear the men shouting and yelling words Maddie and Jo were sure were bad ones as Olu fought to keep them back.

"You think you can trick us by giving us *sapphires* instead, Henri?" one of the men yelled at the idling truck.

Henri revved the engine, wishing it would warm up faster.

"And you promised there would be *ten,* not *eight!*" the man shouted frantically, trying his best to get past Olu's muscular arms.

Henri stuck his arm out the window to give a quick wave to Olu, shifted the truck into gear, and sped off down the winding streets of Fes as the girls held on for dear life.

They were already out of town and back on desolate roads before anyone spoke.

"*Ahhhhh!*" Jo let out a high-pitched scream.

"What is it?" Henri sputtered, trying to see the back seat in his rearview mirror. "What? *What?*"

"You're screaming *now?*" Maddie asked, startled by her sister's delayed reaction to the events that had transpired at the café. Her own heart had finally stopped racing, and she was beginning to calm down. *No more excitement,* she pleaded silently. *Just quiet.*

"Exactly what just happened?" Jo fired back. "One moment, we're sitting at a table eating dessert, and the next, we're running through an underground casino, then a kitchen, then jumping into who-knows-whose truck that smells as old and awful and musty as the military ambulance back at the dig site, and then escaping from an angry mob!"

"Actually, that sounds just right," Henri said casually. "Yep, you hit the screw on the head, Jo."

"It's *nail*, Henri," Jo corrected him. "Hit the *nail* on the head. And I think you've left some of the details out of that story. What did you do to those men?"

Henri shook his head. "Do to them? I did nothing. We have a difference in opinion on the authenticity of certain gemstones," he explained. "But in *that* place, their opinions are the only ones that matter. And if you have a different one, well . . ." He shrugged.

"Run," Maddie said between yawns. "We know."

"That's not all, ladies," Henri defended himself. "I learned from a trusted friend that we needed a special vehicle and a secret route to cross the border into Algeria, where your ship departs. As it turns out, that secret route takes longer than the way I'd planned to go."

Maddie let her head fall back against the seat. "I don't suppose our parents know about this part of the trip, do they?" she asked, closing her eyes.

"Not yet. But rest assured, I'll tell them every detail in a telegram, about how brave you both were and how adventurous your journey has been, even from the beginning! It's very exciting, no?"

He waited a few moments for an answer before turning to look at the back seat, where Maddie and Jo were fast asleep.

"*Bonne nuit,*" he whispered, and drove into the night.

CHAPTER FIVE

TAKEN BY SEA

Jo stood on her tiptoes to see over the long line of passengers in front of her, which wasn't easy on the inclined ramp that led from the dock at the Port of Algiers to the ship's deck. "Not even close yet," she moaned. She came back down to her heels and dropped her chin to her chest. The morning sun was getting hotter by the minute, and the smell from the fishing rig beside their dock was beginning to make her queasy.

"Girls, come now," Henri said, leaning against the metal railing. He stretched his arms out and inhaled deeply. "Smell the sea air! I'm sure we'll be at the passenger check-in soon. Until then, look around you . . . enjoy the land and the solid ground. Pretty soon, you'll be confined to the SS *Delfino* for a couple of days. I hope you brought your sea legs!"

"We're not pirates," Jo joked. "I may have left my sea legs at another port."

"As a matter of fact, this port was *full* of pirates a few hundred years ago, doing all sorts of terrible things, I'm sure," Henri told them.

"Like selling phony gemstones and swiping a few from the bag?" Maddie jeered playfully. She wasn't about to let Henri think that she hadn't understood what had happened the night before. "I might know of one such pirate then."

Henri straightened his jacket in the heat. "I'm a *businessman*," he said confidently.

Maddie looked up at the SS *Delfino*, an Italian steamship transporting passengers from the Port of Algiers to Genoa. Its metal body was tall and wide, and hundreds of small, round porthole windows dotted its sides. "When will we get to wear our dresses from Paris?" she asked Henri, unsure of where there could possibly be a ballroom onboard elegant enough to wear such fancy attire. "You did say we'd wear them on the ship, right, Henri?"

"Indeed, Madeline," he said. "At the captain's banquet. It's one of the most coveted meals on the ship, and I made special arrangements: You and Josephine will be seated at the captain's table tomorrow night. Who knows who you'll meet there?" The line of passengers moved forward a few feet, then a few more. "We're almost to the front now, where your Uncle Henri must bid you adieu. Remember what we talked about for Christmas?"

Jo nodded. "You'll come to Madame Molineaux's and get us, then we all go to Paris."

"Exactly."

Maddie narrowed her eyes. "Are there any 'exchanges in exclusive clubs' planned for Paris?" she asked cautiously.

Henri laughed and shook his head. "Not that I'm aware of," he assured them. "But you never know what may happen between now and then." He winked and nudged the girls forward. "It's your turn," he said.

Maddie stared at the woman checking passengers in at the podium. *Shouldn't Henri be taking us all the way to our cabin?* She straightened her shoulders and reminded herself that she and Jo were world travelers who had watched their parents check in a dozen times. *I guess we don't need him to hold our hands as if we're children. Besides,* she thought with a snicker, *I'm sure he has other "business" to attend to.*

"To tell you the truth," he said as he walked behind them toward the check-in counter, "I've rather enjoyed our little adventure. I hope there are more to come." He felt a pang of sadness as he said good-bye to his charges. In just the twelve hours he had spent with them, they'd found a place in his heart.

The girls turned and hugged Henri, saying good-bye to yet another guardian in Africa. They were boarding the ship alone and would have to fend for themselves until they met their new headmistress in Genoa.

He held out his palm, revealing two souvenir gold doubloons. "Here you go, ladies, one more souvenir from Uncle Henri. Maybe to remind you of the pirate I told you about, and how I met your parents."

"I thought you said he was a treasure hunter?" Maddie questioned him.

"Maybe a bit of both," he winked.

"See you at Christmas, Henri," Jo said quietly, taking her coin from his hand. "Will you write to us before you arrive?"

"*Absolument,*" he said. "I am off then." He shrugged and hesitated for a moment, then turned and made his way back through the line of passengers waiting to board.

⚜

Maddie smiled at Henri one last time, then stepped up to the woman at the podium. "Checking in," she said in her most adult voice. "I'm Madeline and this is Josephine. Last name, Livingston."

The woman flipped through her checklist and stopped. "Two Livingstons," she said. "*Perfetto.* And your dates of birth listed here are . . . ah!" she exclaimed. "You are twin sisters?"

Jo nodded. "That's right," she beamed. "Fraternal twins, that's why we don't look alike. And," she hesitated, "we're coming aboard alone."

"Well, *Twin Sisters Livingston,*" the hostess said in a sing-songy voice, "You did not think we'd leave you all alone on this journey, did you?"

Just then, a handsome young officer came walking up the ship's deck toward the podium. He wore a gray military uniform, and his stern expression turned soft once he saw the two young girls.

The hostess and the young officer chatted briefly in Italian as Maddie and Jo turned to look at each other in surprise. *A new stranger to take care of us,* Maddie thought. *I suppose I should get used to this.*

"*Benvenute al Delfino,*" he said to the girls, tipping his hat. "My name is Gabriele," he stated in a mild Italian accent, "and I'll be making sure you have a safe and enjoyable trip to Genoa. Walk with me, *per favore.*"

Pleased to see someone closer to their age, Maddie and Jo trotted along behind him as he led them into the ship's reception area. Jo flashed a quick smile to her sister, and Maddie, understanding exactly what her sister was smiling about, gave a quick nod in agreement, suppressing her own smile. Gabriele was cute, to say the least.

As they walked through the lavish interior of the ship, Maddie changed her mind about it being elegant enough to wear their dresses. She spotted plenty of places on board where she and Jo could be fancy. The rich carpets and dark wooden walls, the Tiffany lanterns and plush furniture reminded her of the expensive places in Boston where her mother would take her and Jo for high tea on special occasions.

"I can't wait to wander around," Jo gushed to her sister. "We can't get lost on a ship, right?" Jo was already peering down every hallway and looking around every corner, excited to explore their home for the next two days.

"Not unless you go overboard," Gabriele said, half-joking. "But you *do* need to be careful. First of all, stormy seas can knock you off balance. Hold on to the wall railings, and reach for these if you need them," he said, sliding his hand through the loop of a leather strap attached to the upper part of the wall.

Jo reached up and grabbed one. "How clever," she chirped. "Just in case I don't have sea legs, after all."

Maddie stood on her highest tiptoes and flailed to reach a leather strap but was still inches away. She grasped the wall railing with two hands instead. "This feels sturdier," she insisted.

"All right, come along," Gabriele said, satisfied that the girls knew how to keep themselves upright on the ship. "I'll take you to your cabin to settle in, and your luggage will arrive shortly. We depart in about three hours." He hesitated, looking up at the sky through a nearby window. "*If* the weather holds out. We noticed a storm coming over from the coast of Spain. Hope it misses us."

They climbed a small staircase and walked down a quiet hallway. "In here," Gabriele motioned, stopping in front of an open door. "The washroom is just inside on your left, and your beds and window are inside. We'll meet again just before dinner."

"The fancy dinner?" Jo asked eagerly. "The one with the captain?"

"That's tomorrow," he said, smiling. "Tonight, you'll be in the lower deck dining room with the rest of the guests. I'll come to get you." He tipped his hat, turned on his heel, and left the girls alone.

Drip.

Drip.

Drip, *drop.*

As rain pounded against the glass of the small, round window, a tiny leak in the wall dripped every few moments and landed on the night table.

Jo pulled her legs in tighter as she tried to read on her narrow canopy bed. The up, down, up, down of the rolling waves kept her feeling queasy.

"The reading won't help," Maddie said, offering her sister a ribbon bookmark to keep her place. "It'll just make the seasickness worse and give you a headache. Trust me."

"All right then, what are we supposed to do? We can't be on the outside decks, and officers are watching every hall," Jo complained.

It had been raining on the decks of the SS *Delfino* since that afternoon. When the girls had first seen the large boat, they'd been thrilled. They'd imagined the cool sea air blowing against their cheeks and hours of discovery as they explored the inside of the ship.

However, just hours after they'd hugged Henri good-bye on the coast of Africa, the sky turned the darkest gray and storm clouds pummeled the decks of the ship with endless rain. Men in yellow slickers ran around securing loose dinghies and ropes, while the captain gave orders for all guests to return to their cabins.

"I'm hungry," Jo complained. "And dinner was supposed to be served an hour ago. I think it's okay if we leave our room to go to *dinner*." With that, she hopped down off the narrow bed and went to the door. She opened it, letting out a long *creeeak* into the dimly lit hallway.

"Good evening," a surprised-looking Gabriele said from the hallway, his fist poised in the air as if he were just about to knock. "I'm glad you're safe in your room." The ship groaned and leaned far to the right, catching him off guard. He grabbed on to the leather strap above him, and Jo braced herself in the narrow stateroom doorway.

"We're safe, all right," Maddie called out as she jumped off the canopy bed. "But we're getting a bit hungry. No one came and got us for dinner."

"Ah yes, dinner," Gabriele sighed. "As it turns out, your fellow voyagers who ventured out for dinner became quite, well . . . sick."

Maddie tucked her chin and widened her eyes. "Sick?" she asked. "Like, *seasick*?"

"I'm afraid so. I do not recommend going into the corridors." Gabriele held on tighter as the ship lurched in the other direction. "For multiple reasons." The girls nodded in understanding. "But I do have a solution, so I invite you both to stay in your stateroom while I visit the kitchen. Wait here, young ladies, and your dinner will arrive shortly." He tipped his hat to Maddie and Jo, and closed the door behind them.

"Room service?" Maddie asked Jo, feeling very fancy all of a sudden. "We've never had room service, unless you count Dad bringing us biscuits from breakfast in his coat pockets." She laughed lightly, but her smile quickly turned into a frown. She looked down and was silent for a few moments.

Jo sat down on the bed and slung her arm over Maddie's shoulders. "I know, Sis," she said. "I miss Mom and Dad, too. And Boston. And the biscuits. And—"

A knock at the door interrupted her.

"Room service!" a woman's cheerful voice called from the other side of the door.

Jo leaped to the door and threw it open. A plump, rosy-cheeked woman in an apron held a basket of fresh bread and cookies, and Gabriele stood behind her, holding a silver platter of sliced meats and cheeses draped with bunches of purple grapes.

"All of that, for us?" Maddie asked, clearing off the tiny table that was anchored to the wall. "Thank you very much!"

"Yes, thank you! We were getting so hungry," Jo added, eyeing the cookies as the woman put the basket down.

"Is just a little, *ragazze*," the woman said in her thick Italian accent. "So sorry you having no dinner! But glad you stayed in room."

This alternative was more than fine with the girls. They pulled down wooden seats from the wall and looked at the feast in front of them.

"No, honestly," Jo said gratefully, "this is wonderful. We've never had room service before." She took a hot slice of bread from the basket, spread brown mustard on it, and piled it high with salami and cheese.

"We thought you might want something to do," Gabriele chimed in. "Have you ever played 'Walk the Plank?'" He pulled a worn deck of cards from his pocket and placed it on the table. "It's what we play on ships, since it doesn't matter if you don't have a full deck. After all, cards are easy to lose when nothing stays put."

Gabriele and the woman took a few moments to teach the girls how to play.

"I think we already know a similar game," Maddie jumped in after a few moments. "Where you ask the other player if they have a match to one of your cards. I think we called it 'Happy Families.'"

"Aye, but here on the high seas," Gabriele said in his best pirate voice, "we call it 'Walk the Plank.'"

Jo nodded and smiled. "Got any sevens, Sis?"

"Walk the plank, Jo!" Maddie spat back, laughing.

"No stay up too late, *ragazze*," the woman said as she and Gabriele left the girls to enjoy their snacks and play cards. "Tomorrow is your captain's dinner."

Jo stared at her reflection in the floor-length mirror on the back of the wardrobe door. She had never seen such a beautiful dress, and the fact that it had been made in her favorite color, yellow, was even better. The silk bodice hugged her waist, and a ballerina skirt made from layers of tulle spilled onto the floor. Her brown hair was assembled in rows of pinned curls, and she wore a glass-and-polished-wood necklace one of the dig site helpers had given her as a going-away gift.

Although the tiny stateroom on board the SS *Delfino* was tight for two twelve-year-old girls, they'd managed to slide the large dress boxes underneath their canopy beds for storage. Bringing them out and putting them on in such a small space had been challenging, but it was just part of the dressing-up fun.

"You look like a princess," Maddie said as she squeezed in beside her sister to look in the mirror. "A real, live princess, especially with that necklace to match."

"I feel like one," Jo replied as she turned to inspect her sister. "And you! You might as well be a baroness!"

Maddie spun around, ruffled her skirt, and bowed to her sister. Her gown was long and blue, with sheer sleeves and a gathered silk skirt. Her blond hair sat in a high chignon, and she'd even managed to pinch her cheeks enough times to make them a beautiful peachy pink.

"Not without jewelry, I'm not," she said with a twinge of remorse. She hunted around the room quickly for something shiny when the porthole window caught her eye. "Perfect!" she exclaimed, taking the silver-threaded curtain tie from around the hook in the wall and weaving it into her hair.

Jo admired her sister's handiwork. "It's beautiful, Sis." She took Maddie by the hand and led her out of the stateroom.

"Where's Gabriele? He said he'd be back in an hour. Do you think it's been an hour?" Jo wondered aloud as she looked back and forth down the long hallway.

"Sure it has," Maddie said confidently. "Longer than that, actually. Let's go and find him." She spun down the empty corridor, cinching her waist with both hands. Nearly twenty feet in front of her sister, she stopped to strike an elegant pose. "Ta-dah!" she called out, pushing her nose high into the air. "Do I look fabulous?"

"*Ohhhh yes, dahhhhhling,*" Jo replied in her best movie-star voice. She galloped after her sister, occasionally kicking one leg out from under her massive skirt in an imaginary cancan dance.

Maddie doubled over laughing and clapped in rhythm while Jo perfected her high kick behind a line of velvet ropes that sectioned off a service hallway.

"Watch *this*," Jo called, out of breath. She hurled herself over the loose velvet ropes, back and forth at a furious pace.

All of this excitement had, in fact, attracted more of an audience than the girls knew.

"*Ahemmmm,*" a familiar voice said from the entrance to the lobby.

Maddie whirled around so fast she nearly fell to the ground. Jo, surprised in midair, caught her toe on the velvet rope and sent two brass poles tumbling to the floor with a loud clatter.

Gabriele, in a more formal gray military uniform this time, stood facing the startled twins and smiled down at the ground for a few moments while Jo put the ropes and poles back in place, and Maddie untangled herself from her skirt. When he was sure that the girls had sorted out what went where, he looked up and spoke.

"I believe they've just begun," he said, turning toward the lobby and holding out an arm for each girl. "This way, ladies."

Inside the captain's dining room, men in white tuxedo jackets and gloves dashed about, fussing over the finishing touches on every table. A small string orchestra tuned their instruments in the corner. Their host had spared no expense, and Maddie and Jo felt like royalty as Gabriele ushered them through the heavy wooden doors.

SIGNORINA MADELEINE LIVINGSTON read the beautifully scripted place card on the table. Maddie picked it up and tilted it toward the light, making the gold paint on the edges sparkle. The time and date of the captain's dinner were written across the bottom of the card: HALF PAST SEVEN O'CLOCK ON THE TWENTY-NINTH DAY OF AUGUST, NINETEEN HUNDRED THIRTY-TWO.

"Jo!" she exclaimed, holding the card up in the air. "Where is yours?"

Jo reached under the hem of her bodice and pulled the card out, showing it to her sister. SIGNORINA JOSEPHINE LIVINGSTON it read, in the same beautiful writing. Some of the gold had already rubbed onto Jo's dress from the edge of the card, and Maddie snatched it from her sister's fingers.

"You'll ruin it, Jo!" she said, and bent the card back and forth to straighten it out. "Looks like we're the first to arrive. Let's explore!" She placed both cards on the table and turned back toward the doors, but Gabriele cocked his head and narrowed his eyes from beside the entryway. He flattened his hand, made a downward gesture in the air, and smiled gently.

"I guess we have to sit down," Jo surrendered. The girls walked back to their seats on the side of the large rectangular table. "At least we're only a few seats away from the captain."

Just then, another couple entered the captain's dining room. They walked to the two seats in between the twins and the captain's chair, and sat down.

"Hello, girls," the woman said, sliding in next to Maddie. "What gorgeous dresses!"

"Thank you. They're from Paris," Jo said politely.

"Ooh, Paris," the woman crooned. "Are they from the House of Fournier?" she asked playfully, winking.

"Actually, yes," Maddie replied, "they are."

The woman laughed and threw her head back. "Oh, hun, *I'm sure they are.*" She patted Maddie's head and smiled as if she were speaking with a toddler. "One day, I'm sure you'll have a real House of Fournier. Until then, these are very, very pretty. And I *love* that ribbon in your hair," she said to Maddie, cocking her head to the side. "Seems to match the ship's decor," she said before turning back to chat with her husband and the other adults who now sat at the table.

"She—she doesn't believe me," Maddie whispered to her sister. She looked around the room now full of adults, engaging in grown-up conversations. "Why should she? We're just children, after all. Playing dress-up, on a boat with our . . ." She turned and stared back at Gabriele as he scanned the room carefully from the doors. "Nanny?"

"Don't worry about him, or her. Or anyone else at the table," Jo said, looking around. "This is supposed to be fun, remember? Besides, I see *food.*" Indeed, the waiters were serving bread and butter to each guest before the first course. Jo placed her napkin in her lap, took half of her pat of butter and spread it over the top of her dinner roll, then took a large bite. "Dinner," she said between swallows. "We're just here to have dinner."

Maddie sighed and pinched a tiny bite of bread from her roll. "Okay," she grumbled.

Jo, nearly finished with her own roll, slid her knife under the remaining butter on her plate. As she lifted it up, it slipped off the knife and dropped to the ground. Eyes wide, Jo looked around to see who had seen it, but no one was paying attention except Gabriele, who held back a smile and left his post. She turned to her sister. "Maddie, do you have any extra butter?"

"Walk the plank," Maddie shot back, finally grinning again at her own joke.

Jo fished around under the hem of her bodice again. "Ha! Did you want to play?" she asked, edging her hand toward the table with part of the tattered deck in her grasp.

Maddie clasped both hands around Jo's fistful of cards. "Jo! Not at the dinner table!" she hissed. "Ugh. No wonder no one will take us seriously. We're at the captain's table in fancy dresses and you bring out 'Walk the Plank'—"

"Did you say, 'Walk the Plank?'" a gravelly voice boomed out. Both girls froze as the captain stood up to peer across the table. "Why, I've been playing that game at sea since I was fifteen," he chuckled. "I'd say I was good at it, but it's mostly a game of luck, lying, and cheating. So, the only ones who were really good at it were—"

"Pirates?" a bald man with a mustache answered from the seat next to him, smiling without looking up from his food.

"Pirates, exactly!" the captain exclaimed, and the whole table erupted in laughter. "And the occasional stowaway."

The bald man with the mustache smirked. "Can't be too careful these days, of pirates and of stowaways." He looked directly at the twins. "Especially not with *children* on board."

"Where are your parents, dears?" the woman next to Maddie chimed in, looking at the girls as if they were a pair of lost puppies.

"We're, uh . . ." Jo answered slowly. "We're traveling alone. Well, kind of alone," she said, looking around for Gabriele.

"Traveling alone, you say?" the bald man with the mustache inquired. "Why? And where?"

"Your parents let you come all by yourself?" the woman pushed. "My, my."

Maddie leaped to her parents' defense. "They had the chance to lead a once-in-a-lifetime excavation in Siberia," she explained. "We're heading to boarding school in Switzerland for a year and then going back home."

The bald man with the mustache sighed with a sense of relief. "I was wondering what two young ladies were doing alone at the captain's table. But this makes more sense. Tell me, which boarding school? I've been to Switzerland many times in the past few years."

"Madame Molineaux's," Jo said, making sure she pronounced it right. "In Saint-Marcel."

Just then, Gabriele appeared, leaned over Jo's shoulder, and placed a small saucer with two pats of butter on it next to her dinner plate.

"Thank you," Jo mouthed to him silently, happy that he had noticed her spill earlier.

The bald man with the mustache raised his nearly empty goblet in the air. "You, there," he called to Gabriele, assuming he was part of the staff. "Get me another glass of wine."

Gabriele cleared his throat and forced a smile. "I'll make sure you get one, *signore*," he said before leaving the table.

"As a matter of fact," the man continued, "I've heard wonderful things about Madame Molineaux's. A castle turned into a school, with an extensive art collection. Tapestries, sculptures, portraits . . . why, it's almost a museum."

Gabriele arrived moments later to refill the goblet of the bald man.

"Yes, thank you," the man said without looking up, and he settled into his dinner without saying another word.

"School at a museum, that sounds so exciting," the woman next to Maddie gushed. "Maybe you'll get to wear your fancy dresses there, too," she said, winking. "Oh, waiter." She waved her empty glass in the air above her head. "Do you have a glass of wine for me, too?"

Gabriele swallowed a sigh and walked the long way around the table, a subservient smile pasted on his face. Just before he reached her, he ducked down in between the twins, wiping the crumbs off the tablecloth, and whispered, "Walk the plank."

Maddie and Jo shoved forkfuls of food into their mouths to stifle their laughs as he stood up.

"Of course," he crooned to the woman, poured from the bottle into her goblet, then answered an imaginary shout from across the room. "Be right there," he called, then escaped into the kitchen.

Once again, Maddie and Jo flanked Gabriele's sides, each linking an arm with his as they walked down the hallway from the captain's dining room back toward the lobby.

"Did you enjoy yourselves?" he asked the girls.

Maddie and Jo leaned their heads back behind him to give each other looks but quickly faced forward again and answered in unison.

"Oh yes, thank you," they said, trying their best to be polite after what turned out to be a bit of a boring evening of eating snails and aspic, drinking mineral water, and listening to adult conversations.

Maddie giggled. "I *did* think it was funny when that man thought you were a waiter," she said, and Jo let out a quiet snort.

Gabriele shrugged his shoulders and shook his head. "It happens all the time, people mistake me for someone else. I have a familiar face, I suppose."

But you were wearing a military uniform, Maddie thought to herself. *Not a white tuxedo.*

"Shall we step out onto the deck?" Gabriele offered. "It has finally stopped raining, just in time for us to arrive in Genoa tomorrow morning."

"Yes!" Jo practically shouted. "We've been stuck inside since we came on board. We'd love to take a stroll."

Gabriele turned right, into the lobby, and exited onto the warm, breezy promenade deck of the SS *Delfino.* Jo looked over the railing, but there was only darkness in front of her. Maddie squinted and looked down to the white, foamy wake of the ship as it crawled through the ocean.

"At least the stars are out," Gabriele reassured them. "Should be clear until we pull into port." They walked up the deck toward the front of the ship, Gabriele trailing behind the two girls.

"It reminds me of Morocco," Jo whispered, taking Maddie's hand and gazing up at the night sky. "Even the breeze." They moved in silence up the deck until they heard a voice behind them.

"Paulo! Paulo! Hello!" an unfamiliar man's voice called out from a few yards away.

The twins turned around to see Gabriele lowering his head to avoid the man's eyes.

"I'd recognize you anywhere," the man said jovially to Gabriele, patting him on the back and trying to shake his hand. "Remember me? Arturo! From the job. The job in Spain."

Gabriele looked nervously at the twins, who were staring blankly at the awkward interaction. "I'm afraid, my friend"—he shook his head—"that I don't know what you mean. We've never met."

"I'm sure of it. Remember that night on the Plaça de Catalunya?" the man regaled him. "We were only victorious because of you. I'll never forget it!"

Gabriele grabbed onto the man's shoulder tightly. "I'm sorry, *signore*. You've mistaken me for someone else. I have a familiar face, I suppose. Ladies?" he called to Maddie and Jo. "It's time to go back to your stateroom. Lots to pack." And he hurried them back inside the ship without another word.

Unfamiliar sounds outside the window woke Jo. Instead of rain, she heard excited voices on deck and the laughing call of seagulls flying by. The sun shone through the tiny porthole window, and she jumped to life, kicking her quilted blanket to the floor. "Maddie, wake *up, we're here!*" she squealed.

The girls stared out at the beautiful coast of Genoa. Rust-colored palaces sat on the very tips of the land, their elaborate porches hanging off into the blue-green water. Pink and white buildings were stacked one on top of the other, and stone walls and staircases formed a maze between lush gardens and the sea.

"*Italy,*" Jo breathed out and stepped back from the window.

"Let's go, let's go!" Maddie sang, rushing around the closet-sized cabin to find her clothes. She crammed two pieces of leftover bread in her pocket and grabbed a bunch of grapes from the table. "Come on, Sis, breakfast is on deck today."

The girls ran through the empty corridors and found the rest of the passengers already outside, marveling at the breath-taking view. Maddie leaned against the metal rails and closed her eyes as she breathed the salty air in through her nose. She had never been so happy to be back out in the sunshine.

"See, Maddie," Jo said, putting her arm around her sister. "It's better that we're here. Dad was right. We would be miserable in Siberia at the excavation site. No friends, no sun, and no playing outside."

Maddie nodded, enjoying her simple breakfast in silence as she and Jo watched the bow of the SS *Delfino* move closer to the color-splashed coastline of Genoa.

"Ladies, time to get your things from the stateroom," a familiar voice said behind them. "You'll be the first passengers off the ship."

"First?" Jo asked, turning around to face Gabriele.

"Yes, first. Your transport is waiting, and you will meet your party at once."

Maddie looked up at his stern expression, narrowing her eyes. "And who, if I may ask, is the party we are meeting?"

"The writer of this letter," he explained, pulling a folded piece of paper from his jacket pocket, "whose instruction I have been asked to follow without question."

"What does it say?" the girls blurted out at the same time.

He read aloud. "*. . . and please escort the twins and their trunks off the ship first, as the driver and I will be waiting in an automobile bound for Switzerland. My kindest thanks . . .*" He paused and then held the letter in front of the girls, his finger on the signature: *Klara Kronenberg.*

CHAPTER SIX

THE WOMAN FROM CROWN MOUNTAIN

Klara Kronenberg pulled nervously on the hem of her jacket sleeve. She sat up straight in the back seat of the automobile, smoothed her brown hair away from her face, and cleared her throat for the tenth time since arriving in Genoa.

Calm down, Klara, she said to herself. *This isn't the first time you've escorted new students to the school.*

But this *was* the first time that she would be escorting two American girls to Saint-Marcel. She assured herself once again that the decision to admit Madeline and Josephine had been a good one. After all, she had vowed to protect the school in every way possible, and while the welcoming of two Americans would be unconventional, it was certainly in the best interest of Madame Molineaux's.

She laid her head back on the leather seat and closed her eyes. She replayed the scene that had flashed through her mind every day for more than twenty years.

"I promise," she said to the woman lying in the bed. "I will never let anything happen to your beloved school. Not on my watch."

The woman, frail and barely able to speak, looked up at Klara with an expression of gratitude and hope. Her blue eyes were watery and tired, but to Klara, they still looked as compassionate and loving as the day the two had met.

"Do what you can to keep my involvement a secret," the woman whispered. "If my family ever knew..." Her voice faded and she shook her head from side to side slowly, as if it took a great deal of effort just to say the words.

"No one outside the staff will ever know," Klara whispered. She wrapped her warm hands around the woman's thin fingers. "Your secret—and your school—are safe with us."

She kissed the woman's cold hands, tucked them back into the blankets, and made sure her feet were bundled under the heavy quilts at the foot of the bed. She curtseyed and bowed, as she had done countless times before, and made her way out of the palace to her carriage.

A bump in the road jolted the headmistress out of her reminiscence. "How far are we from the port?" she asked the driver.

"We're nearly there," he answered. "Can you hear the gulls?"

Klara had been so nervous and lost in daydreams that she hadn't noticed the beautiful scenery outside the window. She gazed at the colorful row houses and whitewashed stone buildings, admiring the shoppers, all sharply dressed and strolling down streets paved with cobblestones. They were lovely, but her mind was racing with other thoughts.

She pictured the two smiling girls from the photograph. Would they like it at Madame Molineaux's? Would the other girls accept them and befriend them? Or would they be home-sick for America? She sighed, expelling every last ounce of breath in her lungs as she tried to calm herself. It was impera-tive that the twins stay at the school this year.

Suddenly, the buildings gave way to the massive port of Genoa. Docked ships, swaying with the swelling sea, were being tied to heavy wooden poles by deckhands while passengers flooded onto the boardwalks with trunks and suitcases.

"How close do you want me to get to the dock?" the driver asked. "I could let you out here, but that would mean walking with their luggage."

Klara had already opened the door for herself and was on her way out of the car.

"You can wait here," she said. "They've only got a trunk and a few cases. I'll be back with the girls in a few minutes."

She slammed the car door shut and ruffled her skirt around her shoes. The headmistress was plump and poised, and she glided toward the SS *Delfino* as if walking on a cloud.

Remember, she told herself. *Josephine is the tall brunette; Madeline is the petite blond. They think you know all about them already, so not too many questions in the car. Let them tell you what they will.*

She scanned the bustling boardwalk for the pair of girls, weaving back and forth to get a better look between groups of travelers. She squinted her eyes in the sun, reminding herself that these girls wouldn't be in short khaki pants and hats like the photograph, until finally her gaze settled on a handsome face coming toward her out of the crowd.

Gabriele towed their trunk, stacked with suitcases and the dress boxes, and linked arms with his charges, smiling at his longtime friend. "I found two stowaways," he called out as the party moved toward the headmistress. "I suppose you're here to take them off to jail now, Klara?" He tipped his hat, bowed slightly, and gently pushed the girls closer to her.

"Oh, *yes*," the headmistress said, playing along with the joke. "The authorities notified me as soon as they found them on board." Her mouth turned up at one corner, and she bent down to look Maddie in the eyes.

"You must be Madeline," she said warmly. "And you," she said, shifting her attention upward to stare Jo in the face, "must be Josephine. I'm Headmistress Kronenberg, and I'll be taking you to your new home."

Maddie nodded to the woman. "Thank you for coming to get us, Headmistress."

"Are you really from Crown Mountain?" Jo asked. "I looked in my German dictionary, and that's what your last name means. Did you know?"

The headmistress straightened and smiled, amused by Jo's enthusiasm for foreign languages. "Well, Josephine," she said, "I suppose I did know that. But thank you for bringing it to my attention. I wouldn't want to forget."

Jo beamed with pride.

Gabriele tipped his hat once again. "I hate to make such a special delivery and run off," he said, patting the girls on the head and standing their trunk on its end. "But I leave port on another ship in ten minutes. I trust your driver will help you with the luggage?"

Jo stepped up to the trunk, took the handle in both hands, and tipped it onto its wheels. "Don't worry, Headmistress," she said. "I can do it." She fought to keep the trunk from sliding onto the ground, using her knees to prop up the top end.

"And I can help!" Maddie exclaimed, grabbing the rest of their things.

The headmistress didn't know whether to be embarrassed or impressed—the girls looked like two pack mules hauling cargo up the side of a mountain, and yet they didn't seem bothered. In fact, they looked as if they were having fun. She bit her tongue and pasted a smile on her face.

"Right," she said, and cleared her throat. "That will be fine, girls." She shot a puzzled look at Gabriele, who looked at the ground and tried to hide his amusement.

"I'll write when I need you next," Klara said to him, and she turned to follow her new students to the car.

It was getting darker. The beautiful Italian countryside had occupied the girls for most of the drive, and, luckily, Headmistress Kronenberg had packed fruit and cookies to pass the time. The conversation in the car was simple—and mostly one-sided, as the girls told stories of their summer in Morocco. Every few moments, the small talk would lag as Maddie and Jo stared out the windows at the landscape.

"I take it you've never been to Europe," Klara said, noticing the girls' wide eyes as they took in the spectacular views. "It certainly is a beautiful place. And we haven't even crossed into Switzerland yet. I find it the most magical of all on the continent." She gazed out the windows and let her mind wander. Sunset lit just the top of each green hill, and orange lights glowed through the shutters of quaint cottages set back from the road.

"We haven't been to Europe until now," Maddie finally answered. "We thought we were going back to Boston until Mom and Dad told us the news. But," she added, tilting her head thoughtfully, "I'm sure we'll like it in Switzerland."

Jo slumped in her seat and folded her arms across her chest. She was getting tired of sitting still and wished there was something to eat besides cookies. She smiled at the irony of the thought, recalling numerous dinners where she and Maddie had requested nothing *but* cookies. "I was sort of hoping for Paris," she admitted, imagining wearing her dress from Henri every day.

The headmistress looked amused. "Well, you're in luck then, Josephine. Madame Molineaux's is a French-speaking school," she stated, taking on the tone of a cheerful tour guide. "In fact, we'll be just on the other side of the French border— and Paris is only one day away by train. Didn't Henri tell you about the school?"

The girls shook their heads.

"Heavens!" Klara exclaimed. "That explains the long faces, then. Madame Molineaux's is an amazing place for young ladies. After all," she said in a lower voice, "it's not every girl who gets to live in a castle."

As the sun dropped behind the mountains, Maddie and Jo found themselves once again riding through the night in a car with someone they had only just met. The twisting and turning of the mountain roads made them queasy, and they grew quiet.

"It's best to lay your heads back now," the headmistress said. "When you wake, we'll be in Saint-Marcel, and your warm beds will be waiting for you."

The girls didn't argue. Maddie laid her head on Jo's lap, and Jo, being too tired to protest, draped her arm over her sister's back and sank against the car door.

Maddie's eyelids fluttered before she shut them tightly again. *Someone turn off that light!* she thought, not yet awake enough to realize that she was still in the back seat of a car. She buried her face in what she thought was a pillow, but ended up with Jo's knee in her eye instead. She sat up, rubbed her tired eyes, and peered out the windows to find the blinding culprit.

Indeed, light had broken through the darkness of the mountain forest roads. Now the narrow street was lined with glowing amber lanterns hanging from slender evergreen trees. The flames cast quivering shadows on the walls and shutters of cafés, and gave metal railings and doorknobs a shimmering sheen. It was just like something Maddie had read in a story-book, the kind of town where fairy tales were set.

"Jo," she whispered as she patted her sister's knee. "Wake up, we're here."

Jo took a deep breath and exhaled an exaggerated yawn.

"Is this Madame Molineaux's?" she asked, sitting up and leaning over Maddie to see out the other side of the car.

"No," answered the headmistress in a calm voice, still facing the windshield. "This is Saint-Marcel. Madame Molineaux's is up there." She pointed out the window to a hilltop in the distance, where the outline of a castle could be seen between mountain slopes. It was dimly lit, but the castle's parchment-colored walls and golden-brown towers stood out against the night sky.

The engine sputtered softly as the car made its way up the winding road toward the school, leaving the sleeping town of Saint-Marcel behind.

"There are four boundaries around Madame Molineaux's. Two mountain ridges on the sides, an iron gate with stone walls at the front, and the lakeshore at the back. Leaving the boundaries of the school without an escort is absolutely forbidden for first- and second- and third-year students."

"Which year are we?" Jo asked, realizing she didn't know what grade she and Maddie would be in at their new school.

"You are first-years," the headmistress replied. "So, you must not leave the school unless accompanied by myself or another professor. Is that understood?"

The girls nodded.

"Good. That's out of the way," she said with a smile. "Now then. I want to be the first to welcome you to Madame Molineaux's."

The car stopped outside a massive iron gate. The driver got out, turned a brass key in the lock, and pushed with both hands to open the gate. The metal doors groaned as they swung on their hinges, and the driver quickly hopped back into his seat to drive through them. Once the car passed the gate, he got back out, pushed both of the heavy doors closed, and turned his key once more, locking them in.

Tiny garden lanterns lit the way up a curved driveway toward the main castle of Madame Molineaux's, and at the top, the driver parked just outside the front entrance to the school. The headmistress stepped out of the car and opened the door for Maddie and Jo. "Come now, it's almost midnight. Everyone will be asleep. Quiet as we go."

She led them up the steps and under the stone archway that covered two of the tallest wooden doors the girls had ever seen. The same amber lanterns from the streets of Saint-Marcel hung from the walls of the entry, illuminating small bronze plaques laid into the rock. When they reached the doors, the headmistress kneeled, took a match from her pocket, and struck it on the ground.

"Aha," she whispered after looking along the bottom of the stone doorsill. She pulled out a crumbling brick, placed her hand inside the small opening, and felt around blindly for a few moments before finally retrieving a long key with the letters *MM* at its top.

Maddie and Jo gave each other confused looks. "She doesn't have her own key?" Maddie whispered in Jo's ear.

The headmistress unlocked the front door, pushed it ever so slightly, and, with a low creak, it opened wide enough for them to slip inside.

CHAPTER SEVEN

Madame Molineaux's School for Girls

Maddie and Jo struggled to see in the darkness of the main hall. The wall lamps and the chandeliers were cold, and the moonlight through the blue stained-glass windows cast an eerie glow into the stone room. The hall itself was enormous, at least four times the size of their townhouse back in Boston. The headmistress started down a narrow carpet toward the far end.

Jo stared up at the ceiling as she walked. It towered more than fifty feet above her head at its highest point, and the arched wooden beams looked like giant outstretched branches of an oak tree. All of her upward gazing caused her to walk off course, and she hardly noticed as she neared the edge of the carpet. Her left heel came down on the hard stone floor with a bright *smack,* and sent a ringing echo through the hall.

"Quiet!" the headmistress hissed in a raspy voice. She stopped and turned around, her finger raised to her lips, her eyes wide and unforgiving.

"Sorry," Jo tried to whisper back, but it came out of her mouth at full volume.

"Shhh! Everyone is sleeping!" she whispered in her most direct low voice.

"Jo can't whisper," Maddie replied quietly, coming to her sister's defense with caution. This wasn't the kind of orientation she had expected. Where was the welcoming party, the cake, the punch? Hadn't Henri told the girls that the school was awaiting their arrival? This was hardly a warm welcome. She grabbed Jo's hand and gave her a worried stare. *Jo looks like a ghost in here,* she thought. She kept following the headmistress, walking quickly and quietly on the carpet with her sister in tow.

They were nearing the end of the main hall now, and the faintest of lights shone from four hallway entrances: one to the west wing of the castle, one to the east wing, another dimly lit and all the way to the right, and one very large corridor directly in front of them. Jo narrowed her eyes to see what was down the hallways leading to the castle wings, but she could see no farther than the stone staircases just beyond their doorways.

The headmistress turned left at the end of the carpet and led the girls into the west wing, where they walked up a short flight of stone stairs into a long hallway. It was cozy and richly decorated, and the air felt warmer than that in the cold stone hall they had just come from. Small wall lamps burned dimly in between friendly-looking portraits; the figures in them smiled down on the girls as if they approved of their arrival.

Maddie and Jo were ushered into a dark room where the headmistress switched on a lamp and closed the door. They were in a library, with row after row of bookshelves, heavy wooden tables and chairs, and a sitting area in front of a stone fireplace. The smell of leather, paper, and burnt wood made Jo want to cozy up in one of the pillowy armchairs.

"This is the first-year dormitory hall," the headmistress said softly. "There are ten bedrooms, a lavatory, and we're in the first-year library now. Each bedroom has six beds, and all the girls are asleep. Once we walk out of this door, you must follow my instructions exactly, so you don't wake anyone. Understood?"

Maddie nodded.

Jo looked very concerned.

"Can we visit the lavatory? Brush our teeth? I'm thirsty, and I normally sleep with my favorite quilt. It's in our trunk, and—"

The headmistress interrupted her.

"We'll stop by the lavatory on our way, and you can brush your teeth in the morning. Water pitchers and glasses are on your night tables. Your quilt will have to wait, but we've left something special for you to sleep with. Now then," she said as she put her fingers on the lamp switch. "You'll find nightgowns folded on your pillows. Change into them, climb into your beds, and go to sleep. Breakfast is served at seven o'clock in the morning, and classes begin at eight. Are you ready?"

She didn't wait for an answer before she switched off the lamp and opened the door into the dim hallway. After a stop by the lavatory, she took the girls farther down the corridor and paused in front of a large wooden door. Jo stared at the worn brass number five hung just above the iron knocker.

"This is where I bid you goodnight, ladies," the headmistress whispered with a kind smile. "My chambers are at the very end of the hallway, and should you need me during the night, just knock and I will answer. The moon should give you enough light to change and get into your beds. Just remember, don't wake the other girls. I'll wait outside the door until I don't hear any noise at all, and then I'll leave." She opened the door, waited for Maddie and Jo to step in, and shut the door behind them.

Maddie squinted until she could make out two beds that were still made near the window. She took her sister by the hand and led her toward them, careful not to make a sound. The soft breathing of the other girls in the room could be heard easily now. Looking behind her, she could still see the headmistress's shadow underneath the bottom of the door.

"Maybe . . ." Maddie whispered. "Maybe we could both fit in the same bed . . . just for tonight."

Jo took one look at the tiny beds and shook her head no. She sat on top of her bed and popped back up, having sat squarely on something concealed under the covers.

"Shhh! What is it?" Maddie breathed to her sister, afraid she'd already been too loud. The last thing she wanted was for the headmistress to come back in and scold them.

Jo reached under the covers and pulled out a stuffed animal—a soft, pudgy hedgehog. Maddie checked her own bed to make sure she had one, too, and indeed, the same plush toy was tucked under her blanket. The girls gave each other sheepish grins, but they were glad to have something to hold on to as they slept, no matter how long it had been since either one of them needed a stuffed animal to fall asleep.

They changed into their nightgowns, folding their dresses neatly and placing them under their bedside tables. Maddie slid under her covers and let her head fall straight back on the pillow. She held her hedgehog tight against her chest and turned to look at her sister.

Jo was finishing her third glass of water, almost draining the pitcher completely. She kicked around under her sheets to get comfortable, and the bed springs gave a weak groan under her fidgety legs. She settled in and flipped onto her stomach.

Both girls watched as the shadow of the headmistress's feet under the door grew longer then disappeared, and the room fell silent.

But the stillness lasted for only a few moments. Against the far wall, Jo saw someone sit up in bed.

"*Ten!*" the girl whispered loudly.

Jo was too terrified to speak and lay paralyzed under the covers. She wasn't even able to turn to her sister, who was quietly panicking in the next bed.

Maddie's breathing quickened as she watched whoever was sitting up in the bed start bouncing up and down in a clock-like rhythm.

"*Twenty!*" another voice breathed in a high pitch, almost squealing. This girl began to bounce in unison with the other one, and two more beds sprang to life, their inhabitants on all fours like wild animals.

"*Cre-e-ak…*" one of them uttered. The silence that followed was interrupted by a distant creak from somewhere down the hallway.

"*Click!*" the other one said, and once again, the same sound was heard from down the hall, just audible to the girls. A quiet commotion filled the dormitory room.

The four residents scattered, jumping out of their beds and rummaging around. Maddie sat up awkwardly, and in a desperate attempt to find the lamp, knocked the empty water pitcher onto the floor. It hit the wood with a loud clang, interrupting the padded footsteps and whisper-soft ruckus.

Not a moment later, a brilliant orange light was inches away from Maddie's nose.

"Quiet, or she'll come back," uttered a low voice with a French accent.

A torch-shaped flashlight was held steadily in Maddie's face, as if it were a sword keeping a dangerous opponent at safe distance. Jo was enchanted by the colors—it glowed different shades of orange and gold, and reminded her of a big Christmas tree light.

The three other girls now crowded around the Livingston sisters' beds, waiting to see what would happen next. The girl with the flashlight stepped back several paces and positioned the orange flame under her own chin.

"We've been waiting for you," she said. "Haven't we, ladies?"

She shone the flashlight around to the other girls' faces. Everyone wore smiles except for Maddie and Jo, who were still recovering from the surprise welcome.

The girl, tall and handsome with a loose braid, smirked playfully and rolled her eyes at her new roommates.

"Relax. You're among friends in the best room on this hall. I'm Françoise."

Maddie cut her eyes at Jo, who was staring wide-eyed at the girl with the torch. Her name sounded like "France-was," though Maddie knew that couldn't be how it was spelled.

Françoise Cadieux stood boldly in the middle of the circle with relaxed confidence and square shoulders. Her features were chiseled, her skin was freckled and tanned, and she had mossy green eyes that narrowed and sparkled when she smiled. Her English was perfect, with a warm French accent softening the edges of every word. She stared at the two Americans, calmly waiting for one of them to speak. It was Jo who broke the silence.

"Hi," she said timidly. "I...I'm Josephine but you can call me Jo..." She looked at Maddie, giving her a nod of encouragement.

"And I'm Madeline, err, Maddie," she added. "We...we just thought you were all asleep, and—"

"I *know!*" exclaimed a Scottish girl with a short auburn bob. "It was brilliant, wasn't it? We waited and waited and *waited.* Kronenberg said you'd be here just hours ago, but no one could sleep anyway. We told ghost stories to stay awake until we heard you coming down the hallway."

Jo loved ghost stories. "Ghost stories? About what?" she asked, suddenly believing what her mother had said about this school being like a slumber party every night.

The Scottish girl looked straight at her. "About this place, of course," she said dramatically, taking delight in the growing concern on the twins' faces.

"Don't listen to Millie," said a shorter, cherub-faced blonde wearing her golden curls tied back in a scarf. "Madame Molineaux's isn't *really* haunted, we just pretend it is. It's more fun that way. Besides, this castle is so old, it's hard not to make believe with all the spooky noises at night. It's just *gespenstergeschichten.*"

"That's Nixie for you," Françoise said, half grinning. "You'll learn to speak German whether you want to or not."

Nixie looked offended but gave a bashful smile. She nudged the girl on the end of their half-circle audience. "Say hi, Val," she said, giving the girl a slight push forward.

The olive-skinned girl with a long, raven-colored braid looked back and forth between Maddie and Jo. Her big brown eyes were soft, lined by a thick row of eyelashes.

"Hello. My name is Valentina Dellavalle. It is nice to meet you," she said in a thick Italian accent. It was obvious that she had just begun English lessons, and her effort to greet the two girls put them at ease.

Millie smiled at Val. "You see, that was good!" she said in her bright Scottish accent, praising her friend. She faced Maddie and Jo. "She's not perfect at English yet, but it's coming along."

"I think it's wonderful," Jo said, staring straight at Val. "Does everyone here speak English?" she asked, trying not to sound as if she expected everyone in Europe to speak her language.

"Almost," replied Françoise. "And the ones who don't speak it take lessons, just like you will take French lessons. You do speak *some* French, don't you?"

The twins nodded.

"We just came from Morocco," Maddie said. "And we took a few lessons back in Boston."

"Where is Boston?" Nixie asked sweetly. She had only met an American once before, and was already excited about having the two sisters as her friends.

"It's in Massachusetts, in the United States," Jo answered. "We live there . . . well . . . *lived* there." She got quiet for a moment. Even though being in a new country and a new school was exciting, she couldn't deny that she missed home, nor that she would rather be in her own bed, just down the hall from her parents.

Françoise sat down on the bed and threw her arm around Jo's shoulders.

"Don't feel homesick," she said quietly. "We're all away from our home and parents. But we'll be a family here, too. You'll see."

Millie pounced onto Maddie's bed. "Besides!" she said in her most cheerful whisper. "At home, do you get to stay up past midnight with friends, on a *school* night?"

"And make up ghost stories about the castle you live in?" asked Nixie.

"And sneak into the kitchen for the sausages and the bread?" Val asked shyly, hoping the rest of the girls would agree. She was still used to her Italian dinnertime starting well into the evening, and the new schedule of eating the last meal of the day at six o'clock was leaving her hungry every night.

The other girls groaned.

"Really, Val? Again?" Millie protested. "It's been two weeks already. Surely, you're used to an early supper by now."

Val looked down but made no apologies. "I am *Italian*," she insisted. "I need to eat before I sleep."

Jo saw her opportunity to have a much-needed meal before bed and jumped in. "Actually, Maddie and I didn't get a chance to eat much more than cookies this afternoon. I could use something to eat, too."

Françoise smiled and shook her head. "This is the last night for this, ladies. All right? I won't be sent home after only two weeks at boarding school on account of your stomachs." She sighed and hurried to her bed for her slippers like the rest of the girls.

Maddie and Jo, caught without their trunk, had no slippers to speak of.

"Can we go barefoot?" Maddie asked. "All we have are our dress shoes at the moment."

Millie laughed. "Sure you can, just be warned. The stone floor in the main hall is like ice on your toes, even at this time of year."

Jo shrugged and figured that it would be a safer bet to get frostbite than to risk stepping onto the floor loudly with her heel again, alerting the sleeping headmistress to their midnight snack excursion.

Nixie was the first to the door. "I'll go first and whistle when the coast is clear," she whispered, peeking out the doorway.

"Why her?" Maddie asked, wondering why Françoise hadn't been the first out of the door with the torch.

"She's the cutest, like a baby," Françoise said matter-of-factly. "If she gets caught, she will just cry. She can make a fountain in her eyes at a moment's notice."

Maddie loved how close and clever this team of girls had already become, and felt excited to belong to a new group of friends. After all, she and Jo were only two weeks late to the first year of school—none of the first-year girls had known one another longer than that.

Nixie took a deep breath and slipped into the dim hallway.

CHAPTER EIGHT

THE WELCOME BANQUET

The remaining five young ladies, all in their nightgowns, waited eagerly by the door. Jo was so excited to be headed on a small adventure that she nearly forgot why they were going. A tiny rumble reminded her—it was Val's stomach, giving a small drumroll before they left the safety of their room. Val smiled and giggled through her nose at Jo, happy to have found an ally in her pursuit of food.

A low dove call sounded from down the hallway and Françoise peeked her head out the door. At the far end of the hall near the staircase, Nixie stood with both hands cupped together in front of her lips.

I'm getting really good at that, she thought, and gave the call once more.

Françoise waved her arms furiously at her to stop, and then motioned for the rest of the girls to follow her out of the bedroom.

"We are tiptoeing, yes?" she asked in her quietest whisper. All the girls nodded. "Good. Jo, come with me down the hall to get Safi."

"Who's Safi?" Jo asked, wondering how they planned on opening another dormitory door undetected.

"Come on and find out," she said, ushering the other girls out the door and toward the main hall. "Not a sound—she lives by the headmistress."

Françoise and Jo slipped out the door and closed it gently. They crept down the hallway toward the headmistress's chambers, and stopped two doors before it. Françoise rapped softly on the wood with her index finger knuckle. But before she could finish tapping out the rhythm of "Les Toreadors" from the opera *Carmen*, the door flew open, and a tall, graceful girl with deep brown skin hurried out.

"I thought you might not come," she whispered. "I am glad I stayed awake one more moment!"

"Did we disturb the others?" Françoise inquired as she pulled the door closed.

"Oh, no," the girl said, rolling her eyes. "They are deep in their beauty sleep." She linked arms with Françoise and turned to Jo as they padded toward the main hall. "I am Safietou, Safietou Faye. But you can call me Safi."

Jo smiled and nodded. "I'm Jo," she said at her lowest volume, which was still too loud for the secret snack operation. Françoise and Safi both raised their fingers to their lips and nudged Jo down the stone stairs.

"No talking in the main hall," Millie whispered to them quietly as they approached. "Unless you want to wake the whole school." Carefully, as if stepping onto a frozen pond, she lifted one leg and put her foot down on the floor as delicately as possible.

More than a dozen leaping steps would have to be taken on the icy stone to reach the carpet. Millie was followed by Françoise, Val, Safi, and Nixie, and then it was Maddie's turn. She prepared for the chill of the stone on her bare toes, but once her foot touched the freezing surface, she broke into a sprint. It felt as if she was running without shoes across a snowbank, just not as wet.

Jo was left alone at the starting line. Unlike dainty Maddie, whose scampering footsteps resembled that of a mouse, Jo worried that she would sound like a horse trotting across the stone floor.

Françoise saw the concern on Jo's face and immediately removed one of her slippers. She slid it across the floor, softside down. "One is better than none,." she whispered to Jo as she tried to stuff her other foot into her remaining slipper.

Jo shoved her foot into Françoise's slipper and braced herself. She put her now-covered foot down on the stone first, and then took the quickest step she could with her bare foot. This worked well enough to get halfway to the carpet, but then her icy toes wouldn't let her continue. She stood there in the main hall, as straight as she could on her slippered foot, with the bare one raised in something of a ballet pose. She flung her arms out to her sides and flailed around to keep her balance.

The awkward pose sent the girls on the carpet into fits of muffled laughter. Millie doubled over and used both hands to cover her mouth. Françoise had to turn and look the other way to keep quiet. Maddie was used to these kinds of antics, and rolled her eyes and folded her arms in protest.

"Come *on*, Jo!" she hissed. "It's not that bad!"

But it *was* that bad for Jo. She gave her frosty foot a few more seconds to warm up before she dared to lay it down on the stone floor again, knowing that she'd have to touch it to the icy ground at least three more times before reaching the carpet ahead. She squinted her eyes and held her breath as she laid her bare toes against the frozen slate, then hurried toward the rest of the girls.

Maddie took the slipper from Jo's foot and returned it to Françoise.

"Why," Jo asked, rubbing her frozen toes to warm them, "is the floor like an iceberg?"

Françoise lifted her foot behind her and slid the slipper back on with the grace of a figure skater. "Simple," she replied softly. "The spring that feeds the lake comes from *under* the main hall. It sits deep in the mountain, surrounded by ice."

Millie turned and stared at Françoise with doubtful eyes. "And how, exactly, do you know that?" she asked, crossing her arms.

"My father told me," Françoise whispered curtly. "Now quiet, let's keep moving."

The girls fell into a single line, softly walking down the carpet to the central corridor.

Jo hung back slightly and spoke as quietly as she could to Val. "What are all these different hallways?" she asked, waving an outstretched finger from one side of the main hall to the other.

Val raised her hand and pointed behind the girls. "There, it is the utility corridor," she began in her stilted English. "It is a corridor before ours, but, ah, you can no see now. Is very dark. No students allowed to being in there."

Jo nodded.

"Our dormitory, it is the first floor of the west wing," Val continued. "Second-years are on the second floor, and the third-years, they stay on the top floor." She pointed in front of them. "Here, it is the Grand Corridor: it goes to the dining hall and the doors out to the rest of the school."

Val paused and took a breath, and pointed to the right. She wasn't exactly prepared to be giving a tour of Madame Molineaux's in English, but she was doing the best she could.

"There, it is the east wing of the castle. First floor is for a fourth-years. Fifth-years have only three girls in the room. They get, ah, *trattamento speciale* for being the oldest at the school."

"That means special treatment," Nixie chimed in.

Finally, she pointed behind them again. "Last one is the administration corridor, also all dark at night. Never go down that one—only if you in the trouble." She smiled at Jo and looked down, unsure of whether she had ever said that many words in a row in English.

The girls walked through the Grand Corridor now, a huge hallway with high ceilings. The windows extended from the floor to the exposed beams at the roof line, and they were draped in heavy velvet curtains. Maddie and Jo paused and gazed around the grounds of Madame Molineaux's for the first time.

Maddie walked quickly to catch up with Françoise at the front of the line. "What are all these buildings?" she asked.

"That's the science hall," Françoise said, pointing to a two-story building with a tall glass atrium in the middle. "We study biology, chemistry, and botany there. Math, too. It's surrounded by gardens and a labyrinth." Maddie looked out at the maze of hedges and wondered if anyone had ever gotten lost in there. Françoise continued, "Sometimes at night you can see colored smoke coming from the chimneys of the science hall while Professor Natalio conducts his chemistry experiments."

She turned to face the window on the other side of the hallway. "Out that way is the arts hall," she explained, motioning toward an ornate stone building, its gardens decorated with statues. "Music, dance, painting, the creative subjects."

"And after the arts hall, there are stables," Val added.

Horses! Maddie cheered silently, hoping she'd finally get to have one of her own instead of only being able to ride when her family visited relatives on a farm.

"Off in the distance you can see the lake and the boathouse," Françoise added. "And," she said, moving to the following window and pointing to the building farthest away, "out there is the history hall."

Except for the main castle, the history hall was the largest building on campus by far. Most of the rooftop was flat, and two small towers jutted up from the middle of it. Maddie stared up at the imposing building and stopped in her tracks. "I see *things*," she said, frightened. "There, on the roof. They're white. And they're *moving*."

The girls huddled around Maddie and stared.

Nixie gasped. "I . . . I see them, too," she said dramatically. "I think they're ghosts!" But the fright in her voice wasn't convincing, and she couldn't hold her giggles inside. She laughed and bit her lip, sorry that she couldn't prolong her joke.

Safi gave her a playful shove and put her hands on Maddie and Jo's shoulders. "She's close—but they're not *ghosts*, they're *goats!*"

"Goats?" Jo asked, relieved that so far tonight she had been able to stave off an encounter with a real ghost.

"Indeed," Safi explained. "The rooftop is laid with grass, and the goats do the gardening."

Sure enough, as Jo pressed her nose to the window and looked out toward the towers, she saw them clearly. Three white goats moved around slowly and took turns kneeling in the moonlight.

Jo saw something else though, that was most certainly not a goat. "Those may be goats," she said, "but what is *that*?" She pointed at the larger white animal running recklessly from side to side across the grass.

"It is Albert!" Françoise exclaimed. "We never see Albert! *Mon Chien des Pyrenees.*" The rest of the girls pushed against one another to get a glimpse out the window.

By now, Maddie was even more confused. "Exactly *who* or *what* is Albert?" she demanded, shooting Jo a look of disbelief. Madame Molineaux's was becoming stranger by the minute.

"He's the guardian of the goats," Françoise said, smiling.

"He's a dog," Millie added. "A Pyrenean Mountain Dog, in fact. He sleeps all day long and stays awake at night, so we never get to see him. He protects the goats while they sleep."

"Protects them from what?" Jo asked, wondering what goats on a rooftop would have to worry about at night.

"We don't know," Nixie said quietly. She leaned back from the window and took a few more steps down the hall, turning back to the others with a wicked smile. "Maybe those pesky ghosts?"

Françoise gave a bored laugh. "Ha-*ha,* Nixie. Come on, we'll never make it to the kitchen if we keep this up," she said, and pushed to the front of the group with her orange torch light ablaze.

The kitchen at Madame Molineaux's lay just beside the dining hall, nestled halfway underground. The walls and floors were constructed entirely of stone blocks, and the ceiling, rising nearly two stories high, was supported by the same wooden columns and beams as the main hall. The chimneys rising out from the many stoves hugged the stone walls and broke through the peaked roof, taking all of the heat and smoke from the cooking fires out into the open air. It took nearly two dozen cooks to prepare meals for the students, professors, and other staff at the school, but the oven coals lay cold when the girls arrived to forage for their late-night feast.

Val knew exactly where to go for all the fancy meats. She linked arms with Nixie and led her toward a massive wooden door with an iron ring for the handle, and together they pulled with both hands to open it. Inside, strings of sausages and aging cuts of meat hung from the ceiling, and shelves were stacked high with potted liver and spreads.

Françoise handed the torch to Jo and nudged her toward the meats cellar. "I'll go and get the bread over there," she said, pointing to a pantry at the far end of the kitchen. "You can help the girls with the sausages."

Jo stepped carefully into the dark room, careful not to disturb any of the food hanging above her head. Nixie was standing on her tiptoes, trying to read the label on a particular string. "Duck tonight?" she asked Val, as if she were taking her order in a fine restaurant.

Val shook her head. "I had the duck one last night," she replied. "Tonight I try the chicken." She plucked a single link from the chain of sausages, careful not to rip the casing. "And you, Jo? What will you have?"

Jo looked around with delight. She had never seen so much food in one room. "This is the only night we're doing this, right?" she asked Nixie.

"Hopefully," Nixie answered, staring in Val's direction.

"Well then, I should have something exciting." Jo chirped. "I'll have the duck, too, please."

"Excellent choice," Nixie said as she took two links from the string. "Safi? What about you?"

Safi rummaged through the lower cabinets, finally retrieving a medium-sized jar. "I knew I saw this here the other night," she said triumphantly. "I'll try the pickled herring."

Nixie squealed. "Mmmm, *Bismarckhering,* one of my favorites! I'll join you in that. Val, will you pick for the rest of the girls?"

Val wove in and out of the hanging meats and chose three more sausages for the others. She opened a kerchief and wrapped the links up for safekeeping, tying her bundle closed with a stray piece of twine from the butcher's block. "All right, we go!" she whispered, and the four girls exited the meat cellar into the kitchen, pushing the heavy door shut behind them.

Françoise held two baguettes in her arms like sleeping babies, and Maddie carried a small pot of brown mustard. Millie seemed content not to carry anything until she spotted a jar of winterberry preserves. Thinking she might like some dessert after her midnight meal, she tucked it under her arm. Nixie grabbed a small dish of soft butter from the counter and a spreading knife from the drawer.

The troupe of seven left the kitchen with all the makings of a perfect afternoon picnic. Françoise led the way through the moonlit dining hall, its stained-glass windows gleaming as they passed.

Maddie looked around at the empty room. "We're not going to just sit down and eat, are we?" she asked, running her hand down one of the long, polished wooden tables. Seven girls might be awfully exposed in a room designed to seat four hundred.

Millie laughed and walked backward to face Maddie. "That wouldn't be much fun, now, would it? We'll be eating at that table over there three times a day, every day," she said, pointing to a table in the center. "We have a much better spot in mind."

At the end of the tall stained-glass windows, Françoise turned a sharp corner and stopped in front of a bay window, complete with a curved window seat. "It might be a little more cozy now that you two are here," she said, smiling at Maddie and Jo, "but it's the best seat in the dining room."

Indeed, the view from the bay window was the most picturesque Maddie and Jo had seen all night. It looked out onto an elaborate fountain in the middle of a sweeping lawn, and, past that, they could see the history hall, the boathouse, and the sparkling shores of the lake. Even the foamy crest on each small lakeshore wave seemed dotted with specks of silver.

The girls climbed up onto the window seat and sat in a clumsy half-circle, piling their bounty into the center.

Françoise slid her torch light into a worn iron ring in the wall and rubbed her hands together. "*Santé*, ladies," she said, breaking the baguettes into pieces and handing one to each girl. She held up her own pieces as though she were about to make a toast. "To Maddie and Jo, the last of the first-years to arrive!"

The girls raised their bread to the center of the circle in a chorus of laughter, and ate their picnic with delight.

With full stomachs and heavy eyes, Maddie and Jo looked across the stone floor of the main hall and scowled.

It's like ice skating without skates, Jo thought.

Françoise read her mind and poked her head between the twins. "We won't make you go through that again," she said, teasing. "Once I get across, I'll slide both slippers to you, Jo, and Millie will slide hers to you, Maddie. Just wait here."

She stepped out, but before the tip of Françoise's slipper touched the bare floor, Millie threw her arms out to halt the processional. She cocked her head to the side and, eyes widening, spun around and held a finger to her lips.

Everyone stopped in their tracks. Françoise gave her a puzzled look, but understood her friend's concern not a moment later: there were faint footsteps coming down the stairs near the east wing.

Maddie and Jo froze. Val took Safi's hand. Millie panicked for a moment and then moved like lightning. She waved her arms for the others to follow, and then scampered to reach the shadowy stone wall between the Grand Corridor and the east wing.

Françoise turned off her torch and held the warm light behind her back, knowing it would glow faintly for a few more seconds before going completely dark. The rest of the group fled to safety, the barefoot twins being the last to arrive. While all seven girls stood as tall as they could with their backs pressed into the wall, the shadow of the approaching figure neared the main hall.

My feet are going to freeze and fall off, Maddie thought, and she pictured her mother and father in Siberia wearing the warmest snow boots imaginable. She never dreamed that she, too, would be fending off the biting cold at her fancy Swiss boarding school.

Jo, on the other hand, welcomed the numbness. It was impossible to feel the cold on the soles of her feet if she couldn't feel *anything*. She didn't dare try to stand on one foot or the other—any slight move would bring her white nightgown out of the shadows and into plain view for whoever was about to catch her out of bed.

A figure finally emerged from the east wing. It was a woman, tall and a little older than the headmistress. She was dressed in a floor-length sleeping gown, robe, bonnet, and slippers. Her pace was quick, and she practically bounded into the center of the main hall, with little regard to how loud her footsteps were becoming on the hard stone floor.

Françoise had a decision to make. The girls would certainly be found out should the woman turn down the Grand Corridor. Would she turn that way? It was impossible to know. She laid her hand on Nixie's shoulder. *She'll know what to do,* Françoise assured herself, and with a swift push, she shoved Nixie out into the center of the main hall.

The other girls gasped silently and waited for the confrontation in the middle of the room. The woman came to an abrupt stop and turned to Nixie in shock.

"Nixie Engelhardt," she stuttered shrilly. "What . . .what are you doing out of bed at this hour?"

Nixie stood in silence for a moment. "Ahh . . . I . . ." she mumbled, then took a step to her right. The woman stepped along with her.

"Umm . . ." Nixie managed to squeak out, taking yet another step to her right and turning to face the woman. The woman turned to meet Nixie's worried and watery eyes.

Bloody brilliant, she is, Millie thought. Nixie was intentionally having the woman turn her back to the rest of the girls. Françoise, having caught on to Nixie's plan, too, quietly ushered them along the wall, across the entrance to the Grand Corridor, and back to their dormitory hallway.

Nixie's dramatic performance held the attention of the woman in the main hall. "I . . . I can't sleep and . . ." A few tears spilled from her big brown eyes. "I was just going to get some milk, like . . . like Mama gives me at home . . ." She added a few sniffles to intensify the effect, and it worked. The woman's expression seemed to soften, although it still looked as if she were terribly annoyed by the disturbance.

"Come with me. I'll take you to get some milk," the woman said sternly, and just as she took Nixie's hand, Jo stepped up the stairs to the first-year hallway. She poked her head back out into the main hall just in time to catch Nixie giving a thumbs-up sign behind her back before she and the woman disappeared into the Grand Corridor.

Headmistress Kronenberg stepped out from behind the drapes of the first window in the Grand Corridor. Her view of the girls' hasty return had been front row, and had she not been conveniently next to the window before they ran by, she might have been caught out of bed herself. While she couldn't be sure whether the woman would escort Nixie all the way back to her bedroom, she also couldn't risk being seen out of her chambers so late. She would have to wait until morning to find out what had been taken during the night.

CHAPTER NINE

A NEW HOME

Maddie opened one eye and looked up at the stamped tin ceiling of the Room Five dormitory. The metal tiles had been painted white to match the curtains and bed linens, and the room looked quite different than it had just hours ago when she and Jo had arrived. She let go of her stuffed hedgehog and sat up to gaze around. Six beds, six night tables, six rustic wardrobes, and six round rugs were lined up against the walls. The faint light of sunrise glowed through the windows, and Maddie realized that she wasn't the only one awake.

Nixie pulled her pillow out from under her head and covered her face. "Go back to bed, Maddie," she said with a hoarse voice. "The ringers aren't even here yet."

Maddie looked around at the other sleeping girls and decided she could wait to find out what ringers were. She peeked over at her sister. Jo's toes poked out from under her covers, and her arm was draped over her face to keep out the light.

I hope she slept better than I did, Maddie thought. The excitement of being in another country, meeting new friends, and the anticipation of starting classes had been too much. Her mind simply wouldn't rest, and once the other girls were off in dreamland, she started to imagine what kind of ghosts inspired the stories they told about the school. She assured herself that ghosts weren't real, but being awake in an old castle during the small hours of the night was enough to make even the bravest girl a little afraid.

Jo, on the other hand, slept through the night with ease. Once she had gotten comfortable in her new bed, she fell asleep faster than she had in days. No boat rocking. No leaning against a hard car door. It might not have been the down feather mattress of a fine hotel, nor her own four-poster bed back in Boston, but it would do nicely for the rest of the school year.

Maddie was just about to fall back asleep when the shrill sound of high-pitched bells jolted her out of her twilight state.

Françoise and Millie were out of their beds in an instant and headed to the lavatory to get ready. Nixie pulled her pillow tightly over her ears and snuggled down farther under her covers. And Val, stretching her arms and legs as far outward as they would go, smiled with closed eyes and seemed to hardly notice the noise at all.

Jo stumbled out of her bed, covered her ears in protest, and made her way to the door. She opened it just a crack, enough to look out without letting more of the ringing sound in, and saw the culprit: two older students, already dressed in their uniforms, wheeling a small cart down the hallway. A dozen small bells hung from an iron wheel perched on top of the cart, and one of the girls cranked the wheel around and around so that each bell fell forward and rang as it followed the rotation. To Jo, it looked like something from the Middle Ages, and was far less appealing than the usual back scratch from her mother, or her father's good morning song, when she needed to wake up early.

She closed the door and watched the other girls as they got ready for the day. Nixie, finally out of bed, was brushing out her pin curls at her wardrobe mirror. Val laid her uniform onto her bed and marched to the lavatory carrying her toothbrush and a small can of tooth powder. As she left the room, Headmistress Kronenberg entered, carrying two freshly pressed uniforms on wood hangers.

"I trust you slept well, ladies. I see you're up bright and early," she proclaimed cheerfully into the room. Maddie just smiled back at her, stifling the urge to confess that she had never actually been a morning person, and, on top of that, had only gotten what felt like minutes of sleep after a late-night kitchen raid.

The headmistress walked straight over to the twins. "These are for you," she said, and she hung the uniforms in the wardrobes next to their beds. "Your trunk is on its way up the stairs as we speak. The others will show you how to dress and wear your neckties, and you can follow them to the dining hall since I know you don't know your way around the school yet." She raised an eyebrow, fully aware that Maddie and Jo certainly *did* know their way around after the previous night's outing.

Mille cleared her throat and shot the twins an amused look. "Yes, Headmistress," she said sweetly. "We'll show Maddie and Jo to breakfast."

"I know you will," the headmistress said, playing along and patting Millie on the back. "Maddie and Jo, you'll join me for tea later so that I can explain a few rules and traditions we have here at Madame Molineaux's, considering you weren't here to attend the new student orientation like the other first-years. Here are your schedules."

She handed each twin a card with class names and room numbers written on it. "Your schedules are almost identical. I suggest you keep them with you until you've memorized them—tardiness and unscheduled absences are not tolerated. Not even for being lost on your first day of school," she added. She gave a quick nod and smiled warmly. "Enjoy your breakfast."

Jo swallowed the last bite of her warm croissant before she opened her mouth at the dining hall table. "I was so exhausted when I got into bed last night that I forgot to ask—who was the woman who took Nixie to get milk?"

"She's the history teacher, Professor Troxler," Millie replied. "She's bland. Dry. A bit rough on the outside." She stared down at her toast and smiled as she picked it up, holding it next to her face. "See?" she asked the table. "Like this!"

Nixie agreed. "She's terrible. There isn't a bit of cheer in her. She likes the ugly parts of history, or at least, that's all she ever seems to want to teach us about." The others groaned.

"That reminds me," said Françoise, opening a thick textbook next to her breakfast tray. "I haven't finished reading the chapter on the Punic Wars yet . . ."

"Is she really that bad?" Jo asked.

"You can judge for yourself in a few minutes," Safi offered. "We have history right after breakfast. A full stomach and a lecture from Troxler are the perfect combination to send you right back to sleep. And we could all use it today."

Maddie complained out loud. "I didn't sleep a wink, and everyone was already snoring when I started thinking about ghost stories. Good thing I had my hedgehog!" she joked, and laughed at her own childishness. She scrunched up her face. "Why on earth did we get stuffed hedgehogs in our beds, anyway? Hasn't anyone at this school ever heard of a teddy bear?"

Françoise looked up from her book and smiled. "I tossed mine into my wardrobe the first night," she said, smirking, "but I won't tease you if you like to sleep with it. The hedgehog is the mascot for the first-years. See? It's there on your jacket badge, too."

She pulled her jacket sleeve to the front of her arm. On its side was a hand-stitched teal-and-gold patch, complete with two golden letter Ms, the silhouette of a hedgehog, and a banner showing the school's motto with little stars:

* Scientia * Sophia * Gratia *

Jo peered closer at the patch, reading the Latin words. "Knowledge . . . Wisdom . . . Grace," she said, proud of herself for having paid such good attention during Latin class back in Boston.

"Right," Françoise said. "Each year's patch has an animal symbol. During the first four years, the patch is the same—only the animal changes." She gestured toward a brunette girl standing behind Jo. "See? She's a second-year, so she wears the fox on her patch. And there," she said, pointing to a red-headed girl at the next table over, "is a third-year. She wears the ibex."

"What's an ibex?" Maddie asked, unfamiliar with the animal.

"It's a large mountain goat," replied Safi with ease. "The males have huge horns, and they were thought to be almost

extinct until about twenty years ago, when they were reintro-
duced to the Alps."

The twins stared at Safi.

"What?" Safi laughed. "I like animals. I want to work on a
wildlife preserve in Africa one day."

Françoise stood to look out over the other tables. "There's
a group of fourth-years by the door. You can't tell from this far
away, but they wear the bear . . ." She nodded to Safi.

". . . which actually disappeared from Switzerland just
after the turn of the century, due to hunting and trapping,"
Safi added.

"Right. But they still exist on our patches, at least, and maybe
one day they'll come back to the mountains." She winked at
Safi and continued. "The fifth-years are the only girls who get
to wear the Madame Molineaux's crest on their sleeve. It has all
four animals on it, and the whole crest is clutched in the talons
of a Great Blue Turaco. It's a stunning bird, so exotic."

Safi chimed in once more. "They're not native to Switzerland,
of course, but we have our own private collection of them here
in the conservatory. You can't miss them, squawking from
the aviary."

Jo resisted the urge to ask where the birds came from, and
instead imagined fifth-year students with hardly any room on
their beds to sleep, with all those different stuffed animals. "Do
you keep getting a new stuffed animal every fall?" she asked.

"No, no. A different gift each of the years," Val said excitedly. "I saw the fourth-year yesterday wearing the gold
bear-shaped earrings."

"And I heard that this year's second-years found a quilt
with hand-stitched foxes on them, folded in their wardrobes,"
exclaimed Nixie as she leaned forward over the table. "I can't
wait to get that!"

Maddie felt a tinge of jealousy as she thought about future years' gifts. She knew she and Jo would only be at Madame Molineaux's for this year, but as much as she wanted to return to normal life in Boston, she didn't like the idea of leaving this school. They hadn't even been there for a full day, yet already she felt like they belonged.

The interior of the history hall proved to be just as stately and ornate as the exterior. The foyer was decorated with statues and portraits of famous historical figures, and framed documents dotted the spaces in between. Maddie and Jo followed their roommates under the sweeping staircase to the back of the building, where their classroom was full of students. Everyone had already chosen their seat for the semester, so the twins were left with only two options for desks: one seat was front and center, and the other was in the back corner next to a large ventilation grate.

The twins looked at each other for a mere second before the race to the back of the room began; of course, Jo, with her long legs, always arrived any place faster than her sister. She slid into the corner desk, giving Maddie a playful look of mock sympathy before taking her pens and notebook out of her school bag. She laid her study materials out, staking her claim on the less intimidating seat. Maddie squared her jaw and turned toward the front of the room.

She felt as though all eyes were on her as she walked to her desk, and she looked around to locate her roommates.

Françoise also sat in the front row, just a few seats away from her. Millie was three seats behind her, and Nixie and Val were closer to Jo in the back. She slid into her desk chair and scooted it back slightly, bumping the desk of the girl behind her.

"Careful," the girl said in a cold tone of voice, without any trace of friendliness. Maddie turned around quickly to apologize, but stopped short once she saw the glare in the pretty girl's eyes.

"Oh—um—" Maddie stammered, staring back blankly. The girl showed no interest in being friends or wanting to talk, and she cocked her head arrogantly and folded her arms. She raised her eyebrows at Maddie as if to ask, *What are you staring at?* and widened her light gray eyes. Her complexion was porcelain with just a hint of color on her cheeks to offset the bluish tint of her skin. The way her hair was pulled back from her face and held in place with gold-and-pearl hairpins reminded Maddie of a doll she once had. She looked so perfect that she didn't seem real.

A rapping on the desk brought Maddie's attention back to the front of the room, where Professor Troxler, now in a stiff-looking black-and-blue-striped dress instead of a sleeping gown and robe, held a long blackboard pointer as if it were a scepter.

"Attention! Attention, ladies," she barked at the girls, sternly scanning the room for any evidence of trouble-making. "Please open your textbooks to page two hundred and forty-three." She waited for a moment while the roomful of girls opened their books, then walked to the cabinets and withdrew two books from a shelf. She dropped one carelessly onto Maddie's desk, and then walked swiftly to the back corner to deliver the other to Jo. She examined her roster as she walked back to the blackboard.

"Madeline . . . Livingston," she said, waiting to see which one of the new girls would answer. Maddie raised her hand timidly and forced an awkward smile, trying to make a good impression.

"Josephine . . . Livingston?" she asked, and looked confused for a moment. Jo raised her hand high and gave a bright smile to her new teacher.

Professor Troxler put her roster down and sighed.

"Are you having a joke with me, ladies?" she asked, looking very unamused. "Or do you really have the same last name?"

Jo stood and tried her best to be polite. "No—I mean— yes, Madame, err—" she said, stumbling over the words. "No, we're not having a joke . . . and yes, we really have the same name." She looked over at Maddie, smiling. "We're twins, actually."

Strangers usually responded with delight when meeting the girls, discovering that two young ladies who looked so different from each other were indeed fraternal twins. But Troxler didn't look one bit impressed.

"Is that so?" she asked, still scowling slightly. "How unfortunate for you, having to share the same wretched last name *and* the same birthday. In a duel to the death, I wonder which of you would win."

Maddie's mouth dropped open. *What is so wretched about our last name?*

Jo sat down instantly and stared straight into her book. *She really is morbid,* she thought, refusing to imagine a duel between her and her sister. The other girls hadn't been kidding about the nasty instructor.

Professor Troxler started the history lecture as if she had said nothing shocking. She spoke without pausing until the end of the hour, but neither Maddie nor Jo could concentrate on a single history lesson. If the rest of the classes at Madame Molineaux's were like this, it would be a very long year at school.

"La ... vieille ... femme ... marche ... avec ... le ... petit ... garçon." Madame Lécuyer spoke slowly, underlining each syllable with her long wooden pointer. She faced the class and smiled, trying to make eye contact with each of her students. "Millicent Braithwaite, why don't you read it for us?"

Millie stood reluctantly and cleared her throat. As much as she liked to chat and laugh outside of class, speaking French certainly was not one of her stronger skills, and she hated the way her strong voice sharpened the soft words—especially in front of girls who had been taking French lessons since they were young.

"La, er ... vee-ay ... fim marshay ... ummm ... avec ... lah ... er ... petite garçon." It wasn't perfect but it was enough to please Madame Lécuyer.

"*Bon,* Millicent, very nice, you're already getting better," she encouraged her. "Now, another volunteer?"

The doll-faced girl from Troxler's history class raised her perfectly manicured hand.

"Rosemary Byron," Lécuyer announced, obviously pleased that Rosemary had volunteered.

Maddie turned to look at Rosemary, still wondering why she had been so rude to her earlier. *I hope she messes this up,* she thought, wishing for something to knock this prissy girl off her high horse. But Rosemary would not be messing up. She had been taught lessons in French since she was a small child, and made no secret of the fact that she was very bored sitting with novices in such an elementary class.

"*La vieille femme marche avec le petit garçon,*" she recited without hesitation, and the words rolled off her tongue perfectly, with almost no trace of her British accent.

"*Parfait!*" Lécuyer marveled. "I must say, it seems as if we have two natural speakers in our classroom, does it not?" She gestured toward Rosemary and another girl in the back of the class. "Rosemary Byron and Safietou Faye, I'm sure the others would be grateful for any grammar help you could give them."

Rosemary turned to the back of the classroom and stared at Safi.

"She doesn't speak *real* French," she said out loud in a smug tone.

Maddie recoiled at Rosemary's rudeness. *If only Françoise were here, she'd put that little snob in her place,* she thought. But since Françoise was a native French speaker, she was down the hall studying English.

Madame Lécuyer smiled cheerfully and shook her finger at Rosemary.

"She *does* speak French, Rosemary. *West African* French, perhaps, but French all the same. Certainly, there are some differences, but that is why we are all here in class, is it not?" She nodded and smiled at the class in her jovial manner, drawing in a large breath and sighing with satisfaction.

The bodice of her dress hugged her round torso so tightly that it groaned when she inhaled, and Jo fully expected one of the seams to split open at any moment. Madame Lécuyer was quite plump, and, with her rosy cheeks and jolly demeanor, she reminded Jo of pictures she had seen of Santa Claus's wife at the North Pole.

Jo turned around to make sure Safi was all right, but Safi looked calm and relaxed, and simply continued to look at Madame Lécuyer. She was already used to the sideways looks from Rosemary and a few other girls. Her father had told her that she might not find any other African girls at Madame Molineaux's, but he hadn't said anything about bold-faced snobbery.

Jo leaned over toward Safi. "Where are you from in West Africa?" she asked in her most quiet voice. "Maddie and I actually came straight here from Morocco."

"I'm from Senegal," she whispered proudly. "The capital city, Dakar."

"Well, I'm sure your French sounds just wonderful, Safi," Jo praised. "Don't listen to that girl up front."

"Thank you, Jo," Safi said, looking down at her desk. She raised her head and narrowed her eyes at Rosemary from across the room. "She's made it clear that she doesn't like me very much."

Nixie joined in the conversation from two seats over. "Don't worry, Safi. From what I've seen, she doesn't like *any-one* very much. I'm just sorry you have to share a dormitory room with her." She paused and smiled. "Does she snore in French, too?"

The girls all giggled softly before turning their attention back to Madame Lécuyer at the blackboard.

Maddie and Jo caught up with their roommates as the entire school headed to the dining hall for lunch.

"She's horrible, that Rosemary," Maddie insisted as the group funneled into the large room. "It's bad enough we all have to go to class with her, and poor Safi has to stay in the same room with her. But having to eat with her, too? Ugh!"

"Oh, don't worry about *that*," Millie said sarcastically. "Eating with the commoners? Not Rosemary Byron. She eats with the other highbrow Brits at their own special table. It's invitation only." She winked and gestured toward the smallest table in the dining hall.

"*La Famille Royale*," Françoise joked with her nose high in the air.

Maddie huffed and shook her head. "Royal family, indeed. And I'm the Baroness of Boston."

CHAPTER TEN

A PRIVATE ORIENTATION

The twins entered the serving line just as Headmistress Kronenberg approached and cut in. "Good afternoon, ladies. I'm happy to see that you've made it through the first half of your classes today. I trust you're enjoying your lessons?"

Maddie smiled and nodded politely, wondering when the headmistress would let them alone. By now, she was quite sure she knew everything she needed to know about getting along at Madame Molineaux's. "Yes, Headmistress, we're enjoying them very much," she replied. *Except for nasty Professor Troxler and Little-Miss-Priss Rosemary Byron, that is,* she thought.

"Perfect. I hate to interrupt your lunch, but you and Josephine will join me for tea, just for today." She nodded to the rest of the girls and led Maddie and Jo back through the lines of hungry students and down the Grand Corridor.

The main hall was bright, with each of the blue windows sparkling in the midday sun. The headmistress stopped at the edge of the administration hallway and faced the girls.

"As a matter of respect, ladies, we ask that students not come down this hallway without permission. Is that understood?"

Maddie and Jo nodded in agreement, trying to see past the headmistress and farther into the hallway. As they continued toward the office, both girls looked around in wonder. The finest of the school's collection of art and statues had been reserved for this corridor. The portraits looked as if they were hundreds of years old. In them, men stood clutching shields and swords, and women wore ornate gowns and held books.

"Almost there now," the headmistress said to the girls, but she stopped when she didn't hear them padding down the hall behind her. She turned back to see what had distracted her students. The twins stood shoulder-to-shoulder, staring up at a beautifully painted figurehead carved out of wood.

The headmistress approached them slowly. "She's lovely, isn't she?" she asked them quietly. "It's a mermaid figurehead, just like the ones from the front of a ship."

The mermaid leaned into the hallway from the wall and looked down over the girls' heads. Her golden curls spilled down over her shoulders halfway to her waist, and she wore a necklace of pearl and coral. Two tiny starfish adorned her earlobes, and an elaborate seashell crown lay across her forehead.

Jo reached up to touch the glossy wood, but pulled her hand away at the last second and looked back at the headmistress.

"It's all right, Josephine," the headmistress said, smiling gently. "She's fastened tight to the wall. You can't break her or knock her down."

Jo traced the grooves in the mermaid's golden curls with her fingers, amazed at the lifelike detail. "Was she ever on a ship?"

"I don't think so," said the headmistress. "She doesn't look like she's ever been out in a storm, does she?"

Maddie shook her head. "She looks perfect," she confirmed. "Even the jewels still sparkle."

The mermaid clutched a small red heart in her hands, holding it to the middle of her chest. Embedded in the wood, dozens of tiny red rubies glittered in the sunlight.

"Does she have a name?" Jo asked, bending down to inspect the mermaid's curved tail.

The headmistress just smiled. "That's enough about the mermaid, girls. Let's go ahead into my office."

Just steps away from the figurehead, two sets of knights' armor guarded a large arched wooden door with a brass plaque reading DIRECTRICE.

Maddie and Jo followed the headmistress into her office, a room that was as richly decorated and draped as the hallway they had come from. The curtains were pulled back from the windows, letting the sunlight bathe each trophy and plaque in a stately blue glow. Tea was set out on a low table, complete with sandwiches and tarts.

"Please, ladies, sit down. Verbena or jasmine tea?" the headmistress offered, taking her own seat in a chair across from the sofa.

Jo held her cup and saucer out and gazed around the room, up at the walls, at each of the relics carefully displayed there. It was like having tea in a museum.

"Your office is beautiful," she remarked as she dropped two lumps of sugar into her tea. "It's a shame students have to get into trouble to get to see it."

"Ah, well." Kronenberg smiled as she finished pouring her own tea. "Rarely would a girl in trouble find herself in my office. Detention is held down the hall in a room not quite as nice. She paused and looked thoughtful for a moment. "Unless, of course, you serve detention outside, working on the grounds . . . but I doubt very much either of you will be serving detention any time soon, so not to worry."

Maddie pursed her lips to avoid smiling broadly. *You must not know us very well yet,* she thought. As innocent as their schemes always started out, she and Jo usually ended up in some sort of trouble.

The headmistress continued. "Madame Molineaux's is more than just a boarding school. It's a home, and we're a family. Do you see all the families we have had here in the past?" She pointed to dozens of framed pictures lining the walls. "One for each year we've been open, taken at the end of the school year. You can count them, but there are thirty-two in all."

"So, the school has been here since . . . 1900?" Maddie asked. She searched the wall for the photograph for that first year. It was black and white, like half the other photographs. Only about fifty girls stood on bleachers, and their uniforms were different from the ones the students wore now. The skirts were longer, the collars higher, and the girls wore pointy black boots. They stood in groups of ten or so and held their grade's shield, which looked like larger versions of their patches. The fifth-year girls stood in the center, waving the Madame Molineaux's flag on a high pole.

Jo scanned the room and settled on a large frame on the opposite wall. "What's that over there?" she asked, trying to make sense of the black-and-white shapes in the picture.

The headmistress turned her head to see what Jo was pointing at. "Well, that's something you might find handy right about now, as you make your way around the school for the first time." She got up and walked over to the wall, motioning for the girls to follow. "Does it look at all familiar?" she asked.

Jo studied the frame carefully and finally made sense of the wavy lines, circles, and squares. "It's a map!" she said, stepping back to study the layout. "There's the lake, the gate, the labyrinth, and the stables."

"Almost," Kronenberg said, going over to her desk and pulling out two folded sheets of parchment-colored paper. "*This* is a map of Madame Molineaux's," she said, and handed one to each of the girls. "On the wall is an aerial photograph of the school."

"Aerial? Like from an airplane?" Maddie asked.

"Yes, we had it taken two years ago." She opened the folds of Jo's map. "From the photograph, we were able to make this map for the new students. It tends to help them in the beginning, and I suppose it becomes more of a keepsake after they learn their way around."

Jo thought for a moment. She had only been at the school for twelve hours, and she felt as though she already knew her way around pretty well, even without a map. The school grounds were big, but not *that* big.

"You flew a plane over the school and had photographs taken just so you could make a map for new students?" she asked.

"Well, that, and . . . well," the headmistress stammered. "We were looking for something else at the time."

"Looking for something?" Jo pressed. "Looking for what?"

"Did you find it? Can you see it in the photograph?" Maddie asked, seconds after Jo had finished.

Kronenberg fumbled for words. "Ahh, well, no. It's not important, we were just looking to see if something was there. It was nothing, really." She led the girls back to the tea table. "Sometimes, when you're looking for something, you need to step as far away from it as you can. Often, it will help you find what you're looking for. But not this time."

Jo gave Maddie a puzzled look, and her sister's eyes made it clear that she was wondering the exact same thing—*What was the headmistress hiding?*

The headmistress sat back down and changed the subject. She opened Jo's map and spread it on the table. "Here we are, in the castle. We arrived last night and came in through the front doors from the main drive, and this morning you exited through the doors at the end of the dining hall to go to your classes."

Both girls nodded.

"Now. Leaving the castle through the dining hall and going left will take you to the science hall and the gardens. Not only does Professor Natalio teach botany and biology, but he and his staff also grow and harvest much of the food we eat. A stroll through his gardens is often what students need to clear their heads during exam time." She followed the edge of the gardens with her finger until it reached the shore of the lake. "This, of course, is the lake that borders the school, *Le Lac aux Diamants Bleus.* It's a very large lake, and students can take canoes and kayaks out from the boathouse to explore."

"Lake of . . . the blue diamonds?" Jo asked, translating the words. "Are there really diamonds in the lake?"

The headmistress shook her head and laughed gently. "I don't think so, but every now and then, we see people sifting through the silt on the shore, looking for treasure. The man who named the lake—and built this castle—was a bit eccentric. It already had its strange name when we got here—much like the name of the forest that surrounds the lake," she said, moving her finger along the lakeshore to the thickly wooded area that crept up the mountain. "*La Forêt des Flammes.* The forest of the flames."

Jo let her focus drift for a moment to contemplate the two names; they didn't make any sense to her. Then again, she had named two of her dolls Tonsillitis and Malarkey when she was younger, for no other reason than she liked the way the names sounded. Maybe this man had done the same.

"Can we go into the forest?" Maddie asked, imagining leisurely picnics and naps under the trees in spring. "Jo and I lived in the Amazon jungle for a summer once. We love to explore the woods."

"Yes, you can go into the forest. Just take a dachshund with you. And make sure they have a little sweater on if it's cold out." replied the headmistress, as if it were a perfectly normal thing to say.

Maddie and Jo didn't ask *why* they should take a dachshund with them. Or what a dachshund's sweater might look like. If they asked every question they had about the grounds of Madame Molineaux's, they might be at tea for hours.

"You can sign them out at the boathouse," Kronenberg continued. "Just don't take the dachshunds back to your rooms with you. We have a strict policy against having pets in the dormitories." She saw the perplexed looks on the girls' faces and decided to move on with the map.

"Ahem." She cleared her throat. "At the far end of the campus is the history hall—you've already been there this morning. I assume you saw our rooftop residents there?"

"We *did*," Maddie said, nodding at Jo. "They keep the grass short and live in those little towers on top. Um . . . why is there grass on the roof again?"

Kronenberg laughed. "Again, we're not sure," she said playfully. "It was like that when we got here. It was Professor Natalio's idea to put the goats up there to keep the grass trimmed."

"Who's idea was it to put Albert up there with them?" Jo asked innocently. Maddie's eyes widened and she dug the heel of her shoe into the top of Jo's foot.

"Oh, you've seen Albert?" the headmistress asked, putting on an air of surprise. She figured the girls must have seen him during their midnight escapade the night before, but she couldn't let them know that. "How interesting. He usually only comes out late at night."

Jo got flustered and hastily protested. "Well, *we* didn't see him of course, but the girls in our room told us about him this morning on the way to class."

Kronenberg cocked her head to the side calmly. "Oh? Which one of your roommates has seen Albert?" she asked, wondering if Jo would implicate one of her new friends.

Maddie looked up at the cuckoo clock above the door. "Oh! We do hate to be rude, but we'll be late for biology if we don't finish our sandwiches and get to class. Thank you so much for having us. This has been lovely, right, Jo?"

Jo smiled sweetly and nodded, making sure her mouth was too full to speak. The girls finished their tea and excused themselves, barely making it down the Grand Corridor and out the dining hall doors before class began in the science building.

"That was a close one," Maddie said to her sister as they hurried across the lawn. "How could we have known about Albert if we hadn't been out of bed at night?"

"I know," Jo said, apologizing. "I'm going to have to work on my secret-keeping. *Especially* if we're going to sneak back into Kronenberg's office to get a better look at that aerial photograph. What do you suppose they were trying to see from up there? Something in the lake? In the forest?"

Maddie shook her head. "I don't know, but I bet she locks the door at night. We're going to have to come up with something pretty clever to get back in there."

Church bells off in the distance struck one o'clock as the girls approached the science building.

"Is there a chapel on the grounds?" Maddie asked her sister, unfolding her map as they ran. "I don't remember Kronenberg telling us about it."

"I don't think so," answered Jo, out of breath from running. "It must be coming from town." They darted into the building and into class just before Professor Natalio turned around to begin his biology lesson for the day. On the blackboard, he had drawn a picture of a wolf in chalk. Underneath it in large letters read, *Les loups.*

Jo walked leisurely down the science building steps. "I think I'll take one of those strolls through the gardens Kronenberg mentioned," she said, rolling her jacket sleeves up to feel the sun on her tanned arms. "I could use a head-clearing, I suppose—it's been a whole summer since I've had to sit in a classroom."

Françoise caught up with her. "I'll come with you, Jo. Walking in the gardens reminds me of being in Paris." She tossed her books down on the lawn and scooted them under a bush, removing her own jacket to cover them up. "Did you know," she asked, "all the statues were brought here from France?"

"Coming, Maddie?" Jo called to her sister.

Maddie looked up from her schedule card, scowling. "I . . . I can't. I have . . . laboratory?" She looked at her friends in hopes that someone else would have the same class.

Safi shook her head no, and Nixie took a closer peek at Maddie's schedule. "It looks like you're in the *other* first-year laboratory," she fretted. "Maybe there weren't enough stools left in our class."

Maddie was disappointed. The others all had laboratory together, and she was the only one who had to march off to another class. She sighed and put her schedule back in her pocket. "Well, I guess I'll be going, then," she muttered. "Where is the lab?"

"Turn right when you get into the hall, then another right and a quick left to go upstairs," Françoise said over her shoulder.

"No, she should turn *left* into the hall, then right and another right to go upstairs," Safi chimed in, tracing the path with her finger in the air.

Maddie put her bag onto her shoulder and turned back toward the science building. "I have a few minutes," she said, smiling back at her friends. "I'm sure I'll find it eventually." She watched Jo and Françoise slip into the gardens and, for the first time in months, was without her sister by her side.

The science building was nearly empty, as most of the classes at Madame Molineaux's ended at two-thirty each day to allow the girls time for studying, music and dance classes, or enjoying the outdoors. Maddie stopped at the end of the foyer and looked left and right. Each of the hallways would eventually lead to stairs, she thought, so she turned right and wandered past the open classroom doors.

The floors of the science hall were checkered with black and white marble tiles, and framed scientific prints of plants and animals hung from the walls. As she strolled toward the end of the hallway, she stopped periodically to examine the glass display cases that held the preserved skeletons of different species.

Good thing I don't have to be in here at night, she thought, scowling at some of the larger animal skeletons. She turned the corner at the end of the hall and searched the doorways for staircases. Her elbow bumped something in midair, and she recoiled when she realized what she had almost collided with.

A fully reconstructed skeleton of a horse was suspended just inches from Maddie's face. Its bones, strung together and hung from the ceiling with fishing line, clacked against one another like bamboo wind chimes as they settled back into their positions. The skeleton seemed to float along the wall, its hundreds of bones arranged carefully to make it appear as though it were galloping.

Maddie shuddered as she watched the horse skeleton become still again. She smoothed the hair from her face, tugged on the cuffs of her sleeves, and walked with a quickened pace toward the conservatory doors at the end of the hall. With one turn of a brass doorknob and a step across the threshold, she felt instantly transported to another world. Maddie closed the door behind her and took a deep breath.

Inside, the smell of damp soil and tropical flowers filled the atrium while palm and fruit trees leaned over thick patches of lush vegetation. An enormous wooden aviary stretched from the floor to the ceiling at one end of the room, and brilliant blue-green birds, resembling miniature peacocks, flitted between the rafters with ease as their low, hiccuping squawks wafted out of their large cage into the indoor wilderness. Ferns and vines crept along winding pathways, and their leaves rustled as tiny finches scratched in the packed earth for insects.

Maddie could feel the sun beating down on her face through the window-paned ceiling, and she sighed out loud as she imagined that she was on a summer excavation with her parents again. She decided it was her favorite room so far at Madame Molineaux's, and that it would be her refuge during the icy Swiss winter. She ruffled her fingers through a planter of lanky purple orchids and smiled as she strolled up the path.

Her eyes relaxed as she walked between the green plants, and she unfocused them, blurring her vision ever so slightly to cast a dreamy veil over the jungle. She slowed her breathing and continued gazing until her eyes settled on something looking out from the cluster of ferns ahead.

It only took a few moments to make out the large pair of yellow eyes staring at her from in between the fronds. They shined like two candle flames and followed Maddie's movements as she came to a complete stop. She stared into the pair of eyes as she bent down to pick up a small rock from the undergrowth next to her, fully intending to startle the animal out of the bushes. But before she could throw the stone at the beast ahead, the largest cat she had ever seen leaped out from the bushes beside her.

Maddie's reflexes were quick, but not quick enough. The cat wrapped its massive paws around her waist as it stood up on its hindquarters, reaching nearly four feet in the air.

The pair of eyes from the ferns ahead emerged in a playful gallop to join in on the successful hunt—it was another enormous cat identical to the first, with black-and-gray spots on a thick, fluffy beige coat, a bearded chin, and big pointy ears. The cat bounced up and landed with its front paws on Maddie's chest, pausing only for a moment before it springboarded off her onto the ground. Fur flew through the air as Maddie lost her balance and stumbled backward.

"Help!" she managed to yell out as her hands broke her fall. She landed in a sort of crab-walk, and before she knew it, the two cats were back for another round. She braced herself for teeth, claws, or worse—but instead, one of the cats curled headfirst onto the floor and rolled at her feet, while the other rubbed its chin across Maddie's jaw. It was as if two small leopards had snuggled up to their prey for a cuddle.

Hurried footsteps echoed through the conservatory as Maddie tried in vain to sit up. Her new furry friends were determined to keep her on the ground, rubbing up and down her legs and arms and emitting low, rumbling purrs.

"Oh," said a disappointed voice from above. "It's just you."

Maddie looked up to see Rosemary Byron standing over her, hands on hips and wearing a scowl of disapproval. The cats were instantly interested in the new visitor and finally let Maddie get back on her feet. They rubbed their backs around Rosemary's legs and let her scratch their bearded chins.

"What *are* these?" Maddie asked, cautiously patting one of the cats on the head.

"They're Nata-lynx," Rosemary replied in her driest tone.

Maddie nodded slowly. "Oh, right. Okay." She didn't have a clue what Rosemary had just said.

Rosemary gave an ingenuous smile and shook her head. "You don't know what they are," she said condescendingly in her cold British accent.

"No," admitted Maddie, "I guess I don't. First day, you know."

Rosemary ran her fingernails down the spine of the larger cat. "This is Marcello," she said, "and Musetta is the smaller one there. They're part of Professor Natalio's hybrid experiments. He's been developing this breed to restore the lynx population in Switzerland. They're almost extinct, didn't you know?" Musetta reared up on her hind legs and demanded equal attention from Rosemary.

"No, I didn't. They gave me quite a scare though. I'm glad that didn't happen at night!"

"You won't see them at night," Rosemary replied, matter-of-factly. "They sleep in their cages in Professor Natalio's office."

"Why aren't they living outside, in the forest, where they belong?" Maddie asked.

"These two were crossed with house cats and can't live in the wild, being this friendly. They wouldn't survive outside the school."

Maddie thought about the biology lecture from that day. "So that's why Professor Natalio goes on and on about hybrids," she thought out loud. "Are there others?"

Rosemary smoothed her skirt and looked bored once more. "If you're headed up to the first-year laboratory, you'd better run. You're almost late." She walked past Maddie without another word, leaving her with the two domesticated wildcats.

Maddie gave Marcello and Musetta each a pat on the head and walked to class alone.

CHAPTER ELEVEN

THE TORN SKIRT OF ELISABETH OF BOHEMIA

Jo heard the faint church bells off in the distance.

Huh. Those don't usually wake me up at three in the morning, she thought. *Especially when it's thundering.* It had been raining all night, which normally kept Jo sleeping soundly. She opened her eyes to look around. She was in her bedroom, at the Livingston family townhouse in Boston. Everything was just as she'd seen it last, her desk tidy and her books all put away.

Jo sat up and slid her feet into her slippers. It was rare that she woke up and needed a snack, but the rumbling in her stomach was undeniable. Only milk and crackers would put her back to sleep now.

She tiptoed out of her room and walked down the hallway to the stairs, careful not to wake her parents. The staircase seemed shorter than she remembered, but she figured she was just tired, and kept walking toward the kitchen.

It's freezing in here. She shuddered as the skin on her legs and arms erupted in goose bumps in the chilly air. She looked around the foyer to make sure a window or door hadn't been left open but found nothing out of place. She did, however, wonder when her parents had switched all the white nightlights to blue ones—the foyer was filled with them.

In the kitchen, Jo opened the cupboard door where the crackers were usually kept. *Why are there books in the cupboard?* she pondered as she pulled out volumes of history texts instead of tins of cookies and cakes. She shook her head and moved to the next cupboard door. More books. She opened the drawer underneath, but instead of whisks and spatulas, there were opera glasses and bottles of brown and black ink. She didn't remember her mother reorganizing the kitchen. She'd have to look through every door and drawer to find her crackers, it seemed. This would take longer than expected.

Maddie rolled her head from side to side on her pillow. Her eyes flew open, and she jolted up—it felt as if she hadn't taken a breath in a few minutes. She inhaled deeply and sighed, looking out the rain-spotted window. *Maybe it's just the thunder that woke me up,* she assured herself. She lay back down and hugged her hedgehog. Maybe Jo was awake, too.

But when she looked over at Jo's bed, it was empty. Her slippers were gone, and her robe was missing from the bedside hook where it hung each night.

She's probably in the lavatory, Maddie reasoned. She snuggled down under her covers again and waited for the dormitory door to creak open, but it didn't. She sat back up and looked around the room—the other girls were asleep in their beds, so Jo wasn't out for a midnight snack with friends. Jo was alone.

Maddie quickly put on her slippers and swung her robe over her shoulders. She tiptoed to the door, opened it just a crack, and stuck her head out far enough to see the lavatory doorway. It was completely dark. Maddie's thoughts wandered.

Maybe she went to Kronenberg's office . . . but without me?

Jo hadn't been able to stop talking about the aerial photograph or what the staff had been looking for when they'd had it taken. It had been weeks since their tea with the headmistress, and they still hadn't come up with a plan to get back in and investigate.

Maddie slipped out the door into the first-year hallway and padded down the stairs to the main hall, scurrying across it as quietly as she could. It was the first time she had ever been alone in the massive room at night, and she looked down at her hands, now tinted an eerie blue from the windows above. She imagined translucent figures flying around the chandeliers, and the thought of bluish ghosts swirling around in the hall made her quicken her step. Each time the lightning illuminated the sky, her eyes played tricks on her. She was practically running now to the administration hallway, narrowly escaping the grasp of imaginary apparitions, when she stopped short at the entryway. There was Jo, sitting halfway down the hall on folded legs in front of an open curio cabinet, its contents strewn across the floor.

She walked carefully up to her sister and studied her face. Jo's eyes were open, and she was inspecting each item she pulled out of the cabinet before laying it on the carpet.

"Jo?" Maddie whispered. "What are you doing?"

Jo looked up at her sister from her seat on the floor and smiled. "Hi, Mom," she said casually. "I'm . . ." She paused and examined the contents of the cabinet. "I'm about to cook something for us." She looked around again and scowled, thumbing through the drawer of eyeglasses and ink. "No, no, that's not it," she said, laughing and putting on a pair of eyeglasses. "I'm getting ready to go to work with Dad."

Maddie stood and stared at Jo with her mouth open in confusion. She had only seen her sister act this bizarrely one other time—it was in Mexico, during the Caribbean hurricane season. *Not again,* she thought. The last time this had happened, she and her mother were up for hours before Jo finally went back to sleep. She replayed scenes in her mind from that night. She remembered her mother kneeling down and telling her, "It's okay, Maddie. Just play along. And remember, never *ever* wake a sleepwalker."

Jo continued to inspect and organize items from the curio cabinet into piles on the floor. Maddie sat down gently next to her and stroked her hair like their mother often did.

"Now, Jo," she said in her most motherly fashion. "Remember, you don't have to go to work with Dad tomorrow. Let's put everything back, and then we'll come back later tomorrow to get what you need."

Jo wasn't having it. "No," she said, shaking her head. "I'm going to need this . . . umm . . ." She looked down at the tiny silver letter opener she held in her hand. "This teaspoon. For digging at the site." Jo slipped the letter opener into her pocket and stood up.

Maddie grew more and more concerned. If they were caught out of bed, they'd be in trouble for sure, especially for having taken everything out of a cabinet and making a mess. But if Jo was caught stealing, she might be expelled. She stood and put her hand on her sister's back, rubbing in a small circle to keep her sister calm. "Okay, sure, Jo," she said. "Now can we put away all of these other tools you don't need?"

Jo looked down and patted her pocket to make sure what she needed was still there. "Yes, let's do that, Mom. Dad would be so upset if he woke up and found all his things out!"

Maddie played along, assuming her role as their mother in this wild illusion of Jo's. She helped her sister put the books and ink bottles back in the cabinet and shut the door. "Well," she said, "I guess we had better get back to bed now. Ready?" Maddie took one of Jo's hands and made sure she could reach into her pocket with the other hand. She was determined to retrieve the letter opener and somehow get it back into the drawer before they left the administration hallway.

Jo walked along cooperatively, yawning. "I'm ready, all right. I'm plain *exhausted!*" Maddie waited for the right moment and then put her hand in Jo's robe pocket, trying to remain unnoticed. She had the letter opener in her fingers and was slipping it out when Jo noticed what she was doing. Maddie took her chances and whipped the letter opener out of Jo's reach, holding it high in the air.

"Mom, I need that!" Jo said, raising her voice. Maddie knew she wouldn't be able to keep the letter opener out of her taller sister's reach for long. She ran a few steps ahead, and Jo stumbled after her with arms outstretched.

Jo grabbed at the letter opener once and then twice, but Maddie was too quick for her. She held her hand up again, and this time, decided to take advantage of the fact that Jo wasn't thinking clearly.

"Jo, don't grab at the teaspoon again, or I'll drop it out of this window." She held the letter opener in the air right next to a large portrait, hoping that sleepwalking Jo might believe that the frame was a windowsill. But once again, Jo wasn't having it. She made one final lunge at the letter opener, forcing Maddie's hand back against the portrait, and dragged it down the canvas.

The ripping sound of the letter opener's blade cutting through the painted canvas jolted Jo out of her dreamy state. She gasped and stared with wide eyes at her sister, who was pinned back against the ripped portrait with a terrified look on her face. "Oh my gosh, Maddie!" she exclaimed. "What are you doing?"

Maddie let go of the letter opener and it fell to the carpet, barely making a sound. She caught her breath and shook her head with worry. "You were *sleepwalking* again, Jo," she said. "I came to find you, and you were there, taking everything out of that cabinet!"

"Uh-oh," Jo said, looking back down the hall. "Did I break anything?"

"Only this painting," Maddie said, stepping back from the portrait to stand next to her sister. "We ripped it with the letter opener when you tried to take it out of my hand."

The girls took another gaze at the damage to the life-size portrait of a woman. The tear started at the woman's waist and went halfway down her skirt. It was certainly noticeable, and the headmistress would surely see it on her way to her office in the morning.

"*Only* this painting?" Jo panicked. "This painting is none other than . . ." She crouched down to see the small brass plaque just under the bottom of the frame. "Elisabeth of Bohemia," she read, looking back up at the portrait of the woman. "She didn't look very happy before, and now she has a torn skirt." Jo tried unsuccessfully to smooth the ripped sides of the canvas back together.

"Don't touch it, Jo. You'll make it worse!" Maddie scolded, but her sister was now peeling back the pieces of canvas, rubbing her fingers against what lay behind it. "There's something behind this portrait," Jo said, ignoring Maddie's warnings. She went to the side of the frame and lifted it slightly, but there was nothing but wall behind it. She let the frame down and returned to the site of the tear, running her fingers behind the canvas again. "I'm serious, Maddie. Come here and look at this."

Maddie cringed. This felt like more trouble. She began to regret getting out of bed at all.

Jo pulled back a small piece of the ripped canvas. "You can barely see it, but you can feel it . . . there's fabric back here." She peered in closer behind the canvas, careful not to tear it even more. "It's some kind of tapestry."

Only a small section of the tapestry was visible behind the ripped portrait, about the width of a ruler, but the designs on it were recognizable. Parts of shields, swords, dragons, and horses could be seen on the entire length of the long tear. The fabric was woven and rustic, and Jo ran her fingers over the patches that were worn thin.

"This has to be really, really old," she continued. "I wish Mom and Dad were here. They'd know when and where it was from."

Maddie felt the tapestry with her own hands and agreed. "Maybe we can sketch it and send it to them, " she said, remembering all the times her parents had opened up their journals to make sketches of symbols, paintings, and rock formations during their digs.

Jo shook her head. "Maddie, we have to fix this, and quick. If Kronenberg sees it, we're done for. There's no time to come back and sketch it, and besides, it's darker than a dungeon back here! What are we going to do?"

"I don't know, " Maddie replied hopelessly. "But we're going to need some help."

Jo shook Françoise's shoulder gently for the second time. She looked over at Maddie and shrugged, not knowing how far she should go to wake their friend. Maddie's patience was wearing thin, and even more important, she had finally looked at the clock—it was three-thirty in the morning, and the ringers would be in the hall by six o'clock. That didn't leave much time to mend Elisabeth of Bohemia's torn skirt.

Maddie grabbed on to Françoise's hand and squeezed tight. "Françoise!" she whispered loudly into the sleeping girl's ear. Françoise's eyelids fluttered and she stared up at the twins, still half asleep.

"Quoi?" she exclaimed, sounding annoyed. She rubbed her eyes and sat up to face the girls.

Maddie began to explain. "Jo was sleepwalking down the administration hallway and we ended up ripping a portrait— it's a big rip—and we don't know what to do. If Kronenberg finds out we did it, we'll be expelled for sure!" Jo nodded and they waited for a response.

Françoise's expression turned from annoyance to amusement. "Dreaming of detention, were you, Jo?" she asked sarcastically. "Tell me about this rip."

"It's right down a woman's skirt on one of the large portraits. It's not so wide, but it's long—and there's an old tapestry hidden behind it, so we can't just glue it back," Jo explained, trying not to sound frantic.

"Did anyone see you?"

"Only the mermaid, but she's not telling anyone," Maddie tried to joke.

Françoise hopped out of her bed and reached under it. She pulled out her paint box and torch. "Right. Let's go then."

"Hold that light steady," Françoise instructed.

Jo swung the torch like a lantern above the ripped canvas.

Françoise had her paint box open and was already squeezing oil paints from tubes onto a small palette, mixing them to create the different shades of the skirt in the portrait. She ran her hand up and down the tear and turned to the girls. "Jo's right. We can't glue the rip back together, this tapestry is in the way. But . . . why is there even a tapestry here?"

"We don't know," Maddie replied. "It's definitely old, though." She pulled Jo's arm down closer to the tapestry to shine the light on the designs. "Do you recognize any of these symbols?"

Françoise shook her head. "No, but I can tell you it is not from France. These dragons here look like German ones . . ."

She traced around the head of one with her finger. "But I can't be sure." She pushed the torch out of the way, as if it were a lamp on an extendable arm. "I'm going to need a piece of someone's robe. Any volunteers?"

Jo sighed. "It was my sleepwalking that got us into this mess, so I guess you can use mine. What do you need?"

Françoise handed Maddie a tiny pair of embroidery scissors from her paint box. "Cut off half of her belt," she ordered as she measured the length of the rip. "Then cut it open at the seam. That should be wide enough to put behind the canvas." Maddie did as she was told and gave the long piece of bathrobe belt to Françoise.

"It's perfect, " Françoise commented as she stuffed it behind the ripped canvas. She finished tucking the long strip of fabric up under the sides of the tear, and smoothed it out until there were no wrinkles left. "Hand me that pot of glue."

Maddie bent down to Françoise's paint box and took out a small glass bottle, unscrewed the cap and pulled up on the little brush inside. Drippy white glue streamed off the end of the brush and back into the little pot. "Will this soak through the belt?" she asked.

"No," Françoise assured her. "The glue won't touch the tapestry, and once I'm done painting, no one will be able to tell there was any rip at all. As long as no one walks by and touches it while it's wet, you are innocent girls. Steady with the torch, Jo."

Thunder echoed throughout the castle hallways as the three girls huddled next to the portrait of Elisabeth of Bohemia. The mermaid, with her unchanging gaze, stared at the headmistress's office door from down the hall as Françoise worked diligently on her masterpiece. Jo kept the light steady, and Maddie watched for professors, the headmistress, or the unlikely wandering ghost.

CHAPTER TWELVE

THE BOY WITH BINOCULARS

November brought a chill to the crisp mountain air at Madame Molineaux's. The tall evergreens swayed slowly in the wind, their needles carpeting the ground and crunching under the students' wool-lined ankle boots. The girls sported waist-length capes over their shoulders, and were outfitted with knitted tights and berets. Walks in the gardens had been replaced by romps through the woods to find pinecones, feathers, and empty birds' nests.

Maddie and Jo left their literature class and headed toward the boathouse instead of the warm library in their dormitory hall.

"Why are we going to the woods again?" Jo asked her sister as she blew hot air into her cupped hands.

Maddie pulled a sheet of paper from her pocket. "I have to find something to bring to my biology laboratory tomorrow."

She showed the paper to Jo, running her finger down the list of acceptable items. "I know for a fact that most of the girls have pulled mussels out of the lake, so I don't want to do that. And I saw the girls at the table behind me with some snail shells." She pointed at the last item on the list. "I'm going to be the only one with an actual pellet, complete with mouse fur and bones."

She spoke the words with confidence, but Jo wasn't so sure. "I don't know, Sis, what if it gets dark before we get out of the forest?" She looked up at the sun. "It's been getting darker earlier and earlier. Let's just hope we don't get Flossie again."

Maddie nodded as she and Jo approached the boathouse. Flossie was one of the dachshunds available to students venturing into the forest. These dachshunds had been trained to find their way back to the boathouse, even from the deepest place in the forest, and even in the dark. However, Flossie was much too interested in digging in search of rabbit dens to lead anyone anywhere. Once she caught the scent of a furry creature, she lost all directional sense and was useless as a guide. Luckily, Maddie and Jo's last trip into the forest hadn't been a long one, and they'd managed to find their way out, thanks to Jo's trusty compass.

The boathouse was a long, narrow wooden structure on the banks of *Le Lac aux Diamants Bleus*, and the air inside was warm and damp. Crew boats and kayaks leaned against the walls, their racing numbers painted in white, and two older students sat behind a heavy desk in the corner.

"Checking out a boat or a dog?" one of them asked the twins.

Jo surveyed the dogs behind a small fence. "We'd like a dog, but who's available?"

One of the older students hopped off her stool and came around to the gate. "Well, let's see here . . . Brina is nursing her pups so she can't go . . . and Bruno just had a bath, so we'd like to keep him clean." She stepped inside the fence and picked up a familiar-looking dog. "You can take Flossie if you like."

Maddie winced and imagined Flossie wasting time chasing squirrels, but thought perhaps her keen sense of smell could sniff out those owl pellets she was trying to find. After all, they were mostly mouse fur. "Okay," she sighed. "Flossie it is."

The older girl brought the dog out of the fence and pulled a tiny, hand-knitted sweater from a burlap sack hanging on a post. "Over your head it goes," she cooed, and she slipped the sweater on, pulling Flossie's miniature legs through the holes. The dog, realizing that she was getting to go outside, bounced around and barked excitedly, nipping at the ankles of her handler. "Oh, *yesssssss*, Flossie, you get to go on an adventure," the girl said as she slid a leash and collar over her head. "And in your snowflake sweater, no less."

"Did . . . did you make that?" Maddie asked, trying to sound curious instead of incredulous.

"I did," the other girl behind the desk stated. "And we need a few more, if you knit."

Maddie nodded, imagining herself sitting in front of the library fireplace, knitting a sweater for a dog. *Only at Madame Molineaux's,* she thought.

Jo signed the checkout form at the desk, and the little troupe headed back along the lakeshore to the forest path. Flossie bounded ahead at her leash's length and turned around to give a high-pitched yap every now and then, hurrying her two companions along. The path into the woods began underneath two arched pine trees and forked immediately.

"Which way to the owl pellets?" Jo asked, stopping at the junction between the two paths.

Maddie shrugged and shook her head. "I don't think it really matters. Owls are all over these woods."

"Maybe under the trees next to the clearing?" Jo asked, referring to the large grassy area in the center of the forest. "If the owls throw up . . . err . . . make the pellets after they eat, maybe they'd be there. It's full of mice."

"Maybe. It's a good start," Maddie said. "Let's take the lakeside trail. At least that way we can find our way back if Flossie decides not to do her job." She turned to the right and walked through the trees toward the shore.

Maddie held on to Flossie's leash and stopped every few steps to let her sniff the ground and root under wet pine needles with her nose. Jo skipped ahead, perusing the forest floor for pinecones, since they would be decorating them with paint and ribbons to make their first-year hallway festive for Christmastime. She gathered a few and tucked them into the pockets of her cape. "I'm going to go on ahead and look for more of these," she said, patting her pocket.

Maddie nodded and tried in vain to convince Flossie to walk forward for more than a few seconds before becoming distracted, but her efforts proved useless. She resigned her hopes of a quick walk and instead sat on a fallen log, hoping the little dog would soon allow her to continue the hunt. Jo disappeared from sight, heading up the path along the rocky shore.

Within a few minutes, Maddie's daydreams of being the only girl in her laboratory to have found an owl pellet were interrupted by Jo's frantic footsteps, her cape flying out behind her back as she ran.

Jo was out of breath but didn't look scared at all; she looked excited, with wide eyes and a half-smile as she stopped short in front of her surprised sister and a very startled Flossie.

"Maddie!" she gasped. "There's—there's a *boy* over there."

"A boy? Where?" Maddie asked, jumping up from the log.

"On the other side of the cove, standing on a big rock. He's got binoculars . . . he looks like he's spying on someone."

The girls looked at each other, unable to decide what to do next. It had been months since they had seen a boy their age.

"Come on, I'll show you," Jo said impatiently. She took her sister by the hand and dashed off, yanking Flossie from her digging spot.

Indeed, there was a boy, and indeed, he was spying. He fought to keep his balance on the uneven peak of a boulder, his free arm stretched out to help him remain steady. The rock was just high enough so that he could see most of Madame Molineaux's, but there was no action today. None that he was interested in, at least. *There's more going on over there at night than during daylight,* he thought, and decided that his nighttime visits to the cove would be worth the ten demerits if he got caught, but not these daytime visits.

He scanned the tops of the trees for falcons in one last attempt to see something exciting, and slowly took the gaze of his binoculars down to the lakeshore, brushing his red hair away from the viewfinder. He was about to give up and head back when—

"Hey!" Maddie shouted from the ground.

The boy pulled his binoculars down from his eyes and looked down at the Livingston twins, their hands on their hips, scowling up at him.

"Were you spying on us?" Jo demanded, wondering if this boy could understand English.

He fidgeted with his pack for a few moments. He hadn't encountered anyone so far on his explorations. "I wasn't spying on *you*," he said defensively in a British accent. He grabbed his pack and climbed down from the rock, curious as to what these two girls were doing so far from Madame Molineaux's.

"Then what were you looking at through those binoculars?" Maddie asked, still not convinced that he hadn't been watching them from afar.

"I don't have to tell you girls anything. I don't even know who you are. For all I know, you've been spying on *me*," he said with a cocky smile as he approached them. He bent down to pet Flossie.

"Well, I'm Maddie and this is Jo. And we haven't been doing anything of the sort," she retorted. "We didn't expect to meet anyone out here, especially a boy, on the outskirts of a girls' school."

Jo folded her arms and put on her best haughty face. "Did we say you could pet our dog?"

He stood up. *"Please,"* he sneered. That's not your dog. And it just so happens that I'm not on the outskirts of a girls' school. At this point on the shore, it's *you* who are on the outskirts of a boys' school, so there," he said, turning his back and heading off in the other direction.

"Hold on," Jo called after him. "We told you our names, now who are you?"

The boy stopped and faced the girls once more.

"I'm Max, Max Hofstetter." He held up his binoculars and gave a half-smile. "I suppose I'll 'see' you later," he said, hoping to annoy the American girls a little more before he left. *Dumb girls,* he thought as he walked back to the other side of the cove.

I'm sure they'd love to know what I was looking for. Maybe if he saw them again, he'd tell them. But maybe not.

Maddie and Jo watched as the boy named Max stomped off behind the large rocks. "Come on," Jo said, disappointed by Max's hasty departure. "Let's go find your owl pellet before it gets dark."

"You *forgot*?" Maddie asked with bewilderment in the Room Five dormitory, unable to believe that her roommates had failed to mention such an important detail about Madame Molineaux's.

Millie shrugged and looked innocent enough.

"Honestly, I hardly think about it," she admitted. "We're not allowed to go there anyway, and I've never seen any boys around. You should ask a third-year, though. Apparently, there's a fare-well dance at the end of the spring for second-years."

"Well, *I* think about it every day," Nixie chimed in, flopping down onto her bed and taking her pillow in a tight embrace. "I miss having boyfriends. I mean, friends who are boys. I mean—" she giggled and blushed.

Françoise rolled her eyes and paced around the room. "Enough of your swooning, Nixie. What we really need to know is *why* there was a boy spying on us." She turned to Jo. "You say his name is Max?"

"Yes," Jo answered. "With red hair and fair skin. He was definitely spying on us. He even had binoculars!"

"And he was rude," Maddie added. "He tried to tell us that Flossie wasn't our dog, in his snippy little British accent." She put her hands on her hips and threw her nose into the air, arranging her lips into a stiff frown. "Yes, that's right," she said, giving an exaggerated imitation of the boy. "I'm Max Hofstetter, and you're on my territory now!"

"Hofstetter?" Nixie asked, puzzled. "That's a Bavarian name. You say he had a British accent?"

Jo nodded yes.

"How odd," Nixie remarked. "Well, was he handsome at least?"

Maddie shook her head in protest. "Oh, no," she insisted. "He was mousy if you ask me. Right, Jo?"

Jo bobbed her head from side to side and looked as if she was considering the question carefully. "I don't know . . . I wouldn't say he was *mousy*. I thought he had nice eyes. In fact," she said, studying Maddie's face, "he sort of favors you, Sis."

Safi leaned over and pulled Maddie's long bangs away from her face. "There, like this?" she asked, stifling a laugh. "Is this the boy you saw, Jo?"

Maddie jumped up from her chair and smoothed her hair back into place. "Very funny, ha-ha," she surrendered, her cheeks ruddy and hot.

Val looked serious. "I think we should take turns checking that rock to see if he's still spying," she suggested. "We can't just have boys sneaking around, watching us here. This isn't a zoo!"

"She's right," Françoise said. "I say we divide up into groups and visit the rock each day to see if he returns. If we catch him again, we report it to Kronenberg."

The rest of the girls agreed.

"Maddie, you and Millie will go together. Jo, you with Val. I'll go with Nixie," she instructed.

"What about Safi?" Jo asked. "You forgot her."

Françoise smirked.

Safi laughed. "Me? *Volunteer* to go outside in this cold? It's a wonder I even arrive to class. In Senegal, our winter feels like the Swiss summer. I'm happy to sit this one out."

"Okay then," Françoise continued. "We start tomorrow."

CHAPTER THIRTEEN

An Unlikely Messenger

Weeks had passed since Maddie and Jo found Max spying on their school. Each day, a different pair of girls took a dachshund into the forest to look for him, but no one came back with anything to report. It was getting even colder as the early days of December went by, and the enthusiasm behind the mission was quickly fading.

Jo jumped down off the large rock on the cove's shore, stuffing her hands into her woolen stole to keep warm. "No sign of him—or *anyone*," Jo said with disappointment. "I don't think the other girls are going to come anymore. Nixie stopped a week ago, so Françoise has been dragging a very unwilling Safi along with her. Even Maddie seems to have lost interest."

Val wrapped her thick hair around her neck like a scarf and looked up into the gray sky. "It's getting too cold to enjoy being outside," she said, looking defeated. "Maybe you and Maddie scared him for good."

"Maybe," Jo agreed. "But how will we get answers out of Max if we never see him again?"

Val put her arm around Jo and led her back toward the lakeside path.

"Come on, Jo, we're missing the hot cocoa and pinecone decorating," she coaxed. "He will come out in the spring. We can start coming back then." The two girls walked back to the school, picking up snow-covered pinecones as they went.

The first-year hallway buzzed with excitement as girls from each room worked among tables of paint, glue, pinecones, sleigh bells, and green and red ribbon. Headmistress Kronenberg even played Christmas music from the phonograph in her room, and everyone sipped mugs of hot cocoa with marshmallows floating on top. Each dormitory room was responsible for the decoration around their door, and the entire hall banded together to drape the portraits and walls with pinecone garlands. Everyone sang along with the carols, each girl belting out Christmas cheer in her native language.

Nixie stood on her tiptoes, teetering on the edge of a desk chair as she hammered a small nail above the Room Five door. "Did you find the boy today?" she asked, motioning for Jo to hand her the small pinecone wreath she had made.

"Not today," Jo replied. "Maybe he's waiting to come back just before the holiday break."

Françoise pinned curls of ribbon along the doorsill. "I think you're on your own, Jo. I can't even get Safi to go with me anymore, can I?" She turned to Safi, who seemed to shiver at the mere thought of going back outside.

"In Senegal," Safi informed the group, "cold like this would mean the end of the world."

Jo nodded and smiled. "That's okay. We'll find him eventually! No more waiting it out in the cold for our mysterious friend. I resign." She perked up at the sound of one of her favorite Christmas songs, "Silent Night."

Maddie sang harmony and Jo swayed back and forth as she recited the words. Nixie sang in the original German, Françoise and Safi in French, and Millie hummed while she held straight pins between pursed lips as she continued working on their door. And shy Val, who knew all the Italian words perfectly, sang with a confidence the others rarely saw in her.

By the time the hallway emptied for dinner, it sparkled from top to bottom with Christmas decorations. Small candle-shaped lamps glowed in each window at Madame Molineaux's, and as the girls enjoyed the crackling fireplaces in the dining hall during supper, snowflakes began to fall from the night sky.

Frosty blades of grass crunched under Jo's boots as she made her way to the boathouse. She carried a small bag across her shoulders, and her teeth chattered as she inhaled the winter air and breathed out a foggy mist. She stopped in the boathouse and warmed her hands at the stove before approaching the desk.

"Not going into the forest *alone,* are you?" one of the girls behind the desk asked with concern in her voice.

"No," Jo answered, smiling at the idea. "No forest exploring for me today."

The other girl leaned out from behind the desk and stared down at Jo's feet. "Well, I can't let you check out a boat without your galoshes or thermal stockings," she said. "You'd freeze in that water if you stepped in!"

Jo shook her head and assured the older girl. "I'm just here for some breadcrumbs," she said, holding up her shoulder bag. "I saw some geese on the lake earlier and I'm sure they'd appreciate a treat this time of year, don't you think?"

The girl smiled and agreed. "Of course, you can have some. Come on over," she said, motioning Jo to follow, and took the lid off a wooden barrel. "I hope they like rye."

Jo scooped some stale breadcrumbs into her bag and fastened the flap closed. "I'm sure rye is positively gourmet to them," she said, and thanked her as she left.

A flock of geese floated quietly in the shallow water just a few dozen feet off the shore. Jo tossed a small handful of crumbs onto the mirrored surface of the lake, and the geese squabbled and squawked softly as they fought to get the soggy bread. It was calming to watch the lake return to stillness after each round of breadcrumbs had been eaten.

Out of the corner of her eye, Jo saw a common duck swimming up to the group of geese. "Poor duck," Jo said out loud. "Swimming around with no mate."

It was odd to see a lone duck on the lake, and Jo knew that the geese wouldn't welcome a newcomer into their breadcrumb buffet. She tossed a large handful of crumbs toward the geese to keep them occupied, and then she threw a small trail toward the duck, luring him toward the shore so he could eat in peace.

"That's right," she called to the duck. "I won't hurt you, just come on over here so you can get your fair share, too."

The little duck swam close to the shoreline, snapping at each and every crumb along the way. When the bread trail reached the pebbles on the shore, he waddled right out of the water and quacked politely, requesting more food.

Jo marveled at how unafraid he was, and she kneeled down to hold out her hand to him. As he approached her to collect his prize, Jo noticed a black cord around his neck. A tiny glass vial hung from it; the vial held a rolled-up scrap of paper.

A message in a bottle! Jo thought, excited to have made such a discovery. She had heard of castaways on tropical islands stuffing a message for help into a bottle and hurling it into the waves, hoping for rescue. But who would be stranded on a lakeshore? She looked behind her to make sure she was alone. "Come on, little one," she cooed softly. She laid one hand on the duck's back and stroked his feathers gently. Her other hand touched the black cord, and with the slightest tug she was able to lift it over the duck's head, almost unnoticed. She opened her bag of breadcrumbs and dumped them out onto the shore as a reward for her little messenger.

The cork was wedged so tightly in the glass vial that Jo struggled to remove it without crushing the glass. After a few moments of wiggling the cork back and forth, it came out with a tiny pop, and Jo shook the coiled note out into her palm. It was folded in half and read, "FOR MADDIE AND JO."

Jo could hardly believe her eyes. A secret note, addressed to her and Maddie! She unfolded the paper and spread it out flat, reading quickly, as if the note would disintegrate into dust at any minute.

Hike and climb and seek you may,
You will not find me during day.
I much prefer the cloak of night,
When thieves on foot come into sight.
They run about with great concern
O'er the fireplace that never burns.
E'en in winter, it's never lit,
And in it golden treasures sit,
Dropped from dusk to early dawn
Down the smokestack growing out the lawn.
—Max

Jo gave the duck a quick pat on the head and rushed back to school to find Maddie.

"Now then, everyone," Professor Natalio said in his dramatic Italian accent, tapping his glass siphon on the side of the test tube. "Put three drops of the yellow liquid into the solution, and be careful not to spill any on your skin or clothes. It's quite hard to wash off."

Maddie turned to her lab partner and held up her own siphon, carefully placing its tip into the test tube. "Professor," her partner asked, "exactly what is this yellow liquid?"

"Ah-ah, yes, w-well . . ." the professor stuttered. "We call it *l'urina del lupo*. Or, for those of you who do not yet speak the lovely Italian language, wolf urine."

Every girl let out a gasp, and Maddie fought to keep her hand steady.

"Just what are we doing with wolf urine?" she asked in a shrill voice, afraid that the slightest move might squirt the foul liquid all over herself or her partner.

The professor clasped his hands together and, for a moment, looked apologetic. He took a deep breath and regained his jovial tone.

"We are creating an attractive spray that will help me in my new experiment!" he exclaimed, looking out at the disgusted faces of the girls in the class. "I'm going to use your solutions to spray on bushes high in the mountains. I'm trying to attract males of a certain species of wild dog so that I can breed them. It's the only way to save the current population from imminent extinction."

Another hybrid, Maddie thought. The professor went on explaining his new experiment, but Maddie's attention was focused elsewhere. She looked up from her table just in time to see Jo's face in the small glass window of the laboratory door.

Maddie shot her sister a bothered look and then scanned the classroom to see if anyone else had seen Jo. Luckily, the rest of the girls seemed trapped in Professor Natalio's explanation of second-generation hybrid breeding.

Jo waved for her sister to come out into the hall and held up the note, widening her eyes to emphasize the urgency of the situation. Maddie could feel it—her sister had stumbled upon something important. She thought fast to come up with a plan.

"Oh no!" Maddie cried, pulling the siphon out of the test tube and holding it next to her arm. "It's—it's on me!" She took her lab towel and wiped her hand furiously, giving a frightened look to the professor.

He rushed over to inspect the situation and took the siphon from Maddie. "It's all right," he said, looking around the room to make sure everyone was calm. "It's okay, she just spilled a little," he assured the rest of the class.

He turned back to Maddie. "You need to go and wash this off immediately! Stay washing for ten minutes! Otherwise, you'll be the most attractive thing a wild dog has ever come across. That is, well, you would be *if* there were wild dogs here at the school." He laughed nervously and shooed her away from the table.

Maddie held her hand as far from her body as possible and made a theatrical show of heading out the door, turning her head away as if the smell on her skin could curdle milk. She walked into the hallway and scowled at her sister. "This had better be good."

Jo silently applauded her sister's performance. "If I had roses, I'd throw them at you," she said, laughing. "You didn't actually get any on you, did you?"

"No!" Maddie hissed, taking her sister's arm and leading her to the lavatory down the hall. "Now what's all this about? Did you find Max?"

"Almost," said Jo, taking one last look through the hallway before ducking into the bathroom. "It's more like *he* found *us*." She pulled the note from her pocket and opened it up.

"What's this?" Maddie asked, scanning the paper. "A riddle?"

"Looks that way," Jo answered, and showed her sister the front of the note. "And Maddie . . . he addressed it to you and me *only*. Should we tell the others?"

Maddie finished reading the note and thought for a moment. "Not yet," she said quietly. "Let's see if we can figure out what this means first. We'll let the others in on it when we know what's going on." She folded the note and handed it back to her sister.

"No," Jo insisted. "You keep it. I'll lose it, or get it wet, or something. Let's take a closer look at it in the library tonight after everyone has gone to sleep."

Maddie nodded and tucked the note away in her jacket pocket. "See you at dinner," she said, and walked back to her laboratory.

CHAPTER FOURTEEN

In Through the Window

Maddie couldn't sleep a wink. It was a good thing she and Jo were waiting up for the rest of the girls to fall asleep so that they could sneak off to the library, because her mind raced anyway with curiosity about the riddle from Max. All evening, the parts of the poem she could remember consumed her thoughts as she played a thousand games of "What If."

She heard the faint stroke of midnight and sat up to look around in the dark. Her eyes moved from bed to bed, each time waiting to see if the girl's breathing was slow and rhythmic. Indeed, it looked as if each of her roommates was sound asleep—even her sister.

Maddie slid out of bed and into her robe and slippers, careful not to make a sound. She shook Jo's shoulder and pulled her up, waving the folded note in her face to remind her of why they were awake at such an hour. Jo's eyes lost their sleepy glaze after seeing the note, and she hurried to get her robe on. The two girls crept out of the room, and only a single silver sleigh bell jingled as they shut the wooden door behind them.

In the library, Maddie switched on the lamps and unfolded the note on a large map table. She fastened her belt tighter around her robe, shivering a little. It felt as if the temperature had just dropped ten degrees.

"Addressed specifically to us," Maddie pondered, turning the paper over to read their names. "Suppose it had been someone else to find the message first?"

Jo agreed. "I think he's been watching us, Maddie. See here in the first line? *'Search and climb and seek you may'*. . . He's seen us looking for him every day. I imagine he noticed that we stopped last week, and figured he had to come up with a way to reach us. I guess he spotted me feeding the geese every now and then and figured it was his best shot."

"Probably," said Maddie. "I guess he's not as dumb as I thought he was."

"Nah," Jo said, giggling. "I think it's time to make friends. He obviously wants us to know whatever it is his spying has uncovered." She mumbled the lines of the riddle over again. "He could use some help in the poetry department, though," she criticized, cocking her head to the side. "This is a little bit childish."

Maddie snatched the note from Jo's hands. "I don't think he was trying to win any literature contests here, Jo," she retorted. "Let's just figure out what this means and get back to bed. If we get caught—"

A window slammed shut and footsteps crept close to the twins from the other side of a bookshelf.

"You won't get caught," a girl's voice stated. "Not unless I tell, that is." Rosemary Byron stepped out of the shadows and folded her arms. She was still dressed in her school uniform, and wore her winter cloak, hat, scarf, and muff.

Maddie ran to the window where Rosemary had entered and looked down—it was nearly fifteen feet to the ground, with not a single ladder or gutter pipe to climb on. "And just where have you been?" Maddie demanded, furious at the intrusion and unsure of how anyone could have climbed inside through such a high window.

Rosemary maintained her blank stare and didn't flinch. "Absolutely nowhere," she said in her cold British accent. She approached the map table where Jo sat, suddenly interested in what the twins were looking at. "What's that you've got there, Jo?" she asked in a sweeter voice with a phony smile.

Jo looked cautious and took the note from the table, folding it up and sticking it down in her pocket. "Well, it's . . ." she muttered, trying to come up with a story she could tell Rosemary.

"It's a letter from our parents," Maddie interrupted. "From Siberia," she said, nodding. "Very private."

"Right. Family stuff, you know," Jo added, looking quite concerned.

Mary didn't look convinced, but she sauntered away from the table anyway. "Very private, I'm sure, considering you went to all this trouble to be alone." She paused and held her finger to her chin. "Well, *almost* alone. Don't worry, I didn't hear much." She flashed her phony grin once more and walked toward the door. "Good night, Livingstons."

Maddie waited until the door had closed to say anything. "I can't *stand* that girl," she said, taking another look out the window Rosemary had seemingly come in from. "She thinks she knows everything about everything and everyone. What was she doing outside this late anyway? And come over here, Jo," she insisted, peering down at the ground far below. "There's no way she came in through this window."

Jo looked around the room, searching for good hiding places. "Maybe she was already here," she offered, "hiding behind the shelves, or under a desk. Maybe she just wanted us to think she had come in from the outside."

"But why the coat and hat? Her cheeks were flushed from the cold," Maddie persisted. "She was definitely outside."

Jo laughed. "True, she looked *almost* alive. A pleasant change from her usual bluish tint, don't you think?"

"This isn't funny, Jo," said Maddie solemnly. "What if she heard what we were saying?"

"Maddie, *we* don't even know what the poem means. And we didn't read much of it out loud. I have no idea what she was doing here or what she heard—but let's keep it at one mystery per night, okay? Come on," she said as she took her sister by the arm, leading her back to the map table. "Let's see what we can do with this riddle, and we'll figure out what Rosemary's been up to later."

The girls sat back down at the map table and got back to work, staying for another half hour in the library until they had solved as much of the riddle as their tired minds allowed.

The next night at dinner, Maddie felt a gentle kick from under the table. It was Jo, and she widened her eyes as if to say, "It's time." Nixie and Val were casually discussing their upcoming dance recital at the fifth-year Christmas Review, and everyone else at the table seemed preoccupied with finishing their food and getting back to their studies. After all, winter exams were only a few weeks away.

Maddie piled her plates in the middle of her tray and stood up.

"Well, I'm off to get more studying done," she said, trying to sound as disappointed as possible. She had barely finished half her dinner.

Millie pushed her own tray away from her and sighed. "You know, I'll come with you, Maddie. I'm so worried about my French test I can barely eat. Are you going to the library?"

Maddie shot a quick look at Jo and shook her head.

"Actually, um, I . . ." She had to think quickly. "I have to go outside and get something from the grounds for my biology lab." She didn't give anyone else a chance to intrude on her plans. She picked up her tray, pushed in her chair with her hip, and gave a hurried good-bye. "Maybe I'll see you in the library afterward, Millie," she called as she ran off.

The halls and grounds of Madame Molineaux's emptied during dinner, and Maddie and Jo had decided that it was the perfect time to investigate the clues from Max. After careful deliberation, they had concluded a few things. First, whatever was going on happened when it was dark out. Second, they were looking for people hiding treasures somewhere near a chimney. The girls had decided to take turns walking the grounds, searching for the *smokestack growing out the lawn.* They had been at school for nearly three months, and neither could recall seeing a chimney coming out of the ground.

Maddie's first mission was to check the area around the stables and the arts hall. As she hurried across the grounds, she looked back toward the lake, trying to imagine how Max could possibly see over the top of the dining hall to the stables or the arts hall from his spying rock—there was no clear line of sight. This was a disheartening thought. Maddie and Jo were sure that the secret chimney would be near the stables, since they hadn't spent much time there at all, and had certainly seen every other chimney at Madame Molineaux's.

The warm, musty air from the horse pens seeped out of the cracks in the boards and into Maddie's nostrils as she clung to the wooden sides of the stables. She walked all the way around the rustic wooden building and examined the roof, but there was no chimney. Only a few metal pipes from the wood-burning stoves inside jutted outside the stables, and those certainly didn't contain any treasures.

The arts hall boasted four tall chimneys, but all of them were coming from the steeply sloped rooftop. There was no grass in sight, and no way anyone could simply place anything inside them. Still, Maddie walked around the building, just to make sure she hadn't missed anything.

The statues guarding the outside of the arts hall stood elegantly among the manicured bushes, the white Christmas roses at their feet bursting with bright blooms in the dead of winter. They posed playing instruments, reading great works of literature, and contemplating the ideas of the Greek philosophers. It was like walking through a museum as Maddie made her way around the building.

She sighed heavily and stared back toward the castle. It wasn't often that she stood outside to gaze at the campus during the evening, and she took a moment to enjoy the moonlit gardens, sparkling lake, and warmly glowing windows of each building.

Where are you, secret smokestack? Maddie wondered. Without knowing its location, it would be silly, not to mention risky, to be sneaking around in the wee hours of the night to look for thieves at every chimney. She and Jo would have to do more thinking in the library before either one of them ventured back out.

Maddie's icy fingers burned as the wind blew harder. She took one last look around for any sign of a smokestack, and raced back to the warm dormitory with nothing to report.

Jo looked relieved. "Well," she said, wrapping Maddie's feet up in a blanket. "At least we can cross those two areas off the list. And at least I don't have to go out in that cold at midnight tonight!"

"Yeah," Maddie agreed, sounding slightly defeated. "We don't really know what day or what time it's going to happen again. And if we don't know exactly where to look . . . well, there aren't that many excuses we can come up with to get outside alone at night. Surely someone will catch us before we figure it out."

Jo remembered their evening in the library the night before. "Maybe we should ask Rosemary," she suggested. "She goes outside late at night, and maybe she's seen something, or can at least tell us why she's sneaking around."

Maddie huffed, offended. "And let her in on our secret? Absolutely not," she almost shouted. "She'd probably just run to Kronenberg and ruin our whole investigation. I'm telling you, Jo, big things are going on here. Max couldn't even spell it out for us in his note. He had to make up a riddle, for goodness' sake! Someone is up to no good, and we don't have any clues as to who it might be. Maybe it's Rosemary who's hiding the treasures in the chimney."

Jo gave her sister an annoyed look. "Really, Maddie, you think a twelve-year-old girl is the mastermind behind all of this? I think you just don't like Rosemary."

"Well, it makes *some* sense, doesn't it? We get a note from Max telling us that someone here is hiding things at night, and then we find Rosemary coming in from the cold after midnight? Hmmmm?"

Jo wasn't buying it. She folded her arms and rolled her eyes.

"Okay," Maddie confessed. "*And* maybe I don't like Rosemary."

"Well, she's not my favorite person in the world, either, but maybe she has some ideas. I'm not saying we should be her best friends," she added, pausing. "But maybe . . ."

"Maybe what?" Maddie insisted, wondering how she could possibly get along with Rosemary Byron long enough to get the information they needed.

"Okay, you're right. She's not going to talk to us," Jo admitted. She stared at the ground for a moment and had an idea. "We should probably just follow her one night."

CHAPTER FIFTEEN

THE TELLTALE LACES

It was exam week at Madame Molineaux's. The chatter that normally filled each dormitory hallway was absent as students tried to memorize as much as they could before tests began. The fireplaces in the first-year library burned day and night to keep the constant flow of girls warm and cozy as they studied. Each evening, the lights-out curfew seemed to arrive faster as time before the exams dwindled. It wasn't the ideal week to be spying, but the Livingston twins couldn't shake the need to find out more about their new target.

Rosemary's morning routine was legendary among the first-year students. She woke up before the ringers came down the hall. She was first into the lavatory, preferring to wash her face slowly and meticulously before any of the other girls arrived and fought for the sinks and mirrors. After applying a liberal amount of expensive French face cream, she took down each of her perfect pin curls and arranged them so that not a single hair was out of place.

Her makeup case was filled with assorted pots and powders, all with shiny silver tops and fancy names. She shaped her eyebrows with wax, tinted the ends of her eyelashes with charcoal, and puffed a light dusting of rouge onto the apples of her porcelain cheeks. When she finished, she exited the lavatory and returned to her room to dress before any of the other girls had even opened their eyes.

Maddie and Jo confided in Safi to see if they could get her to keep an eye on their suspect, but Safi was skeptical.

"Why me, exactly?" she asked.

"Well, you're her roommate. We just need you to let us know if Rosemary does anything out of the ordinary," Jo explained as they huddled by the fire in the library. "We know she's up early every morning, we know where she sits at lunch and in class . . . but if you should see her, say . . . hiding things, or, umm, you know, being secretive, or . . ."

Safi looked puzzled. "Rosemary does not speak to anyone in our room," she reminded the girls. "*Everything* she does is a secret."

"Well, yes," Maddie continued. "But if you should, say, be up really late at night and you see her getting dressed to go outside . . ." She looked at Jo and pursed her lips in frustration.

"Come off it, Maddie," Jo said, giving in. She sighed and took Safi by the hands. "We're spying on Rosemary. We think she's sneaking around at night, and we want to know where she's been going."

"Ohh." Safi nodded, smiling her wide, pearly grin. "You mean her nightly outings."

Maddie and Jo gave Safi bewildered looks.

"You know about this?" Jo asked their friend. "Do all the girls in your room know?"

"No," Safi said, looking smug. "Just me, I think. I can't help waking up when anyone makes noise."

"Light sleeper, huh?" Maddie asked, wondering why Safi had never mentioned this at lunch. There had been plenty of opportunities to tell the others, especially on days when the girls vented about Rosemary's classroom snobbery or outright rudeness.

Safi laughed and rolled her eyes. "Ladies, I spent much of my early childhood outside of Senegal's capital city, in Tambacounda. I've slept in huts, tents, or deserts under the dark sky . . . places where one must always be alert. A moth doesn't flap its wings without my eyes springing open!"

"Hey," Jo interjected. "We've slept in the desert, too, right, Maddie?"

Maddie nodded enthusiastically. "That's right, and even in a rainforest one summer," she said, boasting of their days on excavation with their parents.

Safi leaned in close. "I don't think it counts if you have a full staff and get picked up in a Rolls-Royce," she said sarcastically.

Jo giggled and agreed. "Okay, okay. You win, Safi." She bit her lip and returned to the topic at hand. "But do you know where Rosemary's going at night?"

Safi gave the twins a bored look and offered a few suggestions. "I don't know, maybe she re-powders her nose, or checks the mirror for the hundredth time, or . . ."

"Ha!" Maddie blurted, laughing at Rosemary's vanity. "I'd believe that. But she's fully dressed. We think she's going outside."

"I can find out for you," Safi assured them. "I'll check her boots tonight after she gets back."

"Her boots? Why her boots?" asked Jo.

"Her laces. If she's been walking around in the snow, her boot laces will be frozen and wet. That's my least favorite part about coming inside, having to unlace my frozen boots. I can't stand it when my fingers are cold."

Maddie hugged her friend's shoulders. "Brilliant, Safi," she squealed. "Jo and I have exams tomorrow, so we couldn't have followed her tonight anyway."

"I'll report tomorrow morning in the lavatory," said Safi, using her most militant voice, and saluted the girls as she left for class.

Jo stared at the stamped-tin ceiling tiles through the darkness. Even her sister had already fallen asleep, having studied for their history exam right up until the lights had been turned out. It was quiet now, and she looked around the room at her sleeping roommates, knowing she'd miss them over the school holiday.

Just before they had departed from the Moroccan excavation site for the African coast, their parents had promised them that Henri would arrange something nice for them while school was out. She and Maddie would be boarding a train in two days to meet Henri in Paris for Christmas, and Jo could hardly wait to see the city decorated in lights.

But as happy as she would be to have some time away from Madame Molineaux's for a vacation, there were still far too many puzzles to be solved. It seemed that she and Maddie were no closer to finding any of the answers than they were a month ago, and she turned familiar questions over and over in her head.

What was Kronenberg looking for when she had the aerial photograph of the school taken? Why are there tapestries behind portrait paintings in the administration hall? What was Max spying on at night, and what does his riddle mean? What is Rosemary up to when she goes out after lights-out?

The girls hadn't had an opportunity to snoop around Kronenberg's office alone yet. In fact, Jo hadn't even been back down the administration hallway since Françoise had repaired the painting she and Maddie ripped. The weather had interrupted her search for Max, and his riddle was proving to be more difficult to decode than she had originally thought it would be.

Jo buried her face in her pillow and tried not to get lost in all the possibilities. She had an exam in the morning, and was expecting a report from Safi about the late-night whereabouts of Rosemary Byron. She had a vacation to look forward to, and a chance to spend time with Henri. Worrying about the mysteries at school could wait until the New Year.

Jo closed her eyes and imagined the goats on top of the history building, bleating and jumping over their little houses one by one. She counted them in French until she drifted off into a dreamless sleep.

Maddie's eyes popped open at the first sound of the ringers down the hallway. She leaped out of bed, shoved her feet into her slippers, and shook her sister to wake her. She left Jo grumbling in the bed, and had barely finished tying her robe around her waist before she was out the door and into the hallway, slowing her run down to a calm walk before she strolled into the lavatory.

Safi was already stationed at a mirror, her dark hair pulled back as she patted her face dry with a hand towel. She looked over at Maddie and smiled. "Good morning, Maddie," she said, trying to sound casual. "Did you sleep well?"

Maddie nodded and took her place at the next sink over. "Indeed, I did, thank you, Safi," she replied as she wet her toothbrush under the silver faucet. "And you?"

Safi turned to her and smiled broadly. "Like a baby," she said, winking one eye dramatically. "I have the answer to the test review question you were asking me about last night. You know the one?"

Maddie caught on and played along. "Oh, yes, of course," she said, smiling, and wondered how Safi would disguise the information she was about to give her in front of the rest of the girls. "I really couldn't figure that one out."

"It's easy," said Safi. "The answer is *September.* September is the safest month to hike in the Alps."

Jo entered the lavatory and made her way over to the mirror, hoping she hadn't missed the news.

"Morning, Jo," Maddie said with a puzzled look on her face. "Safi was just telling me about that question we couldn't figure out for the test review . . . and the answer is September."

Jo nodded and shrugged in surrender. "Of course, September," she said, trying to hide the confusion in her voice.

Safi turned from the mirror and leaned back on the sink. "Sure, you know. September is the safest month to hike in the Alps because *there's no sign of ice or snow. It's just really, really cold.*

Cold enough to make your skin and clothes chilled. Even your *boots* would be cold to the touch, freezing almost."

Maddie pressed on. "So, what you're saying is that, in September, you could go hiking in the Alps and you wouldn't get any ice or snow on your boots, but the leather would be freezing cold?"

Safi snapped her fingers and grinned. "Exactly."

Jo laughed out loud. It might have been just as easy to corner Safi in the hallway on the way to breakfast. She could have just whispered, "No snow or ice on Rosemary's laces, but her boots were freezing." But this was a spy game, and to Safi, the cryptic reporting was half the fun.

Safi sprang off the edge of the sink, looking quite proud of herself. "See you at breakfast," she said, and sauntered out of the lavatory.

Maddie brushed her teeth and nodded to Jo, and the girls shared a giggle at Safi's imaginative storytelling. On the way to breakfast, the sisters plotted further.

"Okay, so we know that Rosemary isn't going outside. Why is she getting fully dressed? Why are her boots freezing cold?" Jo asked, keeping her voice as low as she could.

"I'm just as confused as you are," Maddie whispered back. "But this morning is my last exam, and yours, too, right? How about we find a way to follow her tonight?"

"That's just what I was thinking, Sis," Jo replied, and linked her arm through Maddie's. "Now, in all seriousness, who won the battle of Heilsberg?"

Maddie scowled and held up her history textbook. "I'll tell you at breakfast."

Professor Troxler looked especially irritated. "Attention, ladies!" she rattled.

The classroom of girls closed their history books, moaning and sighing at what was coming next. Jo scanned the last page of the chapter and repeated the study song she had come up with the night before:

In 1807 on a Napoleonic Mission, the Battle of Friedland ended the War of the Fourth Coalition . . .

Troxler slapped her ruler on the side of her desk. "I said *attention*, ladies!" She paced the room slowly, eyeing each of the girls as she passed.

"I have a confession to make," she said, her voice dripping with insincerity. "And that confession is, ladies, that I am very, very tired this morning. Would anyone venture to guess why I am so tired?"

The students looked back and forth at each other, uncertain whether this was a trick question.

"Were you cold?" one student asked.

The professor shook her head no.

"Did you see a ghost?" Nixie asked, hoping that Troxler was about to tell a ghost story.

"No, although I did hear plenty of chains clanking, doors slamming, and footsteps down the hall," replied Troxler. "I have a feeling it was a student, or *students*, that kept me awake, very much of the human sort."

She raised her ruler and pointed it around the room. "Let me be quite clear. Today may be the last day of class before the holiday, but the rules still apply to each and every one of you. Anyone caught out of bed after lights out tonight will be severely, severely punished. In fact, guilty students may or may not be accepted back to Madame Molineaux's in the New Year. I can't be certain."

The room was silent.

"*So,*" she said sharply, whacking her ruler on the desk again. "As you and your little friends talk at lunchtime about pranks or other fun you might have tonight before vacation, keep in mind that I have eyes *everywhere.*"

Jo peered to the front of the classroom. Had it been Rosemary who kept Troxler awake all night?

Rosemary stared straight ahead and squared her jaw. Her cool gray eyes didn't even blink. She drew in a deep breath, held it for a few seconds, and let the tail end of a yawn escape from her lips.

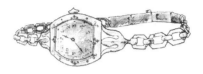

CHAPTER SIXTEEN

A SPECIAL DELIVERY

The dining hall at Madame Molineaux's boasted the tallest evergreen trees from the forest, as Professor Natalio and his staff had chosen only the most perfect fir trees to cut down for Christmas. They had decorated them with red bows and miniature light bulbs, and painted paper angels, and placed gold stars on the treetops. Poinsettias and pinecones had been arranged at each table, and the kitchen served creamy mashed potatoes, boiled ham, roasted carrots, and walnut cakes. Senior members of the school choir strolled from table to table to sing carols while the students ate.

"Don't forget!" a vivacious girl with deep bronze skin and long, curly hair called out as she spun in between the tables. "The fifth-year Holiday Review is tonight! Starring yours truly, of course," she said, tossing invitations onto the trays and plates.

Maddie leaned over to Françoise. "She's wearing the fox on her patch—doesn't that mean she's a second-year? How is she in the fifth-year play, then?"

"That's Isidra Vidal," Françoise replied. "She's almost a professional dancer, apparently. Always away from school to compete in dance competitions."

"I heard her parents made a huge fuss to get her into the Holiday Review," Safi chimed in. "I think Isidra is used to getting exactly what she wants."

And with that, Isidra stomped her foot down on the ground loudly to end her performance.

Millie plopped down at the dining table and held her head in her hands, on the verge of tears. Françoise put an arm around her shoulder as Nixie sat down and tried her best to console her friend.

"I'm sure you didn't do *that* badly, Millie," she said. "It was difficult for certain, but surely you knew at least *half* of the answers!"

Millicent groaned and shook her head. "It's not that, Nixie. I knew the answers last night, and the night before that, and before that! I just can't recall them when I'm anxious. Tests make me so nervous. And Troxler's speech before the exam wasn't exactly encouraging." She slumped down on the table. "Besides. I felt like she was staring at *me* when she said that someone wasn't going to be allowed to come back to Madame Molineaux's."

Francoise puffed her chest out. "How ridiculous, Millie!" she huffed. "Troxler said that about the student who kept her up last night. And I happen to know that you were studying under your blanket with my torch until well after midnight."

Safi exchanged knowing looks with Maddie and Jo. "Yes, Millie. Relax," said Safi. "I'm almost sure I know who it was."

"What? How do you know who it was?" asked Nixie.

⚜

Jo chimed in to explain to the table, hoping that Maddie wouldn't get upset. "She spied on Rosemary for us last night," she said. "We caught her in the library after lights-out a few days ago, and Safi told us that she leaves her bed every night after midnight."

Val spoke up for the first time that day. "What then, Maddie and Jo, were *you* doing in the library late at night?"

Maddie stumbled over her words. "Well, we were . . . you see, we got this letter from . . . um . . ." She stopped short. She didn't want to lie to her friends. "Okay," she sighed. It was time to let everyone in on their secret. "We've got some news," she said, nodding at Jo.

They told the girls about the note from Max, Rosemary's late-night excursions into the cold, and their attempts to locate a smokestack coming out of the lawn on the school's grounds.

"Can we see the note?" Millie asked, completely forgetting about her poor performance on Troxler's exam.

"It's under my mattress," Maddie said. "I'll bring it out tonight and we can all do some detective work after lights-out."

"*After* lights-out?" Nixie whined. "You heard Troxler—if anyone is caught in the halls after lights-out, they'll be expelled!"

"Don't worry. We won't get caught," said Maddie. "We won't go anywhere *near* Troxler's hall. Besides," she said confidently, "we all know who it was that kept her up. The nerve of that girl! Sneaking around, getting the rest of us in trouble . . . I suppose I'm not surprised."

The rest of the girls at the table hushed and stared wide-eyed at Maddie as if she had three heads.

"What? Why are you staring?" Maddie insisted dramatically. She threw her nose into the air for added effect. "I have zero doubt in my mind that it was none other than the perfectly prissy, positively pompous Miss Rosemary Byron!"

Val let out a small gasp.

Maddie felt a pair of eyes staring through the back of her head. She turned around and saw exactly what the other girls had been gawking at.

Rosemary Byron cleared her throat and gazed at the girls with her steely, stoic eyes. She formed her lips into a tight smile and looked directly at Maddie.

"Thank you, Maddie, for that lovely introduction. I suspected your admiration from our first meeting, and now you've confirmed it," she said sarcastically.

Maddie was speechless. Jo looked down at her lap. Val appeared as though she might crawl under the table to hide.

Françoise jumped to her friend's defense. "I'm not sure what you thought you heard, Rosemary, but we generally don't bore ourselves with mindless gossip. Now, what can we do for you?"

Rosemary placed a rectangular box wrapped in brown paper down in front of Maddie and Jo. "Special delivery," she said with a smirk. "Seems it was dropped at my table by mistake."

She rolled her eyes, turned on her heel, and sauntered back to her table.

Jo gasped for air, sure that she hadn't taken a breath since first seeing Rosemary behind her sister.

"Well," Millie said, breaking the tension after Rosemary had walked away, "any hopes you might have had about becoming Rosemary's best mate are probably shot." She laughed out loud. Jo cracked a smile and relaxed her shoulders.

Nixie looked pleased and swallowed the last bite of her food so she could speak. "If you ask me, she had it coming. She is *all* of those things you said, and more." She eyed the box in front of Maddie and Jo. "Aren't you going to open it?"

Maddie was still stunned and slightly embarrassed. Jo reached for the package and read the return address:

Henri Lemaître
Hôtel Lutetia
45 Boulevard Raspail
75006 Paris
France

"It's from Henri!" she squealed. "It must be our train tickets!" She tore off the brown paper, placed the card on the table, and pulled out two small leather boxes. "I'm guessing one of these is for you," she said, handing a box to Maddie. The other girls at the table waited in anticipation to see what the twins had received from Paris.

Françoise picked up the ripped brown paper and examined the address. "He doesn't live far from me," she mumbled with a worried look. The others paused and waited for her to continue, but she immediately turned her frown into a half-smile and changed her tone. "What a coincidence," she quipped.

Inside each box was a jeweled wristwatch—the delicate kind film stars wore, with a thin bracelet and small clockface. Jo's was gold with onyx crystals, and Maddie's was silver with blue stones. All the girls *oohed* and *aahed* over the beautiful jewelry.

"Henri must want to make sure we're on time for our train!" Maddie said excitedly, snapping the tiny silver clasp shut around her wrist.

"I can't believe you get to go to Paris for Christmas," Nixie complained. "You should visit Safi and Françoise for supper one evening."

Françoise shifted in her chair. "It's a shame that my father and I will be so busy. I don't think we have one night without plans."

Safi looked puzzled, but nodded anyway. "My family and I are returning to Senegal during the school break, so I won't be in Paris for long."

"That's okay," Jo said. "I'm sure Henri has every minute of every day scheduled for us to sightsee, shop, and eat at the finest restaurants. He knows the best places in Paris, I'm sure of it!"

She reached for the letter on the table and fiddled with the red wax seal on the back of the envelope, careful not to crack it. It had been stamped with an ornate letter L.

"My dearest Madeline and Josephine," she read aloud from the card, smiling. "I hope you like your gifts from Paris—the jeweler assured me that all the famous actresses here are wearing watches just like these! At once, I knew I had to send them to my special young ladies." She paused for a moment to admire her watch, and Maddie grabbed the note from her hands to continue reading.

"I have so looked forward to seeing your smiling faces in Paris for Christmas, but I regret to say that . . ." Maddie's broad smile turned instantly to a frown.

"What? Regret to say *what*?" Millie asked impatiently.

Maddie scanned the letter, trying to understand why she wasn't going to be in Paris for Christmas. "He—he can't," Maddie stammered. "He can't host us in Paris," she said quietly. She looked down and handed the card back to her sister.

Jo bit her lip and read the rest of the letter to the table. "I regret to say that I have been called out of the country, unexpectedly, on an urgent business matter. We must reschedule our time together in Paris."

The twins' disappointment cast a gloomy shadow over the table of girls. While the rest of the dining hall carried on chatting and laughing, they all sat openmouthed, unsure of what to say.

"But where will you go?" Val asked timidly. "Your parents are still in Siberia, are they not?"

Maddie nodded in defeat. "They are."

Jo flipped the card over and read out loud once more. "I have arranged for you both to spend the holiday with Headmistress Kronenberg, who has been a dear friend of mine for many years." Jo's voice hung on every word as she continued to read. Her eyes widened, her mouth scrunching into a permanent scowl.

"She will take excellent care of you at her home in Bavaria, and I've already sent all of your gifts there for Christmas. Thank you for understanding, ladies, and I will write again soon. My sincerest apologies and all my love, Henri."

Maddie almost jumped out of her seat. "Christmas with Kronenberg? You're joking!"

Nixie shook her head in disbelief. "It will be like . . . being in school . . . instead of on holiday."

Françoise elbowed Nixie in the ribs and pasted a smile on her face. "Do you know what I think?" she asked, looking hopeful for the twins. "I think you're going to have a marvelous time. The headmistress lives in the Bavarian countryside in a beautiful cottage. I visited there with my father, a year and a half ago."

Jo looked doubtful. Françoise was obviously just trying to cheer them up. "Okay, Françoise, I give up. Why in the world were you at the headmistress's house a year and a half ago?"

"Well," Françoise began. "My father was quite concerned about where I would be living and going to school for these five years. He arranged the appointment to interview her personally, just to make sure that I was going to the best boarding school. It was during summer, and we were on holiday in Austria already, so we were close by."

"You missed a card there, Maddie," Millie changed the subject. "See? At the very bottom of the box."

Maddie reached in and retrieved it, sliding her index finger under the unglued edge of the fold. "Let me guess," she sighed. "More bad news from Henri." Inside, there was another sealed letter and a single sheet of stationery. "Also, Maddie and Jo," the paper read, "if you could be so kind as to drop this into the letterbox at 1217 Rue de Vieux-Marcel, that would be most appreciated."

"Old Marcel Street? That must be in town," Françoise offered.

"Maybe you can ask Kronenberg to stop by on the way to her house," Millie joked. But the rest of the group remained silent.

Maddie huffed. "Well, that's fine and dandy. A ruined Christmas, and an errand to run. Ugh. I wish we could just stay here alone and—"

Françoise leaned across the table and narrowed her eyes. "I wouldn't complain if I were you. Some people don't have anywhere to spend the holidays, or anyone to spend them with."

Jo put her arm around her sister. "Françoise is right, Sis. Let's be thankful we have somewhere to go. Besides, we've never been to Germany!"

Françoise folded her arms and smiled. "*And,*" she added, looking quite amused. "You've never met Oma Kronenberg."

"Who is Oma Kronenberg?" Maddie asked, hoping it was a girl or boy their age, someone to have fun with.

Nixie chimed in to give a quick German lesson. "*Oma* means grandma in German, so Françoise is talking about someone's grandmother."

Maddie rolled her eyes and threw out her arms. "Oh, great," she moaned. "What could be better than spending the holiday with not only Kronenberg, but an even *older* Kronenberg?" She shook her head in defeat.

Françoise smirked and shrugged her shoulders. "Just wait and see," she said confidently.

Stockings, shoes, muff, hat, Jo recited silently as she finished packing her things into the twins' black trunk. She held out a fancy black dress and sighed before hanging it back in her wardrobe. It would have been perfect for Paris, but she wouldn't need it at the headmistress's house.

It had been an intense day of ups and downs for the twins. Finding out more about Rosemary's nighttime whereabouts, taking exams, learning that they'd spend Christmas with the headmistress instead of Henri, and finishing the evening with the vibrant and entertaining fifth-year Holiday Review. It was almost time for lights-out, and all the girls in the Room Five dormitory were busily rummaging through drawers to make sure that nothing was forgotten for their holiday.

Jo sat on top of their trunk as Maddie made great efforts to force the metal clasps around it shut, with bits of silk and wool peeping through the gaps in between.

"I can't believe we're all leaving tomorrow," Maddie complained. "There's still so much to talk about and plan, and we've all been so scattered today."

"Don't worry, Livingstons," Val sang. "We have a farewell meeting planned for later. Finish your packing, save the mysteries for later."

CHAPTER SEVENTEEN

THE KNIGHTS OF ROOM FIVE

A clock struck midnight from off in the distance. On the floor of Room Five, the girls sat huddled in the dark around Françoise's torch.

"Was it really tied around a duck's neck?" Nixie asked, crouching as close as she could to the torch to read Max's riddle again.

"It was," Jo replied. "Max must have seen me feeding the geese, so he sent the note by messenger duck."

"But why wouldn't he have just come to the rock when we were looking for him all that time?" asked Millie. "He could just as easily have told you to your face, without all of this riddle nonsense."

"Maybe he got in trouble for spying," Maddie offered. "Maybe he couldn't come to the rock anymore or something bad would happen."

⬧

"Like what?" Val wondered.

"I don't know," Maddie said. "But whatever his reasons, he was confident that Jo and I could help. And we can't solve this puzzle on our own. Getting to the bottom of this mystery has to be something we all do, in sworn secrecy."

Just then, the door creaked open and dim light from the hallway spilled into the room. Safi slipped through the doorway and took the empty spot in the circle around the torch light.

"We were wondering where you were," Françoise said, grabbing Maddie's wrist and twisting it so that the watch faced Safi. "It's after midnight."

Safi held up her hands and explained. "Tonight of all nights," she said defensively. "I waited and waited for Rosemary to leave the room as she always does after lights-out, but she stayed in bed. I had to tiptoe over and make sure she was sleeping before I left."

"See?" Maddie insisted. "I knew it! It was Rosemary who kept Troxler up last night, and she was so scared of being expelled, she didn't sneak out of bed tonight."

"Well, you're here just in time," Jo said to Safi. "We're all going to swear to secrecy about the riddle." She passed the note to Safi.

Françoise rose onto her knees, holding the torch in the air. "I hereby declare us the Knights of Room Five," she said, and she used the torch as a sword and tapped each girl on the shoulders. "Do you pledge your allegiance and swear to secrecy?"

"I do," each girl said when it was her turn.

Jo had never experienced anything so secretive, and she imagined that she was a real knight. After all, this was a castle, and she was on a quest. It made perfect sense.

Val's eyebrows lowered as she concentrated on the riddle. She read the lines over and over again, translating them into Italian in her head. "What do you suppose he means by 'thieves on foot?' Is he saying that thieves are at the school every night?" She shuddered and rubbed the sleeves of her nightgown, looking up toward the wall of picture windows. "Maybe we should pull the curtains."

Nixie jumped to her side.

"No, no, Val. Remember, it's not the thieves you should be worried about. It's the *ghosts*." She winked and giggled, but the rest of the girls groaned.

"Be serious, Nixie," Françoise scolded. "We only have tonight before we all go away on holiday. At the least, we need to figure out a few lines of this riddle."

Jo cleared her throat. "Before we start," she said timidly, "There are two more things that not everyone knows." She looked at Maddie and pulled on her ring finger nervously.

"More secrets?" Val asked.

"Well, not really secrets, but mysteries . . ."

"Come on, then," Millie said impatiently. "What mysteries?"

Maddie nudged her sister. "Go on, Jo, tell them."

Jo sighed. She didn't like feeling as though she had kept something from her friends, but somehow, it hadn't felt right to tell them until now. "First, something strange happened when we were having tea in Kronenberg's office on our first day at school. She was showing us a few photographs of Madame Molineaux's, and one was taken from high up, from an airplane."

"So?" Safi replied. "I've seen that photograph before. It's framed on the wall. It's just an aerial photograph, probably to make a map," she said confidently. "People take them all the time in Senegal, it's the only way they can see the shape of the land and lakes."

Jo shook her head. "It wasn't the aerial photograph that puzzled me," she explained. "It was the fact that Kronenberg got nervous when we asked about it. She accidentally told us that they had the photograph taken because they were trying to find something. But when we asked her what, she changed the subject quickly."

"She was hiding something, for sure," Maddie added. "We planned to sneak in and snoop around, but we never got the chance to go into her office."

"I want to see the photograph," said Val. She looked down at her hands and nodded her head as if she were getting ready to enter a boxing ring. "I'll get into her office."

"Good luck," Maddie said doubtfully. "It's locked whenever she's not in it, even at night."

"Well, then," Val replied with a smile so mischievous it took the rest of the girls by surprise. "I may just have to get into trouble. Trouble so big, I get sent right to the headmistress's office."

The girls giggled. The idea of Val doing *anything* other than following the rules was unheard of, almost impossible to fathom. Quiet, shy Val wouldn't hurt a fly—or even call it names, for that matter. What could she do to be sent to Kronenberg's office?

"I'll believe that when I see it," Françoise said playfully. "But if you really think you can do it, that shall be your quest." She lowered her torch to Val's shoulders once more. "I hereby charge you, Valentina Dellavalle, with the quest to solve the puzzle of the photograph from the sky."

Nixie lit up with delight. "I want a quest!" she squealed. "What will my quest be?"

Françoise thought for a moment. She took Max's note from Val and read over it quickly, moving her lips as she read. She put the note down and picked up her torch again. "We need to find out who these 'thieves on foot' are. Can you stay up to spy on these real-life ghosts?"

Nixie nodded excitedly. "I can! I can. Umm . . ." she hesitated. "Do I have to do it by myself?"

"I thought you liked scary things," Françoise said with a half-smile. "Are you getting afraid now?"

Millie put a hand on Nixie's shoulder. "I'll go with her," she said, and the two girls shook hands. "We'll be brave together, right, Nixie?" Nixie nodded and sat up straight, her chest out and her shoulders back.

Françoise touched the torch to both Nixie's and Millie's shoulders in a knightly fashion. "I hereby charge you, Nixie Engelhardt and Millicent Braithwaite, with the quest to find the thieves on foot."

Excitement grew in the room. The glowing torch made huge shadows on the walls and ceiling as the girls sat around in a circle, and Maddie eagerly waited for her turn to be assigned a quest.

Safi was next, however. She spoke up with her own idea for a quest. "I've been spying on Rosemary Byron," she said slyly. "I know her every move in the dormitory room. My next step is to tag along on her late-night missions. This can be my quest, to track Rosemary like a cheetah hunting gazelle."

Françoise looked impressed. "Very well," she said, once again raising her torch. "I charge you, Safietou Faye, with the quest to discover Rosemary's midnight mischief."

Safi looked pleased and leaned back on her wrists. "You'll see," she assured her friends. "She won't ever suspect she's being followed."

Françoise turned to Maddie and Jo. "You two. Twin Sisters Livingston," she sang with intrigue. "Since the note from Max was addressed to you, you shall be the ones to solve the biggest mystery." She took the note and pointed to the last line of the riddle.

"You shall find the hidden chimney." She took her torch and knighted both the girls. "I hereby charge you, Madeline and Josephine Livingston, with the quest to find the smokestack growing out the lawn."

"We've already started," Jo beamed.

"And you?" Maddie asked, curious as to what Françoise's role in all of this would be. "What will your quest be?"

Françoise held the torch under her chin. "You never told them what the second secret was, did you, Jo?" she said, tilting her head from side to side and smirking.

Jo had been so caught up in the quest assignments that she had forgotten to tell the group the second bit of information she and her sister had been hiding.

"Er, no. I didn't." She looked at Maddie once more. *The whole truth?* she asked silently. Did she have to tell the others everything?

Maddie nodded gently, as if she knew what her sister was thinking.

"Okay," Jo said with a sigh. "I . . . I sleepwalk."

"Is that the secret?" Nixie asked. "Because I already knew." She smiled sweetly and patted Jo on the knee. "I've seen you walk around the room asleep. You even sat on my bed and told me a story about hot dogs from New York City and watching a marching band in a parade."

Jo looked embarrassed. "No, that's not the whole secret, but it's part of the story," she continued, blushing a bit.

Nixie piped up quickly. "Jo, I *loved* the story. And I really, really want to try a New York hot dog and see a marching band in a parade!"

Jo shrugged and looked down. "Well, I was sleepwalking one night just after we arrived, and wandered into the administration hallway, across from Kronenberg's office. Maddie found me unpacking a cabinet, looking for something. I must have thought I was still in my house in Boston."

"I'm pretty sure she was looking for a midnight snack," Maddie chimed in.

"I can understand, Jo," Val said enthusiastically. "In fact . . ." She looked down and patted her stomach.

"No, Val!" the girls cried in unison, laughing. There was no way that they would be taking a trip to the kitchen when Troxler was on the prowl, looking for students to expel.

Jo continued her story. "Maddie and I ended up fighting over a letter opener, and we accidentally tore through a portrait in the hallway. Under the rip in the canvas, we found a hidden tapestry."

Millie leaned into the circle. "And?" she asked.

"And we had to get Françoise to come and repair it," Maddie answered. "But I would be willing to bet that every painting on the administration hallway—no, *every painting in the castle*—has a tapestry behind it."

"That's where I come in," Françoise said proudly. "I'm going to cut each portrait open, just like Maddie and Jo did, to see what lies behind it. Then I'll repair it. No one will know the difference."

"You have to charge yourself with the quest," Safi insisted, looking around to her friends. "Each one of us has to receive the quest."

Françoise kneeled on one knee. "Very well," she said, raising the torch over her head. "I now charge me, Françoise Cadieux, with the quest to find the trapped tapestries."

She tapped each of her shoulders with the torch, and set it back down in the middle of the circle of seven girls.

"We are going to do it, you know," Maddie said with a satisfied smile.

"Do what?" asked Millie.

Maddie placed her hand on top of the glowing torch. The other girls placed their hands on top of hers, until only the faintest orange light could be seen.

"We're going to solve the Mystery at Madame Molineaux's."

Val yawned and pulled her hand from the pile to cover her mouth. "Can we start when we get back?" she asked.

All the girls laughed and agreed that it was time for bed. This would be their last night's sleep at school before the holiday, and everyone would be traveling the next morning.

"Good night, my fellow knights," Jo called to the girls as they snuggled down under their covers. "Until the New Year."

CHAPTER EIGHTEEN

THE NEARLY EMPTY CASTLE

"Bye!" Jo shouted after the forest-green car that had just pulled away from the entrance to Madame Molineaux's. It tottered back and forth along the bumpy, snow-covered driveway and headed for the school gates, leaving a trail of black smoke as it went.

"Did you catch her name?" Maddie asked her sister before cupping her hands to her mouth. "Have a nice Christmas, um . . . friend!" she trumpeted into the cold air.

"I didn't. But maybe she'll smile at us in the hallways now when we come back." Jo kicked her boots against a stone planter to shake off the snow. "I think she might have been the last one, Sis." She opened the enormous front door of Madame Molineaux's just enough to poke her head through to the less-freezing interior of the main hall. Her eyes scanned the bright but empty space, and she listened for any traces of footsteps, trunks being dragged across the rug, or tearful good-byes between friends, which she had heard so many times already today.

Instead, she heard a phrase all too familiar being hollered from inside. "Shut that door, you'll let all the cold air in!" the headmistress called from just inside the administration hallway. Jo had heard this demand countless times from her parents during the harsh winters of Boston, and her old routine sprang to life in Switzerland. She stepped through the doorway, yanked her sister inside, and hugged herself warm while she kicked the door closed—all in one fell swoop. Except this time, her already ice-cold foot smacked against the massive block of carved wood and did little to move it.

"Ow!" Jo yelped, hopping on one foot and holding her injured toes with both hands.

"Calm down," Maddie whispered as she pushed the door back into its frame. "Let's not start our vacation off in trouble, huh? I wonder if Kronenberg has a room in her house just for houseguest detention." She giggled at her own joke as the headmistress approached.

"I take it you've seen the last of the girls off," she said to the twins with a half-smile. She tugged at the hem of her jacket sleeve. "It must be hard watching the others leave with their families and friends. I know you're upset about Henri and Paris, but I'm sure we can have a lovely holiday together."

"It's all right. Thank you for having us, Headmistress," Maddie said softly. "I'm sure you weren't planning on company."

"Come to think of it, I was rather hoping I might have the chance to host someone during the holidays. I just didn't realize it would be two of my students." Kronenberg straightened her shoulders. "Now. I have just a few more things to do before we leave. Can you wait in the first-year library?"

The girls nodded and started toward their hallway.

"I'll come and get you when I'm finished," the headmistress said, and she turned back toward the administration hallway.

Tap tap tap tap tap.

Maddie drummed her index fingers on the freezing-cold glass of the library's central window. "It still doesn't make any sense," she mumbled to her sister, who was draped over a leather armchair, reading *The Adventures of Sherlock Holmes.*

Jo lifted her head from her book with mild interest. "You're not going to figure it out *today*, Maddie. Besides, figuring out where Rosemary's going is Safi's quest, not ours. Remember?" She put her attention back on the pages.

"I know, I know. It's just that, from where we were sitting at that table studying Max's note, the slamming sound came from *right here.* This window, I tell you. And it's even more ridiculous that—" She stopped mid-sentence. "Jo! Get over here!"

Jo recognized her sister's serious tone of voice and leaped up from her comfy reading spot. "What? What'd you find?"

"That," Maddie said, grinning. She pointed straight out the window at the headmistress and two other adults walking the grounds toward the Science Hall. "I don't know what she's doing or who those people are, but I do know one thing."

Jo stared her sister in the eyes and nodded slowly. "Kronenberg's not in her office."

"Finally!" Jo panted, galloping down the first-year hallway steps. "If she didn't lock it, this is our chance to get in again."

The twins scurried across the floor of the main hall and ran into the administration hallway. They stopped in front of the door labeled DIRECTRICE and hesitated.

"I feel like someone's watching us," Maddie said, holding her hand just inches from the doorknob. She cocked her head to the side, listening intently. "I mean, really, Jo—did you hear that? It sounded like paper rustling."

"You're imagining it, Sis. You're letting these guys intimidate you." Jo pointed back and forth to the armored knights on each side of the door. She quickly raised the visor on one, then the other, to reveal nothing but dust and darkness inside their helmets. "See? It's okay if you're nervous to sneak into her office, though. Here, let me." She wrapped her fingers around the brass doorknob, twisted it, and pushed. It opened. "No reason to lock the door if the castle is empty, I suppose. Well, *nearly* empty. Come on." She pulled her sister into the office with her.

Maddie relaxed a little once she was inside. She looked at the sofa where she and Jo had tea with the headmistress and remembered their first day at school. *Seems like ages ago*, she thought to herself.

"I'll take a closer look at the aerial photo," Jo said, marching over to the wall. "See what you can find in her desk."

Maddie hurried over to the headmistress's desk and searched the surface for anything out of the ordinary. "Pens, pencils, magnifying glass, lamp, handkerchiefs, note cards," she recited as her eyes settled on each item. "Nothing strange *on* the desk."

Jo ran to the desk and grabbed a pencil and some note cards. "We don't have much time. I'm going to sketch the photo for later."

She tugged on each drawer, opening it and scanning the contents for a secret map, a tucked-away letter, or a set of keys. But nothing of interest appeared until she pulled the handle on the slide-out writing surface. Laying flat against it was a gray file folder marked *American*.

"Jo," she whispered. "I think Kronenberg is keeping a file on us. It's labeled *American*."

"Then open it, for goodness' sake!" Jo pleaded. Her ears perked up. "I keep hearing things. We need to hurry." She skipped to the doorway and poked her head out, but no one was in the hallway.

Maddie carefully opened the file folder, revealing a thin stack of letters, newspaper articles, and magazine clippings. She leafed through them quickly, reading the headlines one by one.

New York Mother Achieves Top Sales in Hair Care Business. Eleanor Roosevelt Meets with Businesswoman Ida Washington and Others. Harlem's Social Scene is Alive and Well. Mother and Daughter Keep Family Traditions from Jamaican Heritage.

"Jo, I think there's another American coming to school here next year," Maddie explained. "From New York. And she's really . . ." she held up a black and white photograph of the girl and her mother in their living room. ". . . fancy."

"Let me see," Jo said, suddenly forgetting about the aerial photograph. "How neat would it have been to have another American here this year?" She spread out the articles and began to write down an address. "New York's not that far from

Boston, you know. Maybe in the summer we could visit and tell her all about—"

A door creaked somewhere. Ever so softly, but both girls heard it as clearly as thunder.

"We have to go!" Jo panicked. She dropped the pencil and stuffed the note cards into her jacket for later. Maddie slammed the file folder shut, laid it back down where she had found it, and slid the writing surface back into the desk.

The twins slipped out of the headmistress's office, pulled the door shut, and straightened their uniforms.

"Walk casually, Jo, like we're out for an evening stroll. Nothing to see here," Maddie whispered, wondering when they'd finally bump into Kronenberg and her guests. They neared the end of the administration hallway, positioned themselves near the wall, and leaned out to inspect the main hall.

And there, standing still as a statue underneath the entrance to the Grand Corridor, was a petite girl wearing a long, green, silk pleated skirt, a light pink-and-jade printed silk blouse with a high collar that reached the bottom of her wavy onyx bob, and black ankle boots. She stood gracefully with her fingers interlaced in front of her, and stared directly at the twins.

"Were you supposed to be in there?" she taunted, the corners of her mouth turned up into the beginnings of a smile. "I wonder if your headmistress knows." Her accent was delicate, and the way she spoke made the twins feel as though her words arrived at their ears on a gentle breeze.

"Who are you?" Maddie demanded, stepping out of the shadows and toward the girl. "And what are you doing spying on us?"

The girl opened her mouth as if she were going to speak, but closed it quickly, smiled, blinked twice, and darted into the Grand Corridor toward the dining hall.

Maddie and Jo looked at each other in horror. Would this stranger, this teenaged spy, run and tell the headmistress? It took only a moment for the twins to start running down the Grand Corridor after her.

"Wait!" Jo screeched. "Please wait!"

They passed window after window, pulling drapes aside as they went, but there was no one. Maddie's eye caught something in the middle of the rug, and she bent down.

"What's this?" she asked, holding the small, cream-colored tile with a red design up in the air to show her sister.

Jo stopped shaking the heavy drapes and walked over to take a closer look. "Looks like little red flowers and green leaves." She turned the tile over and over in her hand. "Is this part of a game? Like dominoes?"

But Maddie was already farther down the Grand Corridor, down on the carpet again. "Here's another piece, but it's more like a round, flat white stone."

"And I see another up ahead," Jo said as she ran up thirty feet in front of her sister. "It's as if that girl is leaving a trail for us." She dropped the tile into her jacket pocket and bent down to pick up the third piece. It, too, was round, and made from light green stone. It displayed a complex Chinese character engraved in black. "I've never seen anything like this, Maddie."

"Game pieces, indeed," Maddie huffed. "I think we're *in* the game! She's moving us around like chess pieces."

"I love to play chess," a voice called from just inside the dining hall. "But I'll have to defeat you another day. You can keep my treasures as a peace offering, and I won't tell your headmistress about what I saw. *Míngnián zàijiàn*," she said elegantly before turning to walk out the dining hall doors onto the school grounds. She stopped and flashed the girls a smile. "It means, 'see you next year.'" And she was gone.

Jo reached as high as she could to the top of her wardrobe. "I'll hide these in here until we get back." She placed each of the game pieces the mysterious girl had dropped for them on the highest shelf and slid them all the way back. She turned to her sister and smirked. "Too bad you won't actually get to see if she can beat you at chess next year, huh?"

Maddie shrugged her shoulders. "She would have lost anyway."

"Anything else need to go into a hiding place before we leave?" Jo asked, patting down her own jacket. Maddie shook her head no, but Jo had a startling realization as she felt the note card sketches in her pocket. "I dropped her pencil. *I dropped her pencil!* Kronenberg will see it on the floor and know we were in there!"

It was time for one last dash through the castle. The twins ran out the Room Five door and down the hallway, but Maddie grabbed on to Jo's arm and pulled her into the library at the last moment: The headmistress, a man and a woman, and the girl they'd just chased were standing in the middle of the main hall. Maddie and Jo peeked out the library door to eavesdrop.

"It has been a pleasure to meet you, Mr. and Mrs. Lin," the headmistress said with a slight bow. She bent down to meet the girl's eyes. "And you, too, Hui-Ling. I think you'll enjoy being a second-year at Madame Molineaux's next fall."

Mr. and Mrs. Lin bowed their heads and Hui-Ling gave a graceful curtsey.

"We go back to Shanghai tomorrow, by way of Paris, of course," said Mrs. Lin. "Thank you for the tour, Headmistress."

Kronenberg showed them out the huge front doors, then walked toward the administration hallway. Maddie and Jo groaned, slinked back into the library, and awaited their punishment.

Klara Kronenberg shut her office door behind her, leaned back against it, and sighed, relieved that the tour was over. *Would there even be a Madame Molineaux's for Hui-Ling, or any of the girls, to attend next year?* she wondered. She paced back and forth in front of her desk, tugging at her jacket hem. "There's still time, Klara. Still time." She took a deep breath. "Still ti—"

Snap!

She picked up her foot to see what she had stepped on. She picked up the two broken pieces of a wooden pencil, clenched them in her fist, and marched out the door to find the Livingston twins.

Jo shifted in her leather armchair and repeated what she'd just heard back to the headmistress. "So . . . you're having your driver take us into Saint-Marcel alone?"

"I figured you'd be quite bored by now, having stayed here in the library for over an hour," Kronenberg reasoned to her two charges. She let her fingers roll the pieces of broken pencil in her pocket and pasted a smile on her face before continuing. "Besides, I have to lock up all the buildings except one before we leave, and that will take at least an hour."

"Which building are you leaving unlocked?" Maddie asked, wondering why she'd leave one open when, apparently, there were thieves running around at night.

"Professor Natalio will stay on campus for the holiday. He has some rather . . . *explosive* experiments he'd like to test out while no one's here, and he'll be caring for the great blue turacos, Musetta and Marcello, and whatever creatures he has back in his laboratory during the holiday." She gestured for the girls to move toward the door. "Besides, didn't you say you needed to drop a letter in town for Henri?"

"Yes, Headmistress," the girls said in unison.

"Wonderful. We'll pick you up after an hour then, trunks and all, and be on our way to Germany."

CHAPTER NINETEEN

WINTER IN SAINT-MARCEL

Maddie and Jo waved at the driver as he returned to Madame Molineaux's. They hadn't seen Saint-Marcel during the day yet, as the younger students weren't allowed to leave the school boundaries without an escort. The rooftops in the quaint mountain town were padded with thick blankets of snow and smoking chimneys, and, inside each stained-glass door, shopkeepers tended to books, pastries, and hand-knitted winter clothing.

The town center bustled as residents hurried to buy the last of their Christmas gifts, sending sleigh bells a-ringing every time they walked into a shop. The bakery windows, tall and sparkling clear, were lined with children of all ages pressing their noses to the glass, watching as tarts, cakes, and cookies were made from scratch.

Jo lifted her nose into the air, closed her eyes, and took a deep breath. "Mmm," she said, turning toward the bakery. "An hour is plenty of time to try some of *those*." She pointed at the giant plate of star-shaped cookies in the bakery window, wondering how many she could get with the money she had in her coat pocket.

"An hour?" Maddie said, looking at her wristwatch. "That's not very much time to explore. And don't forget, we have to drop the letter for Henri." She looked at the cookies in the window, then back at her sister. "Eat while we walk?"

"Of course," Jo replied, and the two girls ran into the bakery, leaving with a small paper bag full of tiny cinnamon star cookies to occupy them while they walked to the letterbox on Rue de Vieux-Marcel.

"Now then," Maddie said as she slipped Henri's letter through the narrow mail slot at what appeared to be a tailor's shop. "We're done with official business. Where to?" She paused at a street corner and stared up at the narrow signs hanging from the streetlamp and turned to the right. "We can go this way to the inn, the bookstore, and the market," she said, standing on her tiptoes to look as far as she could down the hilly road. "Or, we can go that way," she said, turning in the other direction, "to the college, the ice-skating rink, and the ski lodge."

"Either way is fine with me," Jo mumbled as she shoved in another cookie. "Maybe we could pick out a gift for Kronenberg, for having us during the holiday. Mom always says, 'Don't forget to take something for the host when you're a guest.'"

"Good thinking," said Maddie, and the girls strolled down the steep sidewalk toward the market. Chilly shoppers sipped hot chocolate and coffee in the café, and the restaurant at the inn was full of diners enjoying a hearty winter stew and hot buttered bread. Everyone in town was in a merry mood, and passersby smiled and nodded to Maddie and Jo, still in their school uniforms.

Jo stopped in front of a candle shop and peered in through the stained glass. "What about candles for Kronenberg?"

"Perfect," said Maddie, and she pushed on the tall, narrow door.

Sleigh bells rang as Jo closed the shop door behind them. She stamped the snow off her boots on the bristly doormat and stuffed the remaining cinnamon cookies into her coat pocket. Inside the dark shop, rows of hooks lined the walls, each one draped with pairs of candlesticks. The air smelled of beeswax, vanilla, and cloves, and it warmed the girls instantly from the frosty mountain air.

"*Bonjour, mademoiselles,*" a plump woman greeted, coming out from behind the counter.

"*Bonjour,*" Jo replied. "*Est-ce que vous avez . . .*"

The shopkeeper smiled and shook her finger at the girls playfully. "Your French is good, dear," she said. "But I can tell an American accent in an instant. Many Americans come all the way here to Saint-Marcel, just to buy my candles."

Jo relaxed. "I'm positive your English is better than our French," she said, laughing. "Yes—we're American, but we're studying at Madame Molineaux's."

"I can see that," the woman said, eyeing the crests on their capes. "I know your headmistress very well. Klara hasn't been in the shop lately, though . . . I have wondered about her."

"You know the headmistress?" Jo asked excitedly. "That's great news since we're here to buy a gift for her! We're staying at her house for the holiday." She looked around the shop walls at the candles. "Do you have anything special?"

The woman thought for a moment and snapped her fingers. "For Klara, I have just the pair. One of a kind!" she said. "And they're almost finished. I just need to put the final touches on them in my workshop upstairs."

She motioned for the girls to follow her, and led them to a narrow staircase in the back of the shop. The red carpet on the stairs was worn thin, and the walls were dotted with wax from countless splatters and spills. They climbed three flights of stairs and paused for the woman to catch her breath.

"Um, exactly which floor is the workshop on?" Maddie asked sweetly.

"Just one more flight," the woman said between heavy breaths. "My family and I live on the second, third, and fourth floors of the building, and my workshop is on the fifth."

Jo felt closed in as she walked up the stairs, and she was feeling a bit winded herself after climbing so many steps. Making the trip up and down the stairs more than a dozen times a day might have driven her slightly mad.

You'd have to be skinny as a stick to feel comfortable in these tiny staircases, Jo thought. *A candlestick,* she added, and she let out a tiny giggle.

They arrived at the fifth floor and stepped into an open loft with two dormer windows. Glass jars of wax crowded the work tables, and large spools of colored string were stacked up to make high columns on the floor. A black kettle hung over a wood-burning stove in the corner.

The woman pointed at two red candles propped up in metal holders, their tips joined by a common wick. Each candle was decorated with a colorful holly and ivy pattern and dotted with silver and gold. "I knew I had a good reason for making these!" she said proudly, and sat down to finish the last bit of painting. "You can look around while you wait, if you like."

Maddie walked around each of the work tables, running her fingers over the wax-drop topography on the wood, and finally sat down on one of the window seats. "Jo, come and see how high up we are," she said, pressing her forehead to the glass to get a better look at the town below.

Jo joined her sister and squeezed next to her on the seat. "I see Madame Molineaux's!" Her eyes followed the campus buildings and paths to the lake and forest. She let out a gasp when she realized what was off in the distance. On the other side of the rocky cove, an ominous gray castle towered from the sharp cliffs above the lake.

"That must be Max's school," she said. From up high, it was easy to see how Max made his way over to their side of the forest.

The woman looked up from her decorating. "Finished!" she exclaimed. She blew gently on the last of the drying paint and wrapped the pair of candles in brown paper, tying it with an orange satin ribbon. "You can tell Klara you got them from Claudette's candle shop." She walked to the window where Maddie and Jo sat and handed them the package. "I assume you like the view?" she asked.

"Very much," Jo told her. "We can see our school, and the boys' school, and all of Saint-Marcel."

"*And,*" the woman added. "You can see the very top of the clock tower. This might be the only window in the whole town where you can see it." She pointed to the gargoyles on the clock tower's belfry. "From here, they look scary," she said. "But if you can believe it, they are actually smiling."

Maddie laughed. "I'll remember that. Smiling gargoyles! I'll picture it each time I hear the bells ring. We can hear them all the way at Madame Molineaux's, you know."

The woman gave Maddie a puzzled look. "I doubt that, my dear."

"It's true," Jo said, nodding her head. "We hear them every hour. We can even set our watches by them." She checked her wristwatch to see if it was keeping up with the clock tower.

"Well," the woman said cautiously, "I'm not sure which bells you are hearing, but I haven't heard bells chime in Saint-Marcel since summer."

Maddie and Jo looked at each other with bewilderment. "But why can't you hear the bells ring?" Maddie asked. "You're right next to the tower."

"Look again," the woman said, pointing at the belfry. "Don't you notice something missing?"

Jo peered at the tower, finally realizing that she could see right through the belfry to the blue sky behind it. "It's empty!"

"Yes, my dears," the woman replied solemnly. "Someone has stolen the bells."

CHAPTER TWENTY

THE MITTENWALD MARKET

Jo stretched her long legs as far as they would go under the seat in front of her. *How did we end up on another long car ride with Kronenberg?* she complained silently.

Outside the window, the snow-covered hills could have been the sand dunes of Morocco, had they been yellow instead of white, and had they not been speckled with sparkling, ice-crusted evergreens. Dusk was falling, and Jo wondered how long it would be before she couldn't see anything outside the back seat window at all.

She was supposed to be on her way to Paris. But instead, she and Maddie were bundled under a blanket in the car with the headmistress and the same driver who had taken them to Madame Molineaux's in the fall. Jo pushed off from the window, the space where her forehead had been now foggy with moisture. She used her finger to draw a small Eiffel Tower and two stick-figure girls on the wet, cloudy glass.

As she sat back to admire her artwork, the faintest lights shone through the clear lines she had drawn, making her rustic Eiffel Tower light up like a candle. Jo leaned forward to see out the windshield. "What are those lights?"

The headmistress turned around to answer her. "That's Mittenwald, where my home is. We're almost there."

The dim glow of Mittenwald grew brighter as the car approached the town. Even though it was well past suppertime, curls of smoke rose out of each chimney, up toward the mountain that lay directly behind the village.

"Are we in time for dinner?" Maddie asked, emerging from her cozy pile of blankets.

"Yes, Madeline. Not to worry. Oma Kronenberg has prepared something for our arrival."

Maddie's curiosity got the best of her. "Umm . . . exactly whose grandmother is Oma Kronenberg? Surely, she's not *your* grandmother," she said, doing the math in her head to figure out how old Oma Kronenberg would have to be in order to be the headmistress's grandmother.

The headmistress laughed softly, realizing that the twins probably thought of her as ancient, and very unlikely to have a living grandparent.

"She *is* my grandmother, indeed. She just celebrated her ninety-fourth birthday last month," she said proudly.

Great, Maddie thought. *Good thing we learned how to play Walk the Plank on the ship. I bet we're in for a week of card games with two old ladies.* She vaguely remembered the smile on Françoise's face when she mentioned Oma Kronenberg. *Thanks, Françoise. Very funny.* It was looking as though she and Jo were going to have a long, dull holiday this year.

The headmistress stamped the snow from her boots on the straw mat outside the front door. She looked up at the cottage and smiled as childhood memories filled her with quiet joy. She drew in a deep breath and turned to the girls, who stood behind her.

"Do you smell that?" she asked, her eyes wide. "I told you there would be dinner waiting for us. I bet it's a real feast." The air smelled of gingerbread, warm beef stew, buttery potatoes, and cooked fruit. The fragrance of spruce lingered at the front door where the Christmas wreath hung. The headmistress knocked three times and stepped back. Maddie and Jo peeked out from behind her, unsure of why she would knock at her own home.

And then, in an instant, the door flew open. A spritely old woman erupted into song while playing a vibrant tune on the violin. She sang with the voice of a much younger woman, and she danced around like an elf, wearing red stockings and an ankle-length green dress. The headmistress clapped with delight as Maddie and Jo looked on in shock. This was certainly not the Oma Kronenberg they had imagined—this woman wore gold thread tied into her hair, shook the sleigh bell bracelets around her wrists as she jumped, and, finally, threw back her arms in a dramatic curtsey to her guests, her violin clutched in her left hand.

"I promised myself I wouldn't do it again this year," she exclaimed, pretending to apologize as the headmistress praised her. "But when I heard you had the girls with you, well, I couldn't help it. It's not every day that I have a new audience."

The headmistress stepped forward and hugged her tiny grandmother. "Oma, these are our guests for the holiday, Madeline and Josephine Livingston. Girls," she said, moving out of the way, "say hello." Jo stepped through the doorway and gazed around the small cottage. It was stuffed with furniture, decorated with Christmas garlands, and full of trinkets, figurines, and cuckoo clocks. A fire burned in the sitting room, and the wood-burning oven in the kitchen filled the house with the aroma of freshly baked cakes.

"Hello, Oma Kronenberg," the twins said politely.

Maddie stepped forward and handed her the brown paper package they brought from Switzerland. "We picked these out for you and the headmistress, from a shop in Saint-Marcel."

Oma Kronenberg opened the package and hugged the candles to her chest. "How delightful!" she exclaimed. "They'll look just perfect on our Christmas table." She walked into the kitchen. "I'll cut the wick and find two candlesticks for them."

The headmistress smiled at the girls. "How nice of you, ladies. And from Claudette's! I usually visit her around this time of year, but I haven't had the time. Thank you for bringing them."

Jo shook her head. "No, Headmistress, thank you for bringing us to your home. Our parents must be so grateful that you could invite us, considering Henri couldn't host us in Paris."

"It's been many years since we've had young people in the house for Christmas. We're both glad you're here." The headmistress pushed the girls into the kitchen as the driver took their trunks upstairs.

"You did come hungry, didn't you?" Oma Kronenberg asked with a twinkle in her eye. Spread out on the long, narrow table were cakes, tarts, a pot of beef stew with root vegetables, and myriad other treats the girls had never tasted.

"I think the girls are hungry, and probably a little tired," the headmistress said as she passed plates to Maddie and Jo.

"Eat anything you like, girls," encouraged Oma Kronenberg. "And when you're done, your room is up the stairs, to the left, at the end of the hallway."

"Will you be joining us for dinner, Oma?" Jo asked, hoping the old woman might put on another concert after dinner.

"Ah, no, dear. Things to do, things to do." And with that, Oma Kronenberg flitted out of the kitchen to the back of the house. "See you in the morning," she called. "Good night, my darling Klara."

Maddie slid her finger through the ring on the wooden candlestick and carried it to the bedside table, ducking as she approached the overstuffed feather mattress she and Jo would share. The ceiling sloped downward on one side, following the steep angle of the roof, and it made the girls feel as if they were sleeping under a tent or in a homemade fort. The small woodburning stove in the room made it feel even cozier, and Maddie sprawled out on the floor to look at the book of travel photographs the girls had borrowed from the sitting room downstairs.

"Oma Kronenberg isn't what I expected," Jo confessed. "She looks like fun." She joined her sister on the floor and leafed through the pages of pictures. "I bet you she knows a lot about the headmistress . . . and maybe even about Madame Molineaux's."

"Well, we're here for over a week. I'm sure we can get her alone, without the headmistress, to ask her some questions," Maddie said with a big yawn. She laid the book down, jumped in the bed, and climbed under the covers.

"Lights!" Jo called, mimicking the headmistress's nightly orders to turn off all dormitory lights at school.

Maddie giggled quietly as she picked up the candle. "I wouldn't be surprised if there's a curfew in the Kronenberg house, too." She cupped her hand around the candle flame and blew it out, sending wisps of gray smoke floating past the frosty window.

For the first time in months, Maddie and Jo woke to something other than the ringers coming down their hall at Madame Molineaux's. This morning, the smell of pancakes and spiced pears lured them out of sleep.

Jo was out of bed first. She traipsed over to the icy window and looked out into town. There were people everywhere, having their last look at the Christmas market craft booths. "Wake up, Sis," she sang. "Let's eat breakfast and go to the market!"

Maddie reached over to the night table and found her wristwatch. "What time is it?" she asked. "We're on holiday. We're supposed to sleep in, you know." She picked up her watch to look at the time, but a cuckoo clock from downstairs chimed first. *Cuckoo*, it cried as it dinged, once for each hour. It was nine o'clock.

"It's already *nine*," Jo said impatiently. "The market closes down early since it's Christmas Eve, so get up!"

Maddie groaned into her pillow. Only her sister would want a head start on the first day of vacation. She reluctantly left the toasty bed, pulled her heaviest winter clothes from the trunk, and dressed in front of the wood-burning stove.

Downstairs, Oma Kronenberg had prepared a lavish breakfast, and had even made hot cocoa for the girls. "Klara has already gone out for the day," she told them. "But after we eat, you can do anything you like. There's a market just down the road."

"We saw it from our window when we woke up," Jo said, nodding excitedly. "We might go to get souvenirs for our friends back at school."

"You could buy them cuckoo clocks," Oma Kronenberg suggested. "We are known for them here in Bavaria."

Maddie laughed. "A room full of six girls, each with a cuckoo clock! That might be a little noisy. I think the headmistress might have something to say about it."

"You have a point, my dear," the old woman said, smiling. "Klara sleeps at the end of the first-year hallway, after all! Not *all* the clocks at the market are cuckoo clocks, though. There are some that only chime. You could get one for the dormitory room, and something smaller for each one of your friends."

Jo was sold on the idea. "Perfect," she said, wiping up the last of her spiced pears from her plate with a pancake and tucking it into her mouth in one bite.

"Can we help you with the dishes?" Maddie asked.

"Ah, no, dears. I'm going to cook all day. No sense in cleaning up one mess just to make another! Off you go to the market." She shooed the girls out of the kitchen. "Just be back in time for dinner!" she called as the front door shut.

Jo held a small wooden knight in the palm of her hand and traced over the details of his armor with her finger. There were so many things to see at the market, but the wooden carving had caught her eye. "Look, Maddie," she said as she held him out to her sister. "He looks like the knight from the tapestry. You know, the one in the administration hallway."

Maddie reached into the square bin on the woodcarver's cart and pulled out another knight. "You're right, Sis. Let's tell Françoise. She said the markings on the tapestry could have been German."

Jo took her German dictionary from her cape pocket and flipped through the pages. "*Was Kostet Das?*" she asked the woodcarver. He smiled and held up two fingers. "It's the perfect souvenir for the Knights of Room Five, don't you think?" she asked Maddie. "We each have to have one."

Maddie smiled and dropped the knight back into the square bin. "Absolutely," she said. "I'm going to keep looking around while you buy them, okay?"

Her sister nodded. "*Sieben, bitte,*" Jo said, holding up seven fingers to the man and then sliding three bills across the counter. The woodcarver smiled, packed seven knight figures into a tiny burlap sack, and handed her some coins for change.

"*Frohe Weihnachten,*" he said to her.

Jo nodded. "Merry Christmas to you, too, sir," she said, and ran off to find her sister.

She joined Maddie in front of the clockmaker's booth, which was much longer than the other booths and jammed with clocks of every sort. Some had little houses mounted on the front, and each time the bells chimed, two wooden figures came out of one door, circled around, and went back into another door. It looked as if they were chasing each other around and around in an endless loop.

Others were fashioned with a pair of doors that opened during the chimes, shooting a bird out to make the cuckoo call. Little children pointed at which clock they wanted the clock-maker to make chime, and he fiddled with the backs of them until they made their boisterous calls.

"And which one would you like to hear, young lady?" the man asked Maddie with a heavy German accent.

Jo spoke into Maddie's ear to be heard above the noise. "Pick the biggest one! The one in the back. I don't think I've ever seen a clock so huge."

A pendulum the size of a frying pan swung beneath the large clock, gliding back and forth in front of pinecone-shaped weights hanging from golden chains. Deer and evergreen trees had been chiseled into the massive wooden clock to depict a tranquil forest scene, with squirrels scurrying up the tree trunks and birds flying up in the forest canopy.

"Um . . . can you make the big clock in the back chime?" she asked, pointing behind him.

"Aha! Yes, I can," the man said, laughing. "In fact, the difficult part is making that one stop. Are you going to buy it? How much money do you have?" he joked.

Maddie looked in her cape pocket. "Probably not enough for that," she admitted.

The man laughed harder.

"Don't worry, my dear. No one has enough money to buy this clock. It's not for sale."

"Not for sale?" Jo asked.

"No, this one is priceless. It is one of the original clocks made long ago in the Black Forest. I bring it out at Christmastime for everyone to see, and it makes the little children so happy to hear the bells!" He stepped behind the clock, tinkered and clanked for a moment, and came back out front. Some of the local children put their fingers in their ears in preparation for the great clock to chime. "Get ready, girls—here it comes!" he shouted. The second hand and minute hand on the clock aligned where the clock face read twelve, and a loud click sent the chimes ringing.

Ding, Ding-Dong, the clock struck, each bell ringing out in a low, long chime.

Maddie and Jo exchanged puzzled looks as the town children ran around in excitement. It was a familiar sound, but where had they heard it before?

Ding, Ding-Dong, it struck again, and Jo's eyes widened as she began to realize where she had heard that same exact chime. Maddie cupped her hands around Jo's ear and yelled.

"That's it! That's the sound the bells at Madame Molineaux's make!"

Ding, Ding-Dong, it kept ringing.

"Do you like it?" the clockmaker called out to them, raising his voice over the bells and the commotion.

"Yes—yes, thank you, sir!" Jo called hastily, and she grabbed Maddie and ran up the snow-covered road.

Maddie held on to her sister's arm and slowed to catch her breath just outside the market. "Do you realize what this means, Jo?" she panted.

Jo crouched down on the packed snow and swept her mittens through the white powder, clearing a space to squat down. "I guess so, but I'm still confused. I hear those chimes from all over the school. Surely one clock couldn't ring that loud."

"I've heard those bells every day since we got to Madame Molineaux's. Those *exact* bells," Maddie recalled. "You heard the man from the market: that clock is priceless! There must be another one at school."

"But if there's a clock like that at school, why would Kronenberg tell us the bells were coming from Saint-Marcel?"

Maddie shrugged. "Add that to the mystery list. Maybe we could ask her at dinner."

The faint sound of neighing and laughing came from the other side of the hill where they sat. Within moments, a horse-drawn sleigh pulled up next to the girls. It towed what appeared to be a large farm wagon behind it, and over a dozen children sat bundled up in blankets on warm hay. As it slowed to a stop, the horses stamped their feet and shook their heads, ringing the silver bells on their harnesses.

"Coming aboard?" the driver asked.

Jo ran around to the back of the wagon without hesitation and climbed onto the bed of straw. She had always dreamed of going on a sleigh ride during winter, just like something out of *The Snow Queen.*

"Jo!" Maddie called. "We don't even know where they're headed!"

"We don't have to be back until suppertime, Maddie," Jo reminded her. "Just come on."

Maddie jumped up beside her sister and settled against the wooden side of the sleigh bed. The children began singing a Christmas carol in German, and the driver cracked his whip, sending the horses trotting through the snow-covered streets of Mittenwald.

CHAPTER TWENTY-ONE

CHRISTMAS WITH THE KRONENBERGS

Jo helped herself to more red cabbage, careful not to spill any into her glass of cider as she brought the heaping silver spoon to her plate.

"Your taste for German food is wonderful," the headmistress remarked, happy that the girls were enjoying the traditional Bavarian Christmas dishes that Oma Kronenberg had spent all day preparing.

Maddie swallowed her food and sipped her cider. "We worked up an appetite in town earlier," she said. "I think we were on that sleigh ride for almost three hours!"

Jo nodded. "Mittenwald is so beautiful, and the people are so welcoming. Did you see what we bought our school friends?" She pulled the burlap sack out from under her chair and handed the knights to the headmistress and Oma Kronenberg.

"How nice," Oma Kronenberg said, inspecting the wooden trinkets. "Did you pick out a clock for your room, too?"

Maddie and Jo exchanged anxious looks. "Well, no," Jo started. "We saw some pretty ones, even a great big one, but . . ."

"But we figured that since we already hear the chimes every hour at school, we didn't need another clock. And," Maddie said, holding up her wrist, "we have our wristwatches."

The headmistress smiled and cut into her meat. "I think you mean the clock tower in Saint-Marcel, Maddie," she said, and looked up from her plate to her grandmother. "You remember those bells, don't you, Oma?"

"I do, I do," Oma Kronenberg agreed. She cocked her head to the side. "Well, I think I do. I'm ninety-eight years old, after all. I'm not sure what I remember."

The headmistress shook her head. "You heard them when you were at the school two summers ago. And you're *ninety-four*, not ninety-eight, Oma." The girls giggled. Oma Kronenberg shrugged innocently but didn't look convinced.

"Well," continued Maddie. "Claudette took us to the workshop on the fifth floor of her candle store. We sat and looked out the windows while we were waiting."

The headmistress looked nervous. "Mm-hmm," she said, not looking up from her plate.

"And she told us about the bell tower after she finished your present—"

"*Presents!*" the headmistress exclaimed, cutting Maddie's story short. "I almost forgot, ladies. I have all your gifts from Henri and your parents." She practically knocked over her glass of cider in her hurry to leave the table.

Jo leaned forward, putting both elbows on the table and resting her chin in her hands. Obviously, Kronenberg didn't want to talk about the clock, the bells, or the tower in Saint-Marcel.

But at least it was confirmed: the headmistress was definitely hiding something.

Oma Kronenberg slid her chair away from the table. "In Germany, we open our presents on Christmas Eve," she said with a smile. "Shall we open them next to the Christmas tree? We can come back in for cake afterward."

Maddie gave up on her investigation for the moment. "That sounds perfect," she said, and she took Oma by the hand to lead her to the sitting room.

Jo hung more glass icicles on the tree while she waited for the headmistress to return with their gifts, and Maddie stoked the burning logs in the fireplace.

"I wasn't done hearing your story about the bells," Oma Kronenberg said to the girls. She held her finger to her lips and winked. "We'll chat later," she whispered, and sat in the rocking chair by the fire.

Jo opened her eyes and stared at the bedroom wall, holding her breath as she waited to hear the noise again.

Bang, bang, bang!

She shook her sleeping sister. "Did you hear that?"

"Hear what?" Maddie grumbled. She fumbled for her wristwatch and squinted her eyes to see the time. "It's three o'clock in the morning," she said, and she pulled the covers up over her head.

"It sounds like someone's knocking on the door," Jo said. "I'm going downstairs."

Maddie sat up and groaned. "You're not going to let me sleep this holiday, are you?"

But Jo was already in her robe and slippers. She opened the bedroom door quietly and tiptoed down the stairs, slowing her steps as she neared the bottom. She peered from around the banister to the front door and waited.

"Well?" Maddie whispered, startling Jo from a few stairs above.

"Shhh!" Jo said loudly, and she inched toward the front door. She reached her hand out to the doorknob, and just as she laid her fingers on it, the noise came again.

Bang, bang, bang!

But it was not a knock at the door. Jo swung around to face the sitting room. There on the fireplace stoop, Oma Kronenberg stood in her nightcap and gown, gripping a small hammer in one hand and a nail in the other.

"Oma?" Maddie called softly to her.

She spun around and tucked the hammer behind her back. "Oh!" she gaped. "You frightened me, my dears. What are you doing awake at this hour?"

"We heard banging," Jo replied. "Do you need some . . . er . . . help?"

Oma Kronenberg sighed and stepped down from the fireplace. She set the hammer and nails on the mantel and sat down in her rocking chair. "It's been so long since there were children in the house," she said. "There weren't any nails in the mantel to hang your stockings from." She held up two red stockings, filled with treats for Maddie and Jo. "The children here in Germany hang their stockings early in December, but I know you're missing Christmas in America . . . so here you are. Merry Christmas," she said. "Now's as good a time as any!"

The girls were thrilled. Opening their Christmas stockings was one of their most favorite things about the holiday in Boston.

"They're wonderful," Jo said, her eyes sparkling. Each stocking contained dried fruit and nuts, candy, a tiny bottle of perfume, a wooden whistle, and a knitted hat.

"Did you make these hats, Oma?" Maddie asked.

Oma Kronenberg nodded her head proudly. "I knitted them the night you arrived," she said. "They would have been sweaters if I'd had more time!"

Jo unwrapped the cellophane from a piece of hard candy and popped it in her mouth. "Oma," she said slowly, pushing the candy against her cheek. "Does the headmistress ever tell you about things—well, odd things—happening at Madame Molineaux's?"

Oma Kronenberg examined the glowing logs in the fireplace and fanned them with a leather bellows, sending sparkling orange embers zigzagging up the chimney. "Klara has told me many things about the school," she said carefully. "But not this year. She's been rather quiet about it."

"The story I was telling at supper," Maddie continued. "The headmistress didn't want me to finish it. The bells, the ones we hear at school, aren't coming from Saint-Marcel. They're coming from somewhere inside the school."

"How can you be sure?" Oma Kronenberg asked.

"Well, when we were getting the candles from Claudette's shop in town, she took us up to her workshop. From the fifth-floor windows, we could see the clock tower up close. The belfry is empty. The bells were stolen in the summer."

Oma Kronenberg looked down. "That's certainly troubling news . . . Those weren't just ordinary bells."

"What do you mean, Oma?" Jo asked, rummaging back through her stocking for another treat.

"Those bells came to Saint-Marcel from aboard a ship, long, long ago. And the bells, well—they were already very old when they arrived." She shook her head with worry. "Did Claudette say who might have stolen them?"

Maddie and Jo shook their heads.

"She didn't," Jo said, scowling. "But we think it's related to all the other strange happenings at school."

Oma Kronenberg's eyes lit up and narrowed under her gray, wiry eyebrows. "Strange happenings? Like what?"

Jo was so happy to be telling a grown-up about the mysteries that the words flew out of her mouth. "There's a portrait—a life-size portrait, on the administration hallway by the headmistress's office. It has an old tapestry hidden behind it—and we're almost positive all the other portraits at school have tapestries behind them, too. And there's a photograph that the headmistress has in her office—taken from high up in a plane—of the campus. She started to tell us that she had been looking for something, but never said another word about it."

"And there's a boy who's been spying on the school. He wrote us a riddle telling of thieves who come out at night at the school and hide treasures in a secret chimney," Maddie added.

"*And* there's a girl who disappears somewhere in the school every night, somewhere very cold, after midnight. We caught her in the library once, acting like she had come in from the window. But the window is more than fifteen feet from the ground!"

Oma Kronenberg's curiosity was piqued. She hadn't solved a mystery since the time she found the neighboring shepherd's lost little lamb, Flocki, asleep in her flower garden after a feast of petals. "Tapestries behind portraits . . . that sounds like someone's trying to hide them, don't you think?"

Maddie and Jo nodded.

"And the girl who disappears every night into the cold . . . have you followed her?"

220

"We wanted to," Jo explained. "But the one night we had the chance, she didn't leave her bed. It was the night before we came to Mittenwald."

"Well," Oma Kronenberg said, shrugging, "that will have to wait until you get back to school. But the thieves who come out at night . . . and hide treasures in a chimney . . . have you looked in all the fireplaces?"

"That's the trouble," Maddie said. "This is a special chimney. The boy wrote that the thieves hide the treasures in a smoke-stack growing out of the lawn. And he said that the fireplace is never lit."

The old woman looked confused. "But why would a chim-ney be growing out of the lawn, unless . . ."

She scanned the room aimlessly as she tried to picture it in her mind.

"Unless what?" the girls asked impatiently.

"Unless the fireplace was underground."

Maddie nodded slowly. "That makes sense . . . Who would light a fireplace underground?"

Jo leaned closer to the old woman. "Oma, do you know of any underground chambers at Madame Molineaux's?"

"No," she said quietly. "I've always been told that a frozen lake ran under the school."

"That's what we were told, too," Maddie agreed. "I never considered anything being underneath the school except rock and ice. But a secret underground chamber would explain why a smokestack might grow out of the lawn."

"And maybe that's where Rosemary is going after midnight: *underground*," Jo said excitedly. "That would explain why her boots are freezing cold, but not wet or snowy when she comes in!"

Maddie put her hands on Oma Kronenberg's knee and smiled broadly. "Oma, you've been a great help!"

"I don't know about that, Maddie. I still can't tell you why you're hearing bells at school if they've been stolen from the clock tower in Saint-Marcel."

"First things first," Jo said. "You've helped us crack into the riddle, and, hopefully, that will help us solve the rest of the mysteries!"

The floor creaked above their heads as footsteps stamped across the upstairs hallway.

"Oma?" the headmistress called in a raspy voice. "What's going on down there?"

Oma Kronenberg pulled her finger to her lips to hush the girls. "Nothing, Klara," she answered in her sweetest voice. "I'm just getting some milk. Go back to bed."

Jo giggled at the thought of someone telling the headmistress to go back to bed. It wasn't often that she saw anyone ordering Kronenberg around. The footsteps creaked back toward the end of the hall, and the girls heard the door close with a click.

"It's funny," Maddie whispered when she was sure the headmistress was back in her room. "That's exactly what we do when we're caught out of bed at school. We say we're getting milk, and then we wait for the footsteps down the hall and the click of the door."

"Well," Oma Kronenberg said with a mischievous smile. "We don't have to tell Klara about our detective work *or* that you were out of bed. Just go quietly back to your room. Tiptoe."

She took the girls' stockings and hung them from the single nail she had nailed into the hearth.

"And be sure to act surprised in the morning for your stockings, yes?"

Maddie dropped one last walnut back into her stocking and gave her best surprised face, with an open mouth and her hands on her cheeks. Jo's eyebrows shot up and she covered her mouth with her hand in a dramatic performance.

"That will do," Oma Kronenberg said with a smile, and she shooed the girls back upstairs.

Once the girls were in their room, Jo smiled and held something behind her back. "It may be *very, very* early on Christmas morning," she admitted in the dark room, "but it still counts." She handed a tiny gift wrapped in a handkerchief to her sister.

"Wait," Maddie said, reaching underneath her side of the bed. "I've got one for you, too." She pulled out a paper sack tied with green twine. "You unwrap yours first." Jo untied the twine and reached into the sack. Inside was a wooden slingshot with a bag of three round rocks. "I carved it myself," Maddie stated proudly. "And those were the smoothest rocks I could find along the lakeshore."

Jo placed a rock into the thick rubber-band sling and pulled back, careful not to let go inside the tiny room. She closed one eye and practiced aiming.

"I love it, Maddie," she said, and put the slingshot on the bedside table. "Now you open yours."

Maddie untied the handkerchief and held up what resembled a tiny purse with a long, braided leather strap.

"I—I love it, Jo." Maddie cooed, turning the object every which way. "Umm . . . what is it?"

Jo beamed. "It's a secret pocket. It goes like this," she said, looping the strap around her sister's waist.

"What's so secret about it?" Maddie asked, trying not to sound ungrateful.

"Well, it doesn't work so well over your nightgown. But if you were wearing your school uniform, you'd put it around your waist like a belt, but inside your shirt. That way, you can keep little things in it, and no one can see. Even if someone were to search your pockets, they wouldn't find this one!"

"Where'd you get it?"

"I made it," Jo said, her eyes shining. "I saw one advertised in one of Françoise's French magazines, so I cut up a belt and stitched the burlap on by hand."

"It's perfect. Thank you, Jo."

The girls hugged. "Merry Christmas, Sis," they said to each other, and finally went back to sleep.

Jo folded her arms and looked down at the trunk, already stuffed and overflowing with clothes. It had been almost impossible to close when she and her sister had left school, and now there were more things to take back with them: nesting dolls and hats and gloves from their parents, scarves and leather-bound journals from Henri, and the contents of their Christmas stockings. Even the headmistress had given the girls gifts: fancy black fountain pens and little bundles of Black Forest twigs that had been fashioned into graphite pencils.

Maddie squeezed through the narrow bedroom door from the hallway, carrying two floral-print hatboxes. "Not to worry," she said triumphantly. "Oma gave me these." She put the hatboxes down and filled them with their gifts. When she was done, she closed the lid of the trunk and jumped up to sit on it. "Are you sure we have everything?" she asked her sister.

"Positive. I checked twice." Jo walked around the trunk, forcing the clasps shut on each side. "I think we're ready," she said, looking around their cozy holiday bedroom. It was exciting to go back to Madame Molineaux's, to see their friends again, and to get on with solving the mysteries, but Christmas at the Kronenbergs' cottage had been so lovely, it was a bittersweet departure.

Oma Kronenberg was bundled up in her warmest winter clothes, waiting in front of the house to say good-bye. The headmistress handed the driver the last of her luggage and hugged her grandmother. "Good-bye, Oma. *Ich liebe dich*," she told her. She squeezed the old woman's shoulders tightly, kissed her forehead, and climbed into the car.

Maddie and Jo sandwiched the old woman between them for a hug.

"Good-bye, Oma Kronenberg," Jo said. "I'm so happy we met you."

"And thank you for giving us such a nice Christmas!" Maddie chimed in. "We'll give the headmistress your hatboxes and she can return them to you."

Oma Kronenberg shook her head. "No, no, girls. You keep them, and always remember your Oma Kronenberg." She leaned in and whispered to them, smiling. *"And write to me when you find the smokestack growing out of the lawn."*

Maddie and Jo nodded and joined their headmistress in the car. Oma Kronenberg waved both hands and blew kisses until the car turned onto the main road, heading back to Switzerland.

CHAPTER TWENTY–TWO

A Shortcut to Class

Maddie took a deep breath and gazed around at the lush trop-ical plants. The moist, warm air of the conservatory took the chill from her lungs, and when she closed her eyes, she could almost imagine she was in the jungle.

It had been nearly two weeks since the girls returned to Madame Molineaux's, and the bitter, icy cold of Switzerland in January restricted their detective work. The sky darkened early in the afternoon, the cold wind chapped the girls' faces as they crossed the grounds to their classrooms, and it was far more comfortable to be curled up in front of the library fire or snug-gled in bed with a book.

Luckily, Maddie's winter schedule gave her nearly an hour between morning classes, and she found the perfect bench to sit on, nestled in between banana plants. It was just enough time to relax before heading to Troxler's history lecture.

A low purr brought Maddie out of her jungle daydream. "I see you haven't forgotten about breakfast," she said to Musetta, who rubbed her gray-and-black bearded chin back and forth on Maddie's knee.

Maddie reached into her jacket pocket and retrieved small scraps of sausage and cheese. She had begun this routine with the Nata-lynx only days ago, but already they had grown to expect their morning treats.

"Today, you get the cheese," she said to Marcello, who took a pause from his bath to inspect her offering. "And you, Musetta, can have the sausage."

Marcello sniffed at the cheese politely before taking it between his sharp teeth, crouching down to eat. Musetta snatched the sausage from Maddie's outstretched hand and galloped off into the bushes, rustling the tropical plants as she headed into the most densely planted area of the conservatory.

Maddie shrugged and patted Marcello on the head. "Where did she run off to?" she asked him, half expecting an answer. He narrowed his eyes and purred heavily before standing on his hind legs to search her cape pocket for more breakfast leftovers.

"Ah-ah," she scolded. "That's for me." She held a slice of dry-cured ham and a piece of bread wrapped in a handkerchief, the mid-morning snack she had tucked away at breakfast. Marcello protested, meowing and nuzzling her hand with his nose. The rustling in the tropical leaves began again, this time from the corner of the conservatory, where the foliage and trees tangled themselves together in a wooded knot.

Maddie could see Musetta's tall, pointy ears poke up through the plants as she crept back toward the bench. She shot out of the little jungle and sat directly at Maddie's feet.

"*Meoooowwwwww,*" she demanded, and looked back and forth from Maddie's face to her pocket. She blinked her eyes a few times and flicked her bobbed tail back and forth.

Maddie sighed. "I guess I shouldn't bring it along and then not share, huh? I bet you smelled this ham from a mile away." She took the ham from her handkerchief and started to tear small pieces off for her feline friends, but Musetta had other plans for the meat. She bounded onto Maddie's lap and took the entire piece into her mouth, leaped back into the tropical plants, and headed back into the corner of the conservatory.

"Musetta!" Maddie shouted, more surprised than angry. "Just what do you think you're doing?"

She stuffed her handkerchief back into her pocket and ran after the wild cat. She ducked through the palm trees, brushed past the spindly orchids, and crawled into the small grove of fruit trees. A thick layer of climbing ivy covered the conservatory walls, and Maddie stopped her hunt in front of a messy bramble of vines and sticks.

"Musetta?" she called sweetly. "Musetta, show me where you're hiding."

But there was no response.

Maddie crouched down and picked up a long stick. She poked at the ivy to bring the elusive cat out from her hiding place, but found only an old potting soil sack, wet and ragged under the leaves. She brushed off her knees and began to walk back to her bench when Musetta, peeking out through an opening in the thick vines, gave a quick meow.

"There you are, girl," Maddie said, and took a cautious step toward her. In a flash, Musetta pulled her furry head back into the hole, and with a few more rustling sounds, she was gone. Maddie got down on all fours and peered into the leafy opening with one eye.

Under a canopy of ivy, a clearing had been made in front of a rectangular hole cut into the wall. A rusty metal grille leaned against the wall covering half of the hole, and there, Musetta was provided with the perfect entryway into a secret hiding place. Maddie ripped the vines away and crawled toward the metal grille.

"Musetta?" she whispered into the cavernous space behind the grille. Maddie pushed at the iron grid and slid it all the way over. She took a deep breath and put her head inside.

The air was cold and wet in the dark space, and Maddie couldn't see a thing—not even the floor. She reached backward, picked up a pebble from the ground, and dropped it into the darkness. It landed with a *clack* onto a hard floor within a second of being dropped. *The floor can't be that far below me,* she thought.

She took her head out from the space and sat upright in the clearing under the ivy. She needed the light from the conservatory, but she needed the cover of the vines to keep her exploration a secret. She poked her head back through the ivy, looked twice to make sure no one else was passing through, and then pulled down enough vines from the thick canopy so that the light could shine through and make its way inside the hole.

She poked her head back through the hole. *This isn't a cave,* she thought as she examined the area behind the stone wall. *This is a tunnel.* With enough light to see the tunnel walls and floor, Maddie crept through the hole and lowered herself onto the cold, damp ground.

I'll just go and find Musetta, and then I'll turn back, she promised herself silently. She looked down at her wristwatch. She had twenty minutes before Troxler's history class began, and that was plenty of time to find the cat and be in her seat before the bell rang. She would take Jo back to the tunnel with her after class.

Jo tapped her eraser on her desk. *Where is Maddie?* she wondered. *The bell is about to ring, and Troxler is watching her seat like a hawk.*

She scanned the room from her seat in the back corner of the class. Every desk was occupied. Every one but her sister's. The ringing of the bell called the class to attention, and Troxler's face twisted into a smug grin.

"Well, ladies," she said, smacking her ruler against the palm of her hand as she paced across the front of the room. "It looks as though we will have spotless black boards tomorrow, courtesy of one very tardy Madeline Livingston. Would anyone like to venture a guess as to what is keeping her?" She scowled at Jo. "How about her twin sister? Any idea?"

Jo shook her head no. "I'm sorry, Professor, I'm not sure where she is," she said nervously. "But, I'm sure Maddie has a good—"

Troxler slapped her ruler against her desk. "No, no, *no*, Josephine. There is no need to make excuses for your sister. I shall enjoy having her serve detention, no matter what her reason for being late. Now, then. Open your books to page five hundred and seventy-eight."

Françoise turned around and gave Jo a puzzled look. Maddie was usually early to class, and certainly was never late. But all the students knew—it didn't matter why—any girl who arrived to Troxler's class after the bell rang would serve detention.

Jo couldn't concentrate on Troxler's lecture. *Is Maddie trying to get in trouble, just to get back into Kronenberg's office?* she pondered. *No, that's Val's job, and Maddie knows it.* She doodled aimlessly in her notebook, glancing up at the professor every now and then to appear as though she were listening. She lowered her gaze back onto her drawings and saw something out of the corner of her eye: a small stick poking through the metal grille in the wall next to her desk.

Every ounce of Jo's self-control was not enough to keep her long-winded gasp bottled inside. It escaped right during the introduction to the Franco-Prussian war, and stopped the professor mid-sentence. The entire class whipped around in their seats and stared at Jo. Troxler marched straight toward her desk, and the stick that poked through the metal grille disappeared back into the darkness.

The professor folded her arms. "Josephine, if you think my introduction to the war is frightening, perhaps you should prepare yourself for what's coming in the next few days' lessons. Am I right, Josephine? Is that what has caused your outburst?" Troxler didn't wait for an answer. "Or perhaps," she said, putting on a phony sympathetic expression, "you're just frightened to be in class without your sister."

Jo stared at her notebook, unable to speak. If the stick coming from the grille in the wall wasn't enough to unnerve her completely, Troxler's condescending tone made her feel as though she were an inch tall. She could barely move.

"*Well!?*" the professor demanded, inching her ruler toward Jo's nose.

"Perhaps she could answer you if you would give her enough space to breathe some air," a voice from the front of the class said calmly.

It was Françoise.

She stood beside her desk, unwavering as all the students' eyes turned to focus on her instead of Jo. Troxler spun around on her heel and looked outraged.

"Perhaps," she said slowly, "young ladies who speak without being spoken to should join their truant friend in detention. How does that sound?"

"I suppose that sounds fair," Françoise replied without emotion, and sat back down.

Val had little time to think. If she was going to get into trouble with the rest of her roommates, she had to act fast. "And," Val said in a voice louder than any of her classmates had ever heard her use, "I agree!" She shot up from her desk and stood quivering, looking frantically around the room.

Troxler sighed and looked more annoyed than angry. "Exactly what are you agreeing to, Valentina? Do you even know?"

"I . . . I agree that . . ." She looked back at Jo. "Jo should get some air."

"Let me tell you what I think," Troxler said, her tight lips forming a wicked scowl. "I think you will *sit down* and *remain silent*, and I also think that you shall join Françoise and Madeline in detention. Is that clear?"

Val smiled and sat back down. "Yes," she said, looking satisfied, her cheeks flushed from all the attention.

The professor threw up her hands. "Is there anyone else who would like to be assigned detention before I continue the lesson?"

No one spoke.

"Good. Now, turn your pages." She drifted back to the front of the room.

Jo slowed her breathing. The commotion was making her feel as if the temperature in the room was rising. *Just calm down, Jo,* she told herself, and she turned her head slowly to look back at the grille. There it was again: the small stick poking out from the grille. It came farther and farther through the hole, and then dropped to the ground.

In a flash, Jo recognized the stick. It was one of the twig pencils Kronenberg had given the twins for Christmas. That meant only one thing: Maddie was behind the wall.

Jo bent down and picked up the pencil as if she had dropped it, and squinted through the holes in the metal grille. She couldn't see anything in the darkness except a small flash of white. Seconds later, a small handkerchief was stuffed through the grating to fall silently on the floor.

Jo coughed and bent over once more. She picked up the handkerchief and placed it under her notebook, careful to look as though she were still paying attention to Troxler's lecture. She slipped her hand under the notebook, spread the handkerchief out flat, and read the messy words, scrawled in pencil:

SCIENCE HALL. CONSERVATORY. BEHIND IVY IN BACK CORNER. COMPASS. TORCH.

Jo crammed the handkerchief into her pocket and stood up timidly. "Excuse me, Professor?"

Troxler let her head fall to the side and closed her book. She sighed heavily and closed her eyes. "What could it possibly be now, Josephine?" she asked slowly in an exasperated tone.

"I'm sorry . . . I'm feeling . . . umm . . . queasy. I think I *do* need some air."

The professor shooed her away with a dramatic wave of her hand. "Five minutes. Need I tell you what awaits you if you should fail to return to class?"

Jo shook her head. "No, Professor. I know. Detention." She walked out of the classroom, shut the door behind her, and ran off to the Room Five dormitory.

Maddie let herself down from the ledge as quietly as she could, but the cold soles of her leather boots still made a smacking sound as they hit the floor. She looked back up at the grille. Light from the classroom shone through the holes in the metal, speckling her clothes and the floor with dots of white. She looked down at her wristwatch.

I'll give her twenty minutes, she thought. She squatted down to the ground and wrapped her hands around her ankles.

"Cold leather, cold laces, no ice, no snow," she whispered out loud. "I'm on to you, Rosemary Byron."

Jo rummaged through her wardrobe, tossing her clothes onto the bed. *Where did I put that?* she thought as she struggled to find her trusty compass. She searched through every pocket on every garment, but still couldn't find it. Maddie was stuck in a secret passageway, and there was no use in going to find her sister if Jo couldn't get them both back out.

Finally, Jo spotted it wedged between wooden slats in the back of the bottom drawer. "Aha!" Jo exclaimed, and snatched it from its hiding place. She grabbed the compass and stuffed everything back in her wardrobe. She shoved her hand under Françoise's mattress, retrieved the torch, and dashed off to the science hall.

Maddie looked at her wristwatch. It had been almost twenty minutes since Jo had left Troxler's classroom. *At least I'm not missing history class entirely,* she thought as she listened to the professor's muffled lecture through the metal grating. She had often wondered what could possibly make Troxler's lectures more painful to endure, and now she had her answer: having to sit in the freezing cold to listen to them.

Footsteps tapped the floor from a distance.

"Jo?" Maddie whispered.

The footsteps came closer, and finally, a chilly Jo emerged from the darkness, the torch casting a soft glow around her.

"Maddie!" she breathed. "Where *are* we?"

Maddie pointed up at the metal grille. "We're in history class," she said, smiling. "Just on the wrong side of the wall."

"But how did you find it?"

"I followed Musetta into the tunnels from the conservatory. It felt like I was Alice on her way into Wonderland, with Musetta playing the part of the white rabbit. She disappeared into the ivy with my morning snack."

Riiinggg!

The bell cut Maddie off with a shrill clanging. History class was finally over, and the twins heard their classmates closing their books and walking out of the classroom.

"I guess I'll be in detention, too," Jo said quietly.

"I tried to make it to class," explained Maddie. "I got turned around in the tunnels, but I could tell that I was in the history hall after a while. The tunnels are actually a fast way to get here," she said. "But I couldn't find a way back into the building."

"Well," Jo said, turning in a circle to check her compass. "You managed to cut clear across campus from the science hall! Could you tell that you passed under the dining hall? Did you see any underground fireplaces?"

Maddie shook her head.

"I couldn't tell what was five feet in front of my face, Jo. It's dark in here without a torch."

Jo tilted the compass to show her sister.

"We're at the northernmost point of the school," she said. "If the tunnels go under every building, we could head south and be at the stables."

"It's just before lunch," Maddie said. "I don't think anyone would be around to see us, except the horses."

Jo held her compass with one hand and the torch with the other, and the girls followed the tunnels south. "Let's just hope there's a way out this time."

Millie set her tray down and looked at the two empty chairs across from her. "No sign of them yet?" she asked her friends.

"None yet," said Nixie. "And who knows where Jo stepped out to 'get some air?' I thought she would come back to class for sure."

"Would you have come back after all that?" Françoise asked, raising her eyebrows. "I've never seen Troxler so angry. Jo could have seen straight up her nose, she was standing so close."

"Is that what made you say what you did?" Val asked quietly.

Millie laughed. "What was that, Val?" she said, cupping her hand around her ear. "I couldn't hear you. Louder, please, in your history class voice."

Val smiled bashfully.

"I said what I said," Françoise replied, "because I happen to know that if you serve detention for Troxler, she makes you choose your punishment. And if it's not tedious or boring enough, she makes you choose again."

"Let me guess," Safi said, folding her arms. "You're going to suggest something to do with the paintings so you can check them for hidden tapestries."

"Exactly."

"Then I'm going to choose dusting Kronenberg's office," Val said excitedly. "That way, I can get a good look at that photograph." She tilted her head and narrowed her eyes. "I think I may have to get in trouble more often. That was fun."

Nixie perked up and rose out of her chair.

"Here they come!" she squealed.

Millie yanked Nixie back down into her seat.

"Let's not alert the entire dining hall, Nixie. No one else needs to know why those two were missing."

The girls at Rosemary's table eyed Maddie and Jo as they passed. Rosemary made a comment under her breath, and her friends made lousy efforts at muffling their giggles. She leaned back, narrowed her eyes, and stared down the twins all the way to their table.

Maddie and Jo slipped into their chairs, chilled to the bone and out of breath.

"Have we got a story for you," Jo laughed, grabbing a slice of bread off Nixie's tray.

Safi picked pieces of straw from Maddie's cape. "You smell like a herd of antelope," she said, wrinkling her nose at the twins.

"Correction, Safi," Jo said, giving her own hair a sniff. "We smell like horses."

"I could use a bath for sure," Maddie admitted. "But it was worth it. Ladies, I think we're close to solving this mystery."

"You missed it, Maddie," Nixie gushed. "Jo and Françoise *and* Val all got detention with you. Val was especially dazzling."

"I didn't miss it, Nixie. Just the opposite! I heard the whole thing from behind the classroom wall." Maddie leaned in and lowered her head. "I found secret tunnels that connect the whole school."

The girls drew their breath. Even though the dining hall was loud with chatter, you could have heard a pin drop at the Room Five table.

"How did you find them?" Safi asked.

"Musetta led me to a secret entrance. And," Maddie said, looking straight at Safi, "it was freezing cold down there. The leather on my boots and my laces were chilled, but not wet or icy. I just *know* that's where Rosemary's been going at night."

Safi's eyes sparkled with anticipation. "Then that's where I'll catch her."

"And," Jo continued, "remember when we told you that Oma Kronenberg figured that if the smokestack was growing out of the lawn, the fireplace must be underground?"

The girls all nodded.

"Well, the tunnels are the perfect place for 'the fireplace that's never lit.'"

"You didn't see it while you were down there?" asked Millie.

"Well, no. But we can say for sure that it wasn't on the way from the science hall to the history hall, or from there to the stables."

"So *that's* where you acquired your stunning perfume," Françoise joked, leaning in for a good sniff of the twins' capes.

"I'm just glad we actually found a way out, even if we had to climb up through a trapdoor and into a smelly horse pen," Maddie huffed. "It's a real maze in the tunnels. You'll see."

"When? When will we see? Tonight?" Nixie demanded.

"Everyone's in trouble for now," Jo pointed out. "Let's let things die down for a moment. If we get expelled, then we'll never have a chance at solving this mystery."

Nixie pushed out her lip in disappointment.

"She's right," Françoise agreed. "Everyone act normal. Four of us are already going to serve detention. We don't need everyone's eyes on us. Besides, I believe we already have an audience." She nodded in Rosemary Byron's direction.

"Two weeks," Maddie said. "And then we go."

CHAPTER TWENTY-THREE

THE DETENTION HEARING

"Stop it!" Maddie swung her head around to grimace at Jo, who was intent on tripping her sister as they walked across the grounds to the entrance of the dining hall. It was a small processional: Françoise was first, followed by Val, then Maddie, and finally Jo. The four girls marched quickly behind Professor Troxler through the frosted lawn, awaiting their detention assignments.

"Keep up, ladies, keep up," Troxler barked in her most military tone. "Being tardy for my class is one thing, but being tardy for your detention hearing is quite another." She turned her head back to stare at the twins. "And don't think that being the headmistress's holiday houseguests will help you. You'll serve along with the rest of the girls." Troxler had gathered the girls after history class and led them through the crowds of students, all of whom either looked on them with pity or giggled at their misfortune.

Françoise held her head high, her mouth situated in a subtle smirk, and walked with a relaxed confidence. Val wrung her hands and looked around nervously. The other students were staring, and Val was sure that most of them hadn't ever noticed her before. Maddie was used to getting in trouble, and her mind was on other things besides meeting Kronenberg, like the scheme she would cook up to get back into the tunnels. And Jo, well, Jo didn't seem to be worried in the least, and she plodded along casually, using her sister's heel as a soccer ball when the mood struck her.

They proceeded through the empty dining hall, into the Grand Corridor, and out into the main hall. They turned down the administration hallway, and, as they passed the portrait of Elisabeth of Bohemia, Françoise turned back to the other girls and raised her eyebrows. Her repair of the long rip, while certainly not the work of a professional, was fairly unnoticeable.

"*Parfait,*" she mouthed to them, and gave a proud *okay* sign.

Troxler stopped just before the headmistress's heavy wooden door. "Not a word until you're spoken to, do you understand?"

"Yes, Professor," the girls sang in unison.

Troxler rapped on the door three times with her fist, and the headmistress opened the door graciously.

"Good morning, ladies. Please come in," she said gently. Two pots of steaming tea and six cups and saucers had been put out on the table.

Jo scanned the office for any sign of sandwiches or tarts, but found none. This would certainly be different from the first tea service she and Maddie had there.

The headmistress closed the door once everyone had shuffled in. She gestured for the girls to sit down, but Troxler spoke up in protest.

"Ahem," she cleared her throat. "Klara, the ladies aren't here for a tea party. They're here to be assigned detention, and I have a class beginning shortly. If we could—"

The headmistress held up her hand and smiled.

"Professor, we do not simply cart students into my office and dream up punishments. You must know that by now."

She looked at the girls, who still stood in front of the sofa and chairs, afraid to take their seats.

"It's Professor Troxler's first year at Madame Molineaux's, too, did you know?"

The girls shook their heads.

Troxler stiffened and squared her shoulders.

"It may be my first year at Madame Molineaux's, Headmistress, but I assure you I am no newcomer to discipline and punishment. Surely *you* know that by now, don't you, Klara?"

Val gave a nervous cough and stared down at her shoes. Whatever was going on between the headmistress and the professor was making her very uncomfortable.

The headmistress smiled and changed her tone. "Well, Flora, I suppose I do, and I suppose I don't. Let's just leave it at that. Ladies, sit down now, please. Tea?"

In a moment the girls were seated, ankles crossed, holding their teacups and saucers out in front of their laps.

The headmistress spoke as she poured. "I understand that you, Madeline, were not present for history class. Can you tell me why?"

Maddie looked into her teacup and hesitated. "I—I was in my bed. I didn't feel well."

"Ah," said the headmistress. "And you couldn't tell Josephine to let your professor know? And you didn't see the nurse?"

"Um—ah—" Maddie fumbled with her words. "I couldn't tell Jo because—"

"Because I wasn't with her. In fact, I was feeling ill myself," Jo offered awkwardly.

"Is that why you disrupted class and didn't come back after getting fresh air?" the headmistress coaxed, almost pushing Jo into saying the words.

Jo looked at the headmistress with suspicion. Why was she helping them? "Yes . . ." she replied slowly. "That's right."

The headmistress went on. "And Françoise, I was informed that you were very rude to Professor Troxler. Why was that?"

Françoise lifted her chin and looked the headmistress squarely in the eyes. "I was *also* feeling ill. I barely knew what I was saying, and I apologize."

The headmistress nodded and appeared satisfied. "And Valentina. I understand that—"

"Yes!" Val's teacup rattled against her saucer as she tried to keep a steady hold on it. She set her tea down and sat on her hands. "Yes, Headmistress. I also spoke out because I did not feel well."

The headmistress shrugged and looked to the professor as if to ask, *What more do you need to know?*

Troxler scoffed and folded her arms. "So that's it?" she demanded, glaring at each of the girls. "You were absent, disruptive, and rude because you weren't feeling well? And how is it that not one of you needed to visit the infirmary, or was missing from lunch or your other classes?"

Jo sighed and looked down. "Headmistress, we weren't sick. We were—"

MARY KNIGHT

"Tired!" Maddie shouted, interrupting her sister. Jo was terrible at playing along. "Er . . . we were unable to sleep because of . . . noises . . ." She looked at Professor Troxler. "You know what that's like, Professor, don't you? You were up all night before the holiday. Not one of us slept a wink, and we were so tired the next day that we felt ill."

Troxler looked at the girls sideways and narrowed her eyes. "And what was it that kept you awake?"

All four girls turned to face one another. This story was becoming more and more complicated, and no one had a good answer.

Françoise let the first thought that sprang to her mind escape from her lips. "Howling." She looked as shocked as the rest of the girls that the word had come out of her mouth.

Maddie shot Françoise a desperate look and nodded slowly, wondering how she would explain.

"Yes, the awful . . . howling." She bit her lip and looked to her roommates for help. "You see, we couldn't sleep because, well . . ."

Val's eyes darted around the room for inspiration. She had to come up with something fast. And then she saw it, a photograph of Professor Natalio with Musetta and Marcello, the Nata-lynx.

"Cats!" she spat out frantically. "The cats were howling so very loudly that we couldn't sleep."

And that was it. That was the explanation that all four girls nodded their heads to, the one they would have to stick to and defend, no matter how ridiculous it sounded.

Troxler threw up her hands and shook her head. "Nonsense!" she snarled. "That's the most outrageous thing I've heard all year. Professor Natalio keeps those cats in pens at night, and it's a good thing he does. If I caught them anywhere near my hallway, I'd cut off their ears to match their bobbed tails."

244

The girls' eyes widened. Professor Troxler's morbid disposition was unwavering, even for cats.

"Now, now, Professor, that's *enough*," the headmistress snapped. "I'll talk to Professor Natalio personally about the cats to make sure they stay in their pens during the night. Come to think of it," she said with a warm smile, "I think I might have heard howling the past few nights, too."

"And the detention?" Troxler demanded.

The headmistress nodded reluctantly. "Ladies, I understand you were distressed from not sleeping, but the rules are the rules, you know."

Françoise piped up. They hadn't come all this way to walk away *without* detention—how else would they complete their quests? "We know, Headmistress, and we're very sorry. We understand what we did was wrong, and we'll serve our detention. Maybe we could do something to beautify the school."

Troxler shook her head and smirked. "Oh yes, I bet you'd like that, wouldn't you, dear? Planting bulbs in the flower beds, or combing the kitties? That sounds nice. What it doesn't sound like is *detention*."

"Actually, Professor, I was considering an offer to dust every portrait frame in the castle. I walk by them every day and they are quite dusty," Françoise said coolly.

Troxler didn't budge.

"And, Headmistress," Val added, "perhaps I could dust your office. It's very beautiful, but from where I'm sitting, I can see some . . ." She ran her finger across the outer edge of the tea table. "Unnecessary dirt."

The headmistress looked slightly embarrassed. "Ahem, very well, ladies, as long as Professor Troxler approves, that will be fine. Professor?"

Troxler looked displeased and said nothing.

"Must I remind you, Professor, that we do have an important guest coming to tour the school next month?" the headmistress asked innocently. "I think we want everyone and everything to look their best, don't we?"

The professor forced a tight-lipped smile. "That's right, Klara, we do," she remarked smugly. "A *very* important guest, at that. I suppose that will be fine then, ladies," she said to Val and Françoise. "But how about those two?"

"We could clean the blackboards in the history hall," Maddie suggested dryly. *Surely, that's boring enough for Troxler,* she thought.

Kronenberg tapped her chin with her index finger. "I believe Professor Natalio is in need of some assistance with the goats and Albert up on their rooftop," she said. "Perhaps you could help him with that?"

Jo couldn't help but smile. She had been awaiting the chance to play with the goats and pet the giant, sweet Pyrenean Mountain Dog, and here, at a detention hearing, was her opportunity. "We'll do it, of course," she answered enthusiastically.

"Just what will we be doing?" Maddie asked sweetly. "Feeding them? Combing them?"

The headmistress shook her head and gave them a sympathetic look. "I'm not quite sure, but I don't think he'll need you until the early spring. Something about the thawing of the snow and the droppings."

"The *droppings?*" Jo repeated. "What kind of droppings?"

"I assume droppings from the goats and the dog," the headmistress replied, trying to keep a positive tone. "I'm sure it won't be that bad . . ." Her voice trailed off.

Françoise smiled and looked at her feet. Val looked disgusted, and Maddie and Jo stood in disbelief.

Professor Troxler straightened her bodice and huffed, finally looking satisfied. "Well, ladies," she said, "I think that will do some justice. Thank the headmistress for tea."

"Thank you, Headmistress Kronenberg," the four girls said in unison, and they filed out of the office behind Troxler.

CHAPTER TWENTY-FOUR

A Midnight Meeting

The two weeks after Maddie and Jo came out of the secret tunnels seemed to last two years. The only thing the rest of the girls could do was count down the minutes until they would finally get to go in. But tonight, that moment had nearly arrived.

It was suppertime. The rest of the students in the dining hall were chatting and laughing, but the Room Five table was studying and planning. The girls slid their trays aside and stared at the map Françoise had drawn.

"Okay, Safi," Jo instructed. "I'll be hiding behind the library drapes before midnight. I'm almost positive Rosemary enters and exits the tunnels right here, in this area." She traced a small circle on the map with her finger.

"Right," Safi nodded. "I'll follow behind her when she leaves our room and I'll meet you there. Then we can go in after her."

"But don't forget," Maddie reminded her. "Knock twice on our door before you go into the library so we know to run to our stations. Millie and I are going to wait at the tunnel entrance in the conservatory, and Françoise and Val will be in the stables. Nixie will stand guard in our dormitory."

Nixie crossed her arms and rolled her eyes.

"If you get lost or separated, just whistle," Maddie continued. "Try not to talk too loud. We don't want Rosemary to know we're down there with her. Got it?"

All the girls nodded.

"Eat your suppers, ladies," Françoise ordered. "It's going to be a long night."

Jo slipped behind the drapes in the dark library. The heavy fabric grew hot as she breathed into it, and she wondered how long she'd have to stand straight against the wall before Rosemary got there. Her wristwatch had read 11:45 as she'd left the Room Five dormitory.

I bet she won't come in for a good twenty minutes, Jo reasoned, figuring she could relax for a bit before the excitement started. She crouched down on her knees, settled into a comfortable position, and sighed. "Okay, Rosemary," she announced quietly into the curtains. "I'm ready when you a—"

The doorknob turned. Jo shut her mouth in an instant, held her breath, and poked her head out from behind the curtains. The library door opened, and the dim light from the hallway spilled over the carpet like a wave crashing on the shore, retreating as the door closed again. Rosemary walked toward the window and turned down the last long row of bookshelves.

Jo crawled to an armchair and took cover behind its high back, keeping her eye on her target. Rosemary stopped just before the far wall, pulled the rug up, and lifted a large brass ring from the floor.

A trapdoor, just like the one in the stables! Jo thought. She watched Rosemary disappear down the trapdoor, the rug falling back into place as if nothing had happened. Seconds ticked by. Jo kept her crouched position and waited.

Where are you, Safi?

Safi burst through the library door just as Jo completed her thought.

Jo popped up from behind the armchair. "Let's go, let's go! We're going to lose her!"

"Go *where*?" Safi whispered. "You're the one who saw how she got in. Lead the way!"

Jo ran to the wall and threw the rug aside. She lifted the ring and showed Safi the steep stairs into the tunnel. Safi shuddered from the cold blast of air that came up through the entrance. She switched on the torch and stepped carefully down the stairs with Jo following closely behind.

"Okay, Nixie. You know what to do," Françoise said as she pushed her friend out of the Room Five dormitory into the hallway. Millie, Val, and Maddie crouched behind her, waiting for the signal that the coast was clear.

A few moments later, they heard Nixie's low dove call from the end of the hallway. Françoise and the rest of the girls slipped out the door and ran as lightly as they could down the first-year hallway to the main hall entrance.

"I've decided I need to go, too," Nixie whispered, her eyes hopeful. "Should I come to the stables or the conservatory?"

Françoise shook her head. "Nixie, you're the lookout. If you don't stay, who will make sure it is safe for us to come back?"

Nixie frowned and folded her arms.

"Next time, Nixie, we promise!" Maddie said impatiently. "We have to go *now*."

The girls ran off down the Grand Corridor, leaving a very frustrated Nixie to guard the hallway. She shook her finger in the air and scolded an imaginary version of herself. "*You* have to miss the fun, naughty Nixie," she said. "*You're* supposed to stay here while *we* get to go into the secret tunnels. Hmphh."

She stamped her foot against the hard stone in the main hall, sending a loud smack echoing against the high walls.

"Who's there?" a voice demanded from another hallway.

Nixie froze. Her eyes darted back and forth to each hallway entrance as she tried to figure out where the voice had come from. She could hear the faint, muffled sound of footsteps on the carpet, but still couldn't tell where they were walking.

"Hello?" the voice called again, closer, and Nixie identified the harsh voice. It was, unmistakably, Professor Troxler—and she was approaching the main hall from the administration hallway.

Nixie panicked. She had already used the hot milk excuse at the start of the school year, and if Troxler caught her out of bed now, she would surely think that Nixie was the student responsible for keeping her awake before the Christmas holiday.

Nixie tiptoed quickly back to the first-year hallway and took the stairs two at a time in her hurry to get back to Room Five. But clumsy footing sent Nixie stumbling, and she landed elbows-first on the top step. She lay still for a moment. Had she fallen too loudly? She pushed herself back up onto her feet, looked down the hall, and froze once more: Kronenberg was at the end of the hallway, locking the door to her chambers. She would be turning around at any moment.

Nixie was trapped. Kronenberg was coming toward her from the first-year hallway, and Troxler would enter the main hall from the administration hallway in only seconds. She had to act quickly.

In a flash, she darted into the dark, dungeon-like utility corridor to the left of the first-year hallway. She hid in the shadows and caught her breath, waiting for the inevitable meeting of the professor and the headmistress.

Troxler was first into the main hall. Her slippers tapped on the stone floor, then thudded softly on the central rug. Moments later, two sets of footsteps could be heard. Kronenberg had reached the main hall as well.

The two women met on the rug and stood three feet apart.

Troxler pasted an insincere smile on her face. "Klara! What a surprise to see you out of bed at this hour," she said sarcastically. "Trouble sleeping?"

The headmistress stared intently at the professor's cruel blue eyes. "Just what is it you're taking from us now, Flora?"

"There aren't many more things to take, are there?" Troxler replied, looking around the massive main hall. "That is, as long as you keep hiding them."

Kronenberg didn't even blink. "I don't know what you're talking about, Flora." She cast her arms out wide and gazed around the main hall. "You've searched every inch of this school. I've even taken you to the tunnels and you have found nothing. You *could* take what you have and leave us alone."

"Well," Troxler said, toying with the headmistress. "I *could* take what we already have and leave, but I'm afraid it just wouldn't be enough. I think it is *you* who will be leaving in the end." She curtsied and began walking back to her chambers in the west wing of the castle. "Sleep well, Headmistress."

Nixie could hardly believe what she had just heard. Not only was Troxler taking things from the school, but she *and* Kronenberg knew about the tunnels!

The headmistress hung her head for a moment in the middle of the main hall. She looked so defeated that Nixie contemplated stepping out from the shadows of the utility corridor to console her, but Kronenberg sensed she was being watched.

"Hello?" she called out in a frustrated tone. She searched the darkness for signs of life, getting angrier by the second about her chance meeting with Professor Troxler.

Nixie held her breath and took one careful step backward.

"If I catch a student out of bed, I *will* expel her!" the headmistress called again, her usually pleasant voice wrought with bottled emotion.

Nixie took another step backward down the utility corridor. And another. And another and another, until she was almost to a dead end. She turned and could barely see the outline of a large crate near the back wall. She felt around in the darkness with her hands, and crouched behind it. She poked her head out and watched the distant headmistress walk out of the main hall.

That was close. Too close, she thought. She sighed and unfolded herself out of her crouched position, stretching out to sit cross-ankled on the floor. The floorboards creaked under her, groaning as if they hadn't been sat on in decades.

I need to warn the others. Kronenberg or Troxler—or both—could go down into the tunnels at any time. Maybe now! she thought. *But how will I get into the tunnels?*

She sat quietly and thought for a moment.

I bet I can run to the conservatory quicker than to the stables, she reasoned, and decided that enough time had passed. Surely by now, she wouldn't meet anyone unexpected on her way there. She would be careful.

Nixie grabbed on to a nearby shelf and pulled herself up from her dusty seat on the ground. Steadying herself and brushing off her skirt, she took a single step out of the shadows.

But that would be the last step that Nixie took in the utility corridor. The rotted wooden planks beneath her snapped and crumbled, sending Nixie plummeting feet-first into the darkness below.

CHAPTER TWENTY-FIVE

A CAT AMONG PIGEONS

Maddie sprang to attention. "Did you hear that?" she asked Millie.

"How could I not have heard *that*? I have ears, you know."

A muffled crash and a high-pitched yelp had echoed through the tunnel to Maddie and Millie's station at the conservatory just seconds beforehand.

"Maybe it was Jo and Safi," Millie muttered, not really believing the words herself.

"Or Rosemary," Maddie offered. "Françoise and Val are too far away at the stables to be heard. I think we should investigate."

"We can't leave. What if Jo and Safi come?"

Maddie thought for a second. Safi had taken the only torch. Maddie and Millie relied on the dim light shining from the conservatory through the ivy and into the tunnel entrance. "I've been through these tunnels in the dark before. You stay here, and I'll go see what happened."

"We're not supposed to split up!" Millie protested. The thought of being in the tunnels alone was more than she'd signed up for. *I should have traded posts with Nixie,* she thought in a moment of regret. But it was too late now, and Maddie had a determined look in her eye.

"It's okay," Maddie assured her. "If anything happens, just crawl back up into the conservatory. I'll come back as soon as I make sure the coast is clear."

"If you insist," Millie said, wringing her hands. "Just whistle if you need help."

Maddie nodded and took off down the tunnel.

Safi threw her arm out to bring Jo's steps to a halt. "I heard something."

They had been in the tunnels for a good five minutes with no sign of Rosemary.

"Heard what?" Jo asked.

"A crashing noise. Or maybe it was a door slamming. I don't know."

Jo pulled the hand-drawn map from her pocket. "We've passed under the dining hall already," she reasoned as she looked at the map. "But this tunnel forks ahead. Which way did the noise come from?"

Safi pointed behind them.

Jo shook her head. "That way goes back to the main hall and dormitories. Rosemary should be far ahead of us."

"Maybe it wasn't Rosemary."

Jo shuddered. "Then who would it be, Safi? Maddie and Millie are all the way in the science hall, and Françoise and Val are in the stables . . . If it's not Rosemary, I'm not sure I want to know who it is."

Suddenly, this wasn't the fun game of "Catch Rosemary Byron" that it started out to be. She and Safi were like sitting ducks with only a torch and a map, and the map's accuracy was rather questionable.

"These tunnels could go anywhere . . . *everywhere* . . . and we wouldn't know it yet," Safi said quietly.

Jo stiffened her posture. "Well, we're not going to catch Rosemary standing still. We have to go *somewhere*." She turned to her left. "At least if we go this way, we'll eventually run into Maddie and Millie at the science hall."

"And if Rosemary went the other way?" asked Safi.

Jo thought hard about the decision in front of her and took a deep breath in. "I'm going left toward the science hall. I'll be okay without the light; I've been this way before. You take the torch and head toward the history hall. One of us is bound to find her."

"How am I supposed to know where I am without a map?" Safi demanded.

Jo tore the map, ripping a straight line down the tunnel they were in.

"Here's your half. Just go straight until you come to a dead end and are forced to turn right. Then you'll know you're underneath the history hall. Keep going south, and you'll end up at the stables. Françoise and Val will be waiting for you there."

Safi nodded nervously. "Okay," she said. "I'll whistle if I need help. What if I take a wrong turn?"

"You won't," Jo assured her. "There are plenty of turns to take from the main tunnel, but none of them go far. They're all dead ends. If you get into one by mistake, just turn around." And with that, Jo took off into the darkness alone.

Nixie looked up at the hole in the ceiling. *Hilfe!* she called out in her mind, managing to keep her mouth shut and stay quiet. If Kronenberg and Troxler hadn't heard her crash through the floor, surely they would hear her yelling for help.

She inspected her body for cuts or sprains but found only sawdust shavings covering the back of her cape and stockings. She had landed squarely on a sawdust pile, barely missing a pointy shovel that had been dug into its side.

Nixie sat up and looked around, surrendering any ideas she had for climbing back out of the hole she'd tumbled down into. It was nearly twelve feet above her, and the edges of the wood were so splintered and sharp that any chance of pulling herself up through it was hopeless, even if there had been something to stand on. She looked in front of her and in back.

"Well, Nixie," she whispered out loud. "You got what you wanted. You're in the tunnels."

Her sense of direction was still intact, as she had remained facing the main hall from the utility corridor, even through her fall. The path in front of her led northeast, and likely under the first-year hallway where Jo and Safi had entered the tunnels.

Behind her, the path went west, and since there was no building directly west of where she was, this seemed the riskier option. She picked herself up, dusted her clothes off, and set out on the path in front of her.

Nixie had only taken a few dozen steps when she arrived at what appeared to be a door but was only planks of wood nailed across a sealed entryway.

"Locked out!?" she gasped. "No, no, please open," she pleaded quietly to the wooden planks, pushing and pulling on the rough boards until her fingers hurt. She turned around slowly, looking back toward the sawdust pile with defeat. She was alone. She was without a torch or a map. Not that one of Françoise's hand-drawn maps would have helped her; there had been no mention of a tunnel on the other side of their hallway. She would have to pioneer this tunnel herself.

"One foot in front of the other," she told herself as she walked by the sawdust to go west. She repeated the words she'd heard her father say so many times back home. "That's how you get from here to there." It would be another ten minutes before she knew where she was.

Maddie crept along the tunnel as quietly as she could, the faint light from the conservatory disappearing faster and faster with each step. Her eyes played tricks on her in the darkness, giving human shapes to stacks of crates, finding gnarled faces in the lumpy stone wall, and creating movement where there were only shadows.

Luckily, she had made this trip through the tunnel before. This time, however, she'd have to go only half as far. The tunnel leading back to the first-year library was only a few minutes ahead.

It came faintly at first: a sound easily mistaken for the echo of Maddie's own footsteps on the chilled stone floor. But within moments, it was unmistakable. Here were footsteps walking— no, *running*—toward her.

Her eyes searched for traces of orange light, or any sign that the person running toward her was carrying Françoise's torch. But none came. That meant the runner wasn't Safi or Jo. It had to be Rosemary.

We're supposed to catch her down here, not be bowled over by her! Maddie thought. She jumped into the nearest dead-end hallway and ducked into the corner, holding her knees as she crouched on the floor. She watched as a figure ran past the doorway, the gold Madame Molineaux's crest on the girl's cape gleaming for an instant as it caught the tunnel's last remaining light.

"Millie," Maddie said worriedly out loud. "Rosemary's headed right toward her." She peeked out the doorway of the dead-end hallway, turned back toward the conservatory, and ran on her tiptoes as quietly as her leather soles would let her.

Safi turned the corner underneath the history hall. She looked down at her half of the map. *Finally, this will take me to Françoise and Val,* she thought, the idea soothing her cold, goose-bumped skin. No amount of layered winter clothes could have made her comfortable in the damp, chilly air of the tunnel.

And then she heard it: a high-pitched, softly uttered squeal. *Was that a whistle?* she thought, trying to remember where each girl was supposed to be. *I shouldn't be close to anyone but Rosemary, and she doesn't know our whistle-for-help call.*

It came again, closer this time. Safi's ears perked up. It was definitely *not* a whistle.

She practically threw herself into the nearest dead-end hallway, standing tight against the wall. She turned off the torch and peered out of the shadows just in time to see a flash of gray run by the doorway. She rubbed her eyes and squinted in the dark.

Now, there were two little squeals.

Please don't let that be giant rats, she prayed silently. Safi could handle gazelle, monkeys, even elephants with ease, but rodents were another story. Especially giant rodents who lived in dark, secret tunnels.

Two more gray animals ran past the doorway. No sooner had they passed, then she heard the tiny squeak again, and one of the passersby turned around to look down Safi's way.

Nothing in here for you, nasty rodent, she thought, holding her breath and trying to stand still as a statue.

It came closer to her, creeping next to the stone wall.

"Go away! Get out of here!" her coarse whisper called. "Go away . . . kitty?"

A miniature version of a Nata-lynx looked up at Safi as it rubbed in and out of her ankles, its eyes glimmering a yellow-orange color in the darkness. She bent down and studied the little cat. Indeed, it was a petite copy of Marcello and Musetta: It had the same dotted gray-and-black coat, big fluffy feet, a bearded chin, and a bobbed tail.

"*Mwee-ah!*" it squeaked, arching its back under Safi's hand. She squatted down and lifted the kitten onto her lap. "What are you doing down here, little one?" she cooed to her new friend. Two more small cats dashed past the doorway. "And . . . um . . . how many brothers and sisters do you have?"

By now, the pitiful squeaks from down the tunnel had grown into a small chorus. The little cat looked up at Safi, gave a rumbling purr, and bounded off her lap to join in the commotion. "Wait!" she whispered, sad to lose the comfort of a warm, fuzzy friend in the cold tunnel. *That cat would have made a good scarf,* she thought, and imagined draping the purring kitten over the back of her neck.

She stepped carefully toward the doorway, fully intending to investigate. *They're just cats, Safi. Certainly, you're not afraid of a clowder of cats,* she told herself.

And then, silence.

No more peeps, no more squeaks. Just the sound of Safi's own breath at the doorway. And footsteps.

The footsteps walked casually, clunking around with no particular sense of urgency or direction.

Safi froze. It wasn't Jo. It wasn't Maddie or Millie, and it certainly wasn't Nixie. Was it Françoise? Val? She let out a whistle, just like she and the other girls had practiced, and waited. But no one responded, not even the small cats squeaked.

Instead, the footsteps began again, this time with a quicker pace. But they were going *away* from Safi, not toward her. She left the safe shadows of the dead-end, headed toward the footsteps, and found herself in a large open area. Despite the darkness, she could see what looked like a recessed cellar on the far wall. Two eyes lit up and glared at her from below. "Kitty?" she asked nervously.

All of a sudden, another pair of eyes, and another, and another appeared in the darkness. She switched on the torch.

Perched on wooden crates and iron racks were more than a dozen fluffy Nata-lynx kittens, half of them looking quite a bit older than the others. The kittens sat in front of brown sheets of paper piled with scraps of meat, fish, and cheese. *Quite a feast,* Safi thought.

She approached two kittens perched on a large metal baking rack. "Does Rosemary bring you supper every night?" she asked them, feeling instantly guilty for plotting against her roommate, who, as it appeared, was only leaving her bed at midnight to feed hungry kittens.

She reached for the larger kitten, aiming to give it a good scratch on the chin, but the cat puffed its fur and growled. "Okay, okay," Safi said, backing away. "I understand, you don't know me yet."

But the kitten hissed and shifted uneasily. The Nata-lynx was far from being full grown, but its broad paws and wide stance made a house kitten look like a toy.

"Here," she said, curling her fingers under and holding out the back of her hand from a distance. "You can smell me first." The kitten stood on its hind legs and swiped its paws at her hands.

"*Miyowww!*" it shrieked in protest and sprang off the metal rack into the air. The smaller kitten, startled, leaped high over Safi's head, its clumsy feet pulling the metal shelf down to the floor.

Clang! Bang!

It was chaos. All the cats, skittish and irritated by the bright light, scurried around the room, knocking into this and that. Safi dodged the kittens' attempts to pounce on her and ran into the recessed cellar nearby. It was a miniature room with a grated ceiling so low that she had to bend at her waist to fit inside. The gang of kittens scrambled around the room for another moment, their fright having turned to playfulness. Their leaps and bounds had become a game rather than a legitimate effort to escape from harm's way.

They flicked their bobbed tails and licked their paws, gathering side-by-side in front of the opening of the recessed cellar. Safi stared at the kitten lineup in front of her, amused that they had organized so quickly.

"Hunting Safietous, are you, little kitties?" she asked, snickering at the thought.

"*Hissssssss!*" one of the larger ones warned. Another uttered a low, rumbling growl. Safi's eyes widened as she realized that even though she was joking, the kittens weren't. Perhaps they really *were* hungry, and not just for table scraps.

Don't be scared of kittens, she chided herself. But the older kittens stood higher than her knees, and had feet the size of Madeleine cookies.

She moved slowly to one side, sure that if she could just get out of the recessed cellar and back into the main room, she would have enough space to kick and bat the kittens away. More than a dozen pairs of eyes followed her every move. The Nata-lynx kittens found this game quite entertaining, and one of them licked its chops.

"Eaten by a big, fluffy kitten," Safi whispered out loud, imagining the headlines in the Madame Molineaux's school newspaper. "*Not* the way I want to go." She edged past the last two cats, careful not to break eye contact with the line. Her next step would take her out of the recessed cellar.

She pushed her foot forward and planted her heel on the stone floor, and that's when she felt it: a cold, sharp claw digging into her leg.

"*Yow!*" she wailed at the top of her lungs, and shook her leg to free it from the claw. She glanced at the line of kittens, counting fifteen in all before she realized that it had not been a cat's claw that ripped her tights and scratched her leg. The real culprits of her injury—an iron poker and pitchfork—fell to the floor with a shrill clatter, sending the line of kittens scrambling back into the dark.

Safi tore at the bottom of her tights to free them from the sharp metal, leaving a strip of fabric tangled in the point of a pitchfork prong. *So much for not making any noise,* she thought, and despite her worry of being discovered by Rosemary, took off running down the tunnel to the stables.

A faint, metallic echo found its way through the tunnels to Nixie. She hadn't heard anything but the sound of her own footsteps and water dripping from the ceiling to the floor for the last five minutes. She had made her way through the darkness with cautious, tiny steps, and couldn't tell if her teeth were chattering from the cold or for fear of falling through another floor.

The echo conjured images in her mind of pirate prisoners, raking their copper cups back and forth across the metal bars of a dungeon jail, or wandering ghosts, rattling chains up and down the dormitory hallways.

That's ridiculous, Nixie, she comforted herself. *There aren't any pirate ships that sail on lakes, and you've been waiting all year to see a ghost and haven't yet.*

She gave a huff and a nod, but she was afraid all the same. Nixie liked ghost stories, but not when they involved her own voyage through dark, scary tunnels alone. She shuddered and quickened her pace.

After a few dozen steps, she nearly smacked face-first into a large wooden door. She had reached the end of the tunnel, and there was nowhere to turn. If this door didn't open, she would be trapped underground.

She tugged on the iron ring in the door. It didn't budge. Not even a *crack*, *squeak*, or *creak* came from the wooden planks. She pulled harder, twisting the ring back and forth. She pushed her feet into the stone doorsill, using all her might to pry the door open. It groaned softly with a hint of promise.

"That's it," Nixie coaxed. "Come on. Let me in." She held on tightly to the ring and heaved herself backward off the doorsill, her knees locking as her heels dug in further. The door seemed to sigh, finally giving up its fight to remain closed, and shot Nixie back into the stone wall behind her as it swung open. She let go of the ring and braced herself for yet another fall against the hard stones of the tunnel.

She felt the stone bricks smash into her back, even through her cloak and uniform. But the worst was not over. She fell forward after crashing into the wall, and the newly loosened bricks came tumbling down on top of her. She threw her arms up over her head and pulled her knees in close.

When it seemed as though there were no more bricks to fall, Nixie opened her eyes, relieved at last by the faint light coming down from the staircase on the other side of the door. She turned around and peered through the hole she had made in the stone wall. On the other side of the busted wall was another tunnel, this one sloping down, down, down into the darkness.

Nixie looked longingly at the open doorway above her. Surely, it was the way out of the tunnel and back onto ground level, but she couldn't help but wonder what lay beyond the crumbled stone wall. She bit her lip and looked back and forth at her two options.

Five more minutes won't hurt, she convinced herself, and she stood up and shut the open wooden door carefully. She took a deep breath as she stood just in front of the dark, sloped tunnel on the other side of the wall. The air was even colder inside, and she could almost feel tiny ice shards prickling her cheeks as she moved closer. She took one look back at the closed wooden door before creeping into the damp, cavernous tunnel.

Millie braced herself for the blow that was coming. She knew someone was running directly at her in the dark, but she couldn't see who, and was too afraid to call out a warning.

The runner crashed into her and knocked her to the hard stone floor, and both girls let out a yelp. Stunned, Millie pushed herself up on her knees and scrambled to her feet. She immediately thought of the street brawls she'd seen in her hometown in Scotland, watching the boys duke it out over some silly thing. She raised her fists in front of her face and prepared to punch her assailant.

"Millie?" a voice cried out. "It's me, Jo!"

"Quiet, Jo!" Millie whispered. She lowered her firsts and took Jo's arm in the darkness. "I can't see a thing! We need to get back to the—"

More footsteps. Lighter this time, racing directly toward them at a heart-pounding rate. Jo wrapped her arms around Millie and shut her eyes tight.

Boom!

Maddie plowed into her sister and Millie, and teetered back on her heels from the impact. A hand clamped down around her arm and kept her from falling straight backward.

"Millie?" Maddie whispered after a few exasperated gasps.

"Millie *and* me!" Jo corrected her. "Is anyone else coming behind you?"

"I don't think so. Did you hear all the commotion back there?" Maddie asked, speaking quickly. "Something's wrong. We have to get out of the tunnels and back to the dormitory. Fast!"

The three girls hurried out of the conservatory tunnel entrance, ran through the palm trees and tropical flowers, and burst out the doors of the science hall onto the lawn.

"I can't catch my breath," Millie gasped, her chest heaving up and down. She bent over and rested her elbows on her knees.

"You'd better catch it fast," Jo said, staring off toward the lake. "I think Rosemary's running this way."

Nixie stepped back into the main tunnel and looked down at her boots. Even in the dim light, the slick, wet leather shined bright. She scrunched her toes inside the wet wool of her tights.

I'd better get back to the dormitory before my feet get frostbitten, she thought with concern. She pulled on the brass ring on the wooden door in front of her, and climbed up the steep staircase. Above her head, she could see the outline of a square cut into the ceiling. She pushed up on it and pulled herself into a warm, glowing room.

She was in the boathouse, behind a row of two-man canoes. A fire burned in the wood stove, keeping the sleeping dachshunds warm. She weaved carefully around the leaning boats and walked toward the door.

"*Arf!*" The dachshunds were now wide awake, intent on scaring their intruder away. "*Arrrarrarararf! Arf, arf!*" they yipped, pushing their narrow snouts through the spaces in the fence. For small dogs, they could certainly cause a ruckus. Nixie dashed out of the boathouse and ran as fast as she could on her frozen feet back toward the dormitory.

"There they are!" Françoise exclaimed, pointing across the grounds to the science hall. "Go, go, go, go!" she ordered.

Safi had emerged from the trapdoor in the stables, and she, Françoise, and Val were determined to get back to safety. Safi hadn't even had the chance to recount what happened in the tunnels—only that they needed to get back to the dormitory at once. They darted across the lawn toward their friends.

As the two groups of three girls ran toward the fountain in the middle of Madame Molineaux's campus from opposite sides, Jo waved her arms furiously and pointed toward the lake. When she got in earshot, she yelled across.

"It's Rosemary! She's coming after us!"

Val stopped in her tracks and squinted at the blond girl running from the boathouse. "That's not Rosemary, Jo, it's *Nixie!*" she cried.

The girls stopped and faced the lake.

There she was, a very red-cheeked and out-of-breath Nixie running toward them, pounding on her heels to avoid injuring her frozen toes.

"What is Nixie doing out here?" Jo cried. "She's supposed to be standing watch!"

Millie cocked her head to the side casually. "She doesn't run well, does she?"

"Never mind that, Millie!" scolded Françoise, and she took off to meet Nixie, who was still a good distance away. Once she reached her, she linked her arm through Nixie's and dragged her along.

"Why aren't you at the dormitory?" Françoise asked in between breaths.

"Long . . . story," Nixie squeaked out.

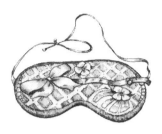

CHAPTER TWENTY-SIX

Rosemary's Performance

Klara Kronenberg sat up in bed. It had taken her a while to calm down enough to go to sleep after her meeting with Troxler in the main hall, so she'd just fallen into deep sleep, and she was very groggy. She didn't know if she had actually heard voices, or if she had been having a dream. She adjusted her sleeping cap and eye mask, yawned, and put her head back on her pillow.

But after only a few seconds, she heard the voices again. She was most certainly awake, and those voices were coming from outside. She raised her eye mask and slid her feet into her slippers. She drew the heavy curtains back and strained to see as far as she could into the middle of the campus grounds, but she could see no one.

Maybe it's the howling cats the Room Five girls were talking about, she thought, and climbed back under her covers. She was just about to place her eye mask back on her face when she came to her senses.

"Howling cats?" she said out loud. "Wake up, Klara. Something's amiss."

All seven girls flew down the Grand Corridor. Safi led the pack, and Nixie held up the rear, panting all the way. When they reached the rug in the main hall, Françoise held both hands out flat toward the other girls.

"Not . . . one . . . sound," she mouthed, and lifted her foot to point at the bottom of her boot.

The girls nodded and took tiny, careful steps across the cold stone floor toward the entrance to the first-year dormitory. Not one of them—not even Jo—made a noise as they tiptoed. Once they arrived at the steps, they took two stairs at a time and ran toward Room Five. Seconds after they passed the library doorway, Rosemary Byron emerged, wide-eyed and furious.

"It was *you!*" she whispered loudly as she stood in the hallway, clenching her fists.

But the girls didn't stop. They piled into Room Five and were about to close the door when everyone—including Rosemary—heard the lock on Kronenberg's door click. As the headmistress opened her door, Françoise shut their door quietly. Rosemary Byron was caught—fully dressed in her uniform—out of bed well past midnight. She froze as the headmistress came walking toward her.

The girls in Room Five pressed their ears to the wooden door.

"She's in for it now, isn't she?" Safi asked, feeling a twinge of regret now that she knew what Rosemary was really doing down in the tunnels.

"Shh!" Millie hissed. "I can't hear what they're saying."

All was quiet for a moment. There was no sound on either side of the Room Five door. The girls held their breath and listened.

"Rosemary Byron," the headmistress said calmly. "I do hope that you have a gripping story to tell me about why you are out of bed and in your uniform at this hour of the night."

"Of course I do, Headmistress," Rosemary said matter-of-factly. "I was in the library."

The headmistress remained calm. "I can see that. The question is, Rosemary, *why* were you in the library?"

"If you must know, Headmistress, I have less than perfect marks in history. You know my father, and you know what he expects. The consequences of being caught studying late at night are nothing in comparison to the punishment I might receive at home this summer for less than perfect marks."

Maddie scowled. "Wow, she's *good.*"

"Shh!" the other girls whispered.

The headmistress paused for a moment. "I *do* know your father, Rosemary. And I believe that he would be proud to know you take your studies so seriously. However," Kronenberg continued, "all students need their sleep. And they must follow the rules. Even *nobility*, Rosemary. Do you understand?"

"I do now," Rosemary said sweetly. "Thank you, Headmistress."

"Good. Now off to bed with you."

The girls heard steps moving toward Rosemary's dormitory room. "Oh, Headmistress," Rosemary added, her voice suddenly becoming syrupy sweet. "Considering you're awake already, perhaps you could come in and check on one of my roommates, Safi."

The girls behind the Room Five door froze. If Kronenberg went into Rosemary's room, she would find Safi's empty bed.

"What's wrong with Safi, dear?" the headmistress asked.

"I'm not sure. It's that, well, she has these fits in the night. She might have a fever . . . I'm not sure. But, as her *friend*, I would feel better if you came and checked on her."

Safi hadn't taken a breath since she first heard Rosemary say her name in the hallway. No one could prove that Rosemary had been in the tunnels, but Rosemary could certainly prove that Safi was out of bed. Jo put her hand on Safi's shoulder.

"That's very kind of you to be concerned for your friend, Rosemary, but we will see how she is feeling in the morning. What everyone needs now is *rest*."

"Of course, Headmistress. Good night," Rosemary said. The girls could practically hear her frowning. Rosemary's door clicked shut behind her.

No one in Room Five moved until they heard the headmistress's door shut and lock.

Safi fanned her face with both hands.

"I thought I was expelled for sure," she sighed. "I need to sit down." She flopped onto Françoise's bed. The rest of the girls gathered around her, and everyone started talking at once.

"Wait, wait!" Françoise ordered. "One at a time!"

"What happened down there?" Millie blurted out impatiently. "I heard two distinct crashes at the conservatory entrance."

"I heard them both, too," Jo added. "Safi and I were together for the first one. Françoise, Val, was it you?"

Françoise and Val shook their heads no.

"It was me," Nixie confessed, shifting uncomfortably on the bed. "Just moments after everyone left, Kronenberg and Troxler came out of different hallways and met in the middle of the main hall. I had to disappear, so I hid in the utility corridor."

"You went in *there*?" Val asked, scrunching her face. "It's so . . . creepy."

"I had no choice!" Nixie insisted. "But I had a front-row seat to listen in on their conversation. Something bad is most certainly happening here."

"What? What is it?" the girls demanded.

Nixie perked up. She liked the attention, especially after she had been cast off as just the lookout. "Well," she said dramatically, "the headmistress accused the professor of taking things *from* the school . . . and the professor accused the headmistress of hiding things *in* the school."

"Did they say what things?" Maddie asked.

"No. It was a short conversation. But Kronenberg said something very important: She said that she had already shown Troxler the tunnels, and that nothing had been found."

"They *know* about the tunnels?" Maddie gasped. "We were all in there . . . We could have been caught!"

"I know! That's why I sat for a moment to think about how I would get into the tunnels to find you and tell you. But when I sat down, I fell through the old wooden floorboards into another section of the tunnels."

"That was the first crash we heard," Safi said, propping herself up on Françoise's pillow. "I knew it had come from the dormitories—didn't I say that, Jo?" She nudged Jo, who shrugged and agreed. "Where did the tunnel lead?"

"To the boathouse, where I came out. It took what seemed like an hour to get there, though, in complete darkness."

"*Just* to the boathouse?" Françoise asked, puzzled that the tunnel hadn't intersected with any of the others.

"Y-yes . . .well . . . y-yes," she stuttered nervously. "There was a boarded-up door that looked like it led in the direction of the first-year hallway, but I couldn't open it. The only other way to go was toward the lake. There were stairs up to the trap-door in the boathouse, but that's it. Nothing else. I woke the dogs up as I ran out, and, well, you know the rest."

"All right, if you're sure there was nothing else," Françoise said cautiously, studying Nixie's face. "How did the conversation between Troxler and Kronenberg end?"

"The headmistress begged Troxler to take what she had already stolen and leave . . . but Troxler said something like, 'In the end, it will be you who must leave,' and then she walked away."

"What did Kronenberg do?" Jo asked.

"She didn't do anything. She looked really . . . sad. And hopeless." Nixie looked solemn for a moment. "I wanted to give her a hug."

Millie's face fell. "Tell us you didn't, Nixie."

Nixie giggled. "I didn't have the chance. She knew she was being watched. She shouted that if there was a student out of bed, she would expel her! So, I walked backward to the end of the corridor. And then I fell."

"Then who made the second crash?" Val asked, wishing she had heard something from the stables.

"I did," Safi chimed in, looking smug. "You won't believe what's lurking down under the history hall."

CHAPTER TWENTY-SEVEN

Not for the Faint of Heart

At breakfast the next morning, no one was hungry. No one except for Val, that is, who tucked away biscuits and sausages as if nothing had happened the night before.

"How can you eat, Val?" Millie groaned. "I'm so tired I feel nauseated."

"Well," Val said after swallowing her food, "I felt bad for lying to Kronenberg about howling cats keeping us awake when we got into trouble with Troxler. But now, it's all come true . . . sort of. So, I feel better. And I'm hungry."

"I bet I know who's excited to sit in front of Rosemary during history lecture," Millie sang playfully, winking across the table at Maddie and nodding toward Rosemary's table.

Rosemary sat with her back to the girls, and she had intentionally avoided their eyes in the hallway.

"It's not like she got in trouble or anything," Maddie complained. "She could at least be her usual brand of nasty instead of ignoring us, too."

"We tried to catch her in the act last night, Maddie," Jo said sympathetically. "And she knows it. She has a right to be mad."

"And we don't? She tried to have Safi expelled. That was wicked."

Jo shook her head. "She's only feeding kittens. We should leave her alone."

"Just because she's nice to cats doesn't mean she won't turn us all in the first chance she gets," Maddie said defensively.

"Look, you two," Françoise interrupted. "This isn't about Rosemary anymore. It's about getting to the bottom of the mystery—the tunnels, Kronenberg, and Troxler. Val and I are serving our detentions tomorrow. We'll see what we can dig up."

Val turned away from the window and covered her face with her hands.

"Ah-choo!" she sneezed as daintily as she could. She had managed to escape the curling swirls of dust all morning, but now the tiny particles were invading her eyes and nose, making it difficult to continue cleaning in Kronenberg's office.

The headmistress stood up from her heavy wooden desk and walked swiftly toward the window.

"Here, dear. Use mine," she said, handing Val a white linen handkerchief.

"Thank you." Val wiped her face gently with the kerchief, folded it neatly, and handed it back to the headmistress.

"Oh, no, no . . . ," the headmistress insisted, resisting the urge to back away. "You keep it, dear. I have plenty in my desk." She sat back down, picked up her bone-handled magnifying glass, and squinted at the tiny lettering on the document in front of her.

"Ah-*choo*!!"

The headmistress sighed and laid down the magnifying glass once more. "You know, Valentina," she said gently. "If you hold the kerchief over your nose while you dust, you won't sneeze as often."

"I am sorry, Headmistress," Val said, fluffing the feather duster around the windowsill with one hand and clutching the kerchief to her face with the other.

"Don't apologize, dear. Obviously, my office was in need of a good dusting! I'm glad you're here, but I do have work to finish. Just try to avoid inhaling the dust. If you can't do it without sneezing, just go right ahead and sneeze. I can always go and work in the library."

Val's eyes widened. Her plan to be alone in the headmistress's office had been thwarted when she'd arrived to find Kronenberg at her desk, finishing up some last-minute work. For two hours, she cleaned quietly, trying to figure out how to investigate the aerial photograph of the school. And now Kronenberg had unwittingly handed her a solution.

"Oh, do not worry, Headmistress," she said in her sweetest voice. "I think I am finished sneez—*ah-choo!!*—ing. The dust bothers—*ah-choo!!*—me hardly at all anymore."

She tilted her head back for added effect. "Ah, ah, ah—*choo!!!*" She blew her nose into the handkerchief and sniffled for a few seconds afterward.

The headmistress looked discouraged. "Are you all right, dear?"

"Of course, I am fine, perfectly," Val insisted. "You stay here and work. I will not give another peep."

The headmistress shrugged and picked up her magnifying glass once more. Val dusted quietly for a few seconds, preparing for her final performance.

"Ahem," she coughed quietly. "Ahem, ahem," she continued, getting louder with each cough. She put the feather duster down and bent over. "Achhh, ahem!!" she coughed again, following the choking sound with another loud sneeze.

The headmistress stood up and gathered her things. "You know, I think I'll just work in the library." She opened one of the desk drawers and pointed into it. "There are more handkerchiefs in here, if you need them."

"No, Headmistress, I assure you I am fine!" Val choked out between forced coughs and phony sneezes.

The headmistress hurried toward the door. "It's quite all right. Thank you again, Valentina," she said, closing the door behind her.

"Don't worry, I will finish dusting off your—*Ahhh—Ahhhhh—*" The door clicked shut. "Choo," Val whispered, smiling mischievously. She ran to the door and turned the lock. She had no idea how long Kronenberg would be gone, and she still had to finish dusting the office. This was going to have to be a snappy investigation.

The bell rang, drowning out the last words of Troxler's lecture on the principles of Roman democracy. Books slammed shut, papers rustled, and students began their between-class chatter.

Françoise ripped a sheet of paper from her notebook and folded it into a small square, stuffing it into her pocket along with a charcoal pencil. "Do you have it?" she asked Maddie.

Maddie nodded. "I do. It's in my secret pocket." She slipped her hand under the hem of her shirt and pulled out a tiny pocketknife, the same one she'd used to whittle Jo's slingshot for Christmas. It had been her father's, but had ended up in her trunk by mistake.

Françoise took the pocketknife and flipped the blade out to inspect it. "Still sharp," she noted out loud, and ran her finger along the blade carefully.

"Put that away!" Maddie whispered. "If Troxler sees it, she'll take it, and I'll never get it back."

Françoise folded the blade down into the handle with a snap, and dropped it into her jacket pocket. "She won't see it," she assured her friend. "And she won't see what I'm doing with it, either. Thanks." The girls stood up and walked out of the classroom into the busy hallway.

"I'd tell you to have fun at detention," Maddie said apologetically. "But that sounds like I'm being snide, doesn't it?"

"Fun?" Françoise asked. "I wouldn't call it fun." She cocked her head to the side. "Secretly slicing open paintings, sketching tapestry patterns, and sneaking out late at night to repair them?" She sparkled with excitement. "I'd call it the best time I've had all year."

Val stood on a stepladder, eye level with the aerial photograph, and ran her fingers around the edge of the lacquered frame.

It looked quite ordinary compared to the gold frames and oil paintings that adorned the other walls in the office. *What are you hiding?* she asked the photograph silently, inspecting each detail with care.

Nothing looked out of place. The buildings appeared exactly where they should have been; the grounds, especially from way up high, looked exquisitely manicured and orderly. She ran her index finger over the coiled walking labyrinth, the rows of gardens, and the sandy lakeshore.

Val stepped down off the ladder and stretched her hands out, holding each side of the frame. With a heave, she lifted the heavy photograph off the wall, struggling to balance under the weight. It pulled her forward, smashing her fingertips between the back of the photograph and the wall.

"Owwww!" shrieked Val, and she instinctively let go of the photograph. It slid down the wall and crashed to the floor, falling facedown.

Val froze. *You've done it now,* she scolded herself. *You must be the only girl in history to get into more trouble while serving detention!* She bent down slowly and lifted the photograph, looking for signs of shattered glass on the floor below.

"Whew!" she sighed with a long breath. Nothing appeared to be broken. Except, perhaps, her fingers. She looked down at her hands, still throbbing after being smashed against the wall.

"Oh no," she said out loud with dread. A thin red line of blood trickled down Val's hand toward her sleeve. She cocked her head to the side, feeling more and more dizzy as each second passed. *Not now!* she pleaded with herself, but it was too late. She closed her eyes and toppled to the ground.

Françoise carried a stepladder in one hand and a bucket of soapy water in the other, splashing suds down the fifth-year dormitory hall as she walked. Normally, junior students weren't allowed down the fifth-year hallways, but this was a special exception. The fifth-year students had been notified that a first-year student would be cleaning up portrait frames today. The artwork in this hallway was more precious, the décor more refined. It felt very grown-up compared to the first-year hallway, and Françoise felt right at home.

I can't wait to be a fifth-year, she thought as she stood next to a large portrait of a horse and rider. She put her bucket on the ground, dipped a rag into the suds, and began to wipe the grooves of the golden frame.

A group of girls emerged from a dormitory across the hall and walked toward her on their way out. Françoise smiled in a friendly manner, fully expecting to be ignored by her older schoolmates. But instead, one of them stopped and took notice of her.

"Hello," the girl said, smiling. Her friends looked amused.

"Hi," Françoise said quietly, and scrubbed harder at a spot on the frame.

"Do you know what?" the girl asked her.

"What?" Françoise asked, pleased that the girl wanted to talk to her. She prided herself on being more mature than other girls her age.

"You missed a spot," the older girl stated drily, smirking and putting her hand on her hip.

The other girls laughed and kept walking. Françoise took a deep breath.

Don't worry about them, she told herself. *You're not here to be their maid. You're here to uncover the truth.*

She looked around to make sure no one else was in the hall, and when she knew she was alone, she drew the pocketknife from her jacket. "Here we go," she said out loud, and in a flash, swiveled the blade from the handle. She leaned in against the portrait and, finding the perfect spot right along the edge of the painting, cut a thin incision along the hind leg of the horse.

She slid the tip of the blade under the canvas, lifted it slightly, and peered behind it. "Voilà," she said, smiling, her face pressed next to the canvas. A burgundy-and-cream-colored tapestry depicted a royal banquet; even in the darkness behind the painting, she could see detailed faces and costumes. Françoise pulled the paper and charcoal pencil from her pocket and made a quick sketch of what she had seen.

She smoothed the open flap in the canvas and stepped back. The slice in the canvas was barely noticeable, and she felt certain that she could come back and repair the painting while the school slept. She finished polishing the frame and picked up the bucket and stepladder. "Next," she said out loud, hoping that each and every portrait she cut open would reveal a beautiful tapestry.

Val's eyes fluttered open and she gazed around at her surroundings. She sat up and rubbed her head, trying to remember what had happened. On the floor next to her legs, she saw a single red drop.

My hand! she thought, and closed her eyes. *My hand was bleeding.* She kept her eyes shut and fumbled around for the linen handkerchief the headmistress had given her, wrapping it around the injured fingers. She opened her eyes and looked down. There was still blood on the edge of her sleeve and a little dried on her hand, but it wasn't much, and it didn't bother her now that she was expecting it.

Val kneeled above the photograph and examined the frame. "How did I cut myself on a picture?" she asked. She ran to Kronenberg's desk and retrieved another linen handkerchief from the open drawer. She rubbed the kerchief on the wood, but couldn't find any traces of blood. She carefully lifted the photograph from the wall and turned it sideways.

"Aha," she said triumphantly. "It was *you.*" On the top corner of the back of the frame, tacks had been hammered through the brown paper dust cover into the wood. One of the tacks had been nailed in crookedly, and the sharp point stuck out ever so slightly from the frame.

Val inspected the tack carefully. Indeed, the point and the frame around it were red with blood from her finger. She wiped around it carefully, staining another of Kronenberg's handkerchiefs with spots of red.

The back of this frame has been opened, she thought. She ran her finger over the tacks in an L-shape around the top corner. In a flash, she was back at the headmistress's desk, plucking a silver letter opener from the leather writing surface. She flew to the photograph and pried each of the tacks up with the edge of the letter opener, popping each one loose with focused precision.

The brown paper backing lay on the wooden frame, no longer secured to the wood by the tacks. Val cleaned her injured fingers and peeled back the corner of the paper. Inside, a small envelope lay with the flap facing up. Val lifted it carefully out of the frame and turned it over. It was addressed simply, "To Klara."

Val hesitated. Opening a letter to the headmistress was risky. She had already made a mess of the headmistress's handkerchiefs, dropped the photograph, and removed the backing from the frame. If Kronenberg came back to the office at this moment, she would have a lot of explaining to do.

Batti il ferro quando è caldo, she thought in Italian before whispering it in English. "Strike while the iron is hot."

The letter was fragile, written in German on delicate ivory paper. She couldn't understand the words, but she knew Nixie would be able to translate it.

She tucked the letter into her jacket pocket and scooped up the line of tacks against the wall.

"Back in you go," she said, using a glass paperweight as a hammer. She carefully placed the paper backing over the frame and inserted each of the tacks into their tiny holes, giving a few quick whacks with the heel of her shoe to secure them in place. She repositioned the last tack, the one that had cut her fingers, to go straight into the wood.

"No more poking for you," Val scolded after she'd hammered it all the way in. She slipped her shoe back on, picked up the framed photograph with both hands and lifted it into the air. She climbed up the stepladder, steadied herself, and tried to hang the wire on the back of the frame on the nail in the wall.

Grittt. The wire scraped down the wall, missing the nail. Val pulled back on the bottom of the frame to get a better look at exactly where on the wall the nail was sticking out. She was making a second attempt to hang the frame when the doorknob turned.

In a panic, Val swung her head around to stare at the office door.

"Valentina?" The headmistress's voice called from the other side of the door. "The door is locked. You must have turned it by accident."

The doorknob turned back and forth again.

"I'm—I'm coming!" Val called nervously. "Just a moment, Headmistress," she said, and desperately tried again and again to hook the frame's wire over the nail.

"Valentina, open this door at once!" The headmistress ordered. "Are you all right in there?"

"I am fine!" insisted Val. She lowered the frame, bent the wire on the back, and made one last effort to hook it over the nail in the wall, finally feeling it catch. She jumped down off the stepladder, scooped up the letter opener, and practically threw it back onto the headmistress's desk.

Exhausted and sweating, she flew to the door and flung it open. "I'm sorry," she said, out of breath. "Please, come in," she continued, trying to hide her distress with a smile.

"You're *bleeding*," the headmistress gasped, her eyes focused across the room at her handkerchiefs, which lay crumpled and spotted with red on the floor. She continued to look around the office, wondering exactly what, if anything, had been cleaned.

"Oh, yes, it is nothing," Val said, showing the headmistress her cut fingers. "I guess I dust too eagerly."

The headmistress ran her finger along the top of the armchair at her side, and held up a pinch of gray dust.

Val opened her mouth to protest. "I make all of my efforts on *that* wall," she explained, pointing at the large row of windows.

"And how did you cut yourself?" the headmistress asked, kneeling down to retrieve the stained handkerchiefs.

"The . . . the wood, on your walls . . . it is very," she paused, searching for the correct English word. "*Splinterful.* Is full of splinters, I mean."

The headmistress nodded. "Well, I will have someone look at that." She threw the splotchy kerchiefs into the wastebasket.

"I'm sorry for your handkerchiefs," Val apologized.

"Don't fret about them, dear. I'm sorry about your poor fingers. That looks like it was painful." She led Val to the door. "Let that be a lesson to you: Detention is a dangerous place to be."

"Yes, Headmistress," Val uttered quietly. She made sure she could still feel the letter in her jacket pocket.

"The next time you decide to act up in Troxler's classroom," the headmistress continued, "just remember this detention and ask yourself: Do I really want to do that again?"

Val nodded, curtseyed, and walked out of the doorway, fighting the urge to run as fast as she could back to Room Five.

Splat!

The murky, soapy water splashed onto the ground from the second-story window, making a small puddle in the already muddy lawn. Françoise placed her dingy rag into the empty bucket, pulled her head back inside the first-year library window, and found a shadowy place to sit on the floor in between the rows of bookshelves. She pulled her sketch paper from her pocket. By now, it had been folded, dripped on, and erased so many times that it threatened to tear apart, but Françoise spread it out delicately on the carpet.

"And now to crack your code," she said. She crawled on her knees down the rows of books, scanning each book title. "No, no, no, no, no," she mumbled as she read each one, and finally stopped short. "Yes!" The tall book was heavy, and a cloud of dust swirled up around Françoise as she threw the pages open. *Eighteenth-Century Tapestries*, the gold foil on the front cover read. She thumbed through the pages and, satisfied with its contents, slammed the book shut. She carried it back to her original sitting place and opened it again, placing the fragile sketch paper flat between the pages of the book. *I'll be back at midnight,* she thought, and slid the book underneath a plush leather sofa for safekeeping.

CHAPTER TWENTY-EIGHT

A LETTER FROM THE PAST

The girls crowded around the bed and stared up at Nixie, watching her every move as she looked back and forth between the sheets of paper. Every now and again, she would giggle or squeal, but she refused to let the other girls know what she had translated until she'd finished the entire letter.

"Come on, Nixie, give us a hint at least!" Millie pleaded. "If it were me translating, I'd tell you what each sentence said right after I knew."

"Yes, well," Nixie said, not looking up from her work. "When I have the need for a translation of a slapstick, pie-in-the-face comedy routine, I'll let you do it your way." She looked up and bit her lip. "Sorry, Millie. I just want to make sure I have everything right before I read this to everyone. It's getting really good, though!"

Millie leaned back on her wrists. "It's okay, I can be patient," she said cordially, and began making water droplet sounds by flicking her cheek and whistling.

"Don't you have a new trick yet, Millie?" Safi asked, reclining onto her back and tossing a rubber ball high above her face, failing to catch it almost every time. "I'm bored with that one."

"Can you do this?" Val challenged, and pinched her nose closed on one side. She took a deep breath, held it for a moment, and whistled out the other nostril in a high pitch.

"No!" Millie shrieked with laughter. "Nor would I want to!"

Maddie and Jo saw the opportunity to show off the hand-clap games they'd learned at school in Boston.

"We did this all the time back home," Maddie announced over the laughter. She and Jo linked their fingers together and shouted, "One, two, ready, go!" Their hands slapped together in rhythm during the tightly rehearsed routine, and they ended it by snapping their fingers high in the air.

"That's brilliant," applauded Millie. "Can you show me and Françoise?"

The twins instructed the two girls in the simple steps of the hand-clap game.

"See?" Jo encouraged her. "It's easy, really. You just have to get it going fast, and people are impressed."

Millie and Françoise practiced the game with each other, only tangling their hands a few times before they were speeding through the routine.

"How do we end this?" Millie cried out. "My fingers hurt!"

Jo leaned in and gave them further instructions. "Simple. All you have to do is wait until you get to the fist-slap part, then clap twice, and snap your fingers high in the air!"

Françoise and Millie went through the routine one more time, and at the right moment, clapped their hands twice. They threw their hands up above their heads, but only Millie's snaps could be heard.

"Hey, Françoise, you didn't snap," Maddie pointed out.

"Sure I did," Françoise said defensively. "See?" She placed the pads of her middle fingers against the tips of her thumbs and flicked—but no sound was made.

Val pounced from her cross-legged position and examined Françoise's repeated attempts to make the snapping noise. "Oh my goodness. I don't believe it . . . There *is* something Françoise Cadieux cannot do after all!"

Safi sat up and laughed with the rest of the girls. "Are you joking? You can't snap your fingers? I was doing that since I was two!"

Françoise looked away and shook her head, smirking. "Snapping your fingers is *not* an important skill. I have plenty of advanced skills, like painting, and drawing, and—"

Millie stuck her boot in Françoise's lap. "Hey, Fran, do you think you could tie my shoe? That is, if you *can* tie a shoe. It's on the same level as snapping your fingers."

Françoise joined in the laughter. "Careful, Millie. I'd hate for you to end up with your foot in your *mouth*," she warned playfully.

"Ooh!" Millie retorted. "Someone's English is getting quite good!"

"I'm done," Nixie said quietly, beaming with pride at her translation skills. No one was listening, though, as the girls on the floor were far too busy teasing one another to hear her. "I'm done!" she called louder, but she still wasn't heard over the shrieking and laughter.

Wheeeeeeeeeeet!

Everyone froze in place. Everyone looked up at Nixie, whose hands were cupped tightly in front of her mouth.

"That's *my* trick," she said, happy to finally have their attention. "And I'm done with the letter."

All eyes were on Nixie as she prepared to read the translated letter out loud, and she couldn't help but feel as though she were on stage, about to recite a famous monologue. She cleared her throat and began her dramatic reading.

"My dearest Klara," she said slowly. "I write this just hours after your departure. The end is still very near, I'm afraid, but I felt as though I had to tell you—my beloved Jesper came back to me in these last hours. Not in a dream, but through the window, and he bestowed to me and my family a great fortune, the fortune we never were able to share together."

"Who is Jesper?" Jo wondered out loud.

"Quiet, Jo! No one knows any more than you do at this point," Maddie fussed. "Keep going, Nixie."

Nixie took a deep breath. "One of my guards came knocking at the door, and Jesper jumped back out the window. He will visit again in the night to give me the map to the treasure."

"Treasure!" Millie blurted. "Map? We've got to find that map!"

"Millie, you haven't even heard the rest!" Nixie pouted. "No more interruptions! Here comes the best part."

Everyone fell silent.

"Klara, my loyal Klara," Nixie swooned. "He has also told me of a secret fortune that lies within Madame Molineaux's, a treasure he placed there for me long ago, and I want that to be yours. You will know where to find it, in my secret chamber." She sighed heavily and clutched the letter to her chest. "It's signed: Forever in my heart, Wilhelmina."

No one said a word for a few moments.

"That's so sad," Maddie murmured. "It sounded like she was about to . . . die."

"At least she got to see her beloved," Val offered, putting her hand on Maddie's shoulder.

"Jespehhhhhr," Safi crooned. "Even his name sounds handsome . . ."

Nixie nodded. "A real love story. I wish I had a beloved." She hugged her pillow tight.

"Enough with the love," Millie scoffed. "What about the treasure?"

"So," Françoise said in a low tone of voice. "There is treasure in the school. Maybe that's what Kronenberg and Troxler were talking about."

"Maybe that's what Max was trying to tell us about," Maddie added.

"And *maybe* that's why Kronenberg hid the letter in the photograph," Val said, shocked at how simple the answer to her quest had become. "She hasn't found the treasure yet— and *that's* why she had the photograph taken from an airplane: she was looking for the secret chamber!"

"Looks like you've solved your mystery, Val," Françoise said with a grin. "Who else has solved their mystery?"

Safi piped up. "I have! We know that Rosemary Byron is just feeding cats in the tunnels."

"And I've solved mine now, too," Françoise informed the girls. "The portraits in the school are hiding ancient tapestries, all from Bavaria, according to the book I found in the library. So . . . who's left?"

"I'm not doing it, I'm just *not*," Maddie insisted, poking at the carrots on her plate with her fork. Six weeks had passed since the twins had been assigned detention with Professor Natalio, and the day had finally arrived.

"Stop complaining," Millie whined. "At least you have some excitement to look forward to. I've been positively *bored* for the last month and a half." Millie and Nixie had yet to discover any ghosts or thieves in the halls or around the castle grounds since they had been assigned their quest.

"And at least you get to play with Albert," Val offered. "That will be fun."

"If I have to pick up droppings to play with Albert, I'd just rather skip it," Maddie huffed.

"Pipe down, Sis," Jo laughed. "Everyone has to serve their detention, and we knew what we were getting into."

"But why couldn't we have gotten something simple like Val and Françoise?"

"I'll have you know," Françoise protested, "that I was up half the night for a *week*, sneaking around to study the tapestry markings and repair all those paintings."

"And I cut my fingers and *fainted* just to get that letter," Val reminded her. "But now we know there's treasure hidden in the school!"

Millie snorted and dipped her finger into her warm tomato soup. "Watch out, Val, I've got a red finger here, and I'm not afraid to use it!" She held her finger up and wagged it back and forth.

Val rolled her eyes. "First of all, Millie, that is orange, not red, and I know it is soup. And second, at least I found something on my quest. That letter is the best thing we have found since the tunnels! You and Nixie have not come up with anything yet."

Millie shrugged. "We're saving the best for last. Right, Nixie?"

Nixie didn't hear Millie. She was staring off in the distance, her mind obviously on other things.

"Nixie?"

"Oh," Nixie said, snapping out of her daze. "Right, I haven't found anything yet. I mean, *we* haven't. Me and Millie. Nothing so far."

"I'm not worried," Jo said with confidence. "We've uncovered so much up until now—the pieces of this puzzle are bound to come together soon. I'm going to get up on that rooftop, clean up the mess, play with Albert and the goats, and who knows? Maybe Max will have another clue for us."

"Better get it looking perfect," Françoise joked. "We want it to look good for our *special guest*."

"Who is he anyway?" Millie asked. "Kronenberg is at her wit's end getting this place ready for his arrival."

"No one knows," Maddie said. "But he'll be here soon. He may have already arrived."

CHAPTER TWENTY-NINE

THE ROOFTOP DETENTION

"Livingston twins!" Professor Natalio shouted jovially. "It's so nice of you to help me today. I wondered who would be so kind as to volunteer to do this dirty job."

Jo winced and looked at her sister. *Volunteer?* she mouthed, and shook her head. *He doesn't know we're in detention,* she thought. "Oh, ahem, yes, Professor," Jo said sweetly. "We jumped at the chance to get to play with Albert and the goats, even if it means cleaning up after them."

The professor handed each of them a small shovel and a bucket. "After you're done cleaning, you can give them a treat," he said, and he placed a jar of melon rinds in Maddie's bucket. "And here's a bone for Albert."

The bone was long and heavy, and didn't look anything like the bones Maddie and Jo had given the neighborhood dogs back in Boston. "Um . . . Professor, exactly what is this?" Jo asked, holding the bone in her hand.

"It's a deer femur!" the professor exclaimed with delight. "I found it on my latest excursion into the Alps. Albert will be busy for days chewing on it."

Jo dropped the bone into her bucket, wiped her hand on her skirt, and forced a smile. "Great."

"Now, ladies, the time is"—he paused to look down at his wristwatch—"five minutes past three in the afternoon. The headmistress has requested that I return you to her office before four o'clock, so I will come up to inspect your work and take you back at three-fifty."

"We get forty-five minutes to clean all of that mess?" Maddie complained politely.

"It shouldn't even take you that long," the professor said. "You'll have plenty of time to play with the animals before I arrive. Again, thank you!" He shooed them into the attic stairwell and closed the door behind them.

Maddie raised the hatch at the top of the narrow staircase, letting the light pour in from the grassy rooftop above.

"Look at this view!" Jo exclaimed as she climbed up onto the roof. "I can see the entire campus." She gazed out at the lakeshore, the tops of the trees, and the unsuspecting students walking to class below.

Maddie joined her sister at the edge of the grass and pointed at a group of girls in the garden. "See what they're doing?" she asked.

Jo squinted. "Not really. They're just standing around talking," she replied.

"Exactly," Maddie said, irritated. "They're not in *detention* like we are. So, let's get this over with so we can rejoin society!"

"*Baa-aa-aah,*" the goats bleated, and casually walked toward the two girls.

"Sorry, little goat, it's cleaning time, not feeding time," Jo said as one goat poked his head into her bucket. She reached down and scratched under his chin, but he had been interested in food, not affection, so he wandered away. "You'll come back when you see the treats we have for you," she sang to the goat, and set to work with the shovel.

"All right. I'll clean out the shelters and you work on the lawn," Maddie instructed, and she toted her bucket and shovel over to the two towers in the middle of the rooftop.

That's strange, she thought as she walked around the first stone tower. *Where's the door in?* She examined the other tower. It was just the same as the first, with solid walls and no doorway inside.

"Jo," she called out, not moving. "Come over here for a minute."

Jo dropped her shovel and ran over to her sister. "What's the matter?"

Madeline took her sister's hand and did a quick figure-eight walk around the towers. "See?" she asked. "No doors. These towers aren't shelters for the goats and Albert like we thought."

Jo looked around the rooftop again. "Um . . . and exactly where *is* Albert?" Her eyes stopped in the far corner of the roof. "Aha," she said, and raced over to a grassy ramp and took a peek down it. "It's like a little barn!"

The ramp led down under the roof into a stone alcove, and Jo ducked down to see inside. In the darkness she could make out several sleeping goats and a large pile of white fur slowly heaving up and down. She stuck her head back outside. "He's in here," she laughed. "Sleeping on the job."

Maddie kneeled down and looked for herself. "He's *supposed* to be asleep, Jo," she said. "Remember? He guards the goats at night."

"Oh, that's right," Jo replied. "But if I don't pet him now, I'll never get to! And he looks so sweet, like a big polar bear." She crept down into the stone alcove and looked back at her sister. "It sure smells like a barn down here," she said as quietly as she could.

Maddie shook her head at her sister. "Get out of there, Jo!"

But Jo's hand was already lost in Albert's big, fluffy white coat. He didn't seem to notice and continued snoring, jerking his legs every few seconds as if he were running.

Jo gave a quiet gasp of delight. "He's dreaming!" she squealed, clasping her hands together under her chin in excitement.

Maddie rolled her eyes. "You can bother the dog *after* we've cleaned everything up. Come on!"

"Fine, fine," Jo mumbled as she got back on her feet in a crouched position. "We'll play later, Albert." She patted the dog on the head gently and crept back toward the ramp. He wiggled a bit, let out a loud snort, and slowly opened his big brown eyes.

He sniffed the air and panted. He sniffed again, and again and again, and suddenly leaped to his feet. Leaning forward, he spotted the rooftop's two intruders, and bounded up the ramp after Jo.

"*Rowowow row!*" Albert barked at Maddie and Jo. He threw his head back and let out a short howl. Circling the girls, he finally got close enough to sniff their clothes and hands.

"It's okay, it's okay," Jo said, scratching the dog's chin. "We're not going to hurt your goats."

Maddie held out the back of her hand. "Here, Albert," she called in a timid voice, not wanting to provoke the white giant further. She had never seen a dog so cuddly and intimidating all at the same time. His head was nearly as high as Maddie's shoulders, and as he panted up at her expectantly, she could feel his hot breath on her face. She patted him on the head and finally hugged him around the neck, happy to be playing with this real-life stuffed animal. Musetta and Marcello were sweet, but they were too fancy and independent for snuggling, or so they thought.

Jo walked over and joined her sister on the grass, and for a long moment, they sat in silence, listening to Albert pant and watching his white coat blow in the wind.

Albert caught the scent of a treat in Jo's bucket and ran off to investigate. He soon returned with the bone, and stretched out his front legs with his hindquarters in the air.

"Not yet, boy," Jo said, taking the bone gently from the dog's mouth. She hopped up from the grass and pulled her sister up by the hand. "We've got work to do. Then we can play."

Whack!

Albert's bone bounced off of the stone ledge surrounding the rooftop.

"Careful, Jo!" Maddie scolded. "If that bone goes over the ledge, he might jump off after it."

Jo ran to the edge of the rooftop and looked over the side. It was more than three stories off the ground, much too high for anyone to be stumbling around carelessly. She picked up the bone and turned around, spotting Albert and a few of the goats keeping their safe distance.

"Good dog," Jo praised him. "You know better than to get too close." She walked to the middle of the rooftop and stood between the two towers. "Here, boy!" she yelled, and lobbed the bone up and over the tower in front of her. It sailed through the air and disappeared behind the other side of the tower, confusing Albert. "Go find it!" Jo called, and she scurried around after him.

Albert pounced and clenched the bone between his teeth, wagging his tail with pride.

"Okay, okay. One more time." Jo took the bone and swung it up in the air in a lofty underhand toss. It flew over the first tower, finally beginning its descent back to the rooftop just above the second tower.

Clank.

It landed on top of the tower's metal cap. Albert positioned himself at the base of the tower, stared up at his stranded bone, and proceeded to bark without stopping.

"Albert!" Maddie shouted at him, covering her ears with her hands. "Stop that!" She ran over to her sister. "What's the matter with him?" she yelled.

"His bone is stuck on the top of that tower," Jo said, pointing up high. "I guess I've got a better throwing arm than I thought."

Maddie sighed and approached Albert, his mouth beginning to foam from the incessant barking. "Come on, Albert, let's go over here."

She picked up her small shovel and threw it across the grassy rooftop like a stick, hoping he would run after it. But Albert looked bored by her efforts, and he continued to jump and bark at the bottom of the tower.

Jo retrieved Maddie's small shovel and turned it back and forth. She peered up at the flat, metal top of the tower and looked her sister up and down.

"Oh, no," Maddie said as she shook her head sternly. "We are *not* going to get up there. Not for a dog bone, Jo!"

But Jo was already on her way over to the tower. "This is easy, Sis," Jo insisted. "I'll hoist you up. You can stand on my shoulders and then use the little shovel to knock the bone down."

Maddie wasn't interested in circus antics today. "Albert will calm down eventually."

"Maybe he will," Jo admitted. "But maybe he won't, and he'll bark all day, and the headmistress will find out we were up on this rooftop playing with the dog during detention."

"Correction," Maddie huffed. "She'll find out *you* were playing with the dog while *I* was cleaning up the yard."

"Come on, Maddie!" Jo pleaded. "If I could, I'd stand on your shoulders and reach for it, but we both know that wouldn't work. It'll be quick, I swear."

Maddie sighed and dragged her feet on the way to the tower. Albert bounced around her, still barking, and rolled over at her feet. "This isn't a game," she scolded. He nipped playfully at her jacket sleeve anyway.

Jo kneeled and linked her fingers together to form a little basket. "Okay, Sis. Just like climbing trees in the jungle, okay?"

Maddie groaned. "Sure, Jo. Except this tree is made of stone and has no branches. But otherwise, yes." She nestled her foot down in Jo's hands, held on to the smooth stone tower wall, and sprang up, placing the other foot on her sister's shoulder.

Jo shuffled back and forth, struggling to balance her sister next to the tower. "Okay, now the other foot!" she grunted, lifting her woven fingers up as high as she could. She felt Maddie's other foot land squarely on her shoulders, and held on to Maddie's boots as her sister balanced.

"Don't move, Jo," Maddie ordered. She took one hand from the stone wall and reached for the little shovel she had tucked into her waistband. She could see the end of the bone resting on the metal ledge. She reached up, clutching the shovel tightly in one hand and desperately trying to hold on to the stone wall with the other. She was just inches away from being able to tap the bone with the shovel.

"I'm going up on my toes," Maddie informed her sister. She held her arms out to her sides, and with one swift motion, raised herself onto the toes of her boots and lunged the shovel at the bone. "Almost!" she yelled. She repositioned herself and held her arms out to her sides once more. Even Albert watched with hopeful eyes, and a few of the goats had gathered to see what all the trouble was for.

As her heels lifted from Jo's shoulders, she swung her arm upward and lunged toward the metal top with all her might. The shovel scraped along the metal with a grating sound, and just as her balance was wavering, the shovel blade caught the end of the bone and pulled it toward her. It slipped off of the metal edge and started to fall.

Maddie raised the shovel back up and tried to pin the bone between the stone wall and the blade, but instead, she sent the bone into the small opening between the top of the stone tower wall and the flat metal top. She plunged the shovel into the opening, scrambling after the bone, but lost her balance and let go of the shovel as she fell from her sister's shoulders.

Clank, clankity clank, clank clank.

In an instant, Jo held out her arms and caught her sister. It was a good thing the girls had once had a whole summer of tree-climbing in the jungle.

"Where did it go?" Jo asked her sister, helping her stand up on the grass.

"It slipped under the metal top," Maddie grumbled. "All that work, and we've still got a lunatic dog."

Albert had resumed his barking fit and ran around in circles. He darted between the towers, and, realizing his bone was gone, resigned himself to playing with the only toy left on the grassy rooftop: Jo's shovel. He carried it over in his mouth to the girls and dropped it on the ground.

"Did you hear that noise?" Jo asked.

"I did." Maddie looked uneasy. "I sent the professor's shovel down into the tower, and now I'll never get it back." She looked the tower up and down with a scowl, squinting her eyes in the sunlight. "No doors, and a metal cap on top . . . It might as well be a chimney."

The girls stared at each other.

"A *chimney*?" Jo asked with disbelief. She looked down and stomped her boots on the grass. "And this rooftop is a *lawn*!"

Maddie's eyes were as wide as saucers. She reached down and grabbed Jo's shovel from the ground. "If this is a chimney, then it must be connected to a fireplace somewhere in this building." She ran to the wall and reached her arms up high. "Give me a boost!"

Jo lifted her sister onto her shoulders once more, and this time, Maddie reached as far as she could into the space between the top of the tower and the metal cap. "Don't say anything, Jo. I'm going to listen to hear how far this shovel falls after I let go." She released the shovel from her fingers. It clanged, banged, and rattled down the long chimney, gaining speed as it fell.

Ding, ding, dong.

The sound of clock chimes echoed up the walls of the chimney and out the top. Maddie let go of the chimney wall and covered her ears.

"Get me down!" she yelled. She could feel the reverberation from the bells' tones as she clenched her teeth together.

Jo kneeled down to the ground, letting her sister slip off her shoulders at a safe distance to the grass. They stared at each other again, unsure of what to do next.

"The clock! Just like the one at the market!" exclaimed Jo. "It's in the chimney!"

"That explains why the chimes sound like they're off in the distance," said Maddie as she brushed her knees off, her eyes sparkling with excitement. "They ring *inside* the chimney!"

Jo swept the dirt from the shoulders of her jacket. "Maddie . . ." She paused for a moment. "We know the history hall like the backs of our hands. There's not a fireplace there we haven't checked. This one has to be—"

"Down in the tunnels, I know." Maddie looked at her wristwatch. "Professor Natalio shouldn't be up to get us for another twenty minutes. If we can go down into the tunnels and look under the history hall, I bet we can find the fireplace." She looked up at the two chimneys. "To think, we've been staring at the 'smokestack growing out the lawn' all this time."

Jo smiled and thought of their reclusive riddle author. "We owe a big thank you to Max."

"We'll thank him *after* we solve the mystery," said Maddie, and she and Jo raced toward the hatch to the stairs.

CHAPTER THIRTY

A Fireplace That's Never Lit

The twins clung to the walls down an empty hallway. The science building had been flooded with students for a few moments as students left their classes, and Maddie and Jo needed to stay out of sight.

"Okay, *now*," Maddie whispered. Jo stepped out of the shadows and into the hallway.

"They're in the cabinet next to the hanging horse?" Jo asked again. She dreaded passing by the horse skeleton, and usually went the long way to class just to avoid it.

"Yes—with matches, too. I'll keep watch while you pick the lock."

The twins scampered down the empty hallway, running faster than they ever had in a school building. They turned the corner, and there, hanging eerily from the ceiling, was the horse. Jo shuddered and pulled a bobby pin from her hair.

"Maybe they're not in there after all, Maddie, and we should just go and get Françoise's torch light."

"There's no time, Jo! Now *go*," Maddie whispered harshly, and gave her sister a push toward the cabinet.

The horse skeleton swayed as Jo passed, its skull bobbing up and down as if it were nodding at her. *Nice horsey*, she thought, and imagined a sweet mare from the stables next to her instead of the stark white bones. She sat down in front of the cabinet and went to work. Her bobby pin slid into the keyhole and she wiggled it a bit, listening for the pin to catch on the lock.

Maddie peeked her head around the corner. "Hurry!"

Jo turned to her sister and scowled. "Do you want to pick this lock or do you want to let me do it?"

"I don't even know how to pick a lock, Jo. How is it that *you* know how?"

Jo smirked playfully. "I learned so I could read your diary," she said, still concentrating on the cabinet door.

"My locked diary?"

Jo raised her eyebrows at her sister and didn't answer.

Click.

The cabinet door popped open, and Jo pulled the bobby pin out of the keyhole. She reached inside, grabbed two white candlesticks and a box of matches, and jumped to her feet. The cabinet door swung closed and latched again.

Maddie was still pouting. "That diary is *private*, Jo!" she continued. "Exactly what have you read in there?"

"Are you seriously thinking about your diary at a time like this? Have you forgotten what we're here for?"

Maddie looked sore and stuck her lip out. "It's just that—"

Jo took her sister by the arm. "Maddie, I was only teasing. I haven't read your diary. Even if it was unlocked, I still wouldn't. I'm not that interested in your secret thoughts."

Her sister looked relieved. "Well, then, where did you learn how to pick a lock?"

"That's in *my* diary," Jo said smugly. "Now let's go."

The air in the conservatory smelled of moss and wet leaves, a heavy veil of condensation fogging the ceiling window panes. As they trekked into the small grove of palm trees in the corner, Jo couldn't help but feel sentimental. Here they were, the Livingston twins, headed off for adventure again. Except this time, their mother wasn't standing by. Their father wasn't twenty paces behind them. They were on their own, and wearing teal jackets and skirts instead of khaki short pants and shirts.

Maddie was first into the tunnel. She shivered as goose bumps sprang up on the back of her neck.

"I forgot how freezing it is down here," Jo said, climbing down from the conservatory entrance. She handed her sister a candlestick and slid the cover off the box of matches, shaking one into her palm. The match hissed as Jo struck it on the side of the box. "Careful with the flame," she told Maddie as they ran. "It's drafty in here."

"This is it," Jo said, holding her compass out in front of her and turning slightly. "We're under the history hall for sure."

"This looks like the place Safi told us about, where her kitten fiasco took place," Maddie observed. "See the metal racks?" She walked to the wall and waved her candle around to show her sister.

"I see it, Maddie!" Jo covered her candle with her hand held flat. Both of their candles had gone out several times as they made their way through the tunnels to the history hall, and the number of matches left in the box was dwindling. "Don't wave it like that, your flame will go out again." But just as she'd said it, a gust of wind blew across the room and extinguished Jo's flame. She looked down in shock and Maddie rushed over.

"It's *you* who needs to be careful, Jo," Maddie scolded. But not a second later, her flame was blown out, too. "Did you do that?!" she demanded.

"*No,*" Jo said firmly, "that wasn't me. That came from somewhere in this room." She held her finger to her tongue for a moment and lifted it into the air, turning every which way to try to figure out where the wind was coming from. But the air stayed still, and the twins stood silently in the darkness as the seconds ticked by.

"Give me the matchbox," Maddie ordered impatiently, but Jo didn't move. She stood, still as a statue, her finger still in the air.

"Stop talking," Jo said, her voice steady and calm. She let her chin fall to her chest, concentrating on her finger. "In fact, stop breathing."

Maddie looked annoyed, but did as her sister said. She stood and held her breath for what seemed like minutes, when finally, Jo spoke.

"There," she said, turning her whole body to the side. "The draft is coming from over there." She crept forward in the dark, toward an area of the room even darker than where they had stood waiting. Maddie followed close behind.

"Be careful, Jo," Maddie whispered. "I can't see a thing. I think it's time we used another one of our mat—"

Clang!

Jo kicked a metal object on the floor and stopped moving. "What was that?" she asked her sister.

"I don't *know* because I can't *see*," Maddie retorted. "Light your candle!"

Jo fumbled with the matchbox in the dark. She rolled the remaining wooden matchsticks under her fingers: there were three left. "We have exactly three matches, Maddie. We have to make them count." She struck a match on the side of the box and lit Maddie's candle first, then her own. She bent down to see what she had kicked.

"That's a pitchfork," Maddie whispered. She moved it across the stone floor with the toe of her boot. "And there . . . there it is!" She reached down and retrieved the strip of knitted wool from the middle prong. "Safi's stocking—we're right where she stood!"

Jo peered into the dark little room, ducking down low to go inside. "And this must be the cellar she was talking about," she muttered. "The ceiling is so low I can barely—" She turned her head to look up and almost dropped her candle.

"What, Jo?" Maddie asked, ducking inside the cellar to join her sister.

Jo was about to answer when a quick gust of wind whooshed down from the ceiling of the cellar, blowing both twins' candles out.

Maddie coughed from the smoke. "Where did that come from?!" she choked.

Jo dropped her extinguished candle and placed her hands on the ceiling. "Aha," she said, her fingers sliding through the square holes. "This isn't a ceiling. This is a metal grate, like the one into Troxler's classroom."

Maddie crept toward the sound of her sister's voice and put her hands above her head, feeling around the metal grate with her fingertips. "This is it, Jo. The chimney. And Safi wasn't in a cellar, she was in a *fireplace!*" She shook her head. "All this time it was right under our noses . . . and we passed right by it."

"We don't know for sure yet, Sis. When I say push, lift up," Jo instructed. She pushed quickly up with one hand above her head, rattling the grate. "It's hinged on your side, so we should be able to push it up to lean against the wall."

The girls laced their fingers on both hands through the metal grate, gripping tightly.

"Push!" Jo grunted, and with great effort, she and Maddie stood up out of their crouched positions, lifting the metal grate on one side to lean it against the side wall. Finally able to stand up straight, the twins huddled close to each other in the enclosed space.

"If we're right about this," Maddie said quietly, "we're standing at the bottom of a treasure trove."

Jo took the box of matches from her pocket and retrieved one of the two remaining matchsticks. "Our candles are on the floor!" she moaned, kicking her foot along the ground to find them.

"It doesn't matter," Maddie said. "Light that match. We only need one good look in here to know the truth."

Jo struck the match on the side of the box and lifted it up into the chimney. As the flame grew brighter, the girls looked up in awe. The walls were lined with treasures of all kinds: crystal goblets and rhinestone jewelry sparkled, twinkling like stars in the shadows. Statuettes and framed artwork were stacked on top of one another as the treasure went up farther and farther, where the faint light from the matchstick couldn't reach. But all these treasures were dwarfed by what was hanging halfway up the far wall—the antique Bavarian clock.

The frying pan-size pendulum, just like the one at the Christmas market in Mittenwald, swept back and forth almost silently along the chimney wall. A beautiful castle surrounded by a forest and waterfalls was carved into the wood, and the lacquered finish gleamed in the dim light. Maddie and Jo stood and gazed at all the beautiful objects as the flame burned farther and farther down the tiny matchstick.

"You know what I *don't* see," Jo observed, "are Albert's bone and our shovels."

Maddie nodded. "They must be wedged in between all of this stuff. After all, the clock chimed when I dropped your shovel down the chimney. It must have slipped behind the clock and flipped some sort of switch," she reasoned. "I wonder if it will go off again at four o'clock . . ."

Jo looked down at her wristwatch and panicked. "The professor is coming to check our work at three forty-five, and that's in ten minutes! We have to get back up there."

"For all we know, Jo, he could be one of the thieves Max is talking about," Maddie whispered desperately. "He's the only one with a key to the rooftop. We can't trust anyone. We have to go straight to Kronenberg before he finds out what we've been up to."

Jo's fingers burned as the flame approached the bottom of the matchstick. She took one last look around the chimney walls and lowered her hand to blow it out, but a final gust of wind swept down the chimney and beat her to it. "To the stables," she commanded, and the girls ducked back into the fireplace, lit their candles with the one remaining match, and ran down the tunnel as fast as they could without letting the flames go out.

Jo threw her shoulder against the trapdoor above her head one more time.

"You're going to break something," Maddie scolded, and pushed her sister out of the way. "And I don't mean the trapdoor." She pushed with her hands as hard as she could, but she could still feel the slide lock holding the door down.

Jo rubbed her aching shoulder. "We don't have time for this, Maddie. We either have to get out of the tunnel here *now*, or we have to run all the way back to the library or conservatory entrance. And we're out of matches, so it will take twice as long for us to get there in the dark, and the professor will—"

Maddie threw her hand over her sister's mouth. Faint footsteps could be heard through the cracks in the trapdoor, and a girl's voice sang quietly. Both girls held their breath as the footsteps neared the tunnel entrance.

Step, step, silence. The footsteps came closer. *Step, step, step,* and then singing. After a few seconds, the girls could hear the voice clearly.

"*Quando se pianta la bella polenta, La bella polenta se pianta così,*" the voice sang.

Jo put her ear up to the trapdoor. "It's Italian," she said, translating as much as she could in her head. "It's about . . . food . . . a food called polenta."

The girls looked at each other in the dark.

"Val!" they said at the same time.

Jo banged on the trapdoor as hard as she could. "Val!?" she shouted. "Val, let us out!"

The singing stopped and the footsteps scampered across the floor. The lock slid off the trapdoor with a loud *clack*, and it opened slowly.

"Maddie, Jo," Val said casually, smiling and helping her friends out of the tunnel. "How was your detention?"

"Boy, are we glad you're here!" Maddie blurted as she and Jo climbed into the horse pen.

"Of course, I am here. I am always at the stables after class," she said, painfully unaware that the twins were in a hurry. "What are *you* doing here?"

Jo brushed the hay off her jacket and skirt while Maddie pulled straw pieces from her hair. "We have to tell you later," she said quickly. "We're on our way to Kronenberg's office!"

"Can I come?" Val asked innocently.

But the girls were already running out of the stables.

"Just meet us back at the dormitory, okay?" Maddie called from the doorway, and she and Jo raced across the lawn toward the dining hall doors.

CHAPTER THIRTY-ONE

THE SPECIAL GUEST

Maddie looked at her wristwatch for the third time that minute. 3:48, it still said, and she pushed her toes off the floor harder to try and keep up with her lanky sister. As the twins barreled down the administration hallway toward Kronenberg's office, Maddie couldn't help but prepare herself for the praise she and Jo were about to get from her. *Imagine Kronenberg's delight,* she thought, *when we tell her we've solved the mystery.*

Jo put her manners aside for a moment. After all, this could be classified as an emergency. She turned the knob and swung the headmistress's door open.

"Headmistress!" Maddie cried out just before stepping inside the office. "We have to tell you someth—"

But she stopped short. She and Jo had interrupted a tea party. And there, at the low-rising table, the headmistress held her teacup halfway between her saucer and her mouth. Professor Troxler shook her head in disgust at the disruptive students, and a familiar bald man smirked as if he had expected such an outburst.

"Oh," Jo stammered. "I . . . we . . . we didn't realize that you had company, Headmistress." She tried to compose herself, smoothing her skirt and pulling on the waist of her jacket.

Maddie was still determined, though. "Headmistress, Professor, Sir," she said confidently, nodding as she addressed the adults in the room. "We're so sorry to interrupt. But if we could speak to you privately, Headmistress, for just one moment—"

The headmistress closed her eyes and took a deep breath. She looked exhausted. "Ladies, I am in the middle of a very important meeting. But do come in. Let me introduce you to our special guest." She turned to the man. "These are two of my most . . ." She searched the girls' faces for a moment. "*Spirited* students, Madeline and Josephine Livingston." The man's eyes widened, and his smirk turned into a smile. He stood and approached the girls.

"Hello, Madeline and Josephine Livingston," he said, his German accent soothing and calm. "My name is Mr. Von Arx. It's a pleasure to meet you formally."

Maddie stared at the man's face, recognizing his mustache. She knew she had seen him before, but couldn't remember where. "It's nice to meet you," she said cautiously. Jo nodded.

"Mr. Von Arx is passing through on his way to France," the headmistress explained as the girls caught their breath.

Jo felt strange, as if she was being introduced to someone she already knew. "How long will you be staying in Saint-Marcel, Mr. Von Arx?" Jo asked, running through a whole year of memories as she tried to recall where she'd seen him before.

Professor Troxler huffed. "You will have to pardon the Livingston twins. They're American."

"That's quite all right, Flora," Mr. Von Arx insisted, holding his hand up behind him and still facing the girls. "I'm not quite sure how long my visit will last. I think the mountain air is good for this old man," he said, taking in a deep breath. "I may stay indefinitely." He turned to the headmistress. "That is, if Klara continues to be such a gracious host."

The headmistress forced a smile but said nothing.

"We should be going then, unless you could spare just a moment to meet with us in the hallway, Headmistress Kronenberg," Maddie persisted, her eyes pleading for the chance to tell what she and Jo had discovered.

The headmistress shook her head. "I cannot. But I can see you tomorrow for tea. Just like the first day of school. All right, ladies?" she said, her voice taking a stern tone that the girls had not heard yet.

"Yes, Headmistress," the girls said with defeat, and they curtsied once more.

"Enjoy your stay, Mr. Von Arx," Jo added politely, taking one last look at his face.

"I'm sure I will, Josephine," Mr. Von Arx said as he sat back down. "I'm sure I will."

"Maybe"—Jo breathed heavily a few times before continuing—"maybe he was one of the gangsters from the tavern in Fes?" Her chest and shoulders ached from all the running they'd squeezed into ten minutes, but her mind wouldn't stop racing with ideas of where they had met the man from Kronenberg's office.

Maddie shook her head. "I didn't catch more than a glimpse of those men, and it was really dark that night. I was paying more attention on how to get out of there in one piece than their faces," she admitted as she wiped the sweat from her brow. "But it's a good theory to start with. Those men were angry at Henri, and Henri knows the headmistress. Maybe that's why he was there? Because of something Henri did?"

"No idea, Sis. We can ask Kronenberg tomorrow at tea."

"And tell her what, Jo? That Henri took us to a *tavern*, at *midnight*, and then loaded us into a truck so we could escape an *angry mob*? Let's wait. Maybe something will jog our memory."

The twins slowed down as they neared the history hall, doubling over to catch their breath once they'd reached its stone walls.

"There you are, Livingston twins!" Professor Natalio shouted, waving down to them from the rooftop of the history building. "Stay there. I'm coming down."

"Don't tell him anything, Jo," Maddie warned.

"But what if he asks what we're doing down here? We were supposed to be up on the roof top when he arrived."

"Just let me do the talking."

Jo nodded nervously as they waited on the lawn.

Professor Natalio clattered and clanged out the history hall doors, carrying the girls' full buckets as far away from his body as he could. "*Accipicchia!*" he said, half smiling and half grimacing. "Not a job for the weak-nosed, eh?" He put the buckets down near the bushes and walked over to the girls. "The roof looks beautiful, and the goats look satisfied," he praised them. "You finished early?"

The girls nodded and smiled.

"Well," Maddie started. "We finished cleaning, and we gave the goats their treats and Albert his bone, so we thought we'd get down off the roof before we got careless and tripped or fell . . . or something." Jo nodded silently.

The professor looked concerned. "Oh yes, ladies. You must be so careful up on the rooftop. It can be a very dangerous place if you become careless! But—ah"—he paused—"where are my shovels?"

Maddie put on her most innocent face. "Oh my, Professor," she said regretfully. "I think we must have left them up on the roof top somewhere. You didn't see them?"

The professor shook his head. "No, no, I didn't. But I will pick them up when I go back onto the roof. It will be sooner than later!"

I'm sure it will, Professor, Jo thought, and imagined Professor Natalio hiding his stolen treasure down the chimney in the night. *Maybe tonight, even.*

"I'll take you back to the headmistress," he said, taking a few steps toward the dining hall.

"Oh, Professor," Maddie insisted. "You don't have to take us *all that way*. We know you have important things to do. We can find our way just fine."

Professor Natalio squinted at the sun for a moment and nodded. "Yes, okay. I have some cleaning up to do myself," he said, holding his dirt-smudged hands out in front of them. "Thank you again for your hard work!"

The girls nodded and turned toward the dining hall just as the clock began to strike four.

"I don't believe it," Nixie said with a scowl. "Sweet Professor Natalio is our thief?"

"Who else could it be?" Maddie asked impatiently.

"Well, what about Troxler?" she offered. "I heard it with my own ears: Kronenberg said she was taking things from the school."

"And maybe that man we saw with her in the office is helping," Jo added.

Maddie shook her head and played with her string of candied nuts for a moment. Her parents had sent a whole box of the candy—enough for all their friends—from a seaside town as they made their way to Switzerland from Siberia. "She may have a part in it, and that man, too, but Professor Natalio is definitely involved. He's the only one with a key to the rooftop, and that's where all the treasures are lowered into the chimney, according to Max. He even said he was going back up *sooner than later*. I bet he goes tonight."

Millie perked up. "This is it, then, Nixie," she chirped. "We know where to look, when to look, and who to look for. Tonight is the night we complete our quest."

"Not a moment too soon," Françoise chided. "Exams are in less than a week."

The words stung Jo's ears. *Exams are in less than a week*, she thought. That meant the end of Madame Molineaux's for her and Maddie, the end of their new friendships, and the end of secret quests. Their parents had been on their way to Saint-Marcel from Siberia for more than three weeks, and would be arriving just after exams finished to take them back to Boston. The end of the school year had never felt so bittersweet.

"Let's go over the plan again," Nixie requested. "Millie and I are going to leave at midnight and hide in the science hall gardens?"

"Exactly," Maddie said, pointing to the gardens on the map she'd received on her first day of school from the headmistress. "You'll head out the dining hall doors and across the lawn together. When you get there, Millie will head into the vegetable garden, and you'll go into the outer ring of the labyrinth. Then watch the history hall rooftop."

Millie raised her hand. "I have a question," she stated as though she were in a classroom. "Why can't we just go through the tunnels to the science hall and into the gardens?"

"It's too dangerous now," Safi warned in her most official voice. "Rosemary, Kronenberg, Troxler, and maybe Professor Natalio could be in the tunnels at any time. It's better to be outside than down there, especially if you have to hide."

"Hide from what?" Millie demanded, feeling the butterflies in her stomach beat their wings faster and faster.

"We don't know, Millie," groaned Françoise. "But Safi's right. If you see anyone, anyone at all, hide. We're not dealing with Rosemary, or kittens, or even ghosts. She gave Nixie a sideways look. "There are real thieves out there, up to no good, and they might not be so kind to two spying students. Not even ones who cry or ask for milk, Nixie."

Nixie gulped.

"Is this enough excitement for you, Millie?" Françoise asked, her stern expression relaxing into a half-smile.

Millie nodded. "Quite enough, yes," she sputtered.

"Don't worry. Just get to the gardens, mind your stations, and keep your eyes open."

CHAPTER THIRTY-TWO

GHOSTS IN THE GARDEN

Millie knotted her boot laces before tying the bow. Tonight was not the night to trip over untied laces, she thought, and she stood up to take another look out the Room Five windows.

It was almost midnight, and the dormitory hallways were dim and silent. The grounds of Madame Molineaux's looked as they usually did: empty and still, except for the front drive. Parked to the side of the massive entryway were four covered delivery trucks.

None of the girls had seen the trucks arrive, or had seen anyone get into or out of them. They took turns looking every few minutes, but now it was just Millie who patrolled the rug in front of the window. She was nervous and hoping that some sort of action near the trucks would persuade her roommates to cancel her and Nixie's mission. But no such action came. The faint chimes of the chimney-concealed clock meant it was time to go.

"You will have safety checkpoints along the way," Val instructed, holding her painstakingly neat list of locations in front of Millie and Nixie. "I will stay at the window to watch the trucks. Safi will be hiding in the lavatory in her robe so she can make sure the dormitory hallway is clear." She pointed farther down the list. "Françoise will be in the shadows of the utility corridor to monitor the main hall, Maddie will be in the Grand Corridor, and Jo will be at the dining hall doors. Are you ready?"

Millie and Nixie exchanged nervous glances.

"We're counting on you two to find out exactly who is up on that rooftop," Jo said, smiling gently. "I know you can do it, and tomorrow at tea we'll be able to tell Kronenberg exactly who is stealing from her."

"Thanks for the pep talk," Millie said, but she wasn't sure it had worked. She took a deep breath and stuck out her chin. "All aboard who's coming aboard," she sang, and pushed Nixie into the hallway.

"Coo . . . coo," Nixie whistled back into the first-year hallway. She was standing on the bottom step of the staircase to the main hall, peeking her head up to watch as the other girls entered the hallway.

Safi was first. She emerged from her room dressed in her robe and sleeping cap, and she stretched out her arm to the side and yawned dramatically while she trudged toward the lavatory. She gave a quick wave of acknowledgment to Nixie and ducked out of sight.

The Room Five door opened next, and Millie, Françoise, Maddie, and Jo filed out silently, creeping up the hall toward the staircase. Val stuck her head out, gave the thumbs-up sign, and closed the door.

At the threshold of the main hall, Françoise patted Millie and Nixie on their backs. "Good luck," she whispered. She tucked her torch under her arm and walked quickly to the utility corridor, disappearing into the darkness.

The four remaining girls tiptoed their way to the narrow rug and continued to the Grand Corridor, where Maddie slipped behind a heavy velvet drape. "See you in an hour," she whispered, and then there were only three girls left.

"Remember," Jo reminded Nixie as they ran through the imposing Grand Corridor, its wall-mounted lanterns and floor-to-ceiling windows casting shadows every which way around them. "You've got to get into the labyrinth. The bushes won't be too dense this time of year, and you can poke your head out wherever you want to get the best view of the history hall."

Nixie nodded. "Just as long as no one sees us on our way there, I'll be completely cloaked in leaves and darkness."

"Right. And Millie, if you crouch down in the vegetable garden, you can crawl up and down the rows of plants as you need to. "

"What if someone comes after us?" Nixie worried out loud.

"No one should be there to see you," Jo assured her. "But if they are, you can always hop behind a statue. They're all over the place." She stopped running. They were at the end of the dining hall, just in front of the pair of doors leading to the rest of the campus. "I'll have the door cracked open," she said as

Nixie grabbed Millie's hand. "So I'll be able to hear . . . at least a little bit."

Millie looked her straight in the eyes. "If Nixie and I do our jobs without being noticed, you shouldn't hear a thing. But if you do," she warned, her eyes growing wider, "run."

"Break!" Millie whispered the word as softly as she could, but loud enough so that Nixie could hear her over their hasty footsteps across the lawn. She let go of Nixie's hand and sprinted to the vegetable garden, finding a hiding spot in between rows of young tomato vines. She bent down, covered her face in leaves, and settled in for the stakeout.

Nixie, having forgotten the precise location of the entrance to the labyrinth, raced along the outer wall of manicured bushes until she found the small doorway. She ran in, turned back toward the vegetable garden, and walked as far as she thought she needed to in order to check in with Millie.

She rustled her hands through a sparsely filled section of the bushes, moved a few flimsy branches out of the way, and climbed in to poke her head through the other side. Across the way, she saw Millie's legs covered in white stocking material, jutting up alongside the tomato plants in the vegetable garden. They were almost glowing in the moonlight compared to all the green surrounding them. *"Donnerwetter!"* she exclaimed softly in German. "You're going to attract the moths with lamps like those!"

While Nixie was bemoaning Millie's bright white legs, Millie caught sight of Nixie's head through the bushes and slapped her hand to her forehead. "Good gosh, Nixie!" she whispered to herself, sure that Nixie's round moonlike face and blond curls in the dark bushes would alert any passersby that they were under surveillance. "She might come in handy as a spotlight later."

All of a sudden, Nixie's face recoiled back into the bushes.

Surely she didn't hear me, Millie thought, and she leaned into the tomato plants to take a closer look at the space where her friend had poked her head through. But there was nothing. No twigs snapping, no leaves rustling. Only silence, until Millie saw what Nixie had hidden from so quickly.

Millie let out a high-pitched yelp and threw her hands over her mouth the moment she saw it—a tall, white, billowing ghost, formless and featureless, approaching inch by inch up the garden path toward her. She bit down on her finger to keep silent and scrambled to the front of the vegetable garden, careful not to stand taller than the rows of tomato plants. She zigzagged in her confusion, but she stopped in her tracks when she saw her partner standing still, as if frozen in ice, at the entrance to the labyrinth. Nixie's face was paler than before, and she stared up at the ghastly figure with fearful eyes.

Millie jumped out of the vegetable garden and ran to Nixie. The ghost was still a good distance away from them, its white body swelling and retracting in the wind as it floated midair. She grabbed Nixie's arm, bent down low, and they started to run toward the dining hall doors.

Nixie snapped out of her daze. She was being dragged along by Millie, who continually looked behind them, ensuring their ghost wasn't gaining on them. But Millie didn't see what was coming over the small hill down to the arts hall: another ghost, just as large and harrowing as the first, that would surely trap them in the middle of the lawn with no clear path to the dining hall.

Nixie took hold of Millie's arm and hurled her in a new direction—toward the three-tiered fountain—and ran like she never had before. In the presence of real ghosts, her feet grew wings, and she barely felt them stomping against the ground. Without a thought, she stopped at the fountain's edge and plunged herself and Millie into the bubbling icy water.

Jo took her foot off the kickplate of the dining hall door and let it shut. She knew what she had heard, and now she had a decision to make: either run out the doors to help her friends, or run back to Room Five, collecting Maddie, Françoise, and Safi along the way.

She backed away from the door and thought for a brief moment. If she went back to the first-year hallway, at least there would be five of them to help the two in need. Besides, Millie *had* told her to run if she heard anything, hadn't she? Jo nodded her head once with conviction, turned on her heel, and dashed through the dining hall into the Grand Corridor with lightning speed.

"Maddie!" she called as softly as she could, trying to recall which curtain her sister had slipped behind. Almost instantly,

Maddie popped her head out from the drapes and motioned for her sister to join her. Jo ran to the window and slipped behind the heavy velvet curtain.

"Something's happened," she breathed heavily. "I heard Millie cry out and I ran back here as fast as I could. We need to get the others."

Maddie leaned back against the stone wall. "All right, go get them. I'll stay here and keep watch in case Millie and Nixie come running," she said, grabbing on to the velvet curtain and gently pushing her sister out of her hiding place. "Okay?"

Jo shook her head. "Either you're coming with me, or I'm staying here with you." She clutched the velvet next to her sister's hand.

Maddie gave her sister a puzzled look. "What's wrong, Jo?" she asked, wondering why her sister had become so clingy.

Jo swallowed hard. "I'm . . . I'm *scared*," she whimpered. "Genuinely scared."

Maddie shoved the drapes out of the way and hugged her sister tight. "It's okay, Jo," she said softly as she pulled her tall sister's head down onto her shoulder. "I'm scared, too. But this is almost over, you know? All of it. The riddle, the thieves, the mystery . . . Mom and Dad's excavation in Siberia, the school year . . . it's all coming to an end." It was the longest hug the girls had shared since arriving at Madame Molineaux's almost eight months ago.

Jo wiped her face on Maddie's sleeve and lifted her head. "You're right," she sniffed. "I guess there's no time to waste, is there?"

Maddie shook her head. "I'll go with you. Let's get back to the others."

The impressive fountain in the middle of Madame Molineaux's was popular among students as a meeting place, thinking spot, and, on occasion, swimming hole for those who dared dip their toes in. A cold spring far beneath the school provided water for the fountain, giving it a year-round temperature just above freezing and the clarity of sparkling crystal.

Stout fish, carved from stone and inlaid with mother-of-pearl, splayed their tails high into the air around the fountain base. Their stoic stares guarded the splash pool and spurted streams of water up to the seashell-shaped top basin, where forest birds often bathed and chattered, even in winter. Pudgy little cherubs, the busiest by far of all the fountain sculptures, wore mischievous smiles as they leaned out from the center column of the middle tier to pour water from vases, pitchers, and giant clam shells into the splash pool below. The fountain had hosted many a private moment for joyous or heartbroken students over the years, and tonight, it would serve as something it never had before: a hiding place.

Nixie couldn't tell if her teeth were rattling against one another from the cold of the fountain pool or for fear of the two ghosts approaching. Both predicaments were bad enough on their own, but combined, they were a recipe for sheer panic. She and Millie were up to their chins in the choppy ice water, gasping for breath as the sculptures splashed them from all sides. The ghosts floated toward each other at a quickened pace, destined to meet only yards away from the fountain.

"Pull your jacket up over your head!" Millie whispered between chokes and sputters. She reached behind her head and pulled the collar of her jacket up and over her hair and eyes, leaving only a small space to see out. Nixie did the same, and only the lower halves of their faces could be seen between their sopping dark coats and the black water.

"What do we do now?" Nixie quavered, her bluish lips trembling just above the splash pool surface.

"You mean you don't have a plan?! What are we doing in the fountain, then?"

"This was the only place to go without being seen by the ghosts," Nixie insisted. "I got us here, now *you* come up with the plan!"

Millie spat water out of her mouth and huffed. "What *can* we do from here? We have to wait. And watch." She strained her neck to see behind them to the history hall roof. Other than Albert and a few wandering goats, the rooftop was empty.

"I can't stay here much longer," Nixie whined. "I can't feel my fingers or my toes! And my face. She pressed on her cheeks with her fingertips. "I can't feel that eith—" Nixie's eyes grew wider. The two ghosts had slowed to a stop and were now inches from each other, their gauzy bodies undulating back and forth the way reeds bent and swayed in the wind.

And then she saw them. Two men, dressed from head to toe in black, emerged from behind the ghosts and began speaking in French and pointing.

Millie was dumbfounded. What was this? A costume parade? She listened to the men's conversation but couldn't make out their words over the splashing sounds in the fountain.

One of the men pulled the black cap from his head and shook it at the other man, plainly arguing with him. He walked from his ghost to the other man's, put his hands on its billowing body, and snatched it away to reveal the real phantom: One of the statues from the garden, which had been covered by a white sheet. Nixie gasped and looked over to Millie apologet-ically, both bewildered and a little embarrassed that she had been so afraid of the "ghosts."

But Millie just stared straight ahead. "What?" she blurted quietly. "They're taking the statues?" *I'd like to see them try and lower those into the chimney,* she thought. The man snatched the sheet from the other statue and made a big show of walking around it and pointing to its face. "That's Calliope, from just outside the arts hall!" she told Nixie. The marble woman stared off across the lake, her thoughtful expression unchanged by the upset and commotion.

One of the men stopped talking suddenly and turned to face the fountain.

"Quiet!" Millie squeaked as softly as she could. But the man took two more steps toward them.

"Down," Nixie whispered, getting ready to hold her breath. "Down."

Millie and Nixie took the deepest breaths they could and sank down into the black pool.

CHAPTER THIRTY-THREE

QUESTS COMPLETED

Françoise, having seen Maddie and Jo enter the main hall, ran out to meet them on the rug. "You are back already?"

"Jo heard Millie yell outside," Maddie informed her. "We should all go together, don't you think?"

Françoise nodded quickly. "Jo, you go and get Val and Safi. Maddie, come with me."

Jo ran up the steps to the first-year hallway, and Françoise led Maddie into the dark utility corridor, switching on the torch as soon as they were halfway down it.

"What are we looking for?" Maddie asked as she looked around at the cobwebs and rusted metal racks.

"I came this way to see where Nixie fell through the rotten boards. But—" Françoise paused and held her arm out to slow

Maddie. "Careful now," she interrupted herself. "This is where it gets tricky."

Maddie stepped cautiously around the old, warped and splintered boards, wondering exactly how long they'd been in disrepair. Everything else at Madame Molineaux's seemed to be properly maintained. Why not the maintenance hallway?

Françoise bent down at the edge of the broken boards where Nixie had fallen and shined her light into it. "Nixie said she fell into a pile of sawdust, nearly landing on a shovel."

Maddie nodded. "So?"

Françoise pointed down to the stone floor beneath them. "Don't you see? Someone has put some burlap sacks on top of the sawdust pile."

Maddie rubbed her eyes. In the orange glow of the torch light, she couldn't tell what was what—but Françoise was right. The area had definitely been furnished with more than saw-dust and a shovel. "Someone's been in that tunnel since Nixie," Maddie whispered.

Françoise nodded. "Let's keep this between you and me for now. I don't want to alarm the others."

"Sure," Maddie said softly. "But we'll tell them later, right?"

"Yes, later." Françoise stood and helped Maddie to her feet, and the two girls walked in silence back toward the entrance to the main hall. They arrived at the doorway just before Val, Safi, and Jo came galloping down the first-year steps.

"Go back!" Val whispered in a raspy voice. "Back!" She pushed the air forward with her arms.

The three girls piled into the utility corridor entrance, nearly knocking Maddie and Françoise down in the process.

"Something, it is happening outside," Val said between breaths. "Lots of the men. They are getting the trucks ready."

No sooner than she had said the words, the front doors of Madame Molineaux's swung open, and several men dressed in all black walked into the main hall.

Françoise pulled Val and Safi in by their jacket sleeves and Maddie grabbed Jo by the arm, bringing the girls out of the moonlight and into the safe shadows of the utility corridor. They huddled together in the darkness and watched as two veiled statues were wheeled into the main hall from the Grand Corridor.

"*Attention! Attention aux fissures du plancher,*" one man said to the men transporting the statues. He continued to bark orders in French.

Françoise kneeled forward at the front of the group. "I'll translate," she said. The men were speaking so fast that even she had a hard time understanding them. She cupped her hand over her ear. "He said to be careful," she whispered. "That the boss can't sell a statue with a broken nose." She listened again. "There are eleven more statues they have to load onto the trucks tonight. He told them to hurry."

Three men gathered around to move each statue, carefully inching the wheels of the hand trucks over the doorstep and out of the school.

Françoise jumped out from the utility corridor and took one quick, sweeping gaze around the main hall. "We have to go back to our room," she said, and began pulling the girls from the shadows.

"What about Millie and Nixie?" Jo reminded her. "Who knows what kind of trouble they're in . . . and now they don't have any safety checkpoints on their way back!"

Françoise kept pushing Jo across the main hall. "We're no good to anyone if we get caught, too. If they're not back in a half hour, we'll go out into the tunnels."

Millie let another puff of air escape her mouth, sending a flurry of bubbles up to the water's surface. She and Nixie had been submerged in the icy water for at least half a minute. It would only be a moment before she had to go back up for air.

She fought for another few seconds, clenching her eyes tighter and shaking her head before she resigned and poked her head above the water. She drew in a much-needed breath as silently as she could and opened her eyes. The men were just in front of the dining hall doors with their statues, trying to prop the doors open and wheel them inside. Millie relaxed her shoulders and breathed hard. She waited for Nixie to surface.

"Nixie!" she snapped, waving her arms around in the water vigorously to find her friend. But Nixie wasn't next to her anymore. Millie trudged through the splashing water in a panicked search, making it halfway around the splash pool before she heard a voice.

"I'm over here!" Nixie whispered, looking quite pleased with herself. Nixie bobbed up and down and squeezed the water from her long, blond hair.

"I thought you were drowned," Millie spat. "What are you, a mermaid?"

Nixie shook her head. "Just good at holding my breath, I guess."

Millie nodded and winced. "The men are gone, but there's no telling when they'll return. We've got to get back to the dormitory . . . Nixie?"

Nixie was staring up at the history hall rooftop, squinting her eyes. "Is that . . . ?"

336

Millie turned around in a flash. On the history hall rooftop, Albert bounded and leaped around a man carrying a long ladder. "It *is*. At least, I think it is." The girls watched as the man pushed the ladder against the far wall of one of the towers. A rotund woman appeared next to him and shooed Albert away from the ladder.

"Then who is *that*?" Nixie wondered out loud. "That looks like—"

"Madame Lécuyer," Millie finished her sentence. "I'd recognize that girlish figure anywhere."

Squish, squash. Squish, squash. Millie and Nixie walked down the Grand Corridor quickly toward the main hall, each clinging to her own wall of windows and drapes for safe cover in case the men in black reappeared. Water dripped out their jacket sleeves and off the hems of their skirts each time they stepped, and every ounce of fabric, skin, and hair on the two girls was drenched beyond even the worst rainstorm's doing.

They reached the main hall and tiptoed from the rug to the staircase of the west wing, careful not to slip in the puddles they were dispensing onto the stone floor. Nixie had never been so happy to see the warm, cozy first-year hallway, not even after her fall through the utility corridor. She and Millie ran up the stairs and burst into Room Five.

"You're all right!" Jo cried, running over to them from the window where the rest of the girls monitored the activity around the trucks. "You're . . . *soaked*." She bent down and took the bottom of Millie's skirt in her hands and wrung it out onto the floor. "Have you been in the lake?"

"The lake might have been warmer," Nixie chattered. She and Millie were noticeably chilled to the bone, and blew on their icy hands to warm them.

"Safi, Val," Françoise ordered from the windowsill. "Get them out of their uniforms and into their robes. Maddie, Jo, get a bucket of embers from the library fireplace. They should still be warm from the late-night studiers."

Val sprang up and yanked Millie's and Nixie's robes from their wardrobes while Safi helped peel the girls' arms from their heavy jacket sleeves. Maddie and Jo crept out of the Room Five door, returning moments later with a glowing bucket of ash.

Françoise stacked her textbooks two-high in a square shape, laid down a metal tray on top, and motioned for Maddie to bring the bucket. Millie and Nixie dashed over to warm their hands and feet at the improvised woodstove.

"You're not afraid it will burn the school books?" Val asked, remembering what Professor Troxler had once told her class about turning in beat-up books at the end of the school year.

Françoise shrugged. "I'm done studying for my exams anyway."

"Yes, but Troxler said if our books were—"

"I don't think a couple of burnt books will matter compared to what Madame Molineaux's is losing at this very moment," Françoise said, taking another look out the window. "Have you seen this, Millie? Nixie?"

"Seen it?" Millie piped up. "We were right in the middle of it!"

"We had to hide in the fountain just to stay out of sight!" Nixie added, nursing her chilly toes with a hot cloth. "But at least we had a good view of the rooftop." She turned to Maddie. "You were right. It was Professor Natalio all along."

"And not just him," said Millie. "Madame Lécuyer was helping him."

Jo shook her head. "My two favorite professors," she moaned. "Who will be next on the list of criminals?"

Safi snorted. "I'm voting for Kronenberg," she said sarcastically, and for the first time all evening, the girls were laughing.

The makeshift woodstove glowed less and less as the girls watched the parade of statues exit the castle. Each one of the life-size sculptures had been painstakingly loaded into the back of one of the trucks and tied down with rope by the men in black. The girls had finally grown tired and uninterested: Val and Safi were asleep on Françoise's bed, Millie was curled up on the floor next to the woodstove, and Françoise flipped slowly through the pages of her library book on ancient tapestries, asking a very sleepy Nixie questions about Bavaria every few minutes. Only Maddie and Jo remained at the window to watch the activity by the trucks.

"I just don't understand," Jo mumbled. "Why would someone steal the school's statues just to sell them? Surely Kronenberg suspects something. We can't be the only ones who know about all this."

"But suppose we *are* the only ones who know," Maddie argued. "What then?"

"Then we'd better tell an adult," Françoise said calmly, walking over to the window where they sat. "If you know one you can trust."

"Why should we have to tell an adult?" Maddie complained. "Why hasn't anyone noticed what's going on around here?"

Françoise smirked and shook her head. "You'd be surprised what adults don't notice, even when it's right in front of their faces."

"We should tell Kronenberg," Jo conceded with dread. "Let's go wake her up."

"Just you and Maddie," Françoise corrected her.

"Why just me and Maddie?"

"Someone has to stay here with the ashes, Jo," she explained softly. "Besides, she'll take the bad news better if it comes from her two favorite students."

Maddie held her fist an inch from the headmistress's door, wincing at the thought of waking her in the middle of the night. *This would have been so much better if we could have strolled into tea tomorrow with all the answers,* she thought, replaying the imaginary scene in her head.

Kronenberg would have praised the two girls for exposing the thieving professors, written a flattering news article for the front page of the school newspaper—LIVINGSTON TWINS SAVE MADAME MOLINEAUX'S FROM MASTERMIND THIEVES!—and created a special award in their honor for Best Students of the Year, for which, of course, she and Jo would be the inaugural recipients. But that wasn't going to happen now, and this would have to do. She sighed and rapped on the door.

"Wait for a few minutes," Jo told her. "She'll have to wake up and get out of bed, and put on her robe and slippers before she comes to the door. And that's if she even heard you knock."

The girls waited and listened for footsteps, but none came. "Maybe you should knock again?"

Maddie looked around. The nearest dormitory room was more than thirty paces away, and she figured she could knock harder this time.

Rap, rap, *rap!* she knocked again. The door rattled inside the doorsill. "It doesn't even sound like it's locked," Maddie said, and she reached down to see if the doorknob would turn. She twisted it in one direction and then the other. On her third turn, the door cracked open.

"Let's get out of here!" she whispered, and scurried back toward Room Five. But Jo wasn't following. Maddie stopped in the hallway and watched as Jo kicked the bottom of the door with her toe.

"What are you doing?" Maddie hissed. "If you were wondering how to get expelled just days before school ends, *this* is how!"

Jo looked unapologetic. "You're the one who opened the door . . . and I think we should check on the headmistress." She gently kicked the door again, and this time, it swung all the way open with a long *creak.*

"She's *not* in here, Maddie," Jo insisted. The bed was still made, the teapot on the table was cold, and the fire was nearly out. "The coast is clear."

"Maybe she's hiding, waiting to pop out and catch us *breaking into her chambers,* Jo! Do you realize the trouble we'll be in if we get caught in here?" She looked around at the headmistress's suite. It was one large room, with a four-poster canopy bed, a sitting area by the fireplace, and a dressing area connected to a bathroom.

"We'll be quick. I just want to take a look around," Jo said as she opened drawers, cabinets, and wooden boxes on the headmistress's dresser. "There may be more clues in here." She ran her fingers over the picture frames in front of the mirror, stopping on one embellished frame in particular and picking it up. "Maddie, come over here."

"Just put that down," Maddie scolded, walking over to where her sister stood. "You've had enough looking arou—" She stopped when she saw what was in the frame: a black-and-white photograph of a young woman in a fancy gown with her arms around a more plainly dressed girl. "Is that Kronenberg?" she asked as she studied the faces in the picture.

"Maybe a much, much younger version of Kronenberg," Jo said. "And who is this?" she pointed to the beautiful young woman in the gown, whose light hair tumbled down her shoulders in curls. "She's so pretty."

"Shh!" Maddie whispered, grabbing her sister's arm tight. "Do you hear that?"

Jo listened intently for a few seconds. "No," she said as quietly as she could.

"Voices," Maddie continued. She walked over to the bay window and turned back to her sister with a worried look. "They're not coming from outside."

Not a moment later, the doorknob turned. Jo dashed back to the dresser and stood the picture frame against the mirror, close to the spot where she'd picked it up. The girls dropped to the floor and slid their way under the headmistress's bed just as the door opened wide.

Smack!

The picture frame tipped forward and fell facedown onto the dresser just as Maddie and Jo saw two sets of boots walk across the doorsill into the headmistress's chambers.

"What was that?" a man's voice asked, his German accent familiar to the girls.

"I don't know, Bastien," the headmistress replied curtly. "But I will ask you once more to please leave me in my chambers."

"You're hiding something, Klara. You know I intend to find it, and I *will* find it, whether I do it now or when the castle is mine at last."

The girls looked at each other in shock. *Mr. Von Arx!* Maddie mouthed to her sister. Jo nodded.

The headmistress stopped pacing. "This castle will *never* be yours, Bastien. It belongs to Wilhelmina, and she left it in my care."

"Ah, yes," Mr. Von Arx sang in a sinister voice. "The deed from her uncle. The one he sent so secretly to her before he died. We both know what happened to that deed, Klara. And if I could speak to the dead, I would thank the king personally for ripping it to pieces."

"This is my home . . . and a home to so many other girls!" she pleaded with him.

"Ah-ah-ah, now, Headmistress," he sneered. "A promise is a promise, and I've stayed true to mine. I haven't told the Council about the missing deed. But you, you have steered me this way and that, leading me on wild goose chases for what I want. And you still haven't found it."

"If you could give me more time . . . over the summer . . . I'm sure I can find it."

"I'm done waiting, Klara," Mr. Von Arx growled softly. "I'll finish taking what I can tonight. In the morning, I'm going straight to my friend, the senior councilman."

"But we don't have enough money to buy back the castle at the auction!" the headmistress cried in desperation.

"Ah, but *I* do," he reminded her. "And maybe, my dear Klara, if I'm feeling especially generous when I'm done raiding your precious school, I'll let you come back. As a servant, perhaps." He laughed and walked out of the room, closing the door behind him.

The headmistress flew to the closed door and locked it. She leaned her back against the heavy wood door, the one she'd opened and closed for so many years, and sighed as she gazed around her chambers.

"Oh!" she wailed. She ran to her dresser and picked up the fallen picture frame. "Broken," she whispered, her voice trembling. She hugged the picture to her chest and began to sob.

Maddie and Jo looked at each other with watery eyes. They knew of only one thing to do, and it was worth getting into trouble for. The girls backed out from under the bed and stood together, watching their headmistress cry.

"Headmistress Kronenberg?" Jo said as gently as she could.

The headmistress whirled around, startled, and choked back her tears. Her expression turned from sadness to fury.

"Madeline and Josephine Livingston," she fumed quietly. "You will tell me at once what you're doing in my chambers."

CHAPTER THIRTY-FOUR

THE SCHOOL'S STORY

The headmistress placed a plate of cookies on the table in front of the girls and walked to the fireplace. "I'm sorry, ladies, for my anger earlier."

"And we're so sorry about the broken glass on your picture frame. Honestly, Headmistress," Jo insisted. "We were only coming to tell you what we saw. The door was unlocked, and, well . . ."

The headmistress bent down to stoke the fire. "I believe you, Josephine. And thank you. It's not every day that a headmistress has her students checking up on *her*, is it?"

Maddie finally felt at ease enough to take a cookie. "I can't believe we actually thought Professor Natalio and Madame Lécuyer were stealing from the school." She laughed nervously as she chewed.

"Ahh, yes. Well, Professor Natalio and Madame Lécuyer have been my most loyal colleagues over the decades. I asked them to hide those things in the chimney."

"So Mr. Von Arx couldn't steal them?" Jo asked.

"Well, yes and no." The headmistress cocked her head to one side. "Mr. Von Arx has only just arrived, after all. It's his assistant, Flora Troxler, who we were hiding things from. He forced me to place her here as a professor so that she could report back to him with any findings." She shook her head in disgust. "That woman is absolutely dreadful. And the furthest thing from a professor that I can imagine."

"I'm afraid I don't understand, Headmistress," said Maddie. "What sort of findings would she report to Mr. Von Arx?"

"Valuables, treasures, anything that could be turned into money," the headmistress went on. "This is all about money, Josephine. And in the end, we will be forced to leave Madame Molineaux's because we don't have enough of it." She sighed once more and looked up at the clock on the wall. "It is so very late, ladies. Perhaps we should talk more about this in the morning."

"No!" the girls cried in unison, leaning forward from the sofa.

"Headmistress, if this is about money, what about the treasure Jesper left here for Wilhelmina? Could that save Madame Molineaux's?" Jo blurted.

The headmistress snapped her head back to stare at the girls in bewilderment as soon as Jo finished her question. "Where . . . where did you hear about Jesper and Wilhelmina?" she asked cautiously.

"We read about them in a letter," Maddie admitted.

"A letter, yes . . . and where did you get the letter?" the headmistress spat, rushing the words.

The girls looked at each other anxiously.

"Um," Jo began. "Well . . . Val found it behind the aerial photograph when she was cleaning your office," she said softly.

The headmistress looked down at her folded hands for a moment, recalling the earlier events of that day. She looked up and nodded. "The blood," she fretted. "I should have known it wasn't splinters." She paused once more and then looked straight into the girls' wide eyes. "Do you still have the letter in your possession?"

The girls nodded.

"Good," she sighed with relief. "They don't have it."

"But why would they want the letter?" Maddie persisted.

The headmistress didn't answer. She stood up, smiled curtly, and paced back and forth in front of the fire for a moment to organize her thoughts. "Let me commend you, ladies." She finally spoke with a reserved tone. "I don't know how you stumbled upon our predicament here at the school, but you have certainly done more than your share of detective work."

"Well, it wasn't just us," Jo stammered. "We owe a lot to our friend Max from the school across the lake. He's the one who spotted the professors on the rooftop of the history hall."

The headmistress nodded. "Ah, yes, I suppose General Gremminger's military school would be a suitable location from which to spy on us. And what did he tell you?"

"He wrote us a riddle," Maddie said. "About thieves who come out at night and drop treasures down a chimney. You . . . you won't tell on him, will you?"

"I wouldn't send a cadet to General Gremminger unless he did something very, very wrong," the headmistress said gravely. "The General is a fair man, but he can be ruthless with his punishments."

Maddie gulped and imagined Max locked in a dungeon cell at the ominous castle across the lake.

"And I can't blame the boy for watching from afar. There was much to be spied upon." The headmistress tapped her chin with her finger for a moment. "But, the letter. I suppose Nixie translated it for you?"

Maddie nodded and hesitated before she asked her next question. "Headmistress . . ." She paused before going on. "Is that Wilhelmina there, in the photograph with you?"

The headmistress's eyes saddened as she walked over to pick up the broken picture frame. She studied the picture for the thousandth time. "Yes, Madeline." She turned the picture around and pointed at the beautiful young woman. "This is Princess Wilhelmina Allerspach."

Maddie and Jo held the picture frame in between them on the sofa, waiting in anticipation for the story they had just been promised.

The headmistress gazed aimlessly out the bay window. "Where do I begin?" she wondered out loud. "At the beginning, I suppose." She reached for the picture and took a deep breath. "Do you know, ladies, I was exactly your age—twelve years old—when my family lost everything in Bavaria?" she said slowly. "All of my brothers and sisters and I were expected to forget about school and fun, and go to work for money. It so happened that a friend of my father's knew the head guardsman for the king personally, and I was placed in the young Princess Wilhelmina's chambers the very next day, as a maid."

The girls couldn't imagine their elegant headmistress as anything else, and certainly not as a servant.

"The princess was ten years older than I, but we became true friends within a month of my arrival. I was the only one she asked to remain in her chambers at night, and we would make up stories about star-crossed lovers and knights in shining armor until she fell asleep. And that summer, just like every summer before it, she was sent to live at her uncle's castle in Switzerland. I was brought along to keep her company."

Maddie and Jo's eyes grew wider.

The headmistress, reading the excitement on their faces, smiled and nodded. "Yes, ladies. *This* castle."

The girls gasped.

"Her uncle was a very eccentric man, a hermit who left the confines of nobility for the quiet isolation of Saint-Marcel, and he stayed here in the castle with only his staff for many years until he died. But he loved Wilhelmina dearly, and he taught her about science and astronomy, math and history. He even taught her how to read."

"That sounds like school," Jo said, looking unimpressed.

"Yes, Josephine, it *was* like school. Wilhelmina loved to learn more than anything else, and she wanted desperately to be educated. But in those days, not every school allowed girls . . . especially 'delicate' princesses. Wilhelmina was only to be concerned with becoming a good wife and queen. So, the chance to learn excited her greatly; it was what she loved most about coming here for the summers. During that particular summer, however, she found a new interest in Saint-Marcel. Or, I should say, he found her."

"Jesper?" Maddie asked.

"Yes, Jesper." The headmistress nodded. "The notorious French treasure hunter and pirate."

French pirate, Jo repeated in her head, remembering what Henri had told her and Maddie on the way from Morocco to the coast. "Headmistress, did this pirate like artifacts? You know, from ancient civilizations?"

The headmistress gave her a puzzled look. "I'm not sure, dear, why do you ask?"

"Oh, it's nothing," Jo replied hastily. "I'm sorry, please go on."

"The pirate had just built himself a castle across the lake, and he spied Wilhelmina reading in the gardens one day. He was so taken by her beauty and her love of books, he decided he had to come to meet her. So, one evening, as she strolled through the castle grounds, he rowed across the lake and surprised her."

Maddie's eyes sparkled. "What did she do when she saw him?"

"She screamed, of course," the headmistress replied, smirking a little. "But she stopped once she saw how handsome he was. She later told me that he kneeled down on one knee and proposed marriage as his first words to her, saying that he had traveled the world over and again but had never seen a sight more exquisite than her smiling face."

"Did you think he was handsome, too?" Jo pried.

The headmistress clasped her hands in her lap and blushed. "He was *terribly* handsome," she crooned. "His hair was long and the darkest black. His blue eyes shone like sapphires, and he was strong and tanned from years at sea. We had never seen anyone like him before."

"Did she say she would marry him?" Maddie asked impatiently.

"Eventually, yes. She did. They would visit each other in the gardens and by the lakeshore at night, and it was my job to watch for Jesper's signal—flaming arrows, shot into the sky—which meant he would be coming over." She smiled again, reminiscing about the sweet romance. "But they were never married." Her expression returned solemn. "The king and queen visited their daughter here unannounced in late summer, and when they learned of Wilhelmina's betrothal to the pirate, they informed the princess that she would be taken back to Bavaria at once. She was so distraught, even I could not console her.

"The king was furious at his brother for allowing Wilhelmina to fall in love with a pirate. He blamed the romance on the uncle's careless watch, and told him she would never be coming to visit again. But that night, we waited, and waited, and waited for the longest time at the window. And the arrows finally came. Wilhelmina was going to tell Jesper about her parents' plans to take her back to Bavaria, and planned to run away with him.

"I watched from the window—this one, right here," she said, walking over to the long bay window, "as she cried in his arms. It was heartbreaking to see how much they truly loved each other, and to know that they would never be permitted to marry."

"So why didn't she run away with him, right then and there?" Jo demanded. "That's what I would have done."

"She didn't have the chance." The headmistress shook her head. "One of the king's servants had seen the flaming arrows across the lake, and he ran to tell him. The king, thinking it a threat to his family, surrounded the castle and grounds with his guards. The princess and Jesper were discovered and dragged back to the castle, where Wilhelmina was locked in her bedroom."

"What did they do with Jesper?"

"They took him to an empty room in the west wing and tied him to a chair to make sure he was there when the king arrived. But Jesper had gotten out of worse situations before."

"He escaped?"

"He did. And fought off four guards with no weapon of any sort."

Maddie and Jo sighed. They were listening to a real, live fairy tale, and it happened right where they lived.

"And he ran to Wilhelmina . . . right, Headmistress?" Jo hoped.

"He tried to, Josephine. But the guards spotted him and chased him all through the castle halls. He dashed up and down the stairs, in and out of rooms, searching for Wilhelmina and trying to disappear, but he couldn't hide for long. That is, until he burst into the humble quarters of an elderly laundress.

"She jumped out of bed and listened sympathetically to Jesper's pleas for help. She did the only thing she could for him—she stuffed him into a laundry sack and shoved him into the back of her closet. When the knocking came at the door, she crawled back into her tiny bed and pulled the covers over her face in the dark."

"Did they find him?" Maddie asked.

"No." The headmistress smirked. "The king was furious that Jesper had escaped his guards, and he sent Wilhelmina back to Bavaria with the queen the next morning, leaving me to pack her things. He pledged to remain at the castle with the guards until they found Jesper, dead or alive. And they did stay, for quite a long while."

"He was in that closet all that time?" Jo marveled. "I thought the tiny cabin on the SS *Delfino* for three days was bad enough . . . but a closet?"

"From what Wilhelmina told me about Jesper, he had seen far worse than a castle closet," the headmistress recalled. "But yes, the laundress hid him there for days."

"Poor Wilhelmina," Maddie gushed. "She probably thought he was captured . . . or dead!"

The headmistress shook her head once more. "On the morning of Wilhelmina's departure, the laundress requested a private moment with the princess to wish her a last farewell. When they were finally alone, she divulged her intentions to save Jesper in hopes that one day he and the young princess could be reunited. Wilhelmina was overtaken with gratitude and promised the old woman that if she saved the pirate, she would be forever indebted to her."

"How did she save him?" the girls asked at the same time, desperate to hear how the story ended.

"The laundress told Wilhelmina's uncle of her plans to sneak Jesper out of the castle. Even though orders from the king strictly forbade anyone from leaving, the old laundress put on quite a show of being gravely ill, and insisted on dying in her real home in northern France. Wilhelmina's uncle asked the king to grant her dying wish, and he did—but only under the condition that two of his men drive her in a horse-drawn carriage all the way. So, she packed her things, buried Jesper under a collection of glass paperweights and figurines in her largest trunk, and set off for her home with a pirate stowaway."

"A pirate in a trunk?" Maddie giggled. "He had to weigh a ton!"

The headmistress looked amused. "I remember Wilhelmina's uncle telling me that right before they left for France, the guards opened the trunk to inspect what was so heavy, and even rummaged through the glass pieces! Jesper had to be terrified . . . But he did escape. And he remained hidden in northern France for almost a year before returning to his castle across the lake."

Maddie took another cookie. "What happened to Wilhelmina?"

"The king arranged her marriage to a nobleman a month after she returned home, and she gave birth to her first son the next summer. She hid her books away, concentrated on her new life, and tried to forget about Jesper. But I heard her cry, almost every night, and I knew that she longed for him."

"And Jesper? Why did he give up?" Maddie asked. "He could have gone to rescue the princess."

The headmistress sighed. "He learned of her marriage and child when he returned, and thought she was happier without him. He was so heartbroken that he emptied his castle of all its treasures and sold it to a wealthy Swiss military man, never to return."

Jo looked unsatisfied. "That's the unhappiest ending to a fairy tale I've ever heard, Headmistress."

"Well, it's not *quite* the end, Josephine. Wilhelmina's uncle died some years later and left his beloved castle to her. He sent his own staff to personally deliver the deed so that she might keep it a secret from her family. For years, she could not think of what to do with it, but finally, she decided: It would be a place where girls could read, learn, and study anything they wanted. The year was 1900. And I, at the age of twenty-five, would be the school's headmistress."

Jo looked at the photograph in the broken picture frame. "So, all this time, you've been staying in the room where you and the princess watched for Jesper?"

The headmistress examined the last cookie on the plate before taking it. "The princess died ten years after founding the school. I suppose I stay in here to keep remembering our grandest times."

Maddie nodded, the wheels in her head spinning faster and faster. "So, the treasure—the one Jesper left for Wilhelmina and her family—did anyone ever find it?"

"I don't believe that anyone has ever found the map she wrote of," the headmistress admitted with regret. "And Wilhelmina died only hours after writing the letter."

"And Jesper?" Jo asked.

"He was never seen or heard from again."

Maddie leaned back and folded her arms. Her brow was furrowed, and she scowled as she thought. "And what about the treasure in the school?"

"We looked for it when we got the letter," the headmistress replied. "We didn't find anything, and we went on about our business as a school. But two years ago, I received an anonymous letter from someone claiming they knew for a fact we couldn't produce the deed to the school."

Jo thought about the conversation they'd just overheard between the headmistress and Mr. Von Arx. "Why did the king rip up the deed?"

"Ah, you *were* listening, weren't you?" Klara raised an eyebrow as a smile played in the corners of her mouth. "He found it years after the school began, and, unaware that his daughter was actually the founder of Madame Molineaux's, he ripped up the deed in hopes that he could keep her away from the castle forever."

"Our dad would never do something like that," Jo thought out loud.

"But what about the anonymous letter?" Maddie pressed. "Why would it matter if you didn't have the deed?"

"The letter said that if we didn't cooperate with their instructions, they would tell the authorities that we didn't own the school and have the school auctioned off to the highest bidder."

"What were the instructions?"

"To find the treasure hidden in the princess's secret chamber by *any means necessary*. To excavate if we had to. And then to turn the treasure, and anything else they desired, over to them as payment for keeping quiet about the missing deed."

"Mr. Von Arx . . ." Maddie's voice trailed off. "He's been stealing from the school and blackmailing you?"

The headmistress nodded in defeat. "And no matter where we look, no matter how high in the air we fly, no matter how far below the ground we dig—we cannot find the treasure."

Maddie shook her head in protest. "That doesn't make sense," she argued. "How could he know about the treasure in the school unless he had read the letter?"

"I'm not sure I'll ever know, Maddie. Mr. Von Arx is a shadowy man who can disappear and reappear anywhere in the world. He is wealthy, powerful, and manipulative. Even if someone knew how he got the information, they would have to be a fool to tell. It is a dangerous thing to be on his bad side."

"He's sure got it out for this pirate, and our school," Maddie complained. "I bet if Jesper found Mr. Von Arx, he'd make him play 'Walk the Plank,' but for real."

Jo stood and looked up at the ceiling. "'Walk the Plank,'" she mumbled as she held both sides of her head in her palms. She closed her eyes. "'Walk the Plank!' Yes!"

"What is it, Josephine?" the headmistress asked cautiously.

Jo put her hands on Maddie's shoulders and stared her straight in the eyes. "We don't know Mr. Von Arx from the café, we know him from the ship! He was at the captain's banquet with us. A-a-and," she stuttered, "he said he knew about Madame Molineaux's and all the art and statues here!"

The twins looked to the headmistress for answers. "Why would he have been on a ship from Algiers to Genoa? And at the same captain's dinner?" Maddie inquired. "It's almost as if he were following us." All the details from that night popped into her mind as she tried to make sense of it.

"Only Henri knew we were on that boat," Jo said quietly. "I wonder if—"

A clock chimed three times in the distance.

"Three o'clock in the morning!" the headmistress cried. "I must insist, ladies, off to bed. We'll have to continue our discussion another time. I don't put it past Professor Troxler to try to give detention to sleepy, irritable students, even on the last day of class."

"Just one more minute," Maddie pressed. "The gigantic clock in the chimney, it's just like one we saw at the Christmas market in Mittenwald."

"Indeed, it is a twin of the clock you saw at the Christmas market, made in the same year and by the same clockmaker. It is priceless." She walked toward the door.

"Why didn't you just turn it off?" Jo blurted.

The headmistress's patience was wearing thin. "One does not simply 'turn off' a clock like that, Josephine. I had no time at all to get a clockmaker to come and turn it off before I hid it from Professor Troxler's greedy eyes. Besides, I needed some sort of bell to ring to keep the students from guessing that the bells of Saint-Marcel were missing."

"Claudette told us they were stolen," Maddie informed her.

"Technically," the headmistress pointed out, "it isn't stealing if you're trying to protect something from someone else stealing it. But yes," she leaned in and nodded. "I took them. Now it's time for bed." She guided the girls toward the door.

"Oma Kronenberg told us they were from a ship," Jo added, desperately trying to squeeze in a few more questions as they were being ushered into the hallway. "Were they from Jesper's ship?"

"Yes. Well. He brought them to the coast on his ship and transported them here, but they were originally on an ancient ship. I suppose you could say they were, as you said earlier, Josephine, artifacts." She opened the door and shooed the girls out.

Maddie kept one foot in the doorway. "Just one more question, Headmistress!" she whispered from the hallway. "The princess told the laundress that if she saved Jesper, she'd be forever indebted to her. What did she do for her?"

The headmistress cocked her head to the side. "Surely you don't mean to tell me, ladies, that you never wondered exactly who Madame Molineaux was?" She waited but got no answers, only blank stares. She pushed on the heavy wooden door. "Goodnight, ladies," she whispered just before it shut, and the girls heard the lock click just seconds after.

CHAPTER THIRTY-FIVE

THE FACE OF A PRINCESS

Jo's eyelids weighed heavy as she tried to appear alert during Professor Troxler's last lecture of the school year. If she hadn't been so tired, she might have glared at the thieving impostor throughout the class period, but instead, she simply tried not to call attention to the fact that she was falling asleep sitting up at her desk.

Maddie, whose desk was positioned front and center in the room, didn't have the luxury of closing her eyes, not even for a second. Professor Troxler turned around from the blackboard at random intervals to make sure her students were listening to the thorough exam review questions she had prepared. Maddie forced herself to find a word on the chalkboard to focus on, and stared blankly ahead.

"I would write these questions and answers down if I were you," she barked at the girls. "I've said it once, but I will remind you again—I will *not* be participating in Eggs-Ham at Midnight, or whatever that ridiculous name is, so you would be wise to pay attention now!"

Eggs-Ham at Midnight was a tradition at Madame Molineaux's, thought up by students in the spring of 1910 as they studied in the libraries well into the night, eating the boiled eggs, ham, and croissants they'd saved from breakfast. Preparing for their year-end English tests, they had laughed at the way the word *exam* sounded like "eggs" and "ham," and thus, the study group was named in accordance.

Throughout the years, the meal-based study session gained popularity, and the professors found it to be a fun and novel way to review with their students on the Friday night before exams. Students wore their pajamas, robes, and slippers, and professors set up banquet stations in their respective classroom buildings with breakfast offerings and blackboards, ready to answer any last-minute questions students had.

"In addition, ladies, remember that I will absolutely not tolerate any tardiness whatsoever on Monday. Your exam begins at eight o'clock, and the classroom door will be locked afterward. Any student arriving after the exam has begun will be—"

Riiing!! The bell interrupted the professor mid-sentence.

"Will be given failing marks!" she shouted over the rustling of books and papers.

Maddie sighed and slumped down in her desk, and Jo laid her head onto her folded arms. The ringing of the bell was the most wonderful sound they'd heard since they dragged themselves from their beds earlier that morning.

"It's really over!" Millie declared quietly as she stuffed her textbook and notes into her bag. "No more history. No more Troxler."

"No more Madame Molineaux's, thanks to her," Françoise corrected her friend as she shot daggers at the professor with her green eyes. "I think I'll draw little pictures of soldiers fighting as my answer to every question on her exam—that is, if I bother to show up for it."

Maddie rolled her eyes. "Come on, Françoise, we're not giving up yet. We still have five more days until we go home."

"Right," Françoise huffed, and walked out of the classroom.

"Look at them," Nixie sneered, watching Professor Troxler and Mr. Von Arx as they admired the artwork in the dining hall, all the while making notes as they secretly decided which paintings and relics to take. "I suppose they're just going to take anything they like."

"That's what Kronenberg said." Jo sighed as she finished the last of her lunch. "And it's all going to be auctioned off."

Val couldn't hold back her tears. "I don't want to go to another school next year," she bawled. "I want to come back *here!*"

"Whoa, whoa, Val," Maddie said gently. "We're sad, too, and we don't get to come back even if Madame Molineaux's stays open! But no one else knows about all this yet. And people are looking at us." She turned around to meet the eyes of Rosemary and her snobby friends, who seemed to be taking great pleasure in the distressed faces of the Room Five dining table.

"Let them look," Safi challenged. "They'll be sorry when they find out what's happening to Madame Molineaux's."

Jo tried to change the subject. "Just think, though," she said, attempting to sound cheerful. "We're the only students at the whole school who know about the princess, and Jesper, and the treasure. That has to count for something."

"Tell us again what she looked like," Safi said. "I've been playing Kronenberg's story in my head all morning, and I can't get Wilhelmina's face quite right. In my version, she looks like . . . Nixie." She scrunched up her face.

"People do tell me I have a royal face," Nixie bragged, beaming while the other girls rolled their eyes.

Maddie looked up at the vaulted ceiling of the dining hall and tried to recall the young woman she'd seen in the black-and-white photograph. "Let's see . . . She was beautiful. She wore a long gown that was cinched around her waist. And her pretty, smiling face was framed with light-colored hair that fell in curls down past her shoulders. She looked magical, like she had just stepped out of a fairy tale."

Nixie giggled. "That really does sound like me, doesn't it?" she asked, batting her long eyelashes.

Millie groaned. "For crying out loud, Nixie, we got it—you look like a princess. Are you happy now?"

Nixie looked pleased. "I'm just *saying*"—now she rolled her eyes—"the way Maddie described her, she could be any pretty girl with curly blond hair. She could be the mermaid outside Kronenberg's office, for goodness' sake."

The whole table fell silent, waiting for Maddie's reply. She looked down at her plate and compared images of the two young women in her head, baffled as to why she hadn't thought of it sooner.

"That's . . . *exactly* who Princess Wilhelmina looks like. She looks like the mermaid."

"Do you think Jesper had a figurehead of Wilhelmina carved for his ship?" Val whispered excitedly.

Nixie clasped her hands under her chin. "That sounds like something a pirate would do for his beloved! How romantic," she squeaked.

"All right, everyone. Calm down," Françoise hushed the girls at the table. "We don't want people to hear us talking about pirates, princesses, and treasure. Especially *them*," she said, nodding at Troxler and Mr. Von Arx, who were inspecting items on an antique table not far away.

"I bet they're still looking for the treasure," Maddie said quietly.

"Maybe if they found it, they'd just take it and leave, and we could all come back for school next year," Val offered hopefully.

Jo shook her head. "Mr. Von Arx went to the Council this morning to tell them Kronenberg didn't have the deed to the school. It will be up for auction soon, maybe even the day after exams end." She narrowed her eyes. "If they find the treasure, they'll just sell it, like everything else they've stolen."

"Then we have to find it first," Françoise whispered. "So Kronenberg can buy the school back! We haven't given up, have we?"

"No," the girls said, trying their best to sound enthused.

"I know we all have exams to study for, and we all have to pack our things to go home," Maddie said. "But just for tonight and tomorrow—forget about the romance. Forget about *them*," she said, looking at Troxler and Mr. Von Arx. "And think, think, *think* about where that treasure could be. It's our only hope at saving the school before it's too late."

Françoise pulled at her teal necktie and leaned in across the table. "Does Kronenberg know we've been into the tunnels?"

Maddie and Jo shook their heads.

"It didn't come up," Jo shrugged.

"Good."

"Let me read it again, just to make sure," the headmistress told the woman behind the desk at the quaint Saint-Marcel post office. She adjusted her wire-rimmed glasses and read the words she had written just moments before.

WE HAVE LOST THE BATTLE -(STOP)- NEED MUCH HELP CLOSING THE SCHOOL-(STOP)- WISHING WE COULD MEET UNDER HAPPIER CIRCUMSTANCES -(STOP)- PLEASE HURRY

She stared at the words on the paper, never having dreamed that she would actually have to write them.

"Ready to transmit, then, Madame?" the woman behind the desk asked.

"Oh, yes. Pardon me," the headmistress mumbled, pushing the paper across the desk.

The woman read it silently and raised her eyebrows for an instant, but her expression returned to normal almost immediately. "Thank you, Madame. Your telegram should be delivered to the receiving party by this afternoon." She stretched her neck to look at the man waiting behind the headmistress. "Who is next, please?"

The headmistress placed the cap on her fountain pen and walked out of the tiny office.

CHAPTER THIRTY-SIX

The Secret Chamber

The conservatory in the science hall bustled as students from each year chatted and wandered in and out of the buffet tables, plucking croissants, smoked meats, and boiled eggs from steaming metal dishes.

"Have you been to the arts hall?" one older student asked a group of her classmates above all the chatter. "They have éclairs and fresh berries in the recital theater!" All the girls cheered in delight. Even the boathouse participated in the late-night banquet, with some of Professor Natalio's workers offering sparkling pear cider as students drifted to and from the other buildings.

Maddie sat cross-legged on her favorite bench in the lush foliage and balanced her full plate on her knees. *Not too much,* she thought, taking a bite of her croissant. *You've still got the arts hall and the history hall meals to eat.*

Françoise and Millie walked up with their plates. Soon, all the Knights of Room Five were seated in a semicircle, flipping through a biology textbook and quizzing each other with sample test questions. Marcello and Musetta roamed in and out of study groups, perusing plates for scraps of meat and egg, and stopping occasionally for chin scratches and pats on the head. Professor Natalio left his place behind the buffet and made his way to a podium and blackboard set up in the front corner of the conservatory.

"Third-years, let's begin your test review at the blackboard!" he shouted over the conversation, his voice echoing off the windowpanes on the high ceiling. Groups of girls stood up from their study camps and followed him to the podium, sitting on the ground with their pencils and paper. "Your exam will be given in two different parts," he boomed. "The written test, and the blank animal diagrams, which you must fill in." He pinned four large pictures to the top of the blackboard.

"Hey, I could ace the third-year exam," Millie laughed. "The first one is a frog, the second is a horse, the third is an elephant, and the fourth is a fish!"

Safi shook her head. "Nice try, Millie. But I think they have to do more than *name* the animals." She pointed at the blank lines next to each of the animals. "See? They have to write out the organs, bones, and muscles," she said. "For instance, the third line on the elephant points to the fibula bone."

All the Room Five girls raised their eyebrows at Safi.

"Have you been eavesdropping on third-year biology lessons?" Françoise asked, looking impressed.

Safi shook her head and smiled. "The veterinary world is very complex," she said confidently. "Knowing the names of bones is just the beginning."

"Maybe they'd let you look in on the horses when the veterinary doctor comes," Val offered sweetly. "He's a nice man who comes to see them in the stables when they're sick."

"If you're so interested in horses, Val, take a look. He's filling in the horse diagram now," Jo said and nodded across the conservatory to the podium.

"Yes, good work, ladies," Professor Natalio beamed as he filled in another blank line with the correct anatomical name. "And this one?" He circled his finger toward the front of the horse's ribcage and just above the legs.

"Liver!" a student called out.

"That's the heart," Safi mumbled, shaking her head. "The liver is much larger and goes farther back."

Professor Natalio cocked his head. "You're close, but incorrect. What's right here?" he asked, circling the area with his finger again.

"Heart!" more than one student called out at the same time.

"Exactly!" The professor wrote the word onto the line. "And here's a question worth extra points on the test—so write it down: How many chambers does a horse heart have?"

"Five!" a student called from the back of the group. All the third-year students giggled.

"Five?" Professor Natalio asked his students, his eyes wide. "I'm afraid the answer is four, dear." He shrugged, laughing. "Unless of course, there's a secret chamber in the heart that I don't know about."

In an instant, Maddie, Jo, Françoise, Nixie, Val, Safi, and Millie froze.

Nixie babbled for a moment without making sense. "Secret chamber . . . heart . . . I mean, Wilhelmina's secret . . . and Jesper's treasure . . ."

Safi nodded and began to squeak out a few words.

Maddie threw herself into the middle of their half-circle. "Don't anyone say another word," she ordered in a hushed voice.

Maddie took her pencil and paper and wrote: THE LETTER. She looked up and around to all the girls, making sure they understood. THE TREASURE IS IN MY SECRET CHAMBER . . . FOREVER IN MY HEART, she wrote, and looked around to everyone again, their eyes giving confirmation that they knew what she was getting at. THE SECRET CHAMBER IS IN WILHELMINA'S HEART! she scribbled, her hand shaking with excitement.

All the girls nodded quickly.

"What do we do?" Val whispered, her soft brown eyes as big as saucers.

"We've got to get to the mermaid," Françoise said quietly as she looked back and forth at both conservatory entrances, each lined with professors and school staff. "We'll never get through those doors unnoticed. We have to go through the tunnels." She looked squarely at Millie and Nixie. "We're going to need a distraction. Think you can drum up some excitement?"

Millie examined the metal dish where the croissants had been. Now, just one lonely pastry lay amid a dusting of flaky crumbs.

She looked across the buffet table to Nixie. "This will be worth all the detention we're going to get, right?" she whispered, looking at the groups of girls sitting on either side of the buffet table.

Nixie nodded and winked. She took a deep breath and straightened her shoulders. "Here goes nothing," she whispered, then cleared her throat. "And let me tell you one *more* thing, Millicent Braithwaite," she shrieked. "If you think he loves you more than he loves me, you're a fool!"

The entire conservatory stopped talking. The staff, the professors, and the students all turned their heads to the buffet line, where Nixie and Millie were improvising a captivating performance.

Millie was nervous. She mentally flipped through the pages of a romantic novel her mother had once left in the sitting room, trying to gain inspiration for a dramatic response. "You don't even know what love is!" she cried out.

Nixie stared at Millie, anxiously waiting for her to keep going, but the words didn't come. Millie gulped and started to look around at the hundred faces gawking at her. "That is, well . . ." she stammered. "You don't, um . . ."

Safi covered her face with her hands. "Millie's not going to pull through," she said hopelessly.

"Just wait," Françoise assured her, although her faith was waning as well. "She'll be fine." All the girls could do was watch their friend try to overcome her stage fright at the front of the crowd of girls.

Millie was sweating now. She breathed hard and wanted to crawl under the table, but she knew that the future of the whole school could rest on her performance. She looked down and grabbed the last croissant. *We'll get this underway, Braithwaite-style,* she thought, recalling the way she and her brothers had settled more than a few arguments at the table.

"You know what I think?" she asked Nixie boldly at the top of her lungs. "I think you can have him!" She dipped the croissant in a bowl of gravy and held the soggy, drippy bread in the air.

"This is it," Françoise whispered to the rest of the girls, a bit surprised by the tactic Millie was about to employ to distract the crowd. "Get ready to run to the tunnel entrance."

"*And,*" Millie yelled, "you can tell him that *this* was from me!" She reared her arm back and launched the gravy-covered croissant at Nixie's head with full force.

But Nixie ducked at the last second. The croissant sailed past her, only grazing the side of her blond curls and leaving a light brown splotch of gravy on her shoulder. It landed with a splat on an unsuspecting Isidra Vidal's head, the thick gravy dripping down the front of her face and pink pajama shirt.

Isidra wiped the gravy out of her eyes and gasped. "What do you think you're doing?!" She inspected her ruined clothes and began a dramatic performance rivaling Millie and Nixie's. "I'll die, I'll just *die,*" she moaned. "This is the finest silk from my father's trip to Japan, and now it's *ruined!*" She glanced around to make sure all eyes were on her and reached over to her plate, fumbling to find the largest piece of food she could.

"Ah-ah-ahhhhhh," Professor Natalio stuttered, running from his podium to the buffet. But before he could get there, Isidra found what she was looking for: a nice, thick, gleaming slice of roasted ham. She pulled her arm back and sent the ham flopping through the air toward Millie.

Nixie shuffled to the side to avoid the flying piece of meat, and Millie ducked under the table, leaving a brunette fifth-year student in the line of attack. The ham slice flew past the table and landed squarely across her face, finally slipping down into her lap.

In the moment of silence that followed, a collective twinkle could be seen in all the girls' eyes. Everyone, even the most perfect of students, felt a sort of primitive energy fill the room. The girl holding the ham in her lap stood slowly with her entire plate of food. She narrowed her eyes at a gravy-covered Isidra on the other side of the buffet table and crushed a boiled egg in her hands, the crack of its shell resonating throughout the conservatory. And from that point, there was no turning back. The room exploded into chaos, with food flying in every direction.

"Go!" Françoise shouted over the commotion. She led the way out of the sweet-and-savory war zone with Maddie, Jo, Val, and Safi trailing behind her to the tunnel entrance.

Back at the buffet table, Nixie and Millie dodged sprays of bread, egg, and ham as they crawled along the ground toward the jungle's edge. They had almost reached a sprawling row of ferns when they heard an angry voice growling from behind them.

"There you are!" Isidra held the dish of gravy from the buffet table above her head. "You can't leave the party without trying the gravy," she sang, pouring the entire bowl slowly onto Millie and Nixie. "Delicious, isn't it?" she sneered as it splattered down their faces and onto their clothes. When the bowl was empty, she shook it one last time for good measure and sauntered away.

The girls swept the gravy away from their eyes, ears, and mouths as they struggled to stand on the slippery floor beneath them.

"Whew," Millie sighed. "At least that's over with. Excellent performance, Nixie." She bowed lightly and flung more gravy from her hands.

Nixie linked her arm through Millie's. "Um . . . not *quite* over, Millie." She stared ahead at Professor Natalio as he tapped his foot against the messy floor in front of them. His clothes were smeared with an assortment of smashed breakfast foods, and his face, dotted with all sorts of jammy pinks and purples, looked angrier than either of the girls had ever seen.

"Professor, we can explain. We just—well, we had to—umm . . . we're . . . sorry?" Nixie said in her sweetest voice, trying in vain to spill tears from her big brown eyes. But the professor just shook his head.

"Right, then," Millie said with defeat, and she and Nixie sat back down on the gravy-covered ground.

CHAPTER THIRTY-SEVEN

BACK THROUGH THE TUNNELS

Val was the last one to enter the tunnels through the ivy-covered entrance in the conservatory. The muffled shrieks and laughter that came from what started as the exam review session but quickly turned into a food fight faded away as the girls inched down the dark tunnel toward the first-year library.

"Suppose Troxler and Mr. Von Arx know about the mermaid?" Val wondered out loud.

"If Kronenberg couldn't figure it out *with* the letter, surely they couldn't have figured it out *without* the letter," Maddie insisted. "But even so—if Kronenberg knew, she'd hide the mermaid down the chimney." She stopped walking and turned to her Italian roommate. "In fact, Val, that's a great idea. Can you get out of the tunnels at the stables and see what's happening on the history hall rooftop? If you see the mermaid being lowered in, at least we know it's safe."

Val looked relieved not to have to tag along to the administration hallway. "I can do that," she said, beaming.

"It's dark down here," Jo warned. "Are you sure you want to go by yourself?"

Val nodded. "It's all right, I know my way. I'll hide out by the stables until one of you comes to get me, yes?"

"Yes," Françoise answered. "We shouldn't be long—we'll sneak into the administration hallway and figure out how to get into the secret chamber. Then we'll take the treasure to Kronenberg."

"What should I do if you're not back soon?" Val persisted.

"If we're not there in twenty minutes, then come find us," Maddie instructed. "And bring help!"

"And watch out for the kittens," Safi added, only half joking.

"Okay," Val chirped. "Good luck." She took off in the other direction, toward the history hall.

"How do we even open the mermaid's heart?" Jo asked. "It's covered in rubies, and I didn't see any hinges or a button or anything . . ."

"Really, Jo? A button?" Maddie scoffed. "This is pirate treasure we're talking about. I think someone as adventurous as Jesper could probably have come up with something more complicated than a button."

"Quiet, both of you," Françoise scolded as they made their way down the dark tunnel. "Someone could be listening to every word you're saying."

"Yes, *someone* indeed," a voice came from the darkness. All four girls stopped in their tracks, looking frantically in every direction for the hidden observer. Rosemary Byron emerged from the shadows. "And this someone doesn't plan to let you pass."

Safi stepped forward and stood inches from Rosemary's face, fed up with her snobbery and condescending tone. "Oh no?" she asked with growing confidence. "And if we keep walking?"

Rosemary swayed her head back and forth calmly and stared ahead as if she were looking right through Safi. "I'll go straight to Kronenberg and tell her about this little game you've been playing since winter."

Jo jumped to Safi's side. "Do it. We dare you," she challenged Rosemary. "In fact," she continued, "let's all go to Kronenberg's chambers together. There's a little something we'd like to tell her about you, too."

"You don't know anything," Rosemary sang, her phony grin irritating Safi and Jo all the more. "And I shall very much enjoy watching the headmistress expel you before Monday's exams."

"You're wrong, Rosemary," Safi replied in a low voice. "We know everything. We even know about your little friends down here."

Rosemary's expression changed from smug to worried.

"That's right," Jo said, the corner of her mouth turned up slightly. "And I'm sure Professor Troxler would be happy to know that the kittens are to blame for her sleepless nights." She looked to Maddie and Françoise. "Correct me if I'm wrong, girls, but didn't she say she would cut off their ears to match their bobbed tails if she found them?"

Jo and Françoise gave her hesitant nods.

"So it's up to you, Rosemary. We can all go on our separate missions and pretend we never met here, or we can all rat each other out to Kronenberg and see what happens. What will it be?"

Rosemary was silent for a moment before she conceded begrudgingly. "Fine then. You go your way, and I'll go mine. This meeting never happened."

"Not so fast." Safi stepped forward. "I know you better than that. You'll tell us what we want to hear, and then run to Kronenberg when we leave. Where were you going, exactly?"

Rosemary tightened the belt on her robe and huffed. "Apparently, you know quite well where I was headed, so step out of the way."

But Safi didn't budge. "I'm going with you. I'll make sure you go where you say you're going."

Rosemary looked horrified at the thought, but Safi linked arms with her.

"Come now, Rosemary, we all want what's best for the kitties," she sang, and pulled her into the darkness.

"I would never, ever *really* tell Troxler about the kittens," Jo insisted as she walked between Maddie and Françoise through the last part of the tunnel. "I was just saying that to make sure Rosemary left us alone."

"I don't know, Jo, I've never seen that side of you before," Maddie marveled. "Usually, *I'm* the one with the sharp tongue."

"Well, I'm learning," Jo smiled. "Sometimes you have to know how to stand up to people. Especially the baddies."

Françoise stopped at the steep staircase to the first-year library and took a deep breath. "When we leave the library, we go straight to our room. I'll bring my torch. Maddie, you bring your pocketknife, and Jo, bring your compass. Who knows where we might end up."

The girls nodded, then climbed up the stone stairs and out through the trapdoor in the library floor.

Maddie rummaged through her wardrobe drawer quietly. *Where did I leave that pocketknife?* she wondered, frustrated that she couldn't remember. She dug in between her folded clothes and lifted the lavender-scented paper lining the bottom of the drawer, but there was no knife. There was, however, the secret pocket Jo had made her for Christmas, lying flat against the wood. She grabbed it and fastened it around her waist under her pajama shirt. *Just in case,* she thought.

At the next wardrobe, Jo dropped her trusty compass into the pocket of her robe. *Tonight calls for a belt,* she thought, taking the belt from Millie's robe to replace the one Françoise had used so many months ago to repair Elisabeth of Bohemia's portrait. Jo tied it around her waist and shoved her clothes back into her wardrobe drawer, but when she tried to push it closed, something kept it from shutting all the way. She opened the drawer, slid her hand to the back of it, and found the culprit: the slingshot Maddie had carved for her Christmas present. *This might come in handy,* she thought, and tucked it into her other robe pocket.

Françoise switched on her torch and walked to the door. "Everyone ready?" she whispered. Maddie and Jo came to her side and nodded.

Françoise opened the door a crack. "Stay close to the wall and stop at the stairs. I have a feeling the main hall will be busy tonight."

But when they arrived at the top of the stairs, the main hall was quiet.

"I thought Von Arx's men would be everywhere. This would have been the perfect night to steal the rest of the valuables from the school," Françoise reasoned. "All the students and professors are at the exam review." She tiptoed down the steps and peeked into the main hall, then turned around and shrugged. "Nothing," she whispered.

But then they heard the bright smack of hastened footsteps on the cold stone floor of the main hall. Françoise leaped up the stairs in an instant, and all three girls crouched down to watch as Professor Troxler walked past the entrance to the west wing. Within a few minutes, she walked back in front of the entrance, and then back again, as if she were pacing the length of the main hall.

"What's she doing?" Maddie asked.

"I'm not sure," Françoise whispered. "But if you're going to go into the administration hallway, I'm going to have to get her out of here." She handed Jo the torch. "Here, take it." She shed her robe, leaving only her gray pajama pants and shirt. "I'm going to take a walk through the utility corridor and make some noise as I go."

"Are you sure? We could just wait until she leaves and then all go together," Maddie offered. Somehow, over the course of the last twenty minutes, they'd gone from a team of seven girls down to three, and now they were about to be a lonely pair.

"I'm sure," Françoise said curtly as she rolled up the sleeves of her pajamas. "As soon as you see Troxler go into the utility corridor, run as fast as you can to the mermaid." She raised one eyebrow and gave the twins a half-smile. "Don't come back without the treasure," she quipped as she took the first step down the stairs. She crept lightly until she was out in the main hall, and then clung to the stone walls, staying in the shadows as much as she could until she reached the utility corridor.

Only seconds after she disappeared into the dark, decrepit hallway, the girls heard a crash as Françoise toppled wooden crates onto the floor. Maddie and Jo waited in silence for the professor to cross back in front of the entryway.

"Hello?" they heard Professor Troxler call from the other end of the hall. She walked to the threshold of the utility corridor and paused. "Who's in there?"

Another crash. This time, it was the metal racks against the stone floor.

Professor Troxler put one foot into the utility corridor. "I've already told the other men," she shouted. "There's nothing more to go. The last truck just left with the final load." She sighed and pulled a matchbook from her pocket, striking one and holding it high in the air. "Come out here at once, or you'll be left behind!" she warned.

Maddie and Jo watched as the professor slipped into the dark corridor. Maddie grabbed her sister's hand, and together they bolted down the steps and across the stone floor of the main hall as fast as they could. By the time they reached the administration hallway, Jo was dragging Maddie behind her, but they both froze in place when they saw the blank wall across from the headmistress's office. The mermaid was gone.

Jo panicked. "Either Kronenberg knew to hide her in the chimney, or . . ."

"She's on one of Von Arx's trucks," Maddie finished.

The girls scrambled toward the front doors of Madame Molineaux's and burst out onto the front entryway just in time to see the last truck barreling down the long drive, the mermaid's green tail sticking out of the back.

CHAPTER THIRTY-EIGHT

Hidden in Plain Sight

"Come on, Maddie, we can catch up!" Jo hollered in desperation. She took two giant strides with Maddie in tow, but tripped and spilled onto the rocky driveway, sending Françoise's torch plummeting to the ground. The orange flame broke into a dozen pieces around Jo's outstretched hand, leaving only shards of colored glass and a lightbulb in the metal base.

"Jo! Are you okay?" Maddie cried as she pulled her sister up off the ground. Tears spilled from her eyes as she realized that her last hope of saving their school was now gone.

"I'm not hurt," Jo sobbed, checking inside her slippers for broken glass and rubbing her knees. "But I'm not okay, Maddie. She's gone, and Madame Molineaux's will go to that awful Mr. Von Arx," she moaned. She sniffed hard and wiped her nose on her pajama sleeve.

Maddie crouched down to inspect the remains of the torch. "Françoise's torch," she said, picking up one of the larger pieces of frosted orange glass. "Maybe her dad can get her another one . . ." She hugged her knees and buried her face in the soft cotton of her pajama pants. "I—I feel like we've let everyone down." It was the first time all year that she was out of options, out of ideas—even out of pep talks. She wept quietly next to her sister as the truck carrying the mermaid drove out the gates of Madame Molineaux's.

"I wouldn't give up yet," a calm voice called from the grassy area next to the front drive. There, saddled on one of two horses, was Val, her white silk pajamas gleaming in the moonlight like a knight's shiny suit of armor. In one hand she wielded a riding crop instead of a sword, and held both horses' reins in the other. The horses stomped their hooves and shook their heads, whinnying impatiently.

"Val?" Jo stood in astonishment. "What are you doing here? And with horses?"

Val gave the girls a puzzled look. "You told me I should come and get you if no one returned to get me in twenty minutes," she said matter-of-factly. "Twenty minutes passed, so I came. And I brought help, just like you asked." She stroked the horses on their heads. "The mermaid, she's getting away, yes?" she asked, looking far in the distance to see if the truck's taillights were still visible.

"Er . . . I don't know how to ride a horse very well," Jo admitted.

"Well, I do," Maddie asserted. She ran to the other horse, wedged her slipper into the stirrup, and flung her other leg over the saddle. "Come on, Jo, you can ride with Val!"

Val scooted back off the saddle and onto the horse's hindquarters. "You ride in the saddle." She pulled Jo up and slid her arms under Jo's, grasping the reins and leaning forward over her shoulders.

"What?!" Jo protested. "I think you need to be driving this thing, Val!"

"I'll drive from here," Val assured her. "Unless you want to be the one riding bareback."

"No, no, I'll stay in the saddle." Jo hoisted herself onto the horse.

Val nodded and let go of Maddie's horse's reins. "Hold on," she told Jo, and with one swift kick to the horse's ribs, the three girls went galloping down the driveway toward the massive iron gate.

Jo leaned her head back to Val as she fought to stay centered on the horse. "What exactly are we going to do when we catch up to the mermaid?" she yelled over the clatter of horse hooves against the driveway.

Val turned to look at Maddie and shrugged.

Maddie thought back to an old western motion picture she'd seen at a theater in Boston. *What does the cowboy do when he catches up to the robber on a speeding train?* she asked herself, playing the black-and-white scene in her head. She looked Jo straight in the eye as the two sisters rode side by side. "You're going to have to jump off the horse onto the train—I mean, the truck!"

Françoise peeked out from her hiding place and saw the faint glow of Professor Troxler's burning match. As she kneeled behind the two tall wooden crates, she felt around in the dark for something else to pull down or throw. *I never thought I'd be playing a game of hide-and-seek with Troxler,* she thought, smirking. Her fingers felt the prickle of a wire-bristled brush on the floor. *Let's confuse her a bit.* She picked up the brush and pulled her arm back, ready to launch it back toward the entrance to the main hall.

But before she could throw it, Professor Troxler spun around and marched out of the utility corridor at a feverish pace.

"Zut!" Françoise exclaimed softly. She stood up and stepped carefully around the toppled crates and metal racks, weaving in and out of the maze of discarded junk in the dark hallway. *Where is she going in such a hurry?* she wondered as she rushed into the main hall, arriving just in time to see the front doors of the school swing closed.

Beep, beep! The muffled horn of a car broke the silence. Through the entrance windows, Françoise saw Troxler waving her arms frantically.

"Get in, get in!" the driver yelled at the professor. He flung open the door and slammed it shut as soon as she was inside. Within seconds, the car sped away, its rubber tires screeching as they spun against the rocky front drive.

Françoise dashed to the front doors and out into the driveway. From where she stood, she saw the faint outline of riders on horses disappearing over the top of a small hill. Troxler's car would be upon them at any moment. She took a step forward to get a better view and winced as her boot crunched down on broken glass. She looked down and saw what remained of her torch, its orange shards sparkling under the light of the moon.

"Oh!" she wailed, bending down to retrieve what she could of her beloved torch. *After all these adventures,* she thought, *you had to break here and now.* For the first time all year, Françoise let herself cry. Her friends were in danger, her school would close in a matter of days, and the only material possession in the world she cared about was lying in pieces amid the dirt and rocks.

No more spy games, she thought, imagining Maddie and Jo in the hands of Troxler and Von Arx. She dried her eyes, sprinted back through the castle doors, and headed for the arts hall.

Jo's eyes widened and she shook her head furiously as she rode awkwardly on the saddle. "Are you joking, Maddie? *You're* the horseback rider, *you* jump off onto the truck!"

"Val will get you really close! Right Val?" Maddie persisted. "She'll steer the horse and you can jump. It's the only way!"

Once they had ridden over the small hill on the driveway, Maddie could see that the gated entrance to Madame Molineaux's was still open. *Good,* she thought. *They left it open after the trucks went through.* But as soon as her thought was finished, her eyes caught the slightest movement at the edges of the gates: Two men dressed in black were moving them inward. Slowly but surely, the gates were closing. She kicked her horse harder and bent down low. "It's closing!" she yelled to Val and Jo.

Val slapped her horse on the hindquarters and dug her heel into his side while Jo leaned forward and shut her eyes tight.

"We're not going to make it!" Jo repeated over and over as the gap between the two gates narrowed.

"We *are* going to make it!" Val screamed. She counted the seconds in her head as the gates were pushed together, calculating how much time she had before the horses wouldn't fit through the opening. "Get behind me, Maddie!" she shouted, and Maddie's horse veered to follow her. "We have to make it in *five . . . four . . .*"

Jo could see the expressions on the men's faces now, and they were changing from dumbfounded to determined.

"*Three!*" Val cried out, the pitch of her voice getting higher as the numbers counted down. "*Two!*"

If Jo had wanted to, she could have reached out and taken either man's hat right from their heads as her horse passed through the narrowing gap in between the gates.

"*One!*"

Maddie's horse slipped through the closing gates with not an inch to spare. His tail whipped back and forth furiously in the space between the iron sides before finally streaming out behind the three victorious girls. Maddie leaned up and gasped for air, not having breathed in what felt like a whole minute for fear that even the slightest motion would slow down her horse. She kicked both heels against his sides and inched her way up next to Val and Jo as they raced down the road toward Saint-Marcel.

"Slow down, Françoise," the headmistress chided, wiping the powdered sugar from her fingers onto her apron. "I can't hear you with all of this chatter." She walked around the table full of éclairs and berries and smiled at Françoise. "What can I do for you, dear?"

Françoise leaned toward the headmistress's ear. "There won't be time to repeat this, so please listen to what I am about to say, as unbelievable as it may sound. At this moment, Maddie and Jo are on horseback chasing Wilhelmina's treasure and are in grave danger."

The headmistress took a deep breath. "Somehow, Françoise, I'm inclined to believe you." She yanked her apron over her head and threw it on the floor.

"You are?" Françoise asked in a mild state of shock.

"Yes. Now where are they?"

"They were headed toward the school gates when I last saw them. Troxler was following them in a car."

The headmistress shook her fists. "And this is the night I let my driver leave! We can't simply run after them . . ."

"Is the car still at school?"

The headmistress nodded. "But it's no use. I don't know how to drive."

Françoise's eyes sparkled under the colored theater lights. "Do you have the keys?"

"Aha! Ha! Ah-haha!" Val could hardly contain her exhilaration. "I can't believe we just did that!" She hugged Jo tightly from behind as they galloped toward Saint-Marcel. "I told you we'd make it."

The road curved around a forest bend, and when they came around the other side, the red taillights of the truck were in sight.

"There it is!" Maddie cried. "Are you ready, Jo?"

Jo patted her compass in one robe pocket and her slingshot in the other. If there was ever a time to be ready for a stunt like this, it was now. "I'm ready. Let's go, Val."

As they gained on the covered truck, the moonlight shone on the other vehicles in the caravan. A shiny black car led in front, followed by two taller trucks and two more like the one the mermaid rode in. Jo took one foot out of the stirrup, then the other, and crouched on the seat of the saddle, holding on to the horse's neck for dear life.

Val inched the horse up to the side of the truck's covered bed, pulling back on the reins to keep his speed consistent. "Whenever you're ready!" she whispered loudly. Jo bit her lip and prepared for the scariest leap she'd ever made.

Maddie rode on the other side of the truck. *You've got to make it, Jo,* she begged silently. *For you, for me, for all our friends, for Kronenberg, for Wilhelmina, and for Jesper.*

Jo lifted her hands from the saddle less than a second before springing off the horse into the air. She threw her weight forward and propelled herself into the bed of the truck, rocketing through the flaps in the canvas cover before landing on top of the hard, rigid mermaid.

Val and Maddie pulled back on the reins to slow their horses, riding at a safe distance behind the barreling truck. Jo's legs stuck out of the back, just like the mermaid's tail, and the girls on horseback watched Jo kick around as she struggled to sit up.

Bang!

The truck backfired, lurching forward and spitting black exhaust at Maddie and Val from its tailpipe. Jo's legs slid down the truck bed until her hips were teetering on the edge, her arms grasping at the mermaid's waist. Val's horse, spooked by the explosion, veered off the road into the forest and dashed away on a moonlight race through the evergreens.

"Val!" Maddie screamed as her own horse reared up on his hind legs, galloping his front hooves in the air as if he were posing for a portrait. Maddie wrapped her arms around his neck and squeezed the saddle between her legs to keep from falling. *They're getting away with the mermaid—and Jo!* She tried in vain to coax her horse back on all four legs. But it would be something else that encouraged her horse to start running again.

Another car, painted a shimmering silver, roared up behind Maddie. She turned around slowly, and, from behind the windshield glass, Professor Troxler's crystal-clear blue eyes gleamed back at her with anger. Maddie and her horse were now trapped between the two vehicles, running at breakneck speed.

Jo pulled herself back into the covered bed of the truck along with the other relics, artwork, and vases that had been stolen from the school. "I'm here, Wilhelmina," she said out loud, pushing on the red heart at the center of the mermaid's chest. Her fingers pressed hard on the rubies laid in the wood, but the heart didn't give. There was no spring, no hinge, and no space to slip her fingers under.

I don't care what Maddie says, she thought. *There has to be a button here somewhere!* She pushed on the large pearl pendant hanging just above the heart. Nothing. *Much too obvious,* she reasoned. She ran her fingers over the crown of shells atop the mermaid's golden hair, but not one shell moved or even wiggled. "Please!" she cried to the wood carving. She pinched each of the blue starfish earrings the mermaid wore, but still nothing. She tapped frantically on every raised scale on the emerald tail but to no avail.

"I don't see a button anywhere," she said out loud. She stopped her search to think for a moment as the truck bumped farther and farther down the road to Saint-Marcel. *This is hidden treasure, meant to stay hidden. If there's a button, it's probably where no one can see it.* She pictured the mermaid hanging on the wall outside Kronenberg's office. *What couldn't we see?*

In a flash, her hands swooped around the mermaid's mane of golden hair. She rolled the carving onto its side and inspected the one place that no one could see from the ground: the back of her head. At the nape of her neck, where her hair parted to spill out over the front of her shoulders, a tiny, heart-shaped pearl joined the two ends of Wilhelmina's coral necklace. Jo laid her finger on it and pushed.

In an instant, the mermaid's clutched heart shot out from between her hands to reveal a small chamber no bigger than Jo's fist. Tucked inside was a lumpy, folded-up sheet of parchment tied with a worn piece of string, and Jo carefully plucked the small package from its hiding place.

Not good, not good, Maddie repeated silently. The first car in the caravan was coming to a stop just outside of Saint-Marcel. "Jo!" she yelled, she and her horse still trapped in between the truck and Troxler's car. "We're stopping!"

Jo stuck her head out from between the two canvas flaps. "I've got it!" she hollered. "I'm going to jump out!"

"No, don't!" Maddie cried. "Troxler's right behind me—you'll get run over!" She kicked her horse in the ribs. "You'll have to jump on with me!"

The back wheel of the truck smacked the edge of a hole in the road, sending Jo flying back against the truck bed. She scrambled to the edge again and took her slingshot from her robe. "Get in front of Troxler!" she yelled.

"What?!"

"Get in front of her! She won't see what I'm doing!"

Maddie squinted back into the headlights of the silver car and steered her horse to block Troxler's view of the truck.

Jo held up her slingshot. "On three!" she shouted.

Maddie's eyes widened as she wrapped the horse's reins around her waist, holding both hands in front of her. There was only one chance to get this right.

"One!" Jo called, sitting up on her knees at the edge of the truck bed. "Two!" She put the small parchment-wrapped package into the pocket of the rubber sling and pulled back. "Three!"

It happened in slow motion for Maddie. She watched as Jo released the rubber sling, as the crumpled bundle of paper and string passed through the Y she had so painstakingly carved and sailed through the air toward her. She held her hands open like a clamshell and barely grabbed onto the parcel as it bounced off the undersides of her wrists.

"Go!" Jo ordered, snapping Maddie back into the present. As the truck came to a stop, she scooped up the red wooden heart and slid it back into the empty chamber between the mermaid's hands. It snapped and locked into place, showing no sign of an opening, and Jo climbed out of the back of the truck just as Professor Troxler stormed out of her car.

The professor marched over and snatched the collar of Jo's robe from behind, twisting it and pulling Jo's shoulder blades back. "Get the other one!" she barked at the men spilling out of the trucks.

Maddie tried to stay calm as she meandered along the side of the road where the trucks were parked, steering her horse away from the men dressed in black. She passed the last truck and looked for an escape route. It was time to get this treasure back where it belonged.

CHAPTER THIRTY-NINE

TINY TREASURES

As Maddie dug her heels in again, preparing to flee back to the castle, the door of the black, shiny car swung open in front of her horse, spooking him back onto his hind legs. Maddie clung to his neck with both arms once again.

"Little girls shouldn't be out riding horses at this hour, should they, now?" a man's voice boomed. Mr. Von Arx stepped out of the shiny black car. "Especially without an escort. That, just by itself, is grounds for expulsion—isn't it, Professor?" he called to Troxler. "I seem to recall seeing that rule underlined twice in the Madame Molineaux's new-student booklet." He smirked at Maddie as she fought to stay on her horse.

Professor Troxler tightened her grip on Jo's robe. "It is the most punishable offense at the school," she assured him. "But then again, these two are no strangers to punishment."

"I'll take those, Madeline," Mr. Von Arx said cordially as he pulled the reins out of her hands. "Let's go and join your sister." He led her horse past the trucks and held out his hand to help her out of the saddle, but she jumped off without help and ran to Jo's side. The two girls exchanged frightened looks and laced their fingers together.

Mr. Von Arx, standing tall and intimidating in his black suit, bent down to the girls' level. "I don't know what you're doing here, ladies, but I would imagine that you have attempted, and perhaps succeeded, at relieving me of some of my property. Am I correct?"

Maddie scowled and leaned forward. "This isn't *your* property, it's the headmistress's!"

Mr. Von Arx shook his head. "I assure you, my dear, none of this belongs to Klara."

"Well, it's still not yours. It's Wilhelmina's!" Jo blurted out.

The group of adults twittered in laughter. "Ooh!" Professor Troxler chided. "They know about the princess, Bastien. You're in trouble now," she sang.

Mr. Von Arx grimaced and faced the girls. "I knew Wilhelmina better than you think," he snarled. He circled the twins in one direction and then the other, looking them up and down several times. "Search them."

Two men dressed in black immediately jumped in and held the girls' arms while Professor Troxler looked through their robes and pajama pockets. She pulled the slingshot out and waved it in the air. "Were you going to slingshot us to death, Josephine?" she laughed. "Surely you learned more about weaponry in my class than to fight with this silly thing." She tossed it into the woods. "I'll let you keep your little compass, though," she jeered, dropping it back into Jo's pocket.

"What, Maddie? Nothing in your pockets?" she asked as she searched the other twin. "I guess nothing of ours caught your fan—" She paused and placed her hand on Maddie's back. "My, my," she declared in an artificial tone. "What do we have under your sleeping clothes?"

Jo's eyes cried out to her sister. *No!* they insisted, begging her to run away and save the treasure. She shook her head once and shut her eyes tight.

Maddie slowly reached underneath the bottom of her shirt. She pulled the secret pocket from around her waist and handed it to the professor. "It's my secret pocket."

Jo opened her eyes and breathed a voiceless sigh.

"Not so secret anymore, is it?" Professor Troxler sneered. She flipped it inside out and examined it closely, but there was nothing hidden there. It was completely empty.

"Enough, Flora," Mr. Von Arx snapped. "They don't have anything and they don't know anything."

Maddie squirmed free from the man's hold. "We know plenty," she shouted. "We know what you're doing, and you're not going to get away with it!"

"Oh?" Professor Troxler smirked. "And what are you going to do about it?"

Neither of the girls said a word.

"As I thought," the professor clucked. She looked at Mr. Von Arx with a sinister grin. "They're just *children*, after all."

Headlights appeared from over the hill, and another car came to a screeching halt behind them. The headmistress, her sleeves still dusted with powdered sugar, rushed out of the back seat and ran to the twins. "Bastien!" she fumed. "You may take what you will from my school, but you will *not* touch a hair on my students' heads!"

"You insult me, Klara," he balked. "I did no such thing." He gestured to Professor Troxler. "I had the good professor do it."

The headmistress huffed and drew the girls close. "Are you all right, ladies?" she asked, inspecting their hands and faces.

Another truck—a different model—pulled up in front of the shiny black car in front, and five men in gray uniforms jumped out of the back to stand at attention. The driver got out of the truck and slammed the door.

"Klara?" the man called, his voice familiar to the girls.

"I'm over here!" The headmistress raised both arms in a desperate greeting, her voice rich with gratitude and relief.

The men in gray walked single file down through the men dressed in black and approached the headmistress.

"I came as soon as I received your telegram," the leader assured her. The girls looked up to see the face of Gabriele, the young Italian officer, who had watched over them on the ship so many months ago.

"Good evening, ladies," he greeted them sternly. He looked back to the headmistress, then turned to address Mr. Von Arx. "I believe you are in possession of a number of items belonging to Madame Molineaux's. I'm not sure how this misunderstanding happened, but my friends and I will be happy to oversee their return. Every last one of them." The five other Italian officers surrounded Mr. Von Arx.

"No need, my young friend," Mr. Von Arx replied haughtily. "By tomorrow morning, all of the castle, campus, and contents of Madame Molineaux's will belong to me. And then, perhaps, I might employ you and your colleagues to assist me in evicting the headmistress and her staff."

As the Italian officers tightened their circle around Mr. Von Arx, yet another car pulled up from over the hill. Its lights flashed for a moment, and out stepped a very dapper, somewhat startled Henri Lemaître.

"Henri!" Jo exclaimed. "What are you doing here?"

Henri smiled at the girls and shot a worried look at Mr. Von Arx. "My goodness, I am early to pick you up, am I not?" he asked playfully.

"*Days* early, Henri," the headmistress said, confused. "Not to mention at the wrong hour of day."

"Henri, our parents are coming to Madame Molineaux's after our exams," Maddie said cautiously, looking back and forth between him and Mr. Von Arx. She could have sworn she saw recognition in both their eyes. "What are you really doing here?"

But Henri didn't have a chance to answer. Two riders on black stallions galloped through the stream of cars toward the girls and the headmistress, towing Val and her horse behind them.

"General Gremminger?" the headmistress wondered aloud. She hadn't seen the headmaster of the boys' school from across the lake since the previous summer. "Why do you have my student on a horse in the middle of the night?"

The general straightened his collar and smoothed his gray mustache. "I found her in the forest on my way here, Headmistress."

"And why were you on your way here?"

The rider on the other black stallion lifted his head.

"Max!" Maddie whispered in astonishment. The girls hadn't seen his face in more than six months. They flashed him a quick smile, but his hardened expression didn't change.

"I caught this cadet spying on Madame Molineaux's," the general reported. "And he alerted me to some . . . shall we say, unusual activity on your premises."

"You must be Max," the headmistress said, cocking her head to the side.

"Yes, Headmistress," he replied. He looked at the general and cleared his throat. "I wish to apologize to you and your students for spying."

The headmistress shook her head. "Not at all, Max. Not at all."

Mr. Von Arx forced his way through the Italian officers. "Well, I must say, this has been such a lovely reunion of old friends. But I really must move along. Back in your trucks," he said, motioning to the men dressed in black.

Gabriele ran after Mr. Von Arx and held him by the shoulders. General Gremminger rode over on horseback.

"I believe we still have the matter of the headmistress's property," Gabriele reminded Mr. Von Arx. "If indeed it becomes yours tomorrow, we will arrange for its transport. But as for tonight, everything is coming back with us. You will unload your trucks at once."

Mr. Von Arx's steely expression broke into a laugh. "Do you really expect me to unload four trucks right here, all at the request of a few foreign officers and one retired army general?" The professor and the men in black chuckled along with him. "I outnumber you by ten men."

"Yes, I do, Von Arx," Gabriele stated calmly. "But if you should need some, shall we say, *encouragement*, perhaps the twenty other officers just down the road from here could persuade you."

"And if that's not enough," General Gremminger pointed out, "there are hundreds more soldiers and cadets just a few minutes' ride away who are also skilled at *encouraging* people to cooperate."

Mr. Von Arx shrugged. "All right, gentlemen. No one needs any encouragement. Men," he called out. "Unload the trucks." He snickered as he walked away from the military men. "Enjoy your things for one last night, Klara," he taunted. "In just hours, you'll officially be a trespasser at Madame Molineaux's."

Maddie stepped out of the headmistress's arms and stood in front of Mr. Von Arx. "Wait," she demanded. "You said that the school is going up for auction tomorrow morning. Is that true?"

Mr. Von Arx closed his eyes and nodded with phony sympathy. "I'm afraid so, my dear. Grown-up business, I assure you. And don't worry. We won't move in until after you're done taking your big tests."

Maddie squared her jaw. "Thank you, Mr. Von Arx. And good luck at the auction."

"I don't need luck, Maddie. I've seen to it that I'm the lone bidder."

"Can we drive you back, Headmistress?" Gabriele offered after the last of the trucks had sped off back toward the school. "You and the girls, of course."

The headmistress shook her head. "You'll be awake all night getting all of those things back inside the castle," she said gently. "I don't suppose the twenty men you spoke of earlier are actually waiting down the road? They could help."

"One of the oldest tricks in the book," General Gremminger laughed. "The I've-got-twice-as-many-men-as-you-do-over-the-next-hill tactic. It's a classic."

Gabriele relaxed his shoulders and smiled. "You wouldn't believe how often it works, Headmistress. I don't have any more men. But I *can* offer you a ride."

"It's all right. I have a driver. But thank you—for everything."

He tipped his hat and ran back to his truck.

"We'll return Valentina and your horses," General Gremminger told the headmistress.

"Thank you, General. Sometimes I wish you were always watching over our school," she admitted.

"If I could spare the men, I would arrange that," he said. "But as of late, we have our own unusual activity at school."

Max looked at Maddie and Jo and nodded, his eyebrows raised.

"Good night, Headmistress," the general said, and he led Max, Val, and Maddie's horse up the road toward Madame Molineaux's.

Henri sauntered up to the headmistress's car and leaned against it. "What a night, eh ladies?" he remarked lightly. "Maddie, Jo, let me apologize again for Christmastime. I was so upset that I had to disappoint you. But I'm here now."

"It's all right, Henri. We had a wonderful time with Headmistress Kronenberg and her grandmother," Jo said, fighting the urge to yawn.

Henri nodded and flicked a wooden toothpick out of his mouth. "I figured you might." He stood and walked toward his car. "I'll just stay in Saint-Marcel for the weekend until your parents arrive. I would swear to you the letter I received said *today*, but it was written in English, so . . . your uncle Henri could have mixed it up."

Maddie let go of her suspicions and ran to give Henri a hug. "It's okay. We're glad to see you, Henri." Jo joined them by his car.

"Would you like me to take you back to the school?" he asked them.

Françoise poked her head out of the headmistress's driver's seat. "They have a driver." She winked and started the car.

Maddie, Jo, and the headmistress stepped out of the car onto the front drive, just outside the doors to Madame Molineaux's.

"I'll park the car and be right in," Françoise promised.

The headmistress nodded.

"I didn't know Françoise could drive," Jo marveled.

"She can't," the headmistress scoffed, rubbing the back of her neck. "But I let her do it when she told me about the trouble you were in. You should have never gone after them," she scolded gently. "They are far, far more dangerous than they might seem."

"Oh, they seem plenty dangerous," Maddie agreed. "But I think it was worth it."

The headmistress gave an exhausted smile. "I suppose we will have our cherished art back for one more night."

"Maybe for longer than that," Maddie said. She stepped out of her slipper and bent down, pulling the folded parchment from inside the toe.

"So *that's* where you hid it!" Jo exclaimed. "I thought we were done for when you gave Troxler your secret pocket."

"I didn't have time to hide it there," Maddie explained. "When I saw Mr. Von Arx step out of the car, I shoved it into my slipper. And it's a good thing I did!" She held the tiny parcel out to the headmistress. "I think Wilhelmina meant for you to have this."

The headmistress gasped and choked back tears. "I don't understand," she uttered. "Wherever did you find it?"

"Wilhelmina was holding it the whole time," Jo smiled. "When she said, 'forever in my heart,' she really meant it."

The headmistress pulled gently on the tattered string and carefully unfolded the parchment. There, sitting in crumpled paper in the headmistress's palm, were ten sparkling blue diamonds, each the size of her thumbnail.

Jo lifted the edge of the parchment and peered at it in the dim light of the lanterns in the doorway. "There's writing," she said.

The headmistress poured the diamonds into her other hand and gave the paper to Jo.

"To my beloved," Jo read aloud from the parchment. "To remind you of the lake where we first met. I love you, Wilhelmina." She straightened the paper with her fingers. "And there's a tiny cursive J here in the corner."

The headmistress was speechless. Tears streamed down her cheeks as she rolled the gemstones in her palm. "Blue diamonds this large are nearly priceless," she whispered, almost to herself. She looked up at the girls. "And there are ten of them . . . I think I'm going to be at that auction tomorrow."

Maddie nodded. "Looks like Mr. Von Arx will have to find another school to steal."

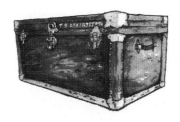

CHAPTER FORTY

Now We Say Adieu

Jo skipped down the steps of the history hall and darted out onto the sunny lawn. She took off her jacket, flung it on the grass, and ran circles around a very grumpy Val.

"Come on, Val, cheer up! It's over! *Fini!* Done!!"

"Let her grieve," Millie laughed. "It's not every day someone's actually *upset* that an exam got canceled."

"Surely you didn't expect Troxler to show up and give the exam after everything that happened!" Nixie argued. "She's banished from the whole country, I heard."

Val shook her head. "Well, I at least thought the headmistress would give us the test. I studied for *two whole days*, Nixie."

"How about this: I'll write to you all summer long, and in each letter, I'll ask you a question from the chapters we read," Safi offered playfully. "Would that make you feel better?"

Val nodded slowly as she seriously considered her friend's offer. "It might, Safi. Thank you."

The girls erupted into laughter.

"I'm pretty sure she was kidding, Val," Maddie said. "Don't worry. You'll have all next year to show everyone how smart you are," she teased.

Val's face fell. "I'm going to miss the two of you."

"We've already gone over this," Jo said, shaking her head. "We'll send postcards all summer long, and Maddie and I will write once a week when we're back in Boston. A deal's a deal."

"It won't be the same," Françoise grumbled. "You'll see. People forget to write."

"Hey, now, don't be that way. We told you, Henri's already invited us to Paris for Christmas!"

"Just make sure he doesn't send you to Kronenberg's instead," Millie joked. "Unless, of course, you get another gift like those wristwatches. In that case, Christmas with Kronenberg is a fair trade."

"Who are those people over there?" Nixie asked, pointing at two men and a woman near the dining hall doors. "They're doing some strange dance."

All the girls stared, watching as the people Nixie pointed to flailed their arms back and forth and jumped up and down.

"Those are our parents! And Henri!" Jo cheered. "That's their version of waving."

"Do all Americans wave like that?" Safi asked, laughing.

"Probably not," Maddie admitted. "Probably just our mom and dad." She dropped her school bag to the ground, and she and Jo ran as fast as they could across the lawn.

"Delicious," Tom Livingston said, cramming another bite of éclair into his mouth. "How many of these did you say you had left over?"

The headmistress laughed. "Too many to count. Apparently, the students preferred the history hall's cinnamon buns at the exam review this year."

"These remind me of the éclairs I get from my favorite patisserie in Paris," Henri remarked, wiping his fingers on his napkin. "You remember the one, Martha?"

"How could I forget? In those days, if we didn't have any dinner prepared . . ." She looked at Tom and Henri.

"Éclairs," they all groaned at once.

"It took me years after we left Paris before I could stomach another one," Tom recalled. "But it's been long enough." He took another pastry from the plate.

Maddie smiled, imagining her parents and Henri as teenagers, eating éclairs for dinner in a tiny Parisian apartment. "Henri," she said, smiling. "How do you know the headmistress?"

"Ah, that fateful day, ten years ago," he began. "I was but a poor young man, peddling statues for a Parisian sculptor. The kind headmistress was one of my very first customers."

The headmistress shook her head. "Henri, you practically *gave* those statues to the school for our gardens! I would have been a fool not to buy them at that price."

Henri snickered. "Yes, well . . ." He looked at the girls. "Your uncle Henri was relieved of his sales position after he sold the statues to your headmistress for next to nothing. It was a minor mathematical miscalculation, that's all . . ."

"And we have remained in contact ever since," the head-mistress finished. "He somehow always managed to stop by and see us in Saint-Marcel."

"You sure have had a lot of jobs, Henri," Jo blurted. "What else do you do?"

Henri shrugged and smiled his charming smile. "I do it all, Josephine. I am, as they say, a *Jacques*-of-all-trades."

The girls giggled.

"What, what?" Henri demanded. "Did I say that wrong?"

"No, Henri," Jo assured him. "You got it right. Sort of."

The headmistress walked to the window and stared out at the line of parents and cars squeezing onto the front drive. "Well, I shall leave you alone to catch up," she said. "I think I'm needed outside to help direct traffic."

Martha joined the headmistress. "It's a good thing you girls only have one trunk," she said as she eyed a fancy car below them. "Who is that girl and why does she have so many suitcases?"

Maddie and Jo didn't need to look. "Rosemary Byron," they said in unison from the sofa.

"Is she one of the nice girls we met?" Tom asked.

"No, she's not exactly our *friend*," Jo explained, careful not to say too much in front of the headmistress. "But we're friendly, I guess you could say."

Maddie grimaced and folded her arms.

"I understand that Rosemary had a very serious conversation with Professor Natalio about some additional resident animals," the headmistress stated matter-of-factly. "Apparently, we might see them this fall."

Let me guess, Maddie thought. *A thousand Nata-lynx kittens roaming the castle halls.* But after she thought it, the idea didn't sound so bad. Three kittens for every girl.

"Stay as long as you like," the headmistress said, finishing the last of her tea. "It's been quite a while since you've been a family."

"Actually, it doesn't matter how far apart on the planet we are. We'll always be a family. Right, Dad?" Jo chirped.

"Right, Jo."

The headmistress nodded. "Of course." She smiled and walked toward the door. "I'll have the porter carry your things out to your car. Enjoy the rest of your afternoon." She exited the room and closed the door behind her.

"So, you liked it here, did you, ladies?" Henri asked the girls.

Maddie and Jo nodded as they ate their pastries.

"Your mom and I thought you hated it," Tom teased. "We figured since we didn't get any letters—not a single one—that they kept you locked in cages without pencils and paper . . . or something."

"We really meant to write, so many times—" Jo began.

"But we had classes, and homework, and friends and—"

Tom held up his hands. "We forgive you," he assured them. "It wasn't as if we had much to report from Siberia, either." He looked at Martha and pulled on his chin.

Martha returned his pointed look and turned to face the girls. "Right, well, it was a bigger project than we expected. It's not done, in fact."

Maddie and Jo stopped chewing and looked at each other.

"What are you saying, Mom?"

"Well, we're not saying anything, exactly," Martha stammered. "It's just that, well, you know. If you thought you might want to . . ."

"What your mother means to say is, I guess, if there was the opportunity to, say . . ."

"Are you saying we get to come back?!" Jo squealed. "Because if you are—"

"All we're saying, honey, is that we've been offered an extension in Siberia and, well, we'd only go if you and Maddie wanted to keep going to school here—"

"Are you joking, Mom?!" Maddie whooped. "Of *course* we want to stay! How did you get the extension?"

Tom shrugged. "A private donor funded the whole thing," he said gratefully. "Can you believe that? He must have a lot of money to give away if he's spending that much on me and your mom."

Jo didn't hear a word after "keep going to school here." She was already thinking about what she would bring from Boston.

"Your headmistress was very complimentary of you both," Martha added. "She said that although you're some of the more . . . *curious* students at the school, you're excellent in your classes and activities, and popular with the other girls."

"Curious as in, strange? Or curious as in, full of curiosity?" Maddie asked.

"Probably a little of both," Tom said. "But she was delighted to hear that she might have you back next year. Go tell your friends good-bye. We'll talk about our summer plans on the long way back to Boston."

"And give your uncle Henri a hug," Henri said, holding his arms out to the girls. "I have to be on my way, but I promise: this Christmas, I'll take you on a fantastic holiday vacation."

Maddie and Jo ran to hug him.

"Thank you for telling our parents about this place, Henri," said Maddie. Jo nodded into Henri's shoulder.

"Good-bye, ladies."

"Not good-bye, but farewell!" Jo sang, jumping toward the door. "Mom, Dad, we'll meet you at the car!"

Françoise admired her own work, holding the newly reconstructed torch out for all the girls to see. "It was nothing, really," she said casually. "I just broke a glass bottle, got out my paints and glue, and voilà! She lives to see another adventure." The torch boasted every shade of gold and orange that Françoise could find in her paint box. Even the glue had been painted over, giving the flame an antique look. "It's a good thing I could do it, too. I'm certain they don't make these anymore." She lifted a layer of clothes in her trunk to pack it underneath, then closed the clasps. "Well, I guess it's time."

"Wait!" Maddie protested. "We have to make our new pact official."

"New pact?" Safi asked. "What new pact?"

"The postcard pact," Maddie beamed.

"You're not serious," Millie moaned.

"I'm serious!" she snapped. "We've already agreed to it, now put your hands in."

All the girls placed their hands on top of one another on the reconstructed torch.

"It has to be *on*, Françoise!" Maddie insisted. Françoise sighed and flipped the switch.

"Okay. So—we'll go around the circle and pledge to send one from our hometown *and* from vacation. Val, you go first."

Val smiled and lifted her chin. "I pledge to post my post-cards perfectly, from Pitigliano and the Mediterranean!"

"I pledge to post my postcards perfectly, from Zurich and Göttingen!" Nixie recited.

"I pledge to post my postcards perfectly, from Dakar and Provence!" Safi sang.

"I pledge to post my postcards perfectly, from Brechin, and, well, Brechin," Millie said with a sheepish grin. "I don't think a holiday is in the cards this year."

Françoise nodded heartily. "Well, I understand, Millie. I pledge to post my postcards perfectly, from Paris and only Paris, because Paris is the greatest city in the world, so who needs to leave?"

Everyone groaned and laughed.

"What?" She shrugged and looked unapologetic, wearing her signature smirk. "You're only mad because you don't live in Paris."

"It's your turn, Livingstons, where are you going for the summer?" Nixie pressed.

Maddie and Jo exchanged looks.

"Okay. We pledge to post our postcards perfectly from Boston," Maddie began.

"And...it's a mystery!" Jo finished. "Our parents said they'd tell us where we were going for the summer on our way home."

"Then we'll be looking out for your mystery postcards, assuming that your mystery holiday spot has a post office," Millie pointed out.

"You'll get them," Jo promised. "The Knights of Room Five never turn their backs on a pledge."

"But if you don't get them for some reason," Maddie added, "we can just tell you everything in the fall . . . when we get back to Saint-Marcel." She pressed her lips together to keep from laughing but couldn't hide her smiling eyes.

"Hold on, say that again?" Françoise stammered. "Did you say you're coming back to Saint-Marcel in the fall?"

The twins nodded excitedly.

"Hoo-ooo-ooo-ray!" Millie howled, and the rest of the girls all piled in for hugs and shrieks of joy. "The Knights of Room Five will ride again! Only, we might have to change our room number . . ."

The girls all laughed, then said good-bye, each of them grateful that this moment was suddenly far more sweet than bitter.

Headmistress Kronenberg held her hands up in front of her as she spoke. "I understand you're angry, Mr. and Mrs. Vidal, but she's simply missed too much class time. She'll have to repeat the second year."

Mr. Vidal stamped his foot and threw his hat to the ground. "Don't you recognize true, global talent when you see it?" he demanded, throwing both hands out to point at a very distraught Isidra. "She missed those classes to compete in worldwide dance competitions. Pursuing excellence!"

"I know, Mr. Vidal. And Isidra is by far the best performer here at Madame Molineaux's. But this is not a competition hall, this is a *school*. And she'll have to re-take those classes if she wants to move on to the third year."

"So small-minded," he sneered. "You fail to see her for what she is."

"No, Mr. Vidal. I see her for exactly who she is. A strong, talented, and smart young lady who deserves a proper education. And that's exactly what she'll get here, if you will let her."

Mrs. Vidal put her arm on her husband's shoulder and sighed. "She can still perform over the summer, and during the holidays," she coaxed.

"And," the headmistress added, "don't forget about our performances here at the school. She was absolutely stunning as the lead in our holiday review. I'm sorry you couldn't be here to see that."

Mr. Vidal glared at the headmistress. "I'm a politician," he grumbled. "I usually have *important* things to tend to."

Isidra looked at the ground.

"I'm sure you do," the headmistress conceded. "Now then. I must also tend to important things. Isidra, I do hope we see you next year." She bowed slightly and walked away.

"I'll tell Oma Kronenberg all about the mysteries when I get home," the headmistress promised the twins as they walked to their car. "But I'm sure I'll leave out the most important bits. She'd much rather hear it from you, I'm afraid."

"Maybe we'll write it to her in a letter," Maddie said with a mischievous grin. "But she'd have to destroy the evidence after she read it."

"She'd enjoy that. The letter, and the destroying of the evidence! You know Oma, always looking for the next mystery."

The girls stopped walking and hugged their headmistress for the last time before they returned to Boston.

"Thank you for everything, Headmistress. And for having us back next year," Maddie said sweetly. "It really does feel like home now."

"It *is* your home, ladies. And because of you, it can continue to be a home to all of us. Remember that always."

"All in a year's work, Headmistress," Jo laughed. "Next year should be just as exciting."

The headmistress sighed. "Let's hope not, Josephine. This has been enough excitement to last me for the rest of my days."

"We'll see!" Maddie chimed. "Good-bye, Headmistress."

"See you in the fall, ladies." The headmistress nudged them gently toward the car. "Oh," she added abruptly. "One more thing, ladies. However did you discover the tapestries behind the paintings?"

Maddie and Jo winced and pasted smiles onto their faces.

"Oh, um—the tapestries?" Jo stammered. "Gosh, I don't even remember. Maddie, do you—"

"Maddie, Jo," Martha called from the car. "We don't want to be late to the train station."

"Wow, sorry, Headmistress!" Maddie exclaimed, grateful for her mother's perfect timing. "We'll be sure to tell you in the fall."

"Mm-hmm," Jo agreed. "In the fall for sure."

The girls waved and jumped into the back seat of the car, relieved that they had the entire summer to figure out how they would tell the headmistress that all of her paintings had been sliced open and glued shut.

Jo rested her head against the car window as the Livingston family rode through the gates of Madame Molineaux's, and, for a moment, she swore she saw a few hairs from a horse tail waving in the wind, caught on a jagged edge of the gate. They drove in silence as Tom and Martha took in the quaint village of Saint-Marcel from behind the windshield, and Maddie only giggled once when she heard the real bells of Saint-Marcel ring as the hour changed. *Finally back where they belong,* she thought.

"So . . . where are we going for the summer?" Jo asked once they had left Saint-Marcel.

"Well," Tom answered. "Boston for a while. And then . . ." He took one hand off the steering wheel and pulled something small and shiny from his pocket. He flipped it with his finger and thumb back to the girls, and it fell into Jo's lap.

She picked it up and inspected it. "A gold coin?"

"Not just any gold coin," Martha corrected her. "It's a gold piece from a sunken port on the coast of Jamaica, in the Caribbean."

"We're going to the beach!" Maddie clapped.

"Palm trees!" Jo cheered.

"And pirates," Tom said, making a *yo-ho* gesture with his arm and squinting one eye. "Ye like pirates, don't ye now?"

"Sure, Dad," Jo replied. "We like pirates just fine." She looked at her sister and hid a smile.

"Just fine?" Tom objected. "Well, that's because you don't know any of the good ones. I could tell you some stories . . ."

Maddie lifted her legs onto Jo's lap and laid her head back against the car door.

"What are you doing?" Jo fussed.

"Getting comfortable."

"But this is my side of the—" Jo started to protest, but then sighed, deciding to give up without a fight and just relax. "Fine. But if I get tired, I get to lay my head in the middle."

"Deal," Maddie grinned.

"Ahem." Their father cleared his throat in the front seat. "I *said*, I could tell you some stories . . ."

The Livingston twins winked at each other and settled in for the long car ride.

"That'd be great, Dad. We're all ears."

THE END

. . . UNTIL THE NEXT BEGINNING, THAT IS . . .

ABOUT THE AUTHOR

Before she started writing historical mystery fiction, Mary studied International Affairs and foreign language at Georgia Tech. After almost a decade as a musician, waitress, and paralegal, she fell into the exciting world of tech startups and developed her entrepreneurial skills. But how to write books and start companies at the same time? She merged her two passions to create the Twin Sisters Livingston brand of stories and Living Lantern Media Group, a company devoted to entertaining, educating, and inspiring girls all over the world through smart, safe, sophisticated media. She lives in Georgia with her two children and a couple of rascal cats.

If you'd like to know when the next of the 24-book *Twin Sisters Livingston* series is coming out, or learn more about Mary's adventures in writing and entrepreneurship, visit the websites below:

www.twinsisterslivingston.com
www.maryknightwrites.com

Made in the USA
Coppell, TX
07 November 2022

85930253R00249